exclusive

SANDRA BROWN

HODDER

First published in America in 1996 by Grand Central, US
First published in Great Britain in 2009 by Hodder and Stoughton
An Hachette UK company

This paperback edition 2010

1

A CIP catalogue record for this title
is available from the British Library

B format Paperback ISBN 978 1 444 70781 6
A format Paperback ISBN 978 0 340 96178 0

Printed and bound by Clays Ltd, St Ives plc

Hodder & Stoughton policy is to use papers that
are natural, renewable and recyclable products
and made from wood grown in sustainable forests.
The logging and manufacturing processes are
expected to conform to the environmental
regulations of the country of origin.

Hodder & Stoughton Ltd
338 Euston Road
London NW1 3BH

www.hodder.co.uk

Chapter One

"*You*'re looking well, Mrs. Merritt."

"I look like hell."

Vanessa Merritt did indeed look like hell, but Barrie was embarrassed for having been caught paying an insincere compliment. She tried to recover gracefully. "After what you've been through, you're entitled to look a little frazzled. Any other woman, myself included, myself *particularly*, would settle for looking like you even at your worst."

"Thank you." She gave her cappuccino a desultory stir. If nerves conveyed sound, Vanessa Merritt's would have clattered like her spoon when she shakily returned it to the saucer. "God. For just one cigarette, I'd let you pull out all my fingernails with pliers."

She'd certainly never been seen smoking in public, so Barrie was surprised to learn that she was a smoker. Although a nicotine addiction might explain why she was so fidgety.

Her hands were never still. She twirled her strand of pearls, played with the discreet diamond studs in her earlobes, and repeatedly adjusted the RayBans that almost concealed the dark, puffy circles around her eyes.

Those spectacular eyes were largely responsible for her beauty. Until today. Today, those remarkable baby blues reflected pain and disillusionment. Today they looked like the eyes of an angel who'd just had her first, horrifying glimpse of hell.

"I'm fresh out of pliers," Barrie said. "But I have these." From her large leather satchel, she withdrew an unopened pack of cigarettes and slid it across the table.

It was obvious that Mrs. Merritt was tempted. Her haunted eyes nervously scanned the outdoor terrace of the restaurant. Only one other table was occupied, by several men, and one obsequious waiter hovered nearby. Even so, she declined the cigarette. "I'd better not. But feel free."

"I don't smoke. I only carry them in case I need to relax someone I'm interviewing."

"Before you come in for the kill."

Barrie laughed. "I only wish I were that dangerous."

"Actually you're better at human interest stories."

It came as a pleasant surprise that Mrs. Merritt was even aware of her work. "Thank you."

"Some of your reports have been quite exceptional. Like the one on the AIDS patient. And the one you did on the homeless single mother of four."

"That was nominated for an industry award." Barrie saw no reason to volunteer that she had entered the piece herself.

"It made me cry," Mrs. Merritt said.

"Me too."

"In fact, you're so good, I've often wondered why you're not affiliated with a network."

"I've had some tough breaks."

Vanessa Merritt's smooth brow wrinkled. "Wasn't there an issue over Justice Green that—"

"Yes, there was that," Barrie interrupted. This wasn't a conversation in which she wanted her failures itemized. "Why did you contact me, Mrs. Merritt? I'm delighted, but curious."

Vanessa Merritt's smile gradually faded. In a low, serious tone, she said, "I made myself clear, didn't I? This is not an interview."

"I understand."

She didn't. Barrie Travis didn't have a clue as to why Mrs. Merritt had phoned her out of the blue and invited her to have coffee. They'd been nodding acquaintances for the last few years, certainly not friends.

Even the choice of today's meeting place was curious. The restaurant was one of several along the shore of the channel that connected the Potomac with the Tidal Basin. After dark, the clubs and eateries along Water Street were filled with people, mostly tourists. Some did a respectable lunch trade, but in the middle of the afternoon, on a workday, the restaurants were virtually deserted.

Maybe this place had been chosen precisely for its seclusion.

Barrie dropped a sugar cube into her cappuccino, then idly stirred it as she stared out over the iron railing of the terrace.

It was a gloomy, overcast day. The channel was choppy. Houseboats and sailboats moored in the marina bobbed in the gray water. The canvas umbrella above their table snapped and popped in the gusty wind that carried the scent of rain and fish. Why were they sitting outside on such a blustery day?

Mrs. Merritt stirred the foamy milk in her cappuccino and finally took a sip. "It's cold now."

"Would you like another?" Barrie asked. "I'll signal the waiter."

"No, thanks. I didn't really want that one. Having coffee was just, you know . . ." She shrugged a shoulder that had once been stylishly slender but was now downright bony.

"It was just an excuse?" Barrie prodded.

Vanessa Merritt raised her head. Through the sunglasses, Barrie saw bleak honesty in the woman's eyes. "I needed to talk to someone."

"And you thought of *me?*"

"Well, yes."

"Because a couple of my stories made you cry?"

"That, and because of the sympathy note you sent. It touched me. Deeply."

"I'm glad it gave you some comfort."

"I . . . I don't have many close friends. You and I are about the same age. I thought you'd be a good sounding board." She lowered her head. A mane of chestnut hair tumbled forward, partially concealing her classic cheekbones and aristocratic chin.

In a quiet voice, Barrie said, "My note couldn't convey how very sorry I am for what happened."

"Actually it did. Thank you." Vanessa Merritt removed a tissue from her handbag and slipped it beneath the sunglasses to blot her eyes. "I don't know where they come from," she said of the tears being soaked up by the tissue. "I should be dehydrated by now."

"Is that what you want to talk about?" Barrie asked gently. "The baby?"

"Robert Rushton Merritt," she blurted forcefully. "Why does everyone avoid saying his name? He had a name, for heaven's sake. For three months, he was a *person* and he had a *name*."

"I guess—"

She didn't give Barrie time to respond. "Rushton was my mother's maiden name," Mrs. Merritt explained. "She would have liked having her first grandchild named after her family."

Staring out over the turbulent waters of the channel, she continued talking in a faraway voice. "And I've always fancied the name Robert. It's a straightforward, no-bullshit name."

The vulgarity surprised Barrie. It was such a departure from Vanessa Merritt's southern-lady persona. In her whole life, Barrie had never felt so bereft of something to say. Under the circumstances, what would be appropriate? What could she say to a woman who had recently buried her baby? *Nice funeral?*

Suddenly Mrs. Merritt asked, "What do you know about it?"

Barrie was caught off guard. Was she being challenged? *What do* you *know about losing a child? What do you* really *know about anything?*

"Are you referring to . . . ? Do you mean the baby's . . . I mean, Robert's death?"

"Yes. What do you know about it?"

"Nobody really knows about SIDS, do they?" Barrie asked, groping for the meaning behind the question.

Obviously changing her mind about the cigarette, Mrs. Merritt tore open the pack. Her motions were like those of a marionette, jerky and disjointed. The fingers that held the cigarette to her lips were trembling. Barrie quickly fished a lighter from her satchel. Vanessa Merritt didn't continue speaking until she'd deeply inhaled several times. The tobacco didn't calm her. Instead, she became increasingly agitated.

"Robert was sleeping, on his side, with one of those little pillows propping him up, the way I'd been shown to position him. It happened so fast! How could . . ." Her voice cracked.

"Are you blaming yourself? Listen." Barrie reached across the table, took the cigarette from Mrs. Merritt, and ground it out in the ashtray. Then she pressed the woman's cold hands between hers. The impulsive gesture was noticed by the men at the other table.

"Robert died of crib death. Losing a baby to SIDS happens to thousands of mothers and fathers every year, and there's not a single one of them who doesn't second-guess their parenting skills. It's human nature to assign blame to a tragedy, so people lay a guilt trip on themselves. Don't fall into that trap. If you start thinking you were responsible for your baby's death, you might never recover."

Mrs. Merritt was vigorously shaking her head. "You don't understand. It *was* my fault." Behind her sunglasses, her eyes darted about. She withdrew her hands from Barrie's, moved them from cheek to tabletop, to lap, to spoon, to neck, in a restless search for peace. "The last few months of my pregnancy were intolerable."

For several moments she covered her mouth with her hand, as though the last trimester had been unspeakably painful. "Then Robert was born. But instead of getting better, as I'd hoped, it only got worse. I couldn't . . ."

"Couldn't what? Cope? All new mothers experience post-partum and feel overwhelmed," Barrie assured her.

She kneaded her forehead with her fingertips. "You don't understand," she repeated in a strained whisper. "Nobody does. There's no one I can tell. Not even my father. Oh, God, I don't know what to do!"

Her emotional unraveling was so obvious that the men at the next table had turned to stare. The waiter approached, looking anxious.

Barrie spoke quickly beneath her breath. "Vanessa, please, get a grip. Everybody's watching."

Whether it was because Barrie had addressed her by her

first name or for some other reason, the emotional collapse immediately reversed itself. Her nervously active hands fell still. Her tears dried instantly. She downed the cold cappuccino she had claimed moments earlier not to want, then finished by daintily blotting her colorless lips with her napkin. Barrie watched the transformation with amazement.

Wholly restored, in a cool, composed voice, she said, "This conversation was strictly off the record, right?"

"Absolutely," Barrie replied. "You made that understood when you called me."

"Considering your position, and mine, I see now that it was a mistake to arrange this meeting. I haven't been myself since Robert died. I thought I needed to talk about it, but I was wrong. Talking about it only makes me more distraught."

"You've lost your baby. You're entitled to unravel." Barrie laid her hand on the other woman's arm. "Be kinder to yourself. SIDS just happens."

She removed her sunglasses and looked directly into Barrie's eyes. "Does it?"

Then Vanessa Armbruster Merritt, First Lady of the United States, replaced the RayBans, slipped the strap of her handbag onto her shoulder, and stood up. The Secret Service agents at the next table came hastily to their feet. They were joined by three others, who'd been standing post along the iron railing, out of sight.

As a group they closed ranks around the First Lady and escorted her from the terrace of the restaurant to a waiting limousine.

Chapter
Two

$\mathcal{B}$arrie dug into her satchel in search of coins for the cold drink machine. "Anybody got a couple of quarters I can borrow?"

"Not for you, sweetcheeks," replied a videotape editor who was walking past. "You've already stiffed me seventy-five cents."

"I'll pay you back tomorrow. Swear."

"Forget it, sugarbuns."

"You ever heard of sexual harassment in the work-place?" she called after him.

"Sure. I voted for it," he retorted over his shoulder.

Barrie gave up on retrieving any coins from the bottom of her bag, deciding that a diet drink was hardly worth the effort of the search.

She wove her way through the television station's newsroom, working the maze of cubicles until she reached her own. One look at the surface of her desk would have made an obsessive-compulsive take a razor to his wrists. Barrie slung her satchel onto the desk, knocking three magazines to the floor in the process.

"Do you ever read any of those?"

The familiar voice caused Barrie to groan. Howie Fripp was the news department's assignments editor, her immediate supervisor, and an all-around pain in the butt.

"Of course I read them," she lied. "Cover to cover."

She subscribed to a number of periodicals. The magazines arrived regularly, creating skyscrapers on her desk until she was forced to throw them away, more often than not unread. She faithfully read her monthly horoscope in *Cosmopolitan*. That was about the extent of the time she spent with the magazines, but on principle alone she wouldn't let her subscriptions lapse. All good broadcast journalists were news junkies, reading everything they could get their hands on.

And she was a good broadcast journalist.

She *was*.

"Doesn't it bother your conscience to know that thousands of trees give up their lives just to keep you in reading matter that you don't read?"

"Howie, *you're* what bothers me. Besides, you're one to preach environmental awareness when the smoke from your four packs a day pollutes the atmosphere."

"Not to mention my farts."

She despised that evil little grin of his almost as much as she despised the small minds that managed WVUE, a low-budget, substandard, independent television station struggling to survive among the monolithic news operations in Washington, D.C. She'd had to beg for the budget to produce the feature stories that had won the First Lady's praise. She had ideas for many others. But the station's management, including Howie, weren't of a similar mind. Her ideas were blocked by men who lacked vision, talent, and energy. She didn't belong here.

Isn't that the belief clung to by prison inmates?

"Thank you, Howie, for not mentioning your farts."

She plopped down in her desk chair and dug tunnels through her hair with her fingers, holding it off her face. Her coiffuer hadn't been much to brag about, but the damp wind on the restaurant terrace had played havoc with it.

Strange choice of meeting places.

Even stranger was the meeting itself.

What purpose did it serve?

On the drive back to the station, Barrie had reviewed each word that was said during her visit with the First Lady. She'd analyzed every inflection in Vanessa Merritt's voice, gauged each hand gesture, assessed her body language, reviewed that disturbing final question that had served as her goodbye, but she still couldn't pinpoint exactly what had happened. Or exactly what hadn't.

"Checked your e-mail?" Howie asked, interrupting her thoughts.

"Not yet."

"That tiger that escaped from the traveling carnival? They found him. He hadn't escaped after all. Ergo, no story."

"Oh nooo!" she said dramatically. "And I was *so* looking forward to covering that."

"Hey, it could've been big news. The cat could've eaten a kid or something." He looked genuinely forlorn over the missed opportunity.

"It was a crap assignment, Howie. You always stick me with the crap assignments. Is it because you don't like me, or because I'm a woman?"

"Jeez, not that feminist routine again. You PMS, or what?"

She sighed. "Howie, you're hopeless."

Hopeless. That was it. Vanessa Merritt had seemed hopeless.

Impatient to explore that avenue of thought, Barrie

said, "Look, Howie, unless there's something specific that's brought you by, I've got a lot to do here, as you can see."

Howie backed up to the partition separating her stall—as she thought of the cramped cubicle—from the neighboring one. Regardless of the season, he wore short-sleeved white shirts. Always. Always with black trousers that were always shiny. His neckties were clip-on. Today's selection was particularly ugly and had a stain on its fraying tip, which reached only the center of his barrel chest, which was far out of proportion to his nonexistent butt and spindly, bowed legs.

Crossing his arms and ankles simultaneously, he said, "A story would be nice, Barrie. You know, a *story*. What you're paid to produce, more or less on a daily basis. How about one for this evening's news?"

"I was working on one that didn't pan out," she muttered as she booted up her computer.

"What was it?"

"Since it didn't pan out, what's the point of discussing it?"

Vanessa Merritt had said that the months leading up to her baby's birth had been intolerable. Even without the strong, descriptive word, her demeanor alone had made it clear that she'd had a very rough time. Following the child's birth, "intolerable" had gotten worse. But what had been so intolerable? *And why tell me?*

Howie rambled on, unaware that she was only half-listening. "I'm not asking for live coverage of somebody getting his head blown off, or man's first steps on Mars, or some extremist from the Nation of Islam holding the pope hostage in the Vatican. A nice, simple little story would do. Something. Anything. Sixty seconds of fill between the second and third commercial breaks. That's all I'm asking for."

"How short-sighted of you, Howie," Barrie remarked. "If that's the best motivational speech you can give, no wonder you get such unsatisfactory results from your underlings."

He uncrossed his limbs and drew himself up to his full height of five feet six inches, and that was with elevators in his scuffed wingtips. "You know what your problem is? You've got stars in your eyes. You want to be Diane Sawyer. Well, here's a news flash for you—you aren't. And you aren't ever going to be. You aren't ever going to be married to a famous movie director or have your own news magazine show. You aren't ever going to have respect and credibility in this business. Because you're a screw-up and everybody in the industry knows it. So stop waiting for the *big* story and settle for something that you and your limited talent can handle. Something I can put on the air. Okay?"

Barrie had tuned him out just after the "stars in your eyes" statement. The first time she'd heard this speech was the day he hired her, out of the goodness of his heart, he'd said. Besides, he'd added, management had been after him to hire another "skirt," and Barrie was "okay-looking." She'd heard the same speech almost every workday since. Three years of them.

There were a few messages on her e-mail, but nothing that couldn't be handled later. She turned off her computer and came to her feet. "It's too late to do anything for tonight, Howie. But I'll have a story for you tomorrow. Promise." Grabbing her satchel, she slung it back onto her shoulder.

"Hey! Where're you going?" he shouted after her as she brushed past him.

"To the library."

"What for?"

"Research, Howie."

As she passed the cold drink machine, she banged it with her fist. A Diet Coke rolled out of the chute.

She took that as a good omen.

Juggling her satchel, an armload of library books, and her keys, Barrie unlocked the back door of her townhouse and stumbled inside. The moment she crossed the threshold, she was subjected to an ardent, wet kiss on the lips.

"Thanks, Cronkite." She wiped the slobber from her face. "I love you, too."

Cronkite and the rest of his litter had been destined for euthanasia at the pound on the day that Barrie decided she needed a four-legged companion after a two-legged one announced he needed space and walked out of her life forever.

She'd had a difficult time choosing which pup to spare, but she'd never regretted her choice. Cronkite was large and long-haired, with definite ripples of golden retriever in his gene pool. Big brown eyes adored her worshipfully now, while his tail beat a happy tattoo against her calf.

"Go do your thing," she told him, nodding toward her patch of backyard. "Use your doggie door." He whined. Barrie sighed. "Okay, I'll wait. But hurry. These books are heavy."

He watered several shrubs happily, then dashed inside ahead of Barrie.

"Let's see if there's anything interesting in the mail," she said as she made her way to the entry where her mail lay in a heap beneath the slot in the front door. "Bill, bill, overdue bill. Invitation to dinner at the White House." She looked at the dog, who tilted his head inquisitively. "Just checking to see if you were paying attention."

Cronkite followed her upstairs to her bedroom, where she exchanged her dress and heels for a Redskins jersey that came almost to her knees and a pair of gym socks. After running a brush through her hair, she pulled it into a pony-tail. Regarding her reflection in the mirror, she mumbled, "Stunning," then put her appearance out of her mind and focused on work.

Over the years, she had cultivated numerous sources—clerks, secretaries, illicit lovers, chambermaids, cops, a handful of people in key positions—who occasionally provided her with valuable information and reliable leads. One was a young woman named Anna Chen, who worked in the administration office of D.C. General Hospital. The juicy scuttlebutt Anna Chen picked up through the hospital grapevine frequently led to good stories. She was one of Barrie's most reliable sources.

Hoping it wasn't too late to catch her at the office, Barrie looked up her number in her home Rolodex and dialed. The hospital operator put her right through.

"Hi, Anna. This is Barrie Travis. Glad I caught you."

"I was on my way out. What's up?"

"What would be my chances of getting a copy of the Merritt baby's autopsy report?"

"Is this a joke?"

"That slim?"

"Nigh to impossible, Barrie. Sorry."

"I thought so, but it never hurts to ask."

"Why do you want it?"

She did some verbal acrobatics as to her reason, which seemed to pacify her source. "Thanks anyway, Anna."

Disappointed, Barrie hung up. An autopsy report would have been a good starting point, although she was still unclear as to exactly what she was starting.

"What do you want for dinner, Cronkite?" she asked as she loped downstairs to the kitchen. She opened the pantry and recited the menu selections. "Tonight's specialties include Kibbles and Bits, Alpo chicken and liver, or Gravy Train." He whined with disappointment. Taking pity, she said, "Luigi's?" Out came his long, pink tongue, and he began panting like a pervert at a peep show.

Her conscience told her to have a Lean Cuisine for dinner, but what the hell? When you spent your evenings at home in a football jersey and gym socks, conversing with a mongrel and having nothing to look forward to except hours of research, what difference did a few hundred fat grams make?

While she was on the telephone ordering two pizzas, Cronkite began whining to go outside. She covered the telephone mouthpiece. "If it's that urgent, use your doggie door." Cronkite glanced disdainfully at the opening cut in the back door. It was large enough to accommodate Cronkite, but not so large that she worried about intruders. As she was reiterating her pizza order, she jabbed her index finger toward the doggie door. Looking humiliated, Cronkite crawled through it. She was off the phone by the time he was ready to come back inside, so she opened the back door for him. "The pizzas are guaranteed in twenty-five minutes or we get them free."

While waiting for the delivery, she poured a glass of merlot and carried it up to the third floor, which she had converted into a home office. She had cashed in a trust fund to purchase the townhouse, located in the fashionable Dupont Circle district. The building was quaint and had character and was also convenient to everything in the city.

Initially she had leased out the top floor, which was a self-contained apartment. But when her renter moved to Europe with six months left on her lease, Barrie used the extra money to convert the three cramped rooms into one large studio/office.

One entire wall of the room was now devoted to videotape storage. She had shelves upon shelves of them. She saved all her own reports, newscasts of historical significance, and every news magazine show. The tapes were alphabetized according to subject. She went straight to the tape she wanted, loaded it into the VCR, and watched it while slowly sipping her wine.

The death and funeral of Robert Rushton Merritt had been thoroughly documented. The tragedy seemed doubly unfair since it had happened to the Merritts, whose marriage was considered the epitome of perfection.

President David Malcomb Merritt could have been a poster boy for any young American male who aspired to hold the office. He was classically handsome, athletic, attractive, and charismatic to men and women alike.

Vanessa Merritt was the perfect armpiece for her husband. She was gorgeous. Her beauty and southern-bred charm somehow made up for any shortcomings. Such as wit. And wisdom. She wasn't considered a dynamo in the brains department, but nobody seemed to care. The public had wanted a First Lady with whom to fall in love, and Vanessa Armbruster Merritt had easily fulfilled that need.

David's parents were long deceased. He had no living relatives. Vanessa's father, however, more than compensated for this lack. Cletus Armbruster had been the senior senator from Mississippi for as long as anyone could remember. He'd survived more presidents than most Americans remembered voting for.

Together they formed a photogenic triumvirate as famous as any royal family. Not since the Kennedy administration had an American president, his wife, and their personal life attracted so much public attention and adoration, nationwide and around the world. Everything they did, everywhere they went, singly or together, created a stir.

Consequently, America went positively ga-ga when it was announced that the First Lady was pregnant with the couple's first child. The baby would make perfection even more perfect.

The baby's birth was given more press than Desert Storm or the ethnic cleansing in Bosnia. Barrie remembered watching, from a newsroom monitor, the umpteenth story on the Merritt baby's arrival at the White House. Howie had sourly remarked, "Should we be on the lookout for a bright star in the East?"

The only event to receive as much news coverage was that same baby's death three months later.

The world was plunged into shock and grief. No one wanted to believe it. No one could believe it. America mourned.

Barrie finished her wine, rewound the videotape for the third time, and watched again as the funeral scenes sadly unfolded.

Looking pale and tragically beautiful in her mourning suit, Vanessa Merritt was unable to stand without assistance. It was obvious to all that her heart was broken. It had taken years for her to conceive a child, another personal aspect of her life that had been explored and exploited in great detail by the media. To lose the child she'd struggled to bear made her a truly tragic heroine.

The President looked courageously stoic as tears streaked his lean cheeks and ran into the attractive furrows on either side of his mouth. Pundits commented on his attentiveness to his wife. On that day, David Merritt was seen primarily as a husband and father who happened also to be the chief executive.

Senator Armbruster wept unashamedly into a white handkerchief. His contribution to his grandson's small coffin was a tiny Mississippi state flag, sticking up among the white roses and baby's breath.

Had Barrie been in the First Lady's situation, she would have wanted to grieve privately. She would have resented the cameras and commentators. Even though she knew her colleagues were only doing their jobs—indeed, Barrie herself had been in the thick of it—the funeral had been a public spectacle, shared via satellite with the entire world. How had Vanessa Merritt held up even as well as she had?

Barrie's doorbell rang.

She glanced at the clock. "Damn! Twenty-four minutes, thirty-nine seconds. You know, Cronkite," she said as they went down the stairs, "I think they do that on purpose just to build our hopes up."

Luigi himself delivered. He was a short, rotund Italian with a rosy sweating face, fleshy cherub lips, and a mop of curly black hair—on his chest. His head was completely bald.

"Miss Travis," he said, *tsk*ing as he took in her attire. "I was hoping the extra pizza tonight was for a lover."

"Nope. The meatball one's for Cronkite. Hope you didn't go too heavy on the garlic. It gives him gas. How much?"

"I put it on your bill."

"Thanks." She reached for the two boxes, whose aroma was causing Cronkite to do an ecstatic do-si-do around her feet. Cronkite's circles, the merlot, and hunger were making her dizzy.

Luigi, however, wasn't going to relinquish the pizzas without the lecture that came as a standing side order. "You're a movie star—"

"I'm on TV news."

"Same thing," he argued. "I say to the missus, 'Miss Travis is a good customer. Two, three nights a week, she calls us. Good for us, but bad for her. She's alone too much.' And the missus says—"

"That maybe Miss Travis prefers being alone."

"No. She says that you don't meet men because all the time you work."

"I meet men, Luigi. But all the good ones are taken. The ones I meet are either married, gay, creepy, or otherwise out of the question. But I appreciate your concern." Again she reached for the pizzas. Again they were withheld.

"You're pretty, Miss Travis."

"I don't stop traffic."

"You got nice hair. Nice reddish color. Good skin, too. And very unusual green eyes."

"Very ordinary hazel." Not spectacular at all. Not like, say, Vanessa Merritt's limpid sapphire pools.

"Kinda small up here." Luigi's eyes moved to her breasts. Barrie knew from long experience that if she allowed it, he would now begin an evaluation of her figure.

"But not too small," he reassured her hastily. "You're slim all over."

"And getting slimmer." She snatched the pizza boxes. "Thanks, Luigi. Add a good tip for yourself to my bill, and give my regards to your wife." She closed the door before he could launch into another lament on her lacking love life.

Cronkite was whipping himself into a frenzy, so she served him his pizza, box and all. Then she sat down at the kitchen table with her pizza, another glass of wine, and the library books she'd checked out that afternoon. The pizza, as always, was scrumptious. The second glass of wine went down even smoother than the first. The research on SIDS was fascinating.

Of the three, the research was the one she finished completely, craving more.

Chapter
Three

$\mathcal{F}$rowning skeptically, Howie Fripp dug into his ear canal with the jagged tip of his car key. "I dunno."

Barrie had a primal urge to leap across his desk and tear out his throat with her teeth. No one else unleashed this feral aspect of her personality. Only Howie. It wasn't only his disgusting personal habits and his flagrant chauvinism that aroused such savage instincts. It was his whining gutlessness and lack of vision.

"What don't you like about it?"

"It's depressing," he replied, executing a shiver for effect. "Babies dying in their beds. Who wants to watch a series about that?"

"New parents. Prospective parents. Parents to whom it's happened. Anyone who wants to be informed and enlightened, which I hope includes at least a portion of our viewing audience."

"You live in a dream world, Barrie. Our audience watches because *Cheers* reruns come on after the news."

Barrie tried to keep the impatience out of her voice. If he knew she was getting riled, he would become even more obtuse. "Because of the subject matter, the series won't be jolly. But it doesn't have to be maudlin, either. I've contacted a couple who lost a child to SIDS two years ago. They've since had another baby, and they're willing to do an on-camera interview about how they've coped."

Coming to her feet, she tried to close the sale. "The thrust will be light at the end of the tunnel. Victory over adversity. It could be very uplifting."

"You already lined up an interview?"

"Subject to your approval, of course," she said, giving him a stroke. "I wanted to get my ducks in a row before I came to you, Howie. I've been researching this for a week, talking to pediatricians and psychologists. It's a timely topic, especially since the death of the Merritt baby."

"Everybody's sick of hearing about that."

"But I'm approaching it from several unique angles."

This wasn't just part of the sales pitch. The more she'd researched Sudden Infant Death Syndrome, the more fascinated she'd become by spin-off subjects that were just as interesting and worthy of exploration as the core. As she'd studied, she'd come to realize that a single, ninety-second piece wouldn't begin to cover them.

Only Howie stood in her way. "I dunno," he repeated. The ignition key was doing a Roto-Rooter on his other ear as he reread her outline. It was detailed but brief. Surely someone of even his limited mental capacity could comprehend it.

She'd asked for three segments, to air on consecutive nights during the two evening newscasts. Each would focus on a different element of SIDS. She'd proposed that they be heavily promoted well in advance.

Ultimately—of course, this wasn't in the proposal—a news producer in the viewing audience would appreciate her work and offer to hire her away from the leper colony of broadcast journalism, otherwise known as the WVUE news department.

Howie belched. The key had produced a glob of brown wax, which he wiped on the top sheet of her outline. "I'm not convinced—"

"I've got an interview with Mrs. Merritt."

He dropped the gooey key. "Huh?"

It was a lie, of course. But desperate times . . . "We recently had coffee together."

"You and the First Lady?"

"That's right. At her invitation. During the course of our conversation, I mentioned doing a series. She endorsed the idea and agreed to share her thoughts."

"On camera?"

Barrie had a sudden vision of Vanessa Merritt trying to hide behind her RayBans, holding a forbidden cigarette with shaking hands—a vision of the woman as an emotional wreck.

"Of course on camera," she said, rolling her eyes.

"You don't say anything about the First Lady in your outline."

"I was saving her as a surprise."

"Okay, I'm surprised," he said dryly.

She'd never been a good liar, but then Howie wasn't an exceptionally good judge of character, so she thought she was safe.

He leaned forward across his desk. "If Mrs. Merritt consents to an interview—"

"She will."

"You still gotta turn out one regular story each day." With that, he sat back and scratched his crotch.

She weighed the condition, then shook her head firmly. "This deserves my full attention, Howie. I'd really like to devote all my time to it."

"And I'd really like to fuck Sharon Stone. But we don't always get what we want, do we?"

Barrie reconsidered. "Okay. Provision accepted."

"Barrie Travis."

"Who?"

The First Lady cleared her throat before repeating the name. "Barrie Travis. She's a reporter for WVUE."

"Oh, yeah. Sort of a breathy voice?" David Merritt, President of the United States, affixed a cuff link bearing the presidential seal. "I called on her at a recent press conference. Her reports on the White House are usually favorable, aren't they?"

"Very."

"So what about her?"

Vanessa, already dressed and seated on a chaise, took a swallow of white wine. "She's doing a series on SIDS and wants to include an interview with me."

Merritt slipped on his tuxedo jacket and checked his reflection in the mirror. When he took office, he had decided against having a personal valet. Not even the most experienced haberdasher knew how to take advantage of his physique better than he himself. The cut of his jacket accentuated his broad shoulders and narrow waist. He kept his hair well trimmed but never lacquered into place. Secretly, he preferred it rakishly windblown. He wore formal clothes with elegance and grace. In blue jeans, he was the boy next door.

Liking what he saw in the mirror, he turned to his wife. "And?"

"And she'll be at the reception tonight. Dalton has promised her an answer."

Dalton Neely was the White House press secretary. He

had been handpicked and well trained by Merritt and his top adviser, Spencer Martin.

"Actually, the formal request came through Dalton's office." Vanessa shook out a Valium from the prescription bottle in her beaded evening bag. "Barrie Travis has been calling my office for several days. I haven't taken her calls, but she's very persistent."

"Reporters make their living by being persistent."

"Well, her persistence has put me on the spot. Dalton approached me this afternoon with her request. Both want an answer from me tonight."

Quickly closing the distance between them, the President grasped her hand and took the small yellow tablet from her palm. He removed the prescription bottle from her evening bag and dropped the pill back into it, then pocketed the bottle.

"I need that, David."

"No, you don't. No more of this, either." He took the wineglass from her and set it aside. "It counteracts your medication."

"That's only my second glass."

"It's your third. You're lying to me, Vanessa."

"Okay, so I lost count. Big deal. I—"

"Not about the wine. About this reporter. She didn't put you in a spot—you did that yourself. She didn't start calling your office until your outing with her a couple of weeks ago. Isn't that the way it happened?"

He'd been informed of their meeting the day it occurred, so he wasn't surprised by Barrie Travis's request for an interview. What bothered him was that, without his consent, Vanessa had initiated a conversation with a member of the media. Vanessa and a reporter, especially one reputed to be less than reliable, was a dangerous combination.

"Did you have me spied on?" she fired.

"Why'd you make that date with her, Vanessa?"

"I needed someone to talk to. Is that a crime?"

"You chose a reporter to confide in?" He laughed skeptically.

"She wrote me a touching note. I thought she'd be nice to talk to."

"Next time try a priest."

"You're making a big deal out of nothing, David."

"If it wasn't a big deal, then why didn't you tell me about it?"

"It wasn't important until she asked for this on-camera interview. Before, our visit wasn't worth mentioning. She promised that anything I said that afternoon was off the record. I needed someone—a woman—to talk to."

"About what?"

"What do you think?" she shouted.

She jumped off the chaise, grabbed the glass of wine, and defiantly drained it.

He struggled to rein in his temper. "You're not yourself, Vanessa."

"You're damn right, I'm not. So you'll be much better off going without me tonight."

The reception, honoring a goodwill delegation from the Scandinavian countries, was to be her first official function since Robert Rushton's tragic death. The small, formal gathering seemed well suited for Vanessa's reemergence into public life. She'd retreated from it following the baby's death. Three months was enough time. The voting public needed to see her back in action.

"Of course you're coming," the President said. "You'll be the belle of the ball. You always are."

"But—"

"No *buts*. I'm tired of making excuses for you. We have to work through this, Vanessa. It's been twelve weeks."

"Is there a time limit on grief?"

He ignored the sting in her voice. "Tonight you'll come through like the Thoroughbred you are. Just be your charming, smiling self, and everything will be fine."

"I hate all those people, looking at me with pity and remorse and not knowing what to say. And when someone does say something, it's so trite, I want to scream."

"Just thank them for the sentiment and leave it at that."

"God!" she cried, her voice cracking. "How can you just resume—"

"Because I have to, dammit. And so do you."

He glared at her with such force that she fell back onto the chaise. Stricken, she stared up at him.

He turned away, and when again he spoke, his anger was contained. "I like your evening dress. Is it new?"

Her shoulders slumped. She lowered her head. Watching her in the mirror, he recognized these reflexive gestures as concessions of defeat. "I've lost weight," she mumbled. "Nothing in my closet fits anymore."

There was a tap on the door. He crossed the room and opened it. "Hey, Spence. Are they ready for us?"

Spencer Martin glanced over David's shoulder and surveyed the room. Spotting Vanessa, and the empty wineglass on the end table, he reversed David's question. "Are you ready for them?"

The President purposefully disregarded his adviser's concern. "Vanessa's got a mild case of stage fright, but, as you know, she always comes through."

"Maybe we're rushing her. If she doesn't feel up to it—"

"Nonsense. She's up to it." He turned toward his wife and extended his arm. "Ready, darling?"

She came to her feet and slowly walked toward them, not looking directly at either man.

One of David's personality traits was to ignore things he didn't want to acknowledge, such as the dislike between his wife and his top adviser. To fill the awkward silence, he said, "Doesn't she look beautiful tonight, Spence?"

"Indeed, Mr. President."

"Thank you," Vanessa replied stiffly. As they stepped into the hallway, she took her husband's arm and asked, "What should Dalton tell Barrie Travis?"

"Barrie Travis the reporter?" Spence cut in. "Tell her about what?" He looked quizzically at the President.

"She's asked Dalton for an interview with Vanessa."

"About anything in particular?"

"SIDS," the President replied.

Barrie was positively giddy. Her words gushed out like water from a broken fire plug.

"I was going through the receiving line with my date. Don't get excited. He's a gay friend who's still in the closet. We scratched each other's back, so to speak. He had an invitation to the reception and needed a female date, and I had an opportunity to speak directly to the President and First Lady.

"Anyhow, I'm gliding along the receiving line, acting real cool and blasé, and when I get to the President, he clasps my hand between his, swear to God, and says, 'Miss Travis, thank you so much for coming. It's always a pleasure to have you at the White House. You look radiant tonight.'

"Actually, I don't remember his exact words, but suffice it to say that I wasn't treated like a stranger, or a passing acquaintance, or even an ordinary reporter. Barbara Walters couldn't have been more warmly greeted."

Cronkite yawned and made himself more comfortable in the center of her bed.

"Am I boring you?" Barrie asked, pausing for breath. "You don't seem to realize the importance of my getting the first exclusive interview with the First Lady since the death of her child.

"Actually the President mentioned it before I did. He said Mrs. Merritt had informed him of my SIDS series. He thinks it's an excellent idea and said that he urged the First Lady to participate. He commended me for raising public awareness on this heartbreaking phenomenon. Then he said that he and Mrs. Merritt would extend me their full cooperation. I was . . . Well, let me put it this way. If it had been sex, I would have been having multiple orgasms."

She climbed in with Cronkite, who took up two thirds of the bed and wouldn't budge an inch. Balancing on the edge of the mattress, she added, "I only wish Howie had been there to see it."

Chapter
Four

$\mathcal{H}$e was aware that the television was on, but it was only background noise until he heard the familiar voice. It brought his head up out of the bathroom sink, where he'd been sluicing cold water over his face. Grabbing a hand towel, he stepped around the corner into the bedroom.

". . . which, unfortunately, you and President Merritt share with thousands of other couples."

He didn't recognize the reporter. She was thirtyish, maybe older. Shoulder-length auburn hair. Wide eyes and bee-stung lips that promised a good time, although both eyes and lips were unsmiling now. Distinctive, husky voice, unusual for a broadcast journalist; most of them sounded as though they'd graduated from the same school of sterile diction. Her name was superimposed at the bottom of the TV screen. Barrie Travis. It rang no bells.

"The President and I were astounded to learn the number of families who experience this tragedy," Vanessa Merritt was saying. "Five thousand annually in our country alone."

This face and voice Gray Bondurant recognized and

knew well, even though it was instantly apparent to him that she'd been coached on how to conduct herself during the interview. She held her hands demurely in her lap, no gestures allowed. Facial expressions carefully schooled.

The interviewer segued into a sound bite from Dr. George Allan, the Merritts' personal physician, who'd had the unpleasant task of pronouncing Robert Rushton Merritt dead in the White House nursery. Dr. Allan explained that medical science is still trying to isolate causes and preventatives of Sudden Infant Death Syndrome.

Then the interview became more personal. "Mrs. Merritt, we all witnessed your and President Merritt's grief during your son's funeral." Scenes from the funeral were edited in. "You've had three months' distance from it. The wounds must surely still be tender, but I know our viewers would be interested in hearing any reflections you might wish to express."

Vanessa took a moment. "My father has a saying: 'Adversity is a great opportunity in disguise.' As always, Daddy's right," she said with a fleeting smile. "David and I feel that we've become stronger, as a couple and as individuals, because we've been tested to the limit of our endurance, and we've survived."

"Bullshit." He balled up the hand towel and hurled it across the bedroom, then picked up the remote control, unwilling to listen to any more.

But he paused. Vanessa was saying, "The President and I hope that others who experience a similar tragedy can draw courage and comfort from survivors like us. Life *does* go on."

Swearing, Bondurant hit the Off button.

Scripted responses, signed, sealed, and delivered to Vanessa to memorize and parrot. Words composed by Dalton Neely. Maybe her father, Clete Armbruster. Possibly even the President, with final approval by Spencer Martin.

However they'd been rehearsed and revised in advance of the interview, they weren't Vanessa's words. She had spoken them, but not spontaneously and not from her heart. He doubted that the reporter with the sexy voice was aware that she'd been duped. Vanessa had been as well programmed as a talking doll with a computer chip in her head. Revealing her inner feelings wouldn't be seemly. It damn sure wouldn't be politic.

Feeling that the walls of the bedroom were closing in on him, Bondurant stalked to the kitchen to get a beer, then went out onto his front porch. Ten feet deep and shaded by an overhang, the porch extended the width of the house. He flung himself into his rush-seated rocking chair and tipped the beer to his mouth. The muscles of his tanned throat worked as he drank half the can in one long swallow.

He looked like a beer commercial. Pictures of him drinking it bare-chested in these rustic surroundings could have sold millions of cans of any brand-name brew, but he didn't realize that, or care. He knew he made an impact on people, but he had never bothered to analyze why. Vanity wasn't in his nature, certainly not during the past year, when weeks would pass without his seeing another living soul. If he drove into Jackson Hole, he might shave. Or he might not.

He was as he was. Take him or leave him. That was, and always had been, his attitude, and he silently communicated it to everyone he met, which was one of the reasons why he hadn't blended in well with the Washington scene. He was glad to be out of it. A certain amount of conformity was required of presidential confidants; Gray Bondurant was a nonconformist.

His blue eyes as hard and cold as a glacier, he stared at the jagged snow-capped peaks of the Tetons. Actually miles away, they looked close enough to touch. Purple mountains' majesty. In his front yard. Imagine that.

He crushed the empty beer can as though it were a foil gum wrapper. He wished he could take back the last ten minutes. Why hadn't he stayed outside a little longer before going in to wash up? What quirk of fate had made him tune his TV to that particular channel at that particular time?

He wished he'd never seen the interview. *Thank you so much, Barrie Travis, whoever the hell you are.* For days now he would be haunted by thoughts of David, and Vanessa, and the baby who had died in the White House nursery.

What galled him most was that the interview might spark a renewed public interest in him. People would begin thinking, supposing, connecting the dots. And then the shit would start flying all over again.

❦

David Merritt paced in front of his desk in the Oval Office. His shirtsleeves were rolled to his elbows; his hands were deep in his pockets. Beneath an errant lock of hair, his brow was furrowed. "I've never heard of it before. What the hell is it?"

"It's called Munchausen syndrome by proxy, named after a German count who got off by inflicting pain on himself."

"I thought that was masochism," Spencer Martin remarked.

Dr. George Allan shrugged and poured himself another scotch from the President's private stock. "It's a little out of my area, and I haven't thoroughly researched it."

"Barrie Travis did." Merritt made it sound like a rebuke, and the doctor took it as such.

Looking abashed, he said, "The 'by proxy' kicks in if the pain is inflicted on someone else, typically a child."

"What's it got to do with SIDS?" Merritt asked. "Why'd Barrie Travis go into it so deeply?"

Dr. Allan took a quick sip of his scotch. "Because

adults afflicted with the disorder sometimes take it to the extreme. They injure their children, sometimes even kill them, in an attempt to get attention and sympathy for themselves. Some mysterious infant deaths, previously attributed to SIDS, are now being reinvestigated as possible murders."

Muttering a curse, Merritt sat down behind his desk. "Why couldn't that Travis broad have stuck to the subject without bringing all those horror stories into it? Pour me one of those, will you?"

The doctor did as asked.

"Thanks." Merritt thoughtfully sipped his drink for a few moments, then looked over at Spence. He didn't like what he saw. Spence was in his thinking mode, and the matter under consideration was troublesome.

"Maybe I shouldn't have encouraged Vanessa to grant the interview," Merritt ventured.

"I disagree. What possible harm's been done?" the doctor asked.

"For God's sake, George, you better than anyone should know," Merritt said testily. "This goddamn series has got her bouncing off the walls again."

"People are noticing," Spence remarked quietly. Merritt gave him a sharp glance that demanded names. "Staff, sir. People have noticed the First Lady's mood swings, and they're concerned about her."

In another implied rebuke, Merritt turned to the physician.

"I can't control her mood swings with medication when she's drinking as much as she is," Dr. Allan said.

Merritt dug his fists into his eye sockets. "Clete's on my ass about that. I keep reminding him that she's lost her baby. That, coupled with her condition, how can he expect her not to be a little unstable."

"Everybody responds to tragedy differently," the doc-

tor said, trying to be helpful. "Some people pitch themselves
into their work, hoping to exhaust themselves so they don't
have the energy to dwell on it. Some people find God, light
candles, and pray. Some—"

"I get it, I get it," Merritt snapped. "My father-in-law
doesn't."

"I'll talk to him if you'd like," Spence offered.

The President barked a mirthless laugh. "Clete doesn't
like you, Spence. You're the last person he'd want com-
menting on Vanessa's emotional health. She's not too crazy
about you either." He turned back to the doctor. "But you,
George—maybe if you spoke with him, explained . . ."

"I'll call him tomorrow and say that you told me about
his concerns. I'll reassure him that she's being carefully
monitored."

"Thanks." Merritt smiled, as though the matter were
closed.

"It's not just Clete we've got to worry about," Spence
said. "Next year is an election year. This administration
needs its First Lady. We need Vanessa, we need her soon,
and we need her well adjusted and ready to campaign." He
turned to the doctor. "Can you deliver?"

"Of course. There's no alternative."

"There's always an alternative."

Spence's rejoinder moved like a chill wind through the
room.

"Jesus, Spence," Merritt said. "You sound about as
cheerful as a death knell. Forget Mr. Gloom and Doom over
there, George," he said, coming to his feet to shake hands
with the physician. "Vanessa's in your good hands, so I'm not
going to worry. And thanks for explaining this Munchausen
thing, although it was irrelevant to Robert's death."

Peering deeply into the doctor's eyes, he added,
"Robert stopped breathing in his crib. Explanation

unknown. That was your official ruling, and you're standing by it. Correct?"

"Absolutely. SIDS." Dr. Allan finished his drink, then said his goodbyes.

"He'd better come through," Spence remarked when he and the President were alone.

"Have no fear. He will."

"But will Vanessa?"

"She always has, hasn't she?"

"Before, yes. Now I'm not so sure she can pull herself together." Only Spencer Martin could have spoken this frankly to the President about the First Lady.

While Merritt appreciated his top adviser's concern, he thought it was disproportionate to the problem. "I stand by my decision. The public needed to see Vanessa do that interview, Spence. She looked great. Sounded great."

Spence was still frowning. "Then why do I wish we'd never consented to it? I'm getting bad vibes. It bothers me that she made the initial contact with the reporter, not the other way around."

"That bothered me, too, at first," Merritt admitted. "But it turned out all right. It was good p.r. for her and for us. As George said, no harm was done."

When Spence failed to reply, the President looked at him sharply.

"Well, we'll see," Spence said, in his foreboding way.

"All right, who is he?"

"Who?" Barrie didn't even look up. In her lap was a pile of phone messages, cards, and letters from viewers, all relating to her SIDS series. In her most optimistic dreams, she'd never expected so great a response.

"You're a sly one, Barrie, hiding this one from us."

Finally she raised her head. "Oh, my God!"

The newsroom receptionist was completely hidden behind the enormous floral arrangement she had carried into Barrie's cubicle. "Where do you want it?"

"Uh . . ." As always, the top of her desk was a hazard zone. "The floor, I guess."

After depositing the arrangement, the receptionist straightened up. "Whoever he is, even if he looks like a toad, to lay out this many bucks for flowers, I say he's a keeper."

Barrie had opened the card attached to the bouquet and was smiling. "I'd say so too, but he's married."

"All the good ones are."

Barrie passed the card to the woman, whose eyes bugged when she read the familiar signature following the handwritten message. Her shriek brought several newsroom staffers crowding into the cubicle.

Barrie reclaimed the card and fanned herself with it. "Just a little token of appreciation from the President, extolling my talent and insight, praising me for the excellence of my series, and thanking me for the patriotic service I've performed."

"One more word and I'm gonna puke." Howie had joined the group.

Barrie laughed and replaced the card in its envelope. It would be something to show her grandchildren. "You're just jealous because you're not a personal friend of the Merritts." Howie and her other co-workers ambled out, a few grousing about the luck of *some* people.

When she was alone, Barrie placed a telephone call. Speaking softly, she asked, "Are you free tonight?"

"Are you serious?"

"What've you got in your freezer?"

"Two steaks."

"I'll bring the wine." She glanced at the bouquet. "And flowers. I'll be there in half an hour."

Chapter Five

"You call that half an hour?"

"Stop bitching and give me a hand." Barrie, carrying the President's bouquet, two bottles of wine, and a grocery sack, wedged her way through the front door of Daily Welsh's house.

"You rob a new grave, or what?" he asked.

"Read the card, smart-ass."

He plucked the card from the floral arrangement and gave a low whistle. "Pretty impressive."

She smiled cheekily. "All in a day's work."

"What are you going to do for an encore?"

"Any other time, I'd offer a scathing comeback about your unfailing talent of throwing a wet blanket over everything good, but I'm tired, so I'll just let it pass and open the wine instead."

"That gets my vote."

Together they went into the kitchen, which was the most appealing room by default. It was a singularly ugly house. Daily arm-wrestled a stuck drawer to get the corkscrew.

"How are you?" she asked, showing her concern.

"I'm not dead yet."

But Ted Welsh—or Daily, as he was known to friends—looked like the next labored breath might be his last. He'd developed emphysema from smoking countless cigarettes during the countless days he had worked to provide the public with news.

Fresh out of high school he had begun working as a gofer on a daily newspaper. Hence, his nickname. He'd worked his way up the ranks and through several journalistic media to become news chief at a network affiliate TV station in Richmond, from which he'd taken an early retirement due to the rapid progression of his disease.

Not yet old enough to receive Social Security—and probably never would be—he lived on a modest pension. The "steaks" thawing on the countertop were actually ground meat patties. Fearing as much, Barrie had picked up two T-bones when she stopped to buy the wine. Daily sipped the Sonoma County vintage while she prepared their dinner.

As he rolled his portable oxygen tank closer to his chair and out of her way, he said, "Cronkite will get a hard-on when he gets a whiff of those bones."

"Unlikely. He's been neutered."

"Oh, I forgot. You castrated even him."

She slammed a jar of meat marinade onto the counter and turned to him. "Don't start *that!*"

"But it's true. You de-ball every guy you meet. It's your way of rejecting a man before he can reject you."

"I haven't rejected you."

"I don't count," he said on a wheezing laugh. "I'm too old and sick to get it up anyhow. I pose no threat. Which brings me to another point. You shouldn't waste your evenings coming to see me. If I'm the best you can do in the way of male companionship, your life's pretty pathetic."

"But I love you, Daily." She closed the distance between them and kissed his cheek.

"Cut it out." He pushed her away. "And don't overcook those steaks. I want mine bloody."

Barrie wasn't deceived by his gruffness. Her affection for him was reciprocated. Their friendship had gotten off to a rocky start, but it was now unshakable. They had reached a comfort level where deprecations were almost equivalent to endearments.

"I'd take twenty years off my life for a cigarette," he remarked as they were enjoying after-dinner coffee in his living room.

"You already have."

"Oh. Right." He was seated in his threadbare recliner, his breathing apparatus at the side of the chair. Plastic tubing fed oxygen from the portable tank directly into his nostrils.

Across the room, Barrie was relaxing on the sofa. She pulled her feet up beneath her and hugged a throw pillow to her chest. "I was with someone else recently who was having a nicotine fit. Someone you would never expect."

"Who?"

"It's confidential."

"Who am I gonna tell? Nobody comes here but you."

"You could have other friends over. You don't invite anyone."

"I can't stand their pity."

"Then you should join a support group."

"Who wants to spend time with a bunch of sickies, sucking wind? Literally."

"We've had this conversation before," she said in a sing-song voice. "Let's not do it again tonight."

"Fine with me," he growled. "Who's the mystery smoker?"

She hesitated. "Our First Lady."

His eyebrows lifted with interest. "No shit? Preinterview jitters?"

"No. That day we met for coffee."

"Now that you've interviewed her one on one, do you still think she's a dimwit?"

"I never thought that."

He gave her a look. "You've called her that a dozen times, sitting right where you are now. Mississippi Belle. Isn't that your nickname for her? You've described her as one of those women who never have an original thought, or pretend not to. All her opinions are formed by men, men she fawns over, namely her father and her husband. She's vacuous and vapid. Have I left out anything?"

"No, that about covers it." Sighing, Barrie absently traced the rim of her coffee cup with her finger. "That's still my opinion, but I also feel sorry for her. I mean, losing your baby. Lord."

"So?"

Barrie didn't realize that she'd lapsed into a thoughtful silence until Daily's question nudged her out of it. "So, what?"

"You're gnawing your inner cheek, a sure sign that something's on your mind. I've been waiting all evening for you to unload it, whatever it is."

She could hide her feelings from everyone else, including herself, but never from Daily. When she was puzzled, or troubled, or otherwise stressed, he homed in on it with the inner radar that had made him an excellent newsman.

"I don't know what it is," she told him honestly. "It's just this . . ."

"Itch at the back of your neck?"

"Something like that."

"Probably means you're on to something, but you don't know what."

Daily leaned forward in his chair, his eyes shining as brightly as those of a firehouse dog at the first clang of the bell. There was color in his cheeks, making him look healthier than he had in weeks, rejuvenated by the scent of a hot lead.

His keen interest made Barrie feel guilty for having broached the subject. She was setting him up for a big disappointment. There probably was no story here. On the other hand, what harm could come from sharing a few thoughts? Maybe he could make sense of them. Either that, or he could tell her there was no life in her sketchy ideas.

"The SIDS series has generated a lot of interest," she began. "Did I tell you I got it on the bird?" Her series had been fed to a satellite, allowing it national coverage.

"It's certainly given your career a kick in the butt," Daily said. "Which is what you wanted, isn't it? So what's the problem?"

She stared into her cup, swirling the coffee that had grown too cool to drink. "When I first met with her, she was having understandable guilt feelings, so I reminded her that no one can be blamed for a crib death—that it just happens. Curiously, she said, 'Does it?'

"It was that question and the way she asked it that prompted me to research SIDS. Then I ran across a bizarre story of a woman who'd had four babies die of the syndrome. Which later proved not to be the case."

"She had that . . . that . . ."

"Munchausen syndrome by proxy," Barrie supplied. "Some crib deaths are now coming under suspicion. Mothers are being charged with killing their own babies to get attention.

"Well . . ." She took a deep breath and held it, raised her head, and gave him a puissant look.

He held her stare for a noticeable length of time. Finally he said, "Maybe I should adjust my oxygen level. I'm either not getting enough, or I'm getting too much. For a minute there I thought you were suggesting that the First Lady of the United States killed her own baby."

Barrie set her cup on the coffee table and came to her feet. "I did no such thing."

"Sounded like it."

"That's not what I'm suggesting, Daily. I swear."

"Then why all this cheek gnawing?"

"I don't know! But something's not right." She dropped back onto the edge of the sofa and held her head between her hands. "I've been with Vanessa Merritt twice in the last few weeks. The first time, she was as strung out as a junkie on the second day of detox—a woman clearly on the verge of emotional collapse. The day of the interview, she was another person entirely. Superior. Cool. Controlled. Correct. And about as . . . as *human* as that coffee table."

"It was a good interview."

"It was passionless, Daily, and you know it," she shot back. His wince told her that he agreed. "The interview with Mrs. Merritt should have been the highlight of the series. Instead, it was the low point. She was plastic. If she'd been like that the first time, I probably wouldn't have noticed. But the contrast between the first Vanessa Merritt and the second was dramatic."

"So she popped a coupla Valiums before she went on camera," Daily said, shrugging.

"Probably. I'm sure she was medicated the night I saw her at that reception—either that or she was drunk. Gorgeous as ever, but vague. Almost . . . I don't know . . . afraid. The President covered—"

"And that's another thing," she said, interrupting herself and launching into another tangent. "He greeted me as though he and I were old chums. Naturally I was flattered by his attention, but I thought it was odd. He was enthusiastic

about the series, before and after it was produced. I me.
look at those flowers. What they cost would have made a
substantial dent in the national debt."

"Then that shoots your theory all to hell, doesn't it? He
wouldn't feel that way toward you and your series if it had
shed an unfavorable light on his wife."

"I'm just surprised by the palsy-walsy treatment. I've
been covering the White House beat for a long time. Why all
of a sudden are the President and I good friends?"

"Barrie, you're a journalist. He's an incumbent facing
reelection next year. He's got to schmooze all journalists.
Win the press, win the election."

She had to concede the validity of Daily's explanation.
David Merritt had, from his first term in Congress, known
how to court the media. The love affair had lasted through his
campaign for the presidency. The gilt was beginning to wear
off the romance, although his media coverage remained
largely favorable. But Barrie Travis was a small-time reporter
who wielded zero influence. Why was he schmoozing her?

Her mind darted from one puzzle to another, as it had
ever since her first meeting with Vanessa Merritt. She didn't
stay with any one thought too long because she feared all of
them were booby-trapped.

"I could probably shrug off the inconsistencies and still
sleep nights, except for one thing," she told Daily. "And I
think this is the real kicker. When we completed the interview, she hugged me. *Me*."

Daily continued playing devil's advocate. "It was good
p.r."

"No, it was an excuse."

"For what?"

"To get close enough to whisper something in my ear
that couldn't be overheard. She said, 'Barrie, please help me.
Don't you know what I'm trying to tell you?' "

...iments exactly, Daily. That was the first and
...e displayed any honest emotion. She sounded
...What do you think she meant?"

...the hell should I know? It could mean, Help me
get my husband reelected. Or, Help me generate public
awareness of SIDS. Or, Help me recover from my grief. It
could mean anything or nothing."

"If it's nothing, it's nothing," Barrie said. "But if it's
something, the implications are explosive."

He shook his head. "I still don't buy it. Why would she
kill her baby after trying so hard to have one?"

"I thought we'd established that. Munchausen syndrome."

"She doesn't fit the profile," he argued. "Women
afflicted with the disorder are usually looking for sympathy
and attention. Vanessa Merritt has outdistanced Princess Di
in terms of press. She gets more attention than any other
woman in the world."

"But does she get it from the one who really counts?"

"The President? You think she's a neglected wife, and
she did this to rattle his cage?"

"It's a possibility."

"A slim one."

"But possible," Barrie stressed. "Look at the public
sympathy Jackie Kennedy received when little Patrick died.
She became an icon."

"For many more reasons than losing a newborn."

"But that tragedy contributed to the legend she became.
Maybe this First Lady wants to create a similar aura for herself."

"Next theory," Daily said with a dismissive gesture.

"HIV. What if one of them is carrying the virus? The
child could test positive. Mrs. Merritt couldn't risk the

humiliation of the world finding out about her or her husband's sexual history."

"Another very slim possibility," Daily said. "If either of them was HIV positive, it would have come out before now—say, when she got pregnant. The President gets routine physical checkups. A secret like that wouldn't remain a secret for very long."

"I suppose you're right." She thought about it for another moment. "Maybe we're overlooking the obvious. What if her motive was plain ol' everyday spite? She impresses me as a woman accustomed to getting her way, a woman who wouldn't tolerate rejection."

"What's your point?"

"She killed their son to punish the President for his affairs."

"*Rumored* affairs."

"Come on, Daily." Barrie groaned. "Everybody knows he's a womanizer. He just hasn't been caught with a naked lady in bed with him, yet."

"And until he is, and the *60 Minutes* crew is there to tape it, and Mike Wallace gets his confession on video, his escapades remain a rumor."

"Mrs. Merritt must know."

"Of course she knows. But she'll smile and pretend that she doesn't, just like every wife of every horny public official has done throughout the history of elected office."

"I still think the woman-scorned motivation is a damn strong one."

Daily tugged thoughtfully on his lower lip. "Barrie, this story has won you industry attention. Positive attention this time."

"My moment in the limelight has nothing to do with this."

"You sure? This series was so good, it's temporarily

overshadowed the Justice Green debacle and proved your critics wrong. You deserve the accolades, but beware of getting greedy. Are you sure that you're not exploiting your sudden attention by inventing another story? Could you be using all this hype as a ticket out of professional purgatory?"

She was about to answer a firm and unarguable no, but she paused to reexamine her motives. Was she shaping the facts to suit her own purposes? Was she letting ambition color her objectivity? Worse, was she falling back into her habit of jumping to the wrong conclusion in order to create a much more dramatic story?

"Honestly, no. I've looked at this objectively and from every possible angle. The woman lost her child. For that, she has my heartfelt sympathy. But isn't it possible that instead of being a victim of cruel fate, she's the victim of unfathomable malice, which drove her to commit the worst crime imaginable? That's the question that's got its hooks into me.

"From the start, it smelled fishy. Why'd she call and invite me to meet her? She's never done that before—not with any reporter I know of. And while we were talking, it was as though she was trying to communicate something without coming right out and saying it. What if that something was a confession?

"If she were anyone other than the First Lady, I wouldn't have waited this long to investigate her story. I think I owe it to myself to dig a little deeper. And, at the risk of sounding incredibly corny, I think I owe it to our nation."

"Okay," Daily said. "Let me ask you just one more thing."

"Shoot."

"What the hell are you hanging around here for?"

Chapter
Six

After a week of zealously following leads that led nowhere, Barrie's ardor began to cool. All she had to show for the time she'd spent pursuing the story of Robert Rushton Merritt's death was frustration.

She'd explored every angle that she and Daily had discussed, but none had panned out. She was trapped in a Catch-22: The story called for a full-fledged investigation, which couldn't be conducted without revealing the story.

To make matters worse, Howie's prostate was acting up again—of course, he had regaled her with all the disgusting details—so he'd been grumpier than usual. Jealous over the success of her series, he was assigning her the stories that other reporters refused to do, the ones placed last in the broadcast lineup. She covered them without complaint, and as quickly as possible, so she could spend more time on the story that consumed her.

Even to consider that the First Lady might have smothered her baby son was treasonous. What was the penalty for treason these days? Public hanging? Firing squad?

Barrie had come to fear that she, not Vanessa Merritt, was suffering a mental breakdown. She was hearing voice inflections that weren't really there, reading hidden meanings into offhand remarks. She should give up this ridiculous notion and concentrate her efforts on the stories Howie doled out to her, rather than hitch her future to a star that would probably explode and form a black hole around her and her career.

But she couldn't give it up. What if, after a few setbacks, Bernstein and Woodward had given up the Watergate story?

She was in her cubicle, studying her notes in search of another new slant, when the director of the evening news interrupted her concentration. "Yo, Barrie. The intro on the story you did for tonight?"

"What about it?"

"There was a hum in the mike. Howie says you should do an intro live from the set."

She glanced at the clock on her desk. They were eight minutes from airtime. "In case you haven't noticed, I got soaked this afternoon, just as we finished shooting the story. My hair's still wet."

"And your eye make-up is all . . ." The hand gestures he made over his own face were discouraging. "But it's either that or ditch the story. Howie says this is your big chance at stardom."

"I'm not holding my breath," she sighed, "but to keep the peace, I'll do it." She grabbed her satchel. "If anybody's looking for me, I'll be in the ladies' room."

"I'll be out here praying for a miracle," the director called after her.

After the newscast, Barrie returned to her desk and checked her messages. One was from a crank who'd been calling her for years claiming that the makers of a popular laxative had put a voodoo hex on him that caused chronic constipation. One was from a newly acquired crank, identifying herself as Charlene and reviling Barrie for being dense and just plain stupid. And one was from Anna Chen, her source at D.C. General.

"Anna?"

"Hi."

Anna Chen's voice was hushed and cautious, and Barrie noticed that she hadn't addressed her by name, although she obviously recognized her voice. Barrie automatically reached for a pad and pencil.

"The matter we discussed a few days ago?" the hospital clerk began.

"Yes."

"There's no copy available."

"I see." Barrie waited, sensing that the woman had more to say.

"The procedure was never performed."

Barrie swallowed hard. "Never performed? Is it . . . an elective procedure? Under the, uh, unusual circumstances, wasn't it mandatory?"

"Ordinarily, yes. But in this instance, the attending doctor determined that it wasn't necessary. He ordered that the procedure be waived, and it was."

Dr. George Allan, the President's personal physician, had ordered the coroner not to perform an autopsy. Barrie bore down so hard on her pencil that the lead broke. "Are you certain?"

"I've got to go."

"Just a few more questions?"

"I'm sorry."

Anna Chen hung up. Barrie stuffed her notes into her satchel, grabbed her raincoat and umbrella, and rushed from the newsroom.

She hadn't actually expected Anna Chen to be waiting for her in her office at the hospital. Nevertheless, she was disappointed to find the office locked and dark. Back in her car, she used her cellular phone.

"Do you have a telephone directory?" she asked Daily the moment he answered.

"Good evening to you, too."

"No time for civilities."

Responding to her urgency, he asked, "Metro D.C.?"

"Start there. Look up a residence listing for Anna Chen. C-h-e-n."

"Who's she?"

"I can't say."

"Oh. A source. What's up?"

"Too long to tell over the phone."

"Saw you on the news tonight," he said. Barrie heard pages flipping in the background.

"How'd I look?"

"I've seen worse."

"That bad? . . . How're you coming on the Chens?"

"No Anna, but there's an A. Chen."

"Give me that one. Phone number and address, please."

The hospital clerk lived in a recently remodeled building in Adams Morgan, a funky, ethnically rich neighborhood. The building's restoration hadn't included an elevator, so Barrie was short of breath by the time she reached the third-floor apartment. Not wanting to give Anna Chen an opportunity to avoid her, she hadn't called ahead. She was relieved to hear a TV through the door.

She rang the bell. The TV was muted immediately. She sensed that she was being viewed through the peephole in the door. "Please, Anna, I must speak with you."

After what seemed a long time, bolts were unlatched, then a chain lock allowed the door to be opened a few inches. Through the crack, Barrie saw only half of Anna Chen's pretty face.

"What are you doing here? You shouldn't have come."

"As long as I did, may I come in?"

"What do you want?"

"What do I *want*? Isn't that obvious? I want to ask why an autopsy wasn't done on—"

"I'm closing the door now. Please don't disturb me again."

"Anna!" Barrie wedged her foot in the door. "I don't understand. You can't just call and dump something like that on me and then not—"

"I don't know what you're talking about."

Barrie was incredulous. "Anna, what's going on? I don't get it."

And then she did. The woman's beautiful, almond-shaped eyes were filled with terror.

Lowering her voice to a whisper, Barrie said, "Have you been instructed not to speak to me?"

"Please, just go."

"Did someone warn you against talking to me? Were you threatened? By whom, Anna? Your superiors at the hospital? Someone in the medical examiner's office? Dr. Allan?" Still keeping her voice low, she said urgently, "You won't be named as my source. I swear it. Just nod if I'm right. Dr. George Allan ordered the coroner's office not to perform an autopsy. Did that mandate come from the President himself?"

Again the frightened young woman tried to close the door, which now felt like a vise on Barrie's instep. "Anna, please tell me what you know."

"I don't know anything. Go away. Leave me alone."

The Asian woman threw all ninety-five of her pounds against the door. Barrie wisely removed her foot. She was left standing in the hallway, staring at the brass figures on the door designating the apartment as 3C, and wondering just who the hell had muzzled Anna Chen. And why.

Vanessa Merritt switched off the TV in her private chambers. She'd been channel surfing when she happened to catch Barrie Travis on the WVUE news set. How could the girl be so stupid? Why hadn't she picked up the hint? But then, in some respects, Vanessa was relieved that she hadn't.

She didn't really want her secret exposed, but she didn't know how long she could stand keeping it to herself. Either way, she was afraid it would kill her.

She poured herself another glass of forbidden wine. To hell with the reprimands from her doctor, her father, and her husband. How could they possibly know what she needed or didn't need? They couldn't possibly understand how she had suffered. They were teamed up against her. They . . .

The thought drifted away before it was completed. That was happening frequently. She couldn't seem to hold a thought for more than a few seconds before it slipped away.

What had she been thinking about?

The baby, yes. Always. But there was something else. . . .

When her eyes strayed back to the TV, she remembered. Barrie Travis. The dumb bitch. Did she have to be hit by a two-by-four before she caught on? Why hadn't she gotten it? Or had she, but was too afraid to act on it. Was she stupid, or was she a coward? Whatever, the result was the same. No help could be expected from that quarter.

Vanessa had thought herself clever to use the reporter as a vessel. The idea had hatched when she'd spotted Barrie at a recent press conference on the east lawn. Wasn't she the one who'd broken the story of Supreme Court Justice Green's "death"? Wasn't it she who'd asked an incredibly dumb question at a press conference that had caused a spontaneous burst of laughter?

Barrie Travis's poor credibility had made her a perfect choice for Vanessa's purposes, which was to drop a few hints to an irresponsible reporter, someone who would get the ball rolling, would begin asking questions that seemed outlandish at first, but to which the important players eventually would seek answers. If Vanessa had planted the seeds of her story with one of the network heavyweights, she would have been dangerously exposed. This way, it would get out, but not directly through her.

Or so she had hoped. Obviously, Barrie Travis had been a poor choice. She wasn't only reckless, she was brainless.

So where could she turn next?

Out of habit, Vanessa reached for her telephone.

"Hi, Daddy."

"Hello!" the senator said. "I was going to call you later. How're you doing?"

"Fine."

"Quiet evening at home?"

"David's making a speech to some labor union convention. I forget where."

"Want me to come over and keep you company?"

"No, but thanks." She couldn't drink as much when her father was around.

"You shouldn't be alone, sweetheart."

"David's coming back tonight. It'll be late, but he promised to wake me."

After a pause, during which she could envision her father's steep frown, he said, "Maybe you should go back to your gynecologist. See if he can give you some hormones or something." He attributed all female ailments to a hormonal imbalance.

"That would hurt George's feelings."

"Screw George and his feelings," the senator boomed. "We're talking about your health here. George is a nice guy, and I assume he's a competent physician for routine stuff like bellyaches and flu shots. But you need a specialist. You need a psychiatrist." ·

"No, Daddy. No, I don't. Everything is under control."

"Losing little Robert has thrown your whole system out of kilter."

Vanessa took a sip of wine to deaden the sharp pain of remorse that his words sent through her. "David wouldn't approve. The First Lady can't have a shrink."

"It can be handled confidentially. Besides, who'd think badly of you for getting some help when you need it most? I'll talk to David about it."

"No!"

"Baby—"

"Please, Daddy, don't worry him. I'll get through it. It's just going to take me a little more time than we thought."

She had learned at the knee of the master, Senator Cletus Armbruster, how to practice politics. By the time they said good night, she had his promise not to confront David about her health.

To calm herself, she washed down another Valium with her wine, then floated into the bathroom and changed into a nightgown and robe. Propped up in bed, she tried to attend to some personal correspondence, but she couldn't control her fountain pen. She tried to read the new best-seller that had everybody talking, but she found it difficult to focus her eyes and make sense of the words. She was about to give up and turn out the lamp when someone knocked on her door. She got out of bed and crossed the room.

"Vanessa?"

She opened the door. "Hello, Spence."

"Were you asleep?"

"I was reading." Spence never failed to rattle her. She ran her fingers through her hair. "What do you want?"

"The President asked me to check on you."

"Really?" she said sarcastically.

"He regretted having to leave you alone tonight."

"Why should tonight be any different?"

Spencer Martin's eyes didn't even flicker. It took a lot more than impertinence to provoke him. Even when provoked, he didn't show it. That had been part of his training.

The Nixon administration had had Gordon Liddy, who bore a scar in the center of his palm from holding it over a candle flame until the flesh melted. Liddy had nothing over Spencer Martin. He was scary in his own right. And invaluable to the President.

"Can I get you anything?" he asked with aloof courtesy.

"Like what?"

"Anything."

"Don't trouble yourself."

"It's no trouble, I assure you. How are you feeling?"

"Fucking great. How are *you* feeling?"

"You're upset. Let me call Dr. Allan to come over."

"I don't need him," she shouted. "What I need . . ." She paused to gather stamina. "What I need is for somebody around here to acknowledge that I had a son, and that he's dead."

"It's been acknowledged, Vanessa. Why dwell on it? What's the point in belaboring the fact that your son—"

"Say his name, you bastard." She lunged forward and grabbed the lapels of his perfectly tailored jacket. "It's hard for you and David to call him by name, isn't it? Your consciences won't let you. Say it!" she shouted. "Say it right now!"

A Secret Service agent rushed into the room. "Mr. Martin, is something wrong?"

"The First Lady isn't well," he said. "Call Dr. Allan to come immediately."

Spence backed her into her room and closed the door. "Going to lock me in my room, Spence?"

"Not at all. If you want to make a spectacle of yourself in front of the staff, be my guest," he said smoothly, gesturing toward the door.

Vanessa lapsed into sullen silence, but defiantly poured herself another glass of wine. By the time the doctor arrived, she had finished that one and was having another.

"She's drunk, George," Spence announced.

She fought off Dr. Allan when he tried to examine her. "Vanessa, your medication doesn't allow you to drink this much."

Spence then ordered him to give her something to shut her up. "I really shouldn't. I have to increase the dosage to make it effective."

"I don't care what you have to do," said the man of steel.

Vanessa bared her arm. "Give me the goddamn drug! The only time I know any peace is when I'm asleep. And, as Spence pointed out, I'm not sleepy, I'm drunk."

As the drug cruised through her system, David came striding into the room. He was obviously furious over the scene she'd created while he was away.

Too damn bad, Mr. President, she thought, although she was too relaxed now to articulate the words.

He and Spence and Dr. Allan conducted a tense, hushed conversation at the foot of her bed. At the conclusion of it, she heard Spence say, "We can't let this go on any longer."

What, precisely, did that mean? She had wished for sweet oblivion, but now she struggled to fight it off.

She was in a deep sleep when they came for her just before dawn.

Chapter
Seven

$\mathscr{P}$resident Merritt concluded his telephone conversation with Barrie Travis and turned to his adviser. "What do you think?"

Spencer Martin had heard every word over the speakerphone. "She was fishing, but you handled it well," he replied. "You declined her request, but you did it graciously. Did her call go through Dalton?"

"Yes. She played it by the book."

"Then it was even more gracious of you to turn her down personally. I guess she thought there was no harm in asking for an exclusive with you to discuss your campaign strategy. Apparently she's now on a first-name basis with Vanessa, and you sent her those flowers. It's natural for her to think she has an inside track to the Oval Office."

David Merritt stared through the windows overlooking the carefully tended grounds of the White House. Visitors were queued up along the iron picket fence, waiting to take the standard tour, during which they'd gawk at the dinnerware of former presidents.

Privately, he scorned the American public, but he loved

being their president, and he was going to hate relinquishing this address, even after his second term. He never considered that there wouldn't be a second. Being reelected was a foregone conclusion. It was in the program he'd set for himself back in that trailer park in Biloxi. With very few deviations, everything had gone according to his master plan. Nothing would be allowed to interfere with the future that David Malcomb Merritt had outlined for himself. Nothing.

As though reading his mind, Spence said, "Wonder why she threw in that last question about Vanessa."

"My wife's well-being is on everybody's mind these days. It would have been more suspicious if she hadn't mentioned her."

"I suppose," Spence said.

His lack of conviction brought Merritt around, a question in his expression.

Spence shrugged. "It's just that several weeks ago, Barrie Travis appeared out of nowhere. Now, every time we turn around, she pops up." He swore beneath his breath. "What was Vanessa thinking when she pulled that stunt? And why is this reporter still hungry? I can understand her snooping around D.C. General before her SIDS series, but why after?"

"That bothered me, too," Merritt admitted. "But her source was made to see the error of her ways. I think Ms. Travis will find it very hard to cultivate another source at that hospital."

Barrie Travis might think her sources were secret, but Spence's were more so. The President hadn't asked in what manner or by whom Anna Chen had been confronted about leaking confidential information to the press. He'd merely been assured by Spence that the matter had been handled—and if that's what Spence said, it was safe to etch it in stone.

Spence was good that way. If a problem arose, he took

care of it. No explanation required. No rationalization. No argument. Spence was hassle-free. Unlike their friend Gray Bondurant, who had insisted on knowing the why and wherefore of every damn executive request.

When action was called for, David Merritt wanted action without having to justify it. He wanted expediency and didn't give a damn about the integrity of the deed. Gray did. Integrity was a big thing to Gray.

"I think Barrie Travis is just an overzealous reporter. She had her fifteen minutes—and that's stretching it—and now she's trying to maximize her brush with fame. Unfortunately, she's become a nuisance." The President chuckled. "She's a screw-up and everybody knows it. Relax. She's not smart enough to do any serious damage."

"I don't know, David," Spence said worriedly. "I think she's smarter than she's given credit for. If not for that one well-publicized gaffe, she could have been a media force to contend with. Her damned tenacity speaks volumes about her character."

"Or her recklessness and blind ambition."

"Either way, if she stays on this, it could hurt us."

Merritt looked at his adviser. Words between them were often unnecessary. Like guerrilla fighters picking their way through an enemy-infested jungle, they could communicate without words, their eyes alone warning each other of possible hazards. This was one of those times.

"If you'd feel better about it, Spence, stay on top of it."

"I'd feel better about it."

⌒≈⌒

Barrie stared thoughtfully at her shorthand transcript of her telephone conversation with President Merritt. She could find no fault with anything he'd said or how he'd said it. It had been a friendly little chat. He'd been firm but polite when refusing her request for an exclusive interview, but that hadn't disappointed or even surprised her. Asking for one had only been a pretext. The purpose of the call had been to inquire about the First Lady.

Since that windy, cloudy day when she'd met Vanessa Merritt for cappuccino, Barrie had been looking for drama beneath every brick in Washington. There was none to be found. Sources had turned mute. The pager she wore twenty-four hours a day, the number of which only her sources and Daily knew, hadn't beeped once, so she'd broken the rules and phoned them. Nobody knew a thing. She'd been ready to concede that her imagination had run away with her, and not for the first time.

Then the mysterious incident with Anna Chen had jump-started her sputtering conviction. The very next morning, Dalton Neely had called a press conference to announce that Mrs. Merritt was going into seclusion for an unspecified period of time. Following that shocking opener, he'd read a brief statement from the President:

"Senator Armbruster and I believe that Vanessa's responsibilities as First Lady haven't allowed her time to wholly recover from the tragic demise of our son. We've impressed upon her how valuable she is to us as an individual and as a patriot. She owes it to her family and to her country to be fully restored, physically and emotionally, before resuming the grueling schedule she imposes upon herself. For that purpose, she's taking an extended rest."

Questions from the floor had been entertained. This recuperative rest would be under Dr. George Allan's supervision, Neely had said in response to one. He had flatly denied that any alcohol or other substance abuse was involved. Barrie herself had shouted above her colleagues to ask when the First Lady might return; she'd been told it was too soon to speculate.

Since then, Neely had given the news-starved media periodic updates on Mrs. Merritt's condition. According to Dr. Allan, she was responding favorably to the rest and relaxation. This morning, when Barrie had spoken to the President, he had thanked her for asking after his wife and promised to pass along her regards. She was improving rapidly, doing exceptionally well. He couldn't be more pleased by her progress.

Everything was just so peachy-fucking-keen.

"Like hell it is," Barrie muttered. The back of her neck was itching again. Something wasn't right. She reached for her telephone.

"D.C. General. How may I direct your call?"

"Anna Chen, please."

"Ms. Chen no longer works here."

"Excuse me?"

"Ms. Chen no longer works here. Can someone else help you?"

"Uh, no. Thanks."

Barrie hung up quickly and tried Anna Chen's home number. A pleasant, computer-generated voice told her the number was no longer in service. In less than five minutes Barrie was in her car, speeding to Anna Chen's apartment building. She jogged up the three flights of stairs and pressed the bell on the door of 3C. After ringing it several times, it became apparent that the apartment was empty.

Frustrated, she rang the doorbell of the neighbor across the hall. Pressing her ear to the door, she heard motion inside and a whispered conversation. "Hello?" she called out, knocking on the door. "I'm looking for Ms. Chen."

The neighbor was a young executive type with a sleek ponytail and a monogrammed shirt, opened to the waistband of his slacks, which obviously had been hastily zipped; a corner of his shirttail was caught in the fly. Looking beyond his shoulder, Barrie saw that he was entertaining a young lady. They were having a picnic lunch on the living room floor.

"I'm sorry to disturb—"

"If you're looking for Anna, she moved," he said, obviously in a hurry to return to lunch. Or whatever.

"When?"

"Sometime last week. Friday, Thursday maybe. Before the weekend, because the super had the apartment cleaned on Saturday. There were workmen in and out all day."

"Do you have any idea—"

"Where she moved? No. But she works at D.C. General."

"Not any longer, she doesn't."

"Huh. Then I'm clueless."

⌒⌒

"Thanks for coming, Daily." Barrie entered her house through the back door. The kitchen was filled with aromatic steam.

"How could I resist such a gracious invitation? 'Be there at seven. Start dinner.' "

Daily was at the stove, stirring a pot of spaghetti sauce, a Christmas apron tied around his waist. She vaguely remembered getting the apron as a gift a couple of years ago and hadn't seen it since. She wondered where Daily had found it.

"Smells delicious." She batted down Cronkite, who was in a frenzy over her arrival. "Have you fed him?"

"A raw meatball, which he swallowed whole." Daily set aside his spoon and turned to her. "How come I had to get out at the corner, walk down the alley, and come in through the back door? Are we playing spy, or what?"

"After dinner."

He held her to that promise. As soon as the dishes were cleared, they made themselves comfortable in her living room. At least Daily was comfortable, seated in an overstuffed armchair, Cronkite's large head resting in his lap. Barrie moved about the room restlessly. Twice she checked the front door to see that it was locked and bolted. She closed the window blinds, making it impossible for anyone outside to see in.

"What in hell is going on?" Daily asked.

She held her finger vertically against her lips and turned on the TV. She set the volume at an ear-splitting level, then moved an ottoman close to Daily's chair.

"You'll probably think I'm overdramatizing," she said, "but I think I'm being watched. I had my cell phone disconnected this afternoon. From here on, I don't want any phone records. When we talk, we have to be very careful about what we say, especially about Vanessa Merritt."

He nodded toward the blaring television set. "You think the house has been bugged?"

"Nothing would surprise me." She filled him in on Anna Chen's disappearance, adding, "I talked to the super of the building. She gave no notice, just paid out her lease, packed up, and took off."

"She could have a dozen reasons for leaving. Another job, another apartment."

"She left no forwarding address either at the hospital or with the super. That's odd for someone who's just relocating."

"Maybe she's trying to shake a bad-tempered boyfriend."

"She was frightened, but not of a violent ex-boyfriend. She was afraid of being seen talking to me. Somebody knew she'd leaked information to me, and she'd been spooked into shutting up."

Daily tugged at his lower lip, saying nothing.

"Why wasn't an autopsy performed on that baby?" Barrie continued. "Dr. Allan wasn't present when he died. In an accidental death, law mandates an autopsy to determine the cause."

"We're talking about the President and First Lady of the United States, Barrie. The law can be bent."

"If your child had suddenly died for no apparent reason, wouldn't you want to know exactly why? Why would the Merritts object to an autopsy if they had nothing to hide?"

"Lots of people object to autopsies." Daily waved his hand in dismissal. "Next argument."

"I keep going back to Vanessa's strange messages to me. *Could* they have been implied confessions?"

"If she murdered her baby, why would she confess?"

"Deep down, she wants her crime to be exposed. She wants to be punished."

"You know, the more you talk, the sicker she gets."

"And where is she?" Barrie asked impatiently, while still keeping her voice low. "At Highpoint?" The Merritts' private getaway on the Shenandoah River was a couple of hours' drive southwest of Washington.

"That would stand to reason," Daily said, "although the official word is that she's resting in an 'undisclosed location.' "

"If she's only resting, and is otherwise healthy, why all the secrecy?"

"If his daughter was seriously ill, Clete Armbruster would be right in the middle of it," Daily said. "He'd have her in the best medical facility in the country, undergoing every kind of test they've got. Have you talked to anyone in his office?"

"I've tried. Neely's statements have become his staff's mantra."

"If her health was at risk, the senator wouldn't be satisfied with an extended rest. He'd fight hell or high water to get the best treatment available."

"Likewise, if the senator knew that she had committed murder, he would fight equally hard to cover it up and protect her."

"Shit," Daily said. "I walked right into that one."

"You keep placing these obstacles in my path," she said crossly. "You don't want me to be right."

"I don't want you to be *wrong*. I don't want you to go out on a limb with a chain saw in your hand like you did with the Justice Green story. And others."

"This bears no resemblance to those. None at all."

"And I don't want it to. After a series of fiascoes, you're just now regaining some credibility. Can you imagine the shit storm these theories of yours will create if they get leaked?"

"Can you imagine how far and fast my career will soar if my theories prove to be right?"

"Before you start fantasizing about your own magazine show, you'd better acknowledge what you've got. A hunch, Barrie. That's it. A hunch, which in journalism amounts to zero."

"No, it doesn't," she argued emphatically. "Unless you're actually there when somebody jumps off a ledge, or an airplane crashes, or a killer is caught standing over the body with a smoking gun in his hand, every good story begins with a hunch, a gut instinct that tells you there's more to the situation than meets the eye.

"You probably won't believe this, Daily, but my motives aren't purely selfish. I'm concerned for Vanessa. She was stretched about as thin as I've ever seen anyone stretched. Say I'm way off base and the baby died of SIDS, as reported. Maybe grief has driven her insane. If she's becoming an embarrassment to the White House, isn't it possible that they shuttled her off somewhere to keep her out of the public eye?"

"You think the President is holding her against her will?"

Put that way, her hypothesis sounded ludicrous. "That would be totally implausible, wouldn't it?"

"No more implausible than anything else we've tossed around." He thought about it for a moment. "Then again, power has its own unique psychology. History has shown that to some presidents, any means justified the end. I guess that could extend to the sequestering of an emotionally unbalanced first lady who might stand in the way of reelection."

Barrie shuddered. "God, our theories only get worse."

"They're still just theories, Barrie."

"Stop reminding me," she muttered.

"That's my job."

"You're no longer my boss."

"True. I'm just your friend. Look, Barrie." He paused to take a few wheezing breaths. "You've got the world's approval now. For once, go easy on yourself."

She resented his tone. "Psychology time, Daily? Time to open up Barrie's head and see what makes her tick?"

"I already know what makes you tick. More importantly, you know, too."

"Then why discuss it?" she said angrily.

"Can you look me in the eye and tell me that your motivation for pushing forward with this dangerous story has nothing to do with winning the approval of two people who—"

"Yes, I can look you in the eye and tell you that. Besides, no matter what my motivation is, it's a story that needs to be told. Agreed?"

"If the story is indeed there, yes," he answered grudgingly.

"Okay, so stop bringing up my scar-inflicting childhood and help me."

"How?"

"Who would talk to me? Senator Armbruster?"

Daily shook his head. "No matter what he believed in his heart, he'd take the company line and defend it with his dying breath. He's a politician down to his toenails. He wouldn't malign anybody his party placed in the White House, even if it was Jack the Ripper. And certainly not his son-in-law. Almost singlehandedly, he put David Merritt in office."

"Okay. So, who else knows the Merritts that intimately? If there was someone close to them who'd had a falling out. Or someone who—" Suddenly a fresh thought yanked her up straight. "That—that . . . soldier who rescued the hostages."

"Bondurant?"

"Bondurant! Yes! Gary Bondurant."

"Gray."

"Right. Gray. He was thick as thieves with the Merritts. Maybe he'd talk to me."

It hurt Barrie to hear the rasp-gasp-rattle in Daily's laugh. "You'd have better luck getting an interview with one of the faces on Mount Rushmore. They're a lot friendlier and more talkative than Bondurant. He's about as approachable as a cobra."

"What's his story? Where'd he come from?"

Daily shrugged. "Your guess is as good as anybody's."

"He didn't just materialize when Merritt appointed him as adviser," she said with frustration.

"But it looks that way," Daily remarked. "Spencer Martin is just as secretive. What's known about them before the Merritt administration wouldn't fill a thimble. My opinion—they cultivate that mysterious aura."

"What for?"

"Effect, I imagine."

"What did Bondurant do before the rescue mission?"

"Planned it, I guess. The three of them—Martin, Bondurant, and Merritt—had Marine recon training. Of the three, the President is the most polished, the natural politician. Spencer Martin is a devious sneak. He fits his role in the administration to a tee. And Bondurant . . . He's the most complex of the trio. Want to know something? The guy always scared the shit out of me. Truth be known, I think he scared the shit out of the President, too."

"I thought Merritt fired him because he had become a little too attached to Vanessa."

Daily grunted. "How come you're so rusty on this? Where were you when this was going on? It wasn't that long ago."

"Howie was mad at me for something or other, so he had me covering alleged misconduct in professional wrestling. I missed out on Bondurant's return and then his split from Washington."

"Actually, there wasn't much to miss. Bondurant had every reporter in Washington frustrated. He dodged cameras and granted no interviews. The tabloids printed their usual tripe, but of course they didn't give the true story."

"What was the true story?"

"I don't know. But if Merritt had thought that Bondurant was humping the First Lady, why would he have picked him to lead that rescue mission? He made Bondurant a national hero. That doesn't sound like the act of a jealous husband, does it?"

Daily wagged his index finger at her. "And there's another fact you've got wrong. The President didn't fire him. Following the mission, he asked Bondurant to resume his position at the White House. Bondurant said, 'Thank you, but no.' "

"How do you know all this?"

"You're not the only one with sources, missy. I may have one foot in the grave, but the other one is still welcome in several camps in Washington."

"If you're so in-the-know, where is Bondurant now?"

"He moved someplace out West. To one of those square states."

Chapter
Eight

She went so far as to invite him to lunch. They went to his favorite deli. She even let him eat before pleading her case.

"Please, Howie. Give me the green light. A few days should do it."

He mopped up the juice from his meatball sandwich with the last scrap of bread and stuffed it into his mouth. Chewing, he said, "Travel's expensive, you know. We've got no budget for it."

"I'll pay as I go with my own money. I'll keep receipts. The station can reimburse me later. But only if I produce the story."

She hoped this self-sacrifice would win him over. It also heightened her incentive to produce an exclusive that would electrify the nation, which she believed she was on the brink of doing. Only a story of this magnitude would have compelled her to break bread with Howie Fripp.

He ruminated—on a raw onion and her request. "Where are you going?"

"I can't say."

"You expect me to give you the go-ahead when you won't tell me where you're going or what the story is?"

"It's explosive. Secrecy is the key to breaking it." She lowered her voice to a hush and leaned in closer, although the onion and garlic fumes emanating from his mouth caused her eyes to tear. "If word got out that I was working on this, it could be dangerous for anyone who knew."

"Gimme a break," he moaned. "Why don't you try selling that crock of shit over at NBC? Some schmuck over there might actually buy it."

"Thanks, Howie. I was hoping you'd say that." She reached for her satchel.

At first taken aback, Howie narrowed his eyes shrewdly. "How come you're not sore?"

"Because now I can go to Jenkins with a clear conscience. I didn't want to jump the chain of command, so I asked you first. Since you've denied my request, I'm clear to go to the G.M."

The mention of WVUE's general manager struck terror in Howie Fripp's heart. "Jenkins will back my decision," he said, feigning confidence. "He'll laugh himself sick because you had the gall to ask for travel time."

"I don't think so," Barrie said cheerfully. "Didn't I tell you about the memo he wrote me?"

Howie narrowed his eyes again.

"It was a glowing review of my SIDS series. He wants me to do more special reports like that. He says my talent is being squandered on crap stories. He'd also like me to do some public service programming. Maybe some outside p.r., too, like personal appearances, speeches, things like that." She frowned. "I thought he would have mentioned it to you by now. No? Well, I guess he's just so busy, he hasn't gotten around to it yet."

She was making it up as she went along, but he was swallowing it. "I'll think about it," he grumbled.

"No need. Really. Forget it. I'll just take it up with Jenkins."

"Wait! Hold it! Give me a minute, for chrissake. You sprang this on me without giving me any warning." While mulling it over, he nibbled on his kosher dill spear. "Do you swear the story is that big?"

"Huge. Gargantuan."

He ogled a young woman jogging past the window, took another bite of pickle, scratched his armpit. "Okay, you can take a few days. But you'd better not be jerking me off."

She shuddered at the thought.

∽∽

"Welcome to the Ponderosa," Barrie said to herself as she drove through the open gate and up the gravel drive to Gray Bondurant's house.

Traveling under an assumed name, using a fake ID made for her by an ex-con—one of Daily's more unsavory sources—and paying with cash so as not to leave a paper trail, Barrie arrived at her destination in the late afternoon. She hoped her safety precautions were overkill, but she was taking no chances.

Even by northwestern Wyoming standards, Bondurant's property was off the beaten path. The single-story ranch house was set against a grove of aspens that were just taking on their spectacular autumn color. In order to reach the house, she'd driven across a stream where clear water gurgled over a stone creekbed.

The house was constructed of log and stone. A covered porch ran the width of it. Three horses were grazing in a paddock. Toward the back were a barn that looked older than the house and a detached garage that stood open and empty except for a snowmobile. Several cords of firewood were stacked against the exterior wall of the garage. Other than the horses, there was no sign of life.

Now that she was here, Barrie suffered a severe case of tummy butterflies. The surrounding terrain was rugged and intimidating. The mountain range made her feel small and insignificant, as no doubt Gray Bondurant would consider her. Alighting from the rental car, she wondered exactly what she would say to him by way of introduction. From what little she'd heard and read about him, she knew chances weren't good that he would welcome her with open arms.

Her flutters were for naught; he wasn't at home. She realized that after several minutes of ringing the doorbell and knocking. Damn. She was mentally pumped up for the encounter with the former Marine. She'd gone to too much trouble and personal expense to retreat this soon. Even an immediate drive back to Jackson Hole held no appeal.

Deciding to wait for Bondurant's return, she sat in the rush-seated rocking chair on the front porch. The view of the Tetons was breathtaking, so she was content to sit and rock while contemplating this marvel of nature. However, it wasn't long before she became aware of another of nature's phenomenons, this one biological. She needed a bathroom.

After another fifteen minutes, she left her satchel in the chair and returned to the front door. Since the garage had been left open, there was a good chance that the house had been left unlocked. It was.

The door opened directly into a living area. Exposed beams supported the high ceiling. An enormous fireplace dominated the stone wall at the far end of the room. The decor was thoroughly masculine. Large pieces of furniture were upholstered in forest-green suede. The windows were unadorned. Woven wool rugs looking like large saddle blankets dotted the hardwood floor. The silence was absolute, without so much as a clock ticking. The room smelled faintly of wood smoke and . . . and man.

The male essence was so strong, so pervasive, that Barrie turned her head quickly, almost expecting to see Bondurant materialize out of thin air.

Chiding herself for acting foolish, she walked quickly through the central room and found her way to a large bedroom. Here again, the surfaces were hard, with the exception of the unmade bed, which she purposefully avoided looking at. She went into the adjoining bathroom.

A single toothbrush hung from the rack above the sink. Towels were folded on a shelf. A shirt hung on a brass hook on the back of the door. She couldn't resist the impulse to touch it. Cotton. Unstarched. Comfy.

The bathroom was basically neat, although she noticed that the cap on a bottle of cologne was dusty from disuse. She was tempted to open the mirrored medicine cabinet and take a peek inside but decided that would be a gross invasion of privacy.

After using the toilet, she rinsed her hands and dried them on a towel hanging from a chrome ring mounted in the wall. The towel was slightly damp. Not too long ago, he'd dried his face or hands on it. She found that slightly disconcerting and experienced a queer sensation in her midsection. Again, she was powerfully aware of the house's occupant, as though he were there, just invisible.

The quiet and seclusion were making her weird, Barrie decided.

She retraced her steps through the bedroom, promising her absent host that as soon as she got a drink of water, she'd be out of there.

She located the kitchen with no problem. There was a six-pack of beer in his fridge. No bottled water. No soft drinks.

She settled on water from the tap, adding several ice cubes taken from a freezer stocked with cuts of beef and little else.

Holding to her promise, she returned to the porch to continue her wait. Surely he would be back before dark. He wouldn't have left his house unlocked if he planned to be away for any significant length of time.

An orange sunset segued into a purple dusk. Stars came out, more stars than she'd ever seen, having lived in a city all her life. The Milky Way cut a ghostly swath directly overhead.

With the onset of darkness, the temperature dropped. For warmth, she wrapped her arms around herself. In spite of the cold, she kept falling asleep, her chin hitting her chest whenever her head dropped forward. Her body was two hours ahead of Mountain Time, and her alarm clock had gone off at five that morning.

"This is nuts," she said, teeth chattering.

Before she could talk herself out of it, she went back into the house and lay down on the long suede sofa. Seconds after laying her head on the cushion, she fell asleep.

Chapter Nine

$\mathcal{T}$he billiard balls clacked, and Howie Fripp emitted an obnoxious snort when his shot sank one into the pocket. "My game. How many's that?"

"Three."

"Whoo-ee! Fifteen bucks. Unless you want to make it the best five of seven."

"No, thanks. You'd clean me out."

Howie reached for the three five-dollar bills his opponent extended toward him. He stuffed the money into his pocket and would have made another cocky comment about his extraordinary win, when something in the other man's eyes warned him that gloating might not be a good idea.

"The least you can do is buy me a drink." The loser of the tournament was smiling, but thinly.

"A drink? Sure, sure," Howie said. "What'll you have?"

He asked for vodka on the rocks. Howie went to the bar and placed the order. He carried the vodka and a beer for himself back to the table where the man had chosen to sit.

"I can't stay out too late," Howie said as he rejoined him. Actually he was ready to leave now. The guy had ordered the vodka by brand. A round or two of drinks with him could liquidate Howie's winnings. "I gotta be at work early."

The man took a sip of his drink. "What line of work are you in?"

"Broadcast journalism," Howie boasted, shaking salt into his beer. "WVUE."

"You're on TV?"

"Nah, I don't do that on-air shit. That's a job for idiots, talking heads. No, I assign news stories to the reporters."

"So, you're more or less responsible for what gets on the air?"

"I'm entirely responsible for what gets on the air." Basking in the man's interest, Howie elaborated and embroidered. "It's up to me which reporter covers which story, which stories get canned, and which get airtime and how much airtime they get. On any given day, I gotta make a million decisions."

"That's a very responsible position."

"I thrive on pressure," he said expansively.

The man seated across from Howie was the man Howie Fripp wanted to see in his own shaving mirror. Sometimes he even deluded himself into believing that he made the kind of impact on other people that this man had made on him. His new friend was a smooth talker. No matter what the situation, he would keep his cool. He hadn't even lost his temper when he was soundly defeated in three straight games of pool. He was the kind of guy who inspired uncontrollable lust in women and fearful respect in men.

"You must be on top of everything going on," the man remarked. "You get the news before anybody."

"That's right."

"So, what's cooking?"

Howie searched his mind for something that would

impress this impressive individual. "Hmm, well, let's see. I had a reporter at the scene of that triple shooting the other night, minutes after it happened. Got video of the bodies before they were covered up."

The man gave a half-smile and glanced down at his wristwatch.

"And, uh, let's see . . ."

"Well, I enjoyed our game. I'd better be going."

"But the biggest thing we've done lately was that series on SIDS. You know, crib death," Howie said, hoping to regain the man's attention.

"Yeah?"

Bingo! "It was my idea to do it. Sort of a follow-up to the President's kid, you know."

"Tragic thing."

"We got an interview with the First Lady."

"That was a real coup. She doesn't grant that many interviews, does she?"

"It was a WVUE exclusive."

"How'd you swing it?"

"You know how it is. I made some calls. Cashed in a few favors." He shrugged in a way that said dealing with the White House was no big deal. "You want another drink?"

"No, thanks. If I get drunk, I might agree to let you whip me in another round." The man grinned.

Howie grinned back. He didn't have any friends to speak of. Maybe he was making a friend. The thought of it made him practically giddy.

"I saw that interview with the First Lady," the man remarked. "Very incisive. What was the reporter's name?"

"Barrie Travis." Howie told his new friend how he had come to hire her. "At the time, she couldn't buy herself a job. I thought, what the fuck? Give her a chance, and win some points with the FCC in the bargain. And she's pretty good-looking."

His new friend chuckled. "If we're forced to work with them, why not hire the pretty ones, right?"

Howie leered. His new friend talked his language. "You got that right, buddy." He winked. "Barrie and me had a thing going for a while, but it got sticky, working with her and all, so I had to break it off. She was okay with it. Didn't cause me any grief like some of them do. Turned out to be a pretty good little reporter. She hustles. May be a little too ambitious for her own good."

"Really. How so?"

"Ah, you know. Because of the success of her series, which I actually produced, she's got her head in the clouds and stars in her eyes. She's driving me nuts about this hot story she's on to."

"Really?" His companion was no longer glancing at his wristwatch. He was leaning back comfortably in his chair, swirling the ice in his glass. "What's the story?"

"Beats me. She won't say."

"Come on. Who am I going to tell?"

"I swear I don't know. But she says if the story pans out the way she thinks, it'll make Watergate look like Mickey Mouse."

The man's smile slipped a notch. "Then it must be hot."

"Hot enough for her to take a few days off to do some research out of town."

"Where?"

The man's voice took on an edge that arrested Howie's fist halfway between the bowl of peanuts on the table and his mouth. Suddenly he felt that maybe he was being indiscreet, that maybe he shouldn't be blabbing so much about Barrie's story. "She wouldn't tell me."

The man's smile returned. "Not even a hint?"

"None."

"Your girl's full of secrets."

"She's a skirt. What can I say? Who can ever figure out a broad?" Howie reached for his beer to wash down the peanuts.

"Well, it's late, and you've got to be at work early. Thanks for the drink."

Howie scrambled up from his chair when his new friend rose. "I enjoyed it."

"You should have, you son of a gun. You're going home fifteen bucks richer."

"Maybe we can do it again sometime," Howie said, hoping he didn't sound overeager. He didn't want the guy to mistake him for a fag. "I'm here a coupla nights a week. Whenever I don't have other plans. Just knocking back with the guys, you know."

"Then I'll probably see you around." They shook hands.

Howie watched him go, envying and admiring the man's confident air, and knowing, almost for certain, that he would never see him again.

For reasons that remained a mystery to him, Howie just didn't seem to make friends easily.

Spencer Martin had driven two blocks before he happened to catch a glimpse of himself in his rearview mirror. Laughing, he reached up to remove the baseball cap that had long, curly hair sewn into the back of it. He also peeled off the fake mustache. It would take a little more effort to get rid of the stench of tobacco smoke and stale beer from the neighborhood dive he'd followed Howie Fripp into.

What an insect, Spence thought as he headed back to the White House.

But he'd learned from Fripp what he and David needed

to know—Barrie Travis was still on the trail of a story she considered hot. Did that story relate to the President or Mrs. Merritt or the death of Robert Rushton Merritt?

He was convinced that Fripp didn't know; otherwise he would have bragged about it. At this point Spence didn't know, either. But finding out was his top priority.

"Well I'm glad you're glad, Mrs. Gaston. . . . No, I'm certain Mrs. Merritt will be pleased with my choice. . . . Good. Now, as to the arrangements for tomorrow, a car will come for you at six-thirty. I know it's early, but . . . Okay. Very good. I'll look forward to seeing you then. Good night."

Dr. George Allan's hand was still on the telephone receiver, and he was staring at it thoughtfully, when his wife came in carrying two steaming cups of coffee. She set one in front of him on the desk and took the other with her to the leather chair facing the desk. "Who was that?"

His home office was on the second floor of their stylish yet comfortable residence just off the section of Massachusetts Avenue known as Embassy Row. George Allan sampled his coffee. "Boys in bed?"

"In bed, but I gave them an extra ten minutes before lights out. Who was that?" Amanda asked again, indicating the telephone.

"A private nurse I hired for Vanessa. To say that Mrs. Gaston is excited over her new patient would be a gross understatement. She can't believe she's going to look after the First Lady."

"Vanessa needs continuous care?"

The Allans had known the Merritts as struggling newlyweds. "Only as a precaution," George replied. "David thinks she should have a medically trained person with her at all times."

"I thought she was just resting."

"She is."

"If she requires constant medical care, shouldn't she be in the hospital?"

"Stop interrogating me, Amanda." George came out of his desk chair so fast, it rolled backward on its casters and bumped into the wall. He went to the liquor cabinet for a decanter of brandy and poured some into his coffee.

"I wasn't interrogating you," she said softly.

"Like hell you weren't. Every conversation we have these days evolves into a cross-examination."

"That's because you're so defensive," Amanda shot back. "Even the most innocent question strikes a nerve."

"Your questions are never innocent, Amanda. They're probing and suspicious."

"And you're paranoid," she shouted. "What is David holding over you that makes you afraid of everything, even me?"

"You don't know what you're talking about."

"I know that since you accepted this job, you've become a different person."

"You're wrong, Amanda!"

"Dad?"

George whipped around to see his two young sons standing in the doorway. They looked extremely sweet and vulnerable in their pajamas, their faces scrubbed shiny. At the sight of them, his anger evaporated. "Hey, guys. Come in."

They hesitated on the threshold until the older one took the first bold step into the hostile arena. His younger brother tagged behind him. George returned to his chair, pulled each of them onto a knee, and hugged them close.

They smelled of soap and toothpaste and shampoo. They smelled like cleanliness. He'd almost forgotten how good *clean* smelled. He hadn't smelled it on himself in a long time.

"I got an *A* on my math paper," the older one told him proudly.

"The teacher called on me to read out loud today. I knew all the words," the younger chimed in.

"That's great! You both deserve a reward. How about this weekend? A movie? Or an arcade? Something special."

"Mom too?"

George glanced at Amanda. "Sure, Mom too. If she wants to come along."

"Do you, Mom?"

She smiled at her sons. "What I want right now is for you two to get into bed."

Following another round of hugs and other delay tactics, she shooed them from the office and down the hallway to their bedroom.

Amanda was in the master bathroom when George caught up with her a half hour later. She was brushing her hair, which she still wore in the same sleek, chin-length bob she'd had when he met her. Like her eyes, her hair was the color of rich chocolate.

She was ready for bed, wearing only panties and a soft tank top. George stood in the doorway for a moment and watched her. He'd fallen into instant lust with her when they were introduced at a Fourth of July party. They began dating, but it took him six months to work up enough courage to ask her to sleep with him. She'd said yes, and wanted to know why he had waited so long. They were married before the next Fourth of July.

She had never resented the demands his profession placed upon them. She was accomplished in her own right and had her own interests. In addition to making a lovely home for their family, she taught art history at Georgetown

University. She was a volunteer counselor at a battered women's shelter. On the tennis court she was capable and competitive. She hosted great parties and had a fair command of several languages. She knew how to dress tastefully and how to comport herself in any situation.

He loved her. God, how he loved her.

He watched the graceful movements of her slender arms as she continued brushing her hair. One hundred strokes a night, as she'd been taught by her Virginian mother. It was an endearing habit. The rise and fall of her breasts entranced him. Her nipples made small impressions against the soft cotton of the tank.

"I'm sorry I lost my temper," he began in a quiet, contrite voice.

Amanda's dark eyes swung up to meet his in the mirror. "I don't want an apology, George." She turned to face him. "I want my *husband*."

He came to her, placed his arms around her, drew her close. "You have me."

Even though she clung to him, she shook her head no. "David has you. He's taken you away from me and from the boys."

He set her away and slid his fingers up through her glossy hair. "That's not true, Amanda."

"Yes, it is. I'm afraid I'll never get you back."

"I'm not going anywhere," he whispered against her lips. "You and the boys mean more than life to me. I couldn't bear to lose you."

She peered intently into his eyes. "You are losing us, George. Every day you slip farther and farther away. No matter how hard I try, I can't seem to reach you anymore. You keep secrets. You're becoming a stranger." Her voice cracked and tears formed in her eyes.

"Please, don't cry. Don't." He kissed her prominent

cheekbones, then her trembling lips. "Everything is all right."

He was lying. Furthermore, he knew that she knew he was lying. He could tell by the way she clutched him to her. Her kiss was more than ardent, it was desperate.

She brought that desperation to their bed, responding to his lovemaking with unbridled passion, as though fierce sex might conquer David Merritt's influence over him. By the time he entered her, each was delirious with need.

Then, sexually replete, naked and damp, they held each other close and whispered professions of eternal love and devotion.

But both knew that George's devotion to the President was just as absolute . . . and far more demanding.

Chapter
Ten

$\mathcal{B}$arrie came awake to find the barrel of a rifle pressed against the underside of her left breast.

Curbing the impulse to jump and run, she moved nothing except her eyes. They followed the length of the rifle up to a pair of eyes that were colder, bluer, and more unyielding than the steel gun barrel.

"It had better be good."

She tried to swallow, but was literally scared spitless. "What?"

"Your reason for being inside my house." He nudged her breast, lifting it slightly with the rifle. "Well?"

"I arrived last evening. You weren't here, so I waited for hours on your porch. It got dark and cold. I was sleepy. The door was unlocked. I didn't think you'd mind."

"Well, I do."

"My name is Barrie Travis." His eyes narrowed fractionally. She would have sworn that he recognized her name, although he didn't acknowledge it. "I came all the way from Washington, D.C., to see you."

"Then you've wasted a trip." He swung the rifle up to

his shoulder. "Since you know where the door is, you can see yourself out." He moved aside so she could stand up.

Barrie slowly uncoiled and came meekly to her feet. Then she hauled off and slapped his cheek hard. "How dare you point a gun at me! Are you crazy? You could have killed me."

His jaw knotted. "Lady, if I'd wanted to kill you, you'd be dead. And I wouldn't have made a mess on my couch in the process."

In one smooth motion, he bent down and picked her satchel off the floor and flung it at her. "Get out, and take your lousy reading material with you."

Before leaving Washington, she had compiled a library of all the tabloids carrying banner headlines about his rumored affair with the First Lady. They were junk, but it made her angry that he'd helped himself to the contents of her satchel. "You went through my bag?"

"You're the trespasser, not me."

"That's not my reading material of choice, Mr. Bondurant. It's research. I'm a reporter."

"All the more reason for you to get out."

Assuming she would do as he'd ordered, he turned and went into the bedroom.

Barrie welcomed a moment to collect herself. She'd had some pretty harrowing experiences in her lifetime, but she'd never before been held at gunpoint. Certainly not at point-blank range. Gray Bondurant was as frightening as she'd been led to believe, although she didn't think he would have shot her.

It had been a scare tactic, nothing more. He'd hoped to frighten her into leaving. Well, she wasn't yet ready to wave the white flag.

She smoothed her hair, straightened her clothing, and cleared her throat. "Mr. Bondurant?" His failure to respond didn't discourage her. She stepped into the open bedroom doorway. "I—Oh!"

He had removed his shirt. Body fat, zero. Everything else, ten. A definite ten. Hair grew in a V shape across his chest and down his tapering torso. There was a nasty but intriguing scar on one of his ribs.

All the tabloids had printed the same grainy snapshot of him, apparently the only picture that was available. His dark aviator sunglasses had comprised most of it. A granite chin and jaw, a narrow slash of a mouth, windblown hair off a high forehead, and the sunglasses. That was it.

Those two-dimensional features in the photograph were quite something else when seen in the flesh. She tried not to stare. "Mr. Bondurant, I've waited hours to see you."

"That's your problem."

"The least you could do—"

"I don't owe you anything."

Stalling, she asked, "What time is it?"

"Around four." He tugged off one boot and sock and let them fall where he stood.

"In the *morning?*"

"Did you come all the way from D.C. to ask me the time, Miss Travis?" Off came the second boot and sock.

"No, I came all the way from D.C. to talk to you about Vanessa Merritt."

That arrested him. He fixed a hard-as-diamonds glare on her. "You've come a long way for nothing."

"It's vitally important that we talk."

He unbuckled his belt, unfastened his jeans, and, when he stepped out of them, he was naked.

Obviously he expected her to scream and run. Barrie refused to show any reaction—although she definitely experienced one. "You can't shock me, Mr. Bondurant."

"Oh, I bet I can," he said softly. He moved past her toward the bathroom. Then he turned suddenly and pulled her against him.

Either the sudden contact with his chest, or profound astonishment, knocked the breath out of her and rendered her speechless and unable to move. His eyes held her spellbound as his hands groped beneath her sweater. The sleeves of it were wide enough for him to push the straps of her camisole off her shoulders. Even then she didn't move. Not until she felt his rough palms on her breasts did she move, and that was to stagger backward into the wall, dragging him with her.

As his mouth descended on her breast, she arched up to meet it, shamelessly eager to feel his lips, his tongue on her flesh. She felt as though every cell in her body were awakening to a blaring reveille. Surging through her was a rush of passion, of *life*, that could not be contained or even disciplined. She had never experienced anything like it, this assault of carnality, this all-encompassing, overwhelming, primal, unconscionable instinct to mate—soon, quickly, *now!*

Together they stumbled blindly toward the bed. She drew her sweater over her head, in the process ripping one of the straps of her camisole and exposing her breast. They fell laterally across the rumpled bed, where caressing became a wrestling match with no rules or boundaries. Reaching beneath her skirt, he removed her panties.

Then he touched her.

Deeply. Inside.

His touch was like a lightning bolt, all sizzle and heat. Moaning with pleasure, she readjusted her hips to accommodate his caresses. His lips moved against her stomach, kissing it lightly. Flicking her skin with his tongue, he nibbled his way back up to her breasts. She laid her hand against his hard cheek and was delighted by the sandpapery texture of it against her palm.

His caressing fingers were so erotic and suggestive, and so well placed, that the orgasm was upon her almost before she realized it. Too enraptured to be embarrassed, she flattened her hand over his, pressing it deeper into her, grinding her body against it, squeezing it hard between her thighs.

When the waves receded, she lay like a victim of a shipwreck—damp, spent, eyes closed, stomach rapidly rising and falling. When she finally opened her eyes, he was gazing directly into them. He took her hand and guided it to his sex.

"Tell me now," he said thickly. "Is there anything you won't do?"

Her lips parted on a startled breath. She swallowed dryly. "What do you have in mind?"

Placing a hand on each of her knees, he slowly pushed them apart again. When he lowered his face into her, her initial cry of surprise dissolved into a moan of pure animal pleasure. He wasn't timid. He wasn't shy about sliding his hands beneath her hips and tilting them up to him.

Tentatively her fingertips explored his hard length. Her thumb glanced the smooth tip. Then she turned and sought him with her lips. He groaned a rich curse when she took him into her mouth.

But even those minutes of absolute, blind sensation couldn't prepare her for the first thrust of his penis into her, nor for the tempered savagery of his strokes. No slow, warm, rippling tide of sensation, this climax. No. It was a meteoric burst of energy and fire that was upon her suddenly, snuffing out everything else, leaving in its wake an airless, soundless, sightless void.

When she finally recovered and opened her eyes, he was standing beside the bed. His skin was dewy with perspiration, which had caused some of his chest hairs to curl. His face was set and tense. At his side, his fists were reflexively clenching and relaxing.

"Don't think you've changed my mind. When I get out of the shower, you'd better be gone." He turned and went into the bathroom, slamming the door behind him.

Barrie closed her eyes and lay perfectly still. It was one of those times when she pretended that she was dreaming. The game was a carryover from childhood. When things became intolerable at home, when her parents' fights got out of control, she would get into her bed and shut her eyes tightly and make believe that her waking world was the nightmare, and that she would soon awaken in another world, one of enchantment, and love, and peace, a world where everything was pleasant and the people in it found joy in one another.

The trick had never worked when she was a child, and it was no different now. When she opened her eyes, she was still in the bedroom of Gray Bondurant, on his bed, and her clothing—what little she still had on—was in disarray.

As was everything else.

She gathered her wits enough to get up and dress. The water in the shower was still running when she left the bedroom. Her satchel was where she'd left it on the sofa. She picked it up, stuffed her ripped camisole into it, and went to the front door.

But there she paused. If she left now, she would have gained nothing except an embarrassment so severe that she could never have fathomed it before. There was no explanation for her behavior, so she didn't insult her conscience with any attempt to justify or rationalize.

It had happened. She had let it happen. Correction: She had actively, avariciously participated in making it happen. It was a fait accompli. She couldn't change history.

The experience had cost her dearly. All she could do now was live with the consequences of her actions, make the best of a disastrous situation, and hope to recapture at least a shred of her dignity. In the process, maybe she could learn something from having come here.

When he entered the kitchen ten minutes later, she was waiting for him, her back to the countertop, on the defensive. "Just for the record, Mr. Bondurant, I don't know what happened in there."

"Just for the record, Miss Travis, I do." Casually, he took a mug from the cabinet and poured himself a cup of coffee from the pot she had taken upon herself to brew. "Get out your notepad. You might want to write this down." Then he turned to her. "It's called 'fucking.' "

Inwardly she flinched; outwardly she kept a stiff upper lip. "You're hoping that if you're horrible enough, I'll leave. It won't work."

"What will?"

"Talk to me."

"No way in hell," he said angrily. "Part of the reason I left Washington was to get away from reporters. Most of you would sell your souls for a story. And if there isn't a story, you make one up." He gave her a derisive once-over. "Although you're in a league of your own, Miss Travis. You didn't even sell anything, you gave it away."

She nodded beyond him toward the bedroom. "That was an . . . accident."

"I don't think so. My cock knew exactly where it was going."

Barrie rolled her lips inward to keep from saying anything. She was also trying to keep from crying, which she had sworn she would not do. "Please, Mr. Bondurant, I'm trying to salvage what's left of my professional integrity."

"I didn't know you had any."

Spreading her arms at her sides, she asked, "Do I look like I came to your house with seduction in mind?"

He took in her dishabille. "Not particularly. But when the situation presented itself, I didn't hear any objections from your side of the bed."

She felt her face color at the memory of the sounds he had heard from her side of the bed. "I came here only to ask you a few questions about the Merritts."

"How many times do I have to say it? I'm not telling you a damn thing."

"Not even that the tabloid stories are lies?"

"They are."

"You didn't have an affair with Vanessa Merritt?"

"None of your goddamn business."

"Was it you who made her so unhappy?"

"If she's unhappy, it might be because her kid just died."

"Are you sure?"

"Am I *sure?*"

"Are you sure he *died?* Or was Robert Rushton Merritt murdered?"

Chapter Eleven

*G*ray turned his back on her, silently swearing. This one went for the jugular. She interviewed with as much ferocity as she screwed.

Even before waking her, he'd recognized her as the reporter who had interviewed Vanessa several weeks ago. Apparently she hadn't gotten all she wanted from that interview. He'd been halfway expecting her, or someone of her ilk, to show up and start dredging him through the shit again. For weeks he'd been stockpiling his resentment against the imminent intrusion.

So he felt no guilt whatsoever over what had happened. He'd been surly and in need of getting laid. She'd been consensual—and that was putting it mildly. Set a stage like that, and naturally something's going to happen.

Actually, he doubted that seduction had been her original plan. Her long skirt, sweater, and boots were not designed to inspire sexual fantasies. Her eyes were still puffy from sleep, and her mascara had flaked off onto her cheekbones. Her lipstick had worn off long ago, and her hair was a mess.

Her voice, however, was incredible. Her voice was a wet dream. It didn't just promise unbelievable sex, it delivered.

But if she thought a good roll in the hay was going to weaken his position, she couldn't be more wrong. He now resented her invasion of his home and his privacy even more than he had before. She had earned his scorn.

Draining his coffee cup, he reached for a skillet and a saucepan and set them on the stove. He took a can of chili from the pantry, opened it, and dumped the contents into the saucepan, then began cracking eggs into a bowl. After beating them to a froth, he poured himself another cup of coffee and sipped it while the chili simmered.

"May I?" She held up an empty mug.

"Go ahead. You made it. I don't want to be responsible for you falling asleep at the wheel when you leave."

He noticed that she cradled the large mug between two very small hands. Feeling his gaze, she looked up at him. "I apologize for slapping you. I've never struck anyone in my life. You're a very provoking individual, Mr. Bondurant."

"So I've been told." He stirred the chili. "How'd you find me?"

"Mostly through sources in D.C. Don't worry. I was discreet."

"I never worry, Miss Travis. It *is* Miss? Or have you just committed adultery?"

That remark, more than the deed itself or any previous insults, set her off. Her eyes sparkled with anger. "No, I haven't committed adultery. I defer to your far greater experience on that subject. And Barrie will be fine, thank you."

Gray turned back to the stove, dropped a teaspoon of butter into the skillet, and turned on the burner beneath it. As he watched the butter melt, he considered how to get rid of her without bodily throwing her out. With very little cerebral effort, he could list a dozen ways to kill a man silently, instantly, and painlessly. But the thought of physically hurting a woman made him queasy.

"You have a beautiful place," she remarked, drawing him out of his thoughts.

"Thanks."

"How many acres?"

"Fifty, give or take."

"You're here alone?"

"Until this morning."

"I'm sure you know that there's a town named Bondurant not too far from here. Is that—"

"No. That's a coincidence."

"Do you keep livestock? Other than the horses in the corral."

"I've got a small herd of beef cattle."

"So that's where all the meat in your freezer came from."

Gray turned and looked at her pointedly.

"I got a drink of water and borrowed a few ice cubes," she said, setting her chin defiantly.

"What else did you find while you were snooping around?"

"I wasn't snooping."

He turned back to the stove, spread the melted butter around the bottom of the skillet, then poured in the eggs. He fed two slices of bread into a toaster, took a plate from the cabinet, then scrambled the eggs with a spatula until they were to his liking. He scraped them into the center of the plate. Over the eggs he ladled the bubbling chili, then topped it off with a liberal sprinkling of Tabasco. The toast popped up as though on cue. He added both slices to the plate, along with a fork, and carried it to the table and sat down, straddling the seat of his chair.

From the corner of his eye, he watched her approach.

She sat down across from him. Ignoring her, he shoveled several bites into his mouth. Not until he paused to take a drink of coffee did he ask, "Hungry?"

"Sort of."

"Want some?"

She looked dubiously at his plate. "I'm not sure."

He shrugged. "It's on the stove."

She left the table and returned a few moments later with a smaller portion of his breakfast. He watched her take a tentative bite. She chewed, swallowed, then began to eat heartily.

"This is a remote area," she remarked between bites. "Don't you get lonely?"

"No."

"Bored?"

"Never."

"Before your, uh, retirement, you led a very adventurous life. Don't you miss the excitement of Washington?"

"If I did, I'd go back."

"How do you pass the time?"

"Any damn way I please."

"How do you earn a living?"

"It's rude to discuss finances."

"Well then, we're safe, because you've already established that reporters are rude." She raised her brows inquisitively.

"I ranch."

The simple answer seemed to surprise her. "Cattle?" He nodded. "Really? Hmm. You know how to do that?"

"I learned as a kid."

"Where?"

"On my dad's place."

"That doesn't tell me much."

"That's the idea, Miss Travis."

Frustrated, she sighed. "You've proven yourself capable in covert military operations, and you've been a presidential adviser. There's definitely no excitement factor to cattle ranching. It's hard for me to accept that you find this new career stimulating and challenging."

"I don't care what you accept."

"You just stay out here and ride horses all day?"

He didn't bother to answer that one.

"You just tend your cattle like a good little cowpuncher?"

"Yeah. When they need tending."

"Is that where you were yesterday? Out tending your cattle?"

"No. Yesterday I went to Jackson Hole."

"I came from there. We must have passed each other on the road." She pushed her empty plate aside. "Breakfast was good. Thanks."

He laughed. "If it had been a cow patty, you'd've eaten it and said it was delicious."

"Why would I do that?"

"Because you want something from me. Since sex didn't get it for you, you thought you'd try being friendly. Isn't all this chitchat just another attempt to disarm me? Frankly, Miss Travis, I enjoyed your first approach better."

"It wasn't an *approach*. I told you, it was—"

"An accident. Tell me, do you hop into bed with every man you meet?"

"Listen—"

"Didn't your daddy love you?"

She dropped her gaze to the tabletop, then almost immediately brought it back up to him. "I guess I can't blame you for forming such a low opinion of me."

"Ah, now we move from pal to penitent."

"Damn you," she shouted, smacking the tabletop hard as she came to her feet. "I'm being honest."

He too stood up. "No, Miss Travis, you're either being brave or stupid. I can't figure out which. But either way, I'm not going to talk to you about myself or the Merritts. And I'm not interested in anything you have to say about them, either."

"Didn't you hear what I said earlier about the death of their baby?"

"I heard it. I ignored it. I'll continue to." He stacked her plate on top if his, then carried both to the sink and ran water over them.

"Why are you ignoring it?"

"Because it's the kind of comment you reporters throw out, hoping that some sucker will bite."

"Do you think I'd make such a serious statement just for the hell of it?"

He turned off the water and faced her. "Yeah. In the short time that we've known each other, I have reason to think that you'd do just about anything to get a gig on *20/20*. Instead of messing with me, why don't you sleep with a network producer?"

"Because none of the network producers I know were Vanessa Merritt's lover."

His surge of rage frightened him. Before he could act on it, he sidestepped her and headed to the back of the house. He could hear her coming after him. She moved so fast that suddenly she was in front of him, her hands on the center of his chest.

She was breathing hard. "You think I came here to swap sex for a juicy story. I didn't. In fact, I'm mortified for the way I compromised myself and my profession. You don't know me, so you'll have to take my word for it when I tell you how badly I wanted to skulk out that front door, and how hard it is for me even to look you in the face."

Something in her voice caused him to wait and listen.

She removed her hands from his sternum and smoothed

them down the sides of her skirt. "That I'm still here should give you some indication of how important this story is, Mr. Bondurant. Not just to me and my career. To everyone. Please hear me out. Then, if you order me to leave, I will. No argument. Five minutes, okay?"

It was a very good act, he thought, but not good enough. His innate caution had been heightened by his recon training, which had taught him never to accept the surface appearance of anything or anyone. Experience had taught him that journalists were vicious scavengers. They would pick your bones clean without the least bit of remorse, then leave you exposed and vulnerable as they moved on to the next victim.

However, despite his statements to the contrary, he was growing interested in what Barrie Travis knew, or had surmised, about the SIDS death of Vanessa's child. Knowing it was a bad idea, and hoping that he wouldn't later regret it too much, he agreed to five minutes. "Outside."

He took the rocking chair. She sat on the top step, her arms wrapped around her shins. She was probably cold, but he didn't offer her anything to ward off the morning chill.

Now that he had granted her an ear, she seemed reluctant to begin, although she had her notepad ready. "It's so beautiful here."

This morning, the valley was shrouded in fog. The mountains were obscured by it, but the imminent sunrise had made the mist as pink as cotton candy. The air was cool and crisp.

"The barn looks older than the house and garage."

Pretty observant. "It was here when I bought the place. It had been built over the original homesite. I just did some refurbishing."

The horses were playing a frisky game of chase in the corral. "What are their names?" she asked.

"They don't have names."

He saw her surprise. "Your horses don't have names? How sad. Why not?"

"Is this the interview, Miss Travis?"

She gave a puzzled shake of her head. "I've never met anyone who didn't name his pets. Part of Cronkite's personality is his name." As she told him about her dog, her face turned soft and animated. "He's a big, floppy, affectionate, spoiled baby. You should have a dog," she said. "It would be good company for you."

"I like my solitude."

"You've made that abundantly clear."

"Time's ticking."

She let him have it then. With both barrels. "I think Vanessa Merritt killed her own baby."

Gray clenched his teeth to keep from saying anything.

She talked nonstop for the next several minutes. He lost track of how many, but certainly more than five. She talked him through several motives for why the First Lady might destroy her child, then detailed for him the steps she'd taken in making inquiries and the roadblocks she'd encountered.

"Now Mrs. Merritt has gone 'into seclusion.' Don't you think that's odd?"

"No," he lied.

"When she retreated from public life after the child's death, that was understandable. Jackie Kennedy did the same when she lost her baby. But it was for a specified time, and we're past that. If she's only resting, as insiders insist, then why isn't she staying with her father? Or why hasn't she gone to their home in Mississippi?"

"How do you know she hasn't?"

"I don't," she admitted with a frown. "But it's been announced that she's in Dr. Allan's care, and he's still in Washington. I don't get what the big secret is all about."

"There is no big secret."

"Then how do you account for Anna Chen's strange behavior? She was always a reliable source, willing to cooperate."

"You pissed her off?"

"I don't know her well enough to make her angry."

"I don't know you at all, and you've made me angry."

"She was scared," Barrie said stubbornly. "I recognize fear when I see it."

"Okay, maybe she was scared," he said impatiently. "Maybe she'd just seen a mouse. And maybe Vanessa's behavior is a little unusual, but doesn't she deserve privacy to do her grieving?"

This Barrie Travis, this reporter with the sexy voice, was bringing up the ambiguities he himself had entertained. His gut in a knot, he stood and walked to the edge of the porch. "Christ, what she must be going through." He plowed his fingers through his hair, squeezed his eyes shut, and tried forcibly to keep his own demons at bay.

Several moments passed before he remembered that she was there. He caught her staring up at him, a strange expression on her face. "It wasn't just an affair. You truly loved her, didn't you?" she said in a hushed voice. "You still do."

Cursing himself for consenting even to five minutes with her, he bent down and, for the second time that morning, picked up her big leather bag and pushed it into her arms. "Time's up."

His hand encircled her biceps as he pulled her to her feet. To steady herself, she gripped one of the posts supporting the porch roof. "After everything I've told you, is that all you have to say?"

"You're on a single track going nowhere, Miss Travis. All these inconsistencies are distortions of the facts, pieced together by your warped imagination and ambitious little mind to create an ugly but sensational story.

"For whatever it's worth, I advise you to drop this thing before you upset somebody in the administration who could really hurt you. Forget about that baby and how he died."

"I *can't* just forget it. Something about his death doesn't ring true."

"Suit yourself. But whatever else you do, forget about me." He went inside and locked the front door.

Chapter
Twelve

When Howie received the summons to the general manager's office, his bowels turned to water. Leaving the men's room, he went directly to the carpeted office on the second floor. An aloof secretary told him that "they" were waiting for him and to go right in.

Jenkins was seated behind his desk. Another man was standing in front of the window, while another occupied an armchair. "Come in, Howie," Jenkins said. Rubber-kneed, he advanced into the office. Typically, an unscheduled meeting like this meant bad news, like a drastic drop in ratings, a major cutback in budget, or a comprehensive ass-chewing.

"Good morning, Mr. Jenkins," he said, trying to appear calm. He purposely kept his eyes on his boss and not on the two austere men who were looking him over like he was in a line-up. "What can I do for you?"

"These men are from the FBI."

Howie's sphincter clenched. The goddamn IRS. He hadn't filed a tax return for the last three years.

"They want to ask you some questions about Barrie Travis."

Howie nearly laughed with relief. Cold sweat had trickled from his armpits and collected around his waist. "What about her?"

"Did you send her on an assignment?" Jenkins asked.

"Uh . . ."

That was a tricky question, and Howie needed time to weigh his answer. If he answered yes, and Barrie was in deep shit, he'd be jumping into the shit right along with her. If he answered no, and her instincts about a top-secret hot story proved correct, then he would be sacrificing his share of the credit.

He glanced at the FBI agent standing silhouetted against the window. The guy looked all business, and so did his partner.

"No," Howie replied. "She asked my permission to take a few days to investigate a story, but I didn't assign it to her."

"What story?" asked the agent by the window.

"I don't know. Something she cooked up on her own."

"She didn't discuss it with you?" the second agent asked.

"Not specifically—not the subject matter. All she told me was that it was hot stuff."

"You don't have a glimmer?"

The new buddy he'd made in the bar the other night had asked him these same questions. "No, sir."

"I find that hard to believe."

"It's the truth," Howie averred. "I tried to pry some information out of her, but she said she didn't want to elaborate until she had something concrete to back up her hunch."

"You're her immediate supervisor, right?"

"Yes, sir."

"And you have no idea what story your reporter is pursuing?"

Howie felt himself weakening, so he immediately turned defensive. "Well, you gotta understand my philosophy of personnel management, which is to let my subordinates take some initiative. When a reporter thinks he's on to a hot story, I cut him some slack. But it's understood that in exchange for my generosity, I expect a damn good piece in return."

Jenkins wasn't impressed. He practically stepped on Howie's last few words. "But Ms. Travis *is* away this week?"

"That's right. She left, let's see, day before yesterday. Said she'd probably be out the rest of the week."

One of the agents asked, "Where'd she go?"

"She wouldn't tell me."

The agents exchanged a meaningful glance. Howie wished he knew what that meaning was.

"Is the station covering her expenses?" This from Jenkins, whose perpetual scowl had deepened during the last few minutes.

"Only if she produces a story." He explained the deal he'd struck with Barrie. "I didn't want her squandering company funds on a wild goose chase." That ought to win him some points.

"What about her politics?"

Howie turned his head to the agent at the window. "Politics?"

"Her political inclinations. Does she generally lean to the left or the right?"

Howie thought for a moment. "I guess you'd say she's liberal. You know, she's always taking up for the underdog. Women, fags, foreigners, people like that. She voted for President Merritt." He smiled all around at the unsmiling group. "The President sent her flowers recently. She got a kick over that."

No comment on that from either agent. The one in the

chair asked, "Is Ms. Travis a member of any organizations? Any activist groups, religious sects, or cults?"

"Yeah," Howie said, nodding enthusiastically. "She's a Methodist."

One of the agents rolled his eyes. The other said, "You wouldn't call her a religious fanatic?"

"No. She's not opposed to letting fly with a four-letter word, or anything like that."

"Does she sympathize with any particular splinter group or radical organization?"

"Not that I know of. But she's participated in some protests."

"Against what?"

"Banning books. Destroying the rain forest. Eating porpoises instead of tuna fish. Stuff like that."

"Nothing subversive?"

"No."

"What about her personal life?"

"She doesn't talk about it much."

"Boyfriends?"

"Nobody regular."

"Roommate?"

"She lives alone."

"Close friends?"

He shook his head. "I've never heard her mention any. She's one of those women who's, you know, married to her career."

"What about her parents?"

"Dead."

"Do you know their names? Where they lived?"

"Sorry. They died before she started working here."

In his eagerness to appear important and be informative, Howie had almost forgotten that they were discussing Barrie and not a hardened criminal. He experienced a twinge of conscience. Barrie could be a pain in the butt, but he felt bad about discussing her so freely with feds.

"Is she in trouble? Has she done something wrong?"

"Just a routine check." The seated agent came to his feet. "She's called routinely to inquire after the First Lady's health, showing what appears to be an inordinate amount of interest in Mrs. Merritt and her whereabouts."

Howie relaxed. "Oh, hell, she's calling as a friend. They got pretty close when Barrie interviewed her."

The second agent said, "The White House tends to get suspicious when someone starts asking nosy questions about the President or members of his family."

The pair thanked Jenkins and Howie for their time and left.

Howie didn't make as clean a getaway. Jenkins's glower was as good as shackles around his ankles. "Do you know something you're not telling?" he demanded.

"No, sir."

"What's her hot story?"

"Just like I told them, Mr. Jenkins, I swear to God I don't know. But Barrie said it would make chicken feed of Watergate."

"So it *is* political?"

"She didn't say. Just that it was big."

Jenkins aimed an imperative index finger at him. "I won't have some radical lunatic working at my TV station."

"Barrie's not a lunatic, sir. She's a good reporter. You told her so yourself in your memo."

"I never sent her any memo. What the fuck're you talking about, Fripp?"

"George?"

Vanessa wasn't sure she'd made herself heard, but the

doctor glanced down at her and smiled. "Glad to see you awake. How're you feeling?"

"Not good." She was nauseated, and it was difficult to focus on his multiple, wavering images. She vaguely remembered a nasty scene. George had given her a shot to sedate her. It seemed like a very long time ago. "What's wrong with me? Where's David?"

"The President and I agreed that you needed absolute bed rest, so we moved you here." He patted her arm, but she probably wouldn't have felt his touch if she hadn't been looking at her hand, where an IV needle was dripping a clear solution into her veins.

Motion on the other side of the bed drew her attention. A nurse was smiling down at her. "I'm Jayne Gaston," she said. She was fifty-five or thereabouts, with a wide, pleasant face and short salt-and-pepper hair.

"Mrs. Gaston's been staying with you round the clock," George said. "She's taking excellent care of you, and so far you've been an ideal patient."

Vanessa was confused and disoriented. The room looked vaguely familiar, but she couldn't remember where she'd seen it before. "Why have I got an IV?"

"To ensure that you don't dehydrate," the doctor explained. "You couldn't keep down any liquids."

The nurse was taking her blood pressure.

"Am I sick?" she asked, suddenly seized by panic. What weren't they telling her? Had she been in an accident and lost a limb? Did she have terminal cancer? Had she been shot?

Those frightening possibilities were instantly replaced by the terrifying reality—David had put her here.

"Where's David? I want to talk to him."

"The President is out on the West Coast today," George told her, pleasant smile in place. "But I believe he's returning tonight. Maybe you can talk to him later."

"Why do I need a nurse? Am I dying?"

"Of course not, Mrs. Merritt. Lie back," George said, pressing her shoulder gently when she tried to sit up. He looked across at Jayne Gaston. "We'd better bring her down some more."

"But, Dr. Allan—"

"Please, Mrs. Gaston."

"Certainly, Doctor." She left the room.

"Where's my father?" Vanessa asked, her voice sounding distant and feeble even to her own ears. "I want to see Daddy. Call him. Tell him to come get me."

"I'm afraid I can't do that, Vanessa. Not without getting David's approval first."

The nurse returned with a syringe. She gave Vanessa an injection in her thigh.

"You'll get better faster if you relax and let us take care of you," George told her gently.

"What's wrong with me? Has the baby come yet?"

Jayne Gaston looked across to Dr. Allan. "Poor thing. She thinks she's still pregnant."

George nodded grimly.

"My baby," Vanessa sobbed. "Have you got my baby?"

"Let's leave so she'll rest now."

"No, please," Vanessa rasped. "Don't leave me. You all hate me. I know you do. What aren't you telling me? My baby's dead, isn't he?"

Dr. Allan signaled the nurse to follow him from the room. Mrs. Gaston quietly closed the door behind them.

Vanessa struggled to remember something. It was important, but she couldn't quite grasp it. She had to think, had to remember. There was something she should remember. What was it?

Then a moan spiraled up from deep within her. She remembered the lifeless body she'd lifted from the crib. She

heard echoes of her own screams, exactly as they'd rever-
berated down the hallways of the White House that night.

"My baby," she sobbed. "My baby. Oh, God. I'm
sorry."

Rather than debilitate her, the anguish galvanized her.
She was unclear as to her goal, but she knew that she couldn't
lie here helplessly any longer. Unaware of the pain, she ripped
off the tape securing the IV needle to the back of her hand.
Once it was out of the way, she swallowed her nausea and
pulled the small catheter from her vein.

When she tried to sit up, she felt as if an anvil were on
her chest, anchoring her to the bed. Calling upon every
ounce of reserve strength she had, she finally willed herself
into a sitting position. The room tilted. The trees she saw
through the window appeared to be growing out of the
ground at a forty-five-degree angle. She retched, but dryly.

Her brain seemed incapable of telegraphing messages
to her legs. It took her five minutes and an incredible amount
of effort to drag them over the side of the bed. Then her feet
dangled above the floor while she staved off nausea and
incessant waves of dizziness. Eventually she worked up
enough courage and stamina to slide down the edge of the
mattress and place her feet on the floor.

Her legs didn't support her. She collapsed in a heap
beside the bed, then lay there sobbing, breathing heavily,
too weak to stand, too weak even to call out for help. She
wished for death.

No. She'd be damned if she would make it that easy for
them.

Determined, she inched along the floor like a crude life
form, using a hand, a foot, a shoulder, a heel like a pseudo-
pod, propelling her forward in minute increments.

When she finally reached the door, she was bathed in
sweat. Her hair and nightgown were plastered to her skin.

She curled into the fetal position and rested, shivering now as her perspiration cooled.

At last, she raised her head and looked up at the doorknob. It appeared as unreachable as the moon. She tried pounding on the door, but her hands made only weak slaps against it. So she pressed her palms against the cool wood and crawled up the door, straining the muscles of her arms and chest, until she could get one leg beneath her, then the other, until she was on her knees.

Then she seized the doorknob with both hands and managed to turn it, at the same time slumping against the door. It burst open, and she fell out into the hallway, landing hard on her shoulder and sending rockets of pain down her arm.

"Mrs. Merritt! Oh, my God! Dr. Allan!"

Shouting voices. Running footsteps. Hands cupping her armpits, lifting her.

Limp, spent, she swayed between two Secret Service agents as they carried her back to the bed.

George Allan elbowed the agents aside. "Thanks, gentlemen."

"Should I call for an ambulance, Dr. Allan?" one of them asked.

"That won't be necessary." He listened to her heart through a stethoscope. "Mrs. Gaston, will you get another IV line going, please?"

The other agent asked if he should call the President or Mr. Martin. The doctor said he would make the call himself as soon as Mrs. Merritt was stabilized. The two agents withdrew.

"Let's put some restraints on her," George told the nurse. "Arms and legs."

"Isn't that excessive?"

"We can't risk her getting out of bed and falling again, Mrs. Gaston."

"I'd be happy to assist her if she wants to get up, Dr. Allan. In fact, it might do her good to get out of bed. I think she's overly sedated."

"I appreciate your input," George said, his tone belying his words, "but I know what's best for my patient. Please follow my orders, which are also those of the President of the United States. Are we clear on that?"

"Yes, Dr. Allan."

Vanessa's eyes were closed, but she had followed most of their conversation, although some of the words were difficult to assign meanings to. Why couldn't she get up if she wanted?

Where was David?

Where was her father?

Where was *she*?

Hell, maybe.

No, hell for sure.

~~

"*Where*?"

"Wyoming."

"Shit!"

Having delivered his bad news to the President, Spence fell silent as he jogged along beside him. The verbal rampage that followed was colorful and then some. Merritt resorted to the language he'd learned from his father, who had worked in Biloxi's shipyard.

Merritt's roots had been exposed during his first campaign for a congressional seat. By the time he ran for President, it was well known by the voting public that he hadn't lived a life of wealth and privilege. His mother had worked as a cook for the public school system, but the dual-income family had rarely been solvent. They had never owned a home. David Merritt's childhood had been spent in a rented unit in a second-rate trailer park.

Rather than try to hide his humble beginnings, the campaign committee had touted him as the embodiment of the American dream. He was the twenty-first century's Abraham Lincoln. He'd overcome incredible odds to hold the highest office in the world. Senator Armbruster's tutelage had been of tremendous help, but it was Merritt's own intelligence and determination that had brought him to Armbruster's attention in the first place.

What wasn't publicized was the ignobility of young Merritt's poverty. It wasn't commonly known that both his parents had been alcoholics. He had been more or less responsible for himself long before his parents had conveniently drunk themselves to death. The one and only time he had allowed himself to become intoxicated was the day he buried his father. He got drunk to celebrate his freedom from two people he had disdained and despised for as long as he could remember.

Spence glanced at the President now.

As usual, his outburst hadn't lasted long. He'd fallen silent except for his aerobic breathing. Spence had chosen this time to break the disturbing news because it was a matter of personal importance and required complete privacy. On the jogging path it was unlikely that they could be overheard even by the Secret Service agents who tagged along a few yards behind. They knew better than to get too close when the President was in conversation with Spence. Everything between them was strictly classified.

"How do you know Barrie Travis went to Wyoming?" the President huffed.

"She hasn't been home in two days. Her dog's boarded at a kennel."

"I didn't ask if she was out of town," Merritt snapped. "I asked how you know she went to Wyoming."

Spence didn't let the dressing-down ruffle him. He considered temper a weakness, even in presidents—*especially* in presidents. "While you were in California, I talked to that bozo she works with." He told Merritt about meeting Howie Fripp in a neighborhood bar. "The guy's a moron. But even so, I don't think he knows where Travis went, because he gave two FBI agents the same story yesterday morning at the TV station. They said his fear stunk. If he'd known something, he would have told."

"Was her house searched?"

"Officially, no," Spence said. "We have no warrant or viable reason to obtain one."

"What about unofficially?"

"Unofficially, it was gone over by the best man in the business," Spence reported with a cold grin. "It looked to him like she was trying to cover her tracks. He didn't find a single note, or scrap of paper, or receipt, anything to indicate that she was leaving or why she was going. What he did find were several overdue books from the library, all relating to women's psychological disorders and SIDS."

Merritt wiped his perspiring forehead. "She's still on it."

"That's my guess. We located her car in a parking lot at National Airport, then started going through the passenger logs of all flights out of there over the last several days. She didn't travel under her own name, and there were no credit card charges on any of her accounts."

The President stopped running. Spence stopped, too. The Secret Service agents halted but kept their distance.

"She's being awfully paranoid," Merritt said.

"Right. When her name didn't appear on any of the logs, we checked airline agents until we found the one who sold her the ticket. Travis was traveling under an alias and paid for her ticket to Jackson Hole with cash. The airline employee identified her from a picture."

"She went to see Gray."

"She went to see Gray." Spence's expression was as somber as the President's. "At least that's what we must assume."

Merritt stared into space, thinking it over. "He hates reporters. I don't think he would talk to her."

"Are you willing to take that chance?"

"Damn." Merritt flicked a bead of sweat off the tip of his nose. "What if we're too late? If she's talked to Gray, if he's told her anything—"

"Then we have a potential problem," Spence said.

"Prior to an election year, we can't afford even a 'potential' problem."

"I agree." Spence locked gazes with Merritt. "I think we have to guarantee this reporter's silence."

The President nodded, then resumed jogging. "Do whatever you deem necessary."

Spence fell into step with him. "I'll see to it immediately."

Chapter
Thirteen

"Are you shittin' me? The FBI?"

"That's what Howie said." Barrie was watching herself in the mirror as she talked long distance to Daily from her motel room in Jackson Hole. Was it the poor lighting in the room or her increasing apprehension that made her look so pale?

"Two agents went to WVUE and questioned him about me." She recounted for Daily everything she could remember that Howie had related to her. "They scared him shitless. Literally. He went into details that don't bear repeating about distress in his lower bowel."

"This is no laughing matter, Barrie."

Another defense mechanism she'd developed during childhood was a sardonic sense of humor. This time her wit did nothing to alleviate the grave situation. She had hoped that Daily would dismiss her concerns. Instead, he was underscoring them. "What do you think it means?"

"I think it means that you've made people nervous."

"What people?"

"Maybe just Dalton Neely. Your repeated calls have

annoyed the White House press secretary; they insinuate that he's being less than truthful about the First Lady's well-being. His way of telling you to back off is to sic the feds on you."

"Or?"

"Or," he sighed, "it could go all the way up to the Oval Office. Did Howie have any theories?"

"He and Jenkins were told that the inquiry was strictly routine, then Howie told them that my interest in Vanessa was a friendly outgrowth of the recent interview."

"Did they buy that?"

"They seemed to. That probably capped it."

"Probably."

After a moment she said, "Daily, we're agreeing on a point that neither of us believes."

They were quiet for a while, the only sound on the line being Daily's wheezing breath. Finally he asked, "I almost forgot—how was Bondurant?"

Her heart executed a flawless swan dive. How *was* Bondurant? In or out of bed? In bed, he was bloody fabulous. Out . . . "About what I expected. Hostile. Taciturn."

"Didn't greet you with open arms, huh?"

In a manner of speaking, he had. "Well, not exactly."

"Did he shed any light on the topic?"

"Not a ray. Not on purpose anyway. I'm convinced that there were some strong feelings between him and Vanessa. At least from his side."

"You think they did the nasty thing?"

"Consummated or not, he's still emotionally attached. In an unguarded moment, he lamented the hell she must be going through. I presume he was referring to her grief over the baby's death."

"Never presume anything, Barrie. Don't you listen? Don't you learn? Get the *facts*."

"Well, I'm not going back for another round with him, if that's what you're suggesting. He told me to forget my story and, short of that, to forget him. I intend to do the latter. I'll get my story, but I'll get it sans Bondurant."

"What's going on with you?"

"Nothing's going on with me." God, she would *die* if Daily ever found out how she had sacrificed her journalistic integrity and objectivity to several minutes of sexual bliss.

"Okay," he said without conviction. "You just sound awfully defensive."

"I'm worried about my story."

"So you're sticking with it?"

"Absolutely. Since when does a minor reporter's employer warrant a visit from the FBI? The more doors that are closed on me, the more convinced I become that somebody has something to hide."

"When are you coming back?"

"Tomorrow. I'll pick up the trail in Washington. Any news about Vanessa?"

"Same old shit."

"I'll call you tomorrow night when I get home. Are you all right?"

"Fine," he said, not sounding fine at all. "Barrie? If you've stumbled over something really ugly . . . Well, just be careful. Okay?"

His concern was touching and made her homesick for him. Even after hanging up, she kept her hand on the receiver, reluctant to break the emotional contact. Daily was more like family than friend, more of a parent than either of her own had been.

Wearily, she went into the bathroom and began removing her clothes. The mirror over the basin was no kinder than the one above the bedroom dresser. She looked a fright. What was left of her makeup was thirty-six hours old. It was caked in the fine lines around her eyes, which seemed to etch themselves deeper on a daily basis. She was thirty-three. What would she look like at forty-three? Fifty-three? She had no basis for comparison. Her mother hadn't lived that long.

Barrie pushed aside the shower curtain and turned on the water. She yelped when the shower spray struck her chest and looked down to see what had caused the stings. There were faint, pink abrasions on her breasts. Whisker burns.

God, what had she done?

She ducked her head beneath the nozzle, wishing the hard spray would pound out her memories of Gray Bondurant. Naked, he was lean and tough and supple. His body didn't have the smooth perfection of youth. It had seen wear and tear. But its dents and dings made it all the more appealing, just as his graying temples and the creases around his eyes made his face more interesting.

She needed rest, she thought, working shampoo lather through her hair. Fatigue and stress were making her emotionally fragile and dangerously reflective. First on Daily. Then on her parents. Now on a tall, rangy man with laser-beam-blue eyes and a cruel mouth.

Didn't your daddy love you?

No, Mr. Bondurant, he did not. He didn't love my mother, either.

If he had, why had he cheated on her? Why had he made a habit of adultery all his married life? Why had he lied and denied her mother's accusations, and engaged her in those vituperative shouting matches that had filled Barrie's nights with misery and terror? Why had he continued torturing his family with his affairs until he died of a heart attack in a Las Vegas hotel room while his bimbo of the month was anointing his loins with coconut-flavored love gel? He hadn't even had the consideration to drop dead in a decent manner.

And what had Barrie's silly, stupid mother done? Had

she ever rebuked him for betraying his marriage vows? Had she reviled him for ignoring his daughter, for being too busy screwing around to notice any of her rites of passage from infancy through young adulthood? Had she ranted and raved at him for being the least affectionate, least attentive parent in history? Even after his death, had she told anyone what a royal son of a bitch he was and always had been?

No. She had buried him in grand style, and then, unable to conceive of life without him, she went home and swallowed a bottle of pills.

One week, two funerals.

Yes, Mr. Bondurant, you surely struck a nerve.

Barrie stepped from the shower and reached for a towel. She'd read the books, listened to the talk shows. She knew the psychology. Girls rejected by their fathers usually went one of two ways: They became nymphomaniacs, looking for love and attention in whatever form, from every man they encountered, or they rejected men altogether, usually in favor of other women.

Barrie had done neither.

She hadn't become a slut, craving male attention and relying on it for her sense of self-worth. Nor had she taken the other path. Her sexual appetite was whetted only by men. When she was with one whom she found physically attractive, charming after a fashion, intelligent to some degree, she enjoyed sex very much. Her one unbendable rule was that she set the time and the place and the parameters of the relationship. She called the shots.

Until this morning's sexual episode.

Never had she lost control like that. That kind of mindless, heedless, reckless plunge into passion was hazardous to one's psyche. Case in point, her own mother. Barrie had vowed not to repeat her mother's fatal mistake of loving blindly and having that love abused.

Barrie would share her body when desire and circumstances permitted. But she had sworn never to let her head, and certainly not her heart, get fucked.

∽∼

Gray woke just in time to see the pillow coming down over his face.

Instinctively he tried to reach for the pistol beneath his pillow, but his arms were pinned down by a pair of knees, one on either side of him, as his attacker crouched over his chest. He strained and struggled. He arched his body. He tried to pull in air that wasn't there.

And the bastard was laughing.

Gray recognized the laughter a split second before the pillow was tossed aside. Spencer Martin's face hovered above his, grinning. "You're going soft out here on the frontier, old man."

Gray threw him off and rolled out of bed. "You damn lunatic. I could've killed you."

"Haven't you got that backward?" Spence said, still laughing. "*I* could've killed *you*."

"What the hell are you doing here, sneaking into my house, playing games? Jesus, what time is it? I gotta pee."

"Glad to see you, too, Gray." Spence followed him as far as the bathroom door. "You've lost a few pounds."

Gray reached for a pair of blue jeans hanging on the back of the door. As he stepped into them, he appraised his former colleague. "You've put on a few. The White House chef must still know his stuff."

Spence kept his rare grin in place. "Know what I've missed most since you left?"

"My charm?"

"Your total lack of it. Most people kiss up to me. I'm the President's trusted adviser and best friend. No matter how rude I am, people go out of their way to kiss my ass. But not you, Gray. You treat everybody the same. Like shit," he added.

"So that's why you're here? You miss me?"

He led Spence through the house and into the kitchen. He had only one clock in the house, and it was over the stove. He checked the time. Almost daylight. It had been twenty-four hours since he'd entertained Barrie Travis in this room. The unsettling symmetry of that didn't escape him.

"You never were much for laughs, Gray. But you were good to have around. You served your purpose."

Gray shot Spence a telling look. "Yeah, I did, didn't I? I was there when you needed me most." He held the stare for several tense seconds before turning away. "Coffee?"

"Please. Got anything to eat?"

He prepared a hearty breakfast similar to the one he'd fed Barrie the day before. As they ate, the silence was broken only by the clink of flatware against dishes. After a time, Spence asked, "Is it always like this?"

"Like what?"

"This quiet."

"No." Gray sipped his coffee. "Usually it's quieter. There's nobody talking."

"Gray the loner," Spence said. "The strong and silent, stalwart, unsmiling hero who eschewed publicity and sought a solitary life. Damn! It's the stuff of legends. Who knows? Maybe a hundred years from now, schoolchildren will be singing folk songs about you."

Gray was silent.

After the hostage rescue mission, he'd been approached by publishers and movie producers eager to turn his real-life adventure into entertainment. They'd offered staggering amounts of money, but he had never been tempted. He'd saved up enough to buy this place and live comfortably for the rest of his life. All he'd wanted was out, and out he was.

Gray removed the dishes from the table, then returned with the coffee carafe and poured each of them a refill. Finally, he brought the topic back to why Spence had come to Wyoming.

"You. Simple as that," Spence said. "David sent me out to Seattle on an errand. I thought as long as I had to fly over, I'd drop in and check on you."

David might have sent Spence on an errand, but nothing Spence did was ever simple. He had a multiplicity of motives for every action. That way, he was covered. He had fallback positions to take if an action came under close scrutiny by one of the checks and balances built into the federal system.

Spence had been the unqualified best of their entire infantry and reconnaissance division. He had aced everything—weapons, intelligence, survival. He knew no fear. Spence was a machine. Gray wouldn't have been surprised to find a computer instead of a brain inside his skull. Or an engine inside his chest where a heart should have been.

He knew with absolute certainty that the man seated across the breakfast table from him had no soul.

"You're lying, Spence."

Spencer Martin didn't even blink. "Fuckin'-A, I'm lying. And I can't tell you how glad I am that you caught it, Gray. You're as sharp as ever. Haven't lost your edge." He leaned forward. "He wants you back."

Although he was surprised, Gray maintained his rigid calm.

"David needs you back in Washington," Spence pressed.

"Like hell he does."

"Hear me out." Spence held up both hands, palms out.

"He's a proud man. Hell, I don't have to tell you that. He's stubborn and determined, and the hardest thing for him to do is back down or apologize for being wrong."

"So he sent you to do it for him."

"I'm not groveling, but I'm asking, on David's behalf, that you get your ass back to Washington, where it belongs."

"My ass belongs right where it is."

Spence glanced at the spectacular scenery through the windows. "You're not Grizzly Adams, Gray."

"I like the mountains."

"So do I. They're great for climbing and skiing and yodeling. Keep the place here for vacations—but return with me to Washington. Your talents are being wasted. The President needs you. I need you. The country needs you."

"That's a stirring speech. Who wrote it for you? Neely?"

"I'm serious."

"The country needs me?" Gray snorted. "Cut the crap. The *country* doesn't care if I'm dead or alive. I did the job I was trained to do. My country asked no more from me, and I sure as hell asked no more from it. That's as it should be."

"Okay, forget patriotic duty. What about David?"

"Hell, he doesn't need me. His ratings are through the roof. The other party will sacrifice some poor bastard to run against him next year, but that'll turn out to be an expensive exercise in futility, because David will serve his second term. He needs me like he needs a boil on his butt."

"Not so."

Spence stood, stretched, and looked out the window. The sun was up now, so the view was breathtaking. The snow on the peaks appeared gold-flecked.

"This thing with Vanessa," Spence said, "is a potential hand grenade."

"What 'thing'?"

Spence turned. "The baby dying. She's freaked out over it."

"As any mother would be."

Spence shook his head. "It's more than that. Grief has exacerbated her other problem. Bottom line, she can't be left alone." He told Gray that she was at Highpoint under the care of George Allan and a full-time nurse. "David's afraid she'll do something crazy."

"You mean like harm herself?"

"It's anybody's guess. Anyway, David thought if you came back, you might have a stabilizing effect on her."

"He's got far more faith in my healing abilities than they warrant. Besides, if he can't hold sway over his wife, what does he expect me to do?"

"Allay the new gossip about their marriage," Spence replied bluntly. "Vanessa's been away a lot recently. You know how people talk. Rumors get started.

"A good marriage would go far toward David's reelection. A marriage on the skids would be disastrous. If you were back, that rumor would be squelched once and for all. David might be a forgiving man, but he would never reenlist a man who'd been his wife's lover."

Gray was grinding his teeth so hard it was making his jaw ache. Beneath the table, his hands were clenched into fists.

"Complicating the situation is this reporter," Spence continued as he returned to his chair. "Barrie Travis. She's been asking some questions that are a little too personal for comfort. She has unimpressive credentials." Resting his arm on the laptop computer he always carried, he summarized Barrie Travis's professional history. "But since Vanessa granted her that interview, she's passing herself off as the First Lady's best friend and confidante. She's just a screw-up—but sometimes a loose cannon can pose the worst threat."

"She is a threat. She was here."

"*Here?* When?"

"Yesterday."

Spence dragged his hands down his face. "We thought she was just poking around Washington, but if she sought you out, she means business."

"Oh, she means business, all right. She had a whole backpack full of tabloid clippings about me and Vanessa. She'd done her homework and had set up shop to get the goodies. I told her I had nothing to say about the Merritts and wasn't interested in hearing anything she had to say about them."

"*Did* she say anything about them?"

Gray chuckled. "Get ready for this one, buddy. She thinks Vanessa killed the baby and only claimed it was crib death."

"I hope you're joking."

"Have you ever known me to joke?"

"Jesus Christ," Spence whispered. "We knew she was out in left field, but . . . She actually believes Vanessa could do that? That's preposterous."

"Of course it is."

"But if Travis even leaks something like that, I don't have to tell you the harm it could do, not just to David and next year's campaign, but to Vanessa. She's very fragile now. George has had to increase her medication to keep her in balance. She's grown real fond of the grape, which contributes to the problem. If Travis's theory became public, Vanessa would fall apart completely."

Gray could envision Spence's mind clicking along its single track: protecting and preserving the presidency for David and therefore for himself.

"Where's the Travis broad now?"

Gray shrugged. "On her way back to Washington, I guess. I told her to get lost."

Spence was on his feet again. "I'd better call Washington. David will want to hear this immediately."

"Phone's in the bedroom on the nightstand."

"Thanks. And, by the way, great breakfast," Spence said over his shoulder as he left the room.

Gray turned on the radio to listen to the news and weather while he cleared the kitchen. Methodically he returned perishables to the refrigerator and staples to the pantry.

In the course of putting things away, he opened the drawer where he kept large utensils and exchanged a long-handled spatula for a Beretta.

Then he turned on the faucets and began filling the sink with hot, soapy water. He dunked the dirty dishes into the sink. As he washed them, he kept both eyes on the toaster. When its chrome surface reflected movement behind him, he yanked the pistol from his waistband, spun around, and fired.

His gun hand dripped soapsuds onto the kitchen floor.

Chapter
Fourteen

*B*arrie's return flight to Washington was long and turbulent. National Airport was as chaotic as a Turkish bazaar. By the time she retrieved her car from the parking lot and reached the TV station, she was frazzled. She hoped to sneak in, check her desk for mail and messages, then leave without being seen or having to talk with anybody.

There were no messages on her e-mail; four were in her telephone mailbox. Two were from acquaintances, one was from the dry cleaners saying they couldn't get the stain out of her blouse, and the last was from Charlene the kook, demanding to know why Barrie hadn't returned any of her previous calls.

Barrie wondered what Charlene's hot news flash was: terrorist infiltration of the Boy Scouts, mafia activity among Eskimos, cyanide in Corn Flakes?

"Poor thing," Barrie muttered as she deleted the phone messages. "She's probably just lonely and wants someone to talk to."

"Who does?"

"Dammit, Howie!" she exclaimed, swiveling her chair around. "Does sneaking up and scaring the daylights out of me give you some kind of sick thrill?"

"You wouldn't've jumped if you didn't have a guilty conscience."

"Don't start. I'm in a black mood."

"*You* are?" he exclaimed in a shrill voice. "What about me? I was the one who covered your ass when the feds came calling. I was the one you lied to and made to look like a fool in front of Jenkins. Memo, schmemo!"

"I'm sorry about that, Howie. Truly. I wouldn't have lied if it hadn't been necessary."

She stood to leave, but he blocked her path. "What are you investigating, Barrie? Tell me."

"Not till I've got more."

"Why didn't you take a photographer with you?"

She had wondered when it would occur to Einstein here that she hadn't requested a video photographer to accompany her when she went in pursuit of a big story. What was a TV news story without a visual?

"It would have been premature to take a photographer. You'll be the first to know when someone's ready to go on record with a statement."

His expression turned nasty. Nastier. "I'm only a few years away from retirement. If you think I'm gonna blow my pension on you, you got another think coming. You were a bad risk to start with, but I took a chance on you."

"For which I'll be eternally grateful. Now, I've crossed the Continental Divide and two time zones. I'm tired, cranky, and none too fresh in the hygiene department. I'm going to pick up my dog and go home to bed. Good night." She squeezed past him.

"Okay, fine, bury yourself. But don't expect to drag me down with you! That's the last time I'll go to the mat for you." She was almost out of hearing when he got in a parting shot: "And you look like hell."

⌒⌒

She considered leaving Cronkite at the kennel overnight but decided she needed the company. Besides, she hated to keep him confined any longer than necessary.

She arrived at the kennel minutes before closing. Both the personnel and Cronkite were overjoyed to see her. "He's well behaved, but terribly spoiled," the young woman said as she relinquished the pet to his owner.

"Yeah, I know. But he's a prince among dogs." Barrie knelt down and ruffled his coat while he enthusiastically lapped at her face.

His exuberance didn't abate on the drive home. "I promise you'll get a treat as soon as we get inside," she told him as they got out of the car. "Just please calm down." Since someone had taken the parking space in front of her townhouse, she'd had to settle on another, half a block away.

"Cronkite, please!" Ninety pounds of dog strained at the leash. Knowing he was close to home, where a treat awaited, he was nearly in a frenzy.

"Okay, okay." Barrie removed the leash from his collar. It was either that or be dragged along behind him. Once freed, he went airborne for a millisecond, then bounded down the street, his nails clicking on the pavement.

"Go in through your doggie door," she called after him.

She leaned into the backseat to retrieve her satchel and luggage.

The concussion of the blast struck her like a giant hand and knocked her backward to the ground.

A gigantic fireball burst into the night sky, washing the entire neighborhood with the eerie red glow of hell.

"Ohmygodmygodmygod." She managed to get onto all fours. For several seconds, she could only gape at the inferno half a block away where her townhouse had stood. Black smoke roiled above it, blotting out a quarter moon.

For several moments, she was too stunned to move. Then adrenaline kicked in. Swaying drunkenly, she came to her feet and began running down the sidewalk. At least she tried to run. Actually it was more a stumble-lurch.

"Cronkite!" Her scream was little more than a croak. "Cronkite! Here, boy!"

She was unaware of the heat as she staggered up the brick walkway that had led to her front door.

"Lady, are you crazy!"

Restraining hands caught her from behind and held her back.

"Somebody help me," a man called out. "She's trying to go inside."

Then several pairs of hands were on her, holding her back. She struggled, but to no avail. They dragged her across the street and into a neighbor's yard, out of harm's way. She tried to make herself understood, but could only sob. "Cronkite. Cronkite."

"I think Cronkite's her dog."

"Not anymore. If he was in that house, he's . . ."

"Does anybody know what happened?"

"Whose house was it?"

Barrie was only vaguely aware of the voices around her. Neighbors poured from their houses. The sidewalk and street were now crowded with gawkers. From a distance came the wail of sirens.

When her well-meaning neighbors were sure that Barrie wasn't going to barge into the conflagration, they released her and drifted away to watch the fire. She shrank back into the hedgerow between lawns and watched in horror as her property continued to disintegrate. No one paid any attention to her. The bystanders were chattering among themselves, trying to piece together the sequence of events.

"Here come the fire trucks. Can they get through?"

"I hope they hose down our roofs."

"Was anyone inside?"

"Only a pet. Somebody said it was the owner's dog."

Unheard, Barrie whimpered, "Cronkite."

That was her last word before a large hand clamped over her mouth and she was yanked backward through the hedge.

She screamed, or tried to, but the hand across her mouth only increased its pressure. Barrie dug her heels into the neighbor's backyard grass, but her captor jerked her off her feet. When they reached the alley behind the house, she kicked his shins hard enough to make him relax his hold, but she was free only long enough to fall and skin her knees on the pavement. She screamed, but there was no way her scream could have been heard above the racket and confusion of the crowds and emergency vehicles.

She scrambled to regain her footing, but once again was swept up into a breath-stealing bear hug. "Shut up or I'll hurt you."

Believing him, she put up no more resistance as she was dragged through another yard, then another alley, and another yard. Finally they reached a car parked at the curb two streets away from hers.

When her abductor reached for the door handle, her teeth came down hard on the meaty part of his palm and she rammed her elbow into his belly. He flinched and grunted a curse; Barrie took off at a sprint. Her freedom was short-lived. He grabbed a handful of her hair and brought her up short.

She was spun around and shaken so hard that she feared she would break. "Stop fighting me, goddammit. I'm trying to keep you alive."

When her brain stopped jiggling, she realized she was in the company of Gray Bondurant.

～⁓

"Do you have your glasses with you?"

He was driving, heading toward a suburb in Maryland. He drove skillfully, but safely within the speed limit. The last thing he wanted was to be stopped for a routine traffic ticket. He kept one eye on the rearview mirror, but after a few blocks, he was positive they weren't being followed. No one was looking for him. Yet.

Realizing that his question hadn't registered with his passenger, he glanced across the car at her. She was staring straight ahead through the windshield, dazed. "Do you have your glasses?" he repeated.

She turned to him, stared at him blankly for several seconds, then nodded. Inexplicably, she'd managed to keep her satchel on her shoulder.

"Take out your contacts and put on your glasses," he instructed.

She wet her lips, swallowed. "How did you know—"

"I know. Just do it. Then tuck your hair up under that baseball cap." He'd brought one along. It was lying in the seat between them.

"What . . . Why . . ."

"Because I don't want to risk your being recognized."

"By whom?"

"By the guys who blew your house to smithereens, who do you think?"

"My dog's dead."

Her voice cracked. The headlights of an oncoming car were reflected in her teary eyes. She began to cry, quietly. Gray took the coward's way and said nothing. He couldn't think of anything to say. He wasn't much good at that sort of thing. But he preferred her crying to acting like a zombie.

He continued to drive, literally going with the flow. When her tears finally subsided, he pulled into the parking lot of a twenty-four-hour coffee shop.

"We've got a lot to talk about," he said. "I can't take you in there if you're going to fall apart on me and attract attention."

He sat by while she removed her contact lenses and put on her eyeglasses. He'd seen the glasses in her satchel when he'd gone through it after discovering her asleep on his sofa.

"Do you have a handkerchief?" she asked.

"No."

She wiped her nose on her sleeve. "Then I'm ready. But forget that cap. Nobody's going to recognize me."

Before he could stop her, she opened the door and got out. He caught up with her as she was greeted by the smiling hostess, who escorted them to a booth. He declined the glossy menu. "Just coffee, please."

It was a well-lighted place. Only a few of the booths were occupied. One section of the dining room had been roped off; the floor was being mopped with a strong solution that compromised the aroma of fried ham and pancake syrup.

"Mr. Bondurant, how is it that you managed to abduct me just seconds after my house was blown up?"

He refrained from answering until after the waitress had poured their coffee and withdrawn. "I didn't do it, if that's what you're suggesting."

"That's exactly what I was suggesting."

"Well, you're wrong." Looking down at his coffee, he added, "Too bad about your dog."

"This from a man who hasn't even named his horses," she said snidely.

"Look, I did you a favor by hauling you away from there."

"But why *hauling*? Why didn't you just escort me from the site?"

"Because you were in no condition to listen to reason. I had to get you away from there, and that was the fastest way. I thought they'd be after you, and I was right. But if you want to split up now, that's fine with me."

"I don't know what you're talking about," she exclaimed, but in a low voice that wouldn't attract attention.

"Then why don't you shut up and let me tell you."

She sat back against the vinyl booth and folded her arms.

He took a few sips of coffee. "First, I want to know exactly what happened. It's fair to assume that Brinkley—"

"Cronkite."

"Cronkite went into the house ahead of you."

"There is—*was*—a doggie door in the back door."

"Is that how you usually go in, through the back?"

"Usually."

"Then they probably tripped that door."

She leaned across the table. "*Who*? And what are you doing here? Why'd you follow me back to Washington? You did follow me back, didn't you?"

"I came to warn you that you've been asking the wrong questions of the wrong people. You're on the scent of a story that the President can't allow to be told."

She turned a lighter shade of pale. Nervously, she pulled her lower lip through her teeth. "How do you know?"

"Less than twenty-four hours after you left my place I had a visit from Spencer Martin."

"Isn't he connected to the White House in some capacity?"

"You could say so. Second only to David Merritt, he's the most powerful man in the country."

"Then why don't we hear and see more of him?"

"Because he doesn't want you to. He moves through the halls of the White House like a ghost, and that's the way he wants it because his anonymity makes him even more powerful. He keeps a low profile, but he's Merritt's chief adviser."

"You've been out of touch, Mr. Bondurant. The President's chief counsel is—"

"Forget Frank Montgomery. He's a figurehead, a lackey. Merritt throws him a bone, he fetches it. He's got a title, a nice office, and privileges, but Spence is David's alter ego. David doesn't take a leak without consulting Spence first. He's in on every decision, no matter how major or how minor. He's what you might call a facilitator."

"What does he facilitate?"

"Chores."

Barrie raised an eyebrow.

"Chores that would compromise the President if he were to take care of them himself."

He didn't have to spell it out for her. "In other words, there are some gray areas to the duties Spencer Martin performs for the President. And you know this because you were . . ."

"Also a facilitator."

"I see."

Her eyes were like mirrors of his conscience gazing at him through her glasses. "But I resigned. I hadn't seen or heard from Spence for more than year—since I left Washington. Then the day after you came to my house, he showed up."

"Coincidence?"

"No. He came to see me because he either guessed or knew that you'd been there, asking me questions about Vanessa."

"What did you tell him? About me, I mean."

Gray knew why she'd asked—she wanted to know if he'd boasted of his latest sexual conquest to his buddy. His hand where she'd bit him was throbbing like a son of a bitch. Seconds after they met, she'd slapped him. In some regards, this Barrie Travis was gutsy and bold. But right now she looked extremely vulnerable, and hell, her dog had just been killed, so although it was a perfect opportunity to embarrass her again, he declined.

"I told Spence that you'd come snooping, that you had this harebrained notion that Vanessa had killed her baby and passed it off as SIDS."

"You told him that?" she exclaimed. "No wonder they incinerated my house."

"If I had denied knowing anything about it, he would have seen straight through the lie, so I had to play along. But I knew immediately that you were on to something. Why else would Spence have been nervous enough to come to Wyoming and check out what I knew?"

"You're absolutely certain that was the purpose of his visit?"

"Yeah," he said. "There was a commercial airline ticket in his breast pocket, round-trip from Washington to Jackson Hole."

"So?"

"So, Spence told me he was on an errand to Seattle for the President. On any errand like that, he would have taken a government plane. Plus, the ticket had been issued in a phony name. Then, in Jackson Hole, he rented a car under another assumed name. He had no intention of going to Seattle. No, Miss Travis, his was not a social call. Your story poses an extreme threat to the administration, and they'll do whatever it takes to keep it from getting out."

"My God," she whispered, raising bloodless fingers to

her lips. "It's just beginning to sink in. I was right. That baby did not die of SIDS."

"When did you first suspect that?" She was staring into space. "Miss Travis?"

"I'm sorry," she said, rubbing her temples. "Hearing my hypothesis from someone else makes it *real*. The implications are staggering—and terrifying."

"Especially to the man occupying the White House. Talk me through it," Gray said. "When did you first suspect that something was wrong?"

"Vanessa called me out of the blue and asked me to meet her. It was immediately apparent to me that she was holding herself together by sheer willpower."

He listened raptly as Barrie told him everything that had happened after that initial meeting and explained the steps she'd taken to produce the TV series.

"I saw it—the segment with Vanessa."

"The Vanessa Merritt I interviewed on camera was totally different from the abjectly miserable woman I'd been with weeks before."

"Not all that surprising," he told her. "Vanessa is manic-depressive."

He watched her full lips open in astonishment. "Are you sure? When was she diagnosed?"

"A long time ago. Shortly after they married, I believe."

Clearly, Barrie was flabbergasted. "How could they keep that under wraps for all these years?"

"Because she's well treated for it and carefully monitored. Her manic episodes made her an excellent campaigner. She was always up. Always on. Of course she's on lithium to regulate the mood swings, so they're apparent only to someone who knows her well. She takes antidepressants and antipsychotic drugs, too. When she's on her medication, she functions well. One truthful thing Spence said was that the baby's death has thrown her off balance. The minute I saw her on TV, I knew that something was drastically wrong," he concluded.

"So you know her very well."

He dodged that missile by saying, "I know David even better."

"You actually believe he and his top aide are responsible for blowing up my house?"

"Haven't you been listening? Hell, yes, I believe it. Spence must have arranged it before leaving for Jackson Hole. When it's discovered that tonight's only fatality was your dog, they'll try to dispose of you by some other method."

Whey-faced, she sucked in a quick breath. In a voice that was huskier than usual, she said, "You're telling me that my life's not worth the paper it's printed on."

"Essentially, yeah."

She rested her forehead in her palm. "I think I'm going to throw up."

"Don't," he said sharply. "We can't create a scene. Breathe through your mouth."

Gray sat tensely until her nausea passed. After a while she asked for a glass of water, and he signaled the waitress. She noticed that Barrie wasn't feeling well. "Is she okay?"

"Morning sickness," Gray said, thinking how goofy his fake smile must look. "Except she gets it at night."

"Oh, that'll pass after the first few months, honey. How far along are you?"

"Uh—"

"Three months," Gray said.

Patting Barrie on the shoulder, the waitress offered to bring her a cup of hot tea. "She'll be fine," Gray said. "But thanks."

Reassured, the waitress moved away. Barrie took several sips of water. "You lie very well."

"You don't."

"I know."

Gray realized that she was still in shock. Tears were close to the surface.

"I've dragged you into this, haven't I, Mr. Bondurant?"

He gave an indifferent shrug.

"I have," she insisted tremulously. "Because I went to see you, your life's in danger too. You share the story they can't allow to be told." The more she talked, the more anxious she became.

"You took an awful risk by coming here. You should have stayed in Wyoming. If you go home now, maybe they'll forget that you know. They'll think that you dismissed me."

He was amused by her naiveté but kept a straight face. "They don't forget. They don't leave any loose ends, either. Geography doesn't matter. They want whatever happened to the baby, and whatever's going on with Vanessa, to be deepsixed. And our curiosity along with it."

"How'd you get here so fast?"

"I trashed Spence's computer and turned in his rental car by dropping the keys and the paperwork into the quickcheckout box at the airport. Then I used the return portion of his ticket."

Knowing there were a limited number of commercial flights into Jackson Hole, Barrie asked, "Were you on my plane?" He nodded. "I didn't see you."

"You weren't supposed to."

"Oh." She paused, trying to figure out how he had escaped her notice. "Why didn't you just warn me somewhere along the way? If you had, Cronkite might still be alive."

"I miscalculated. I didn't expect their first warning to be the coup de grâce. I thought they'd start with a veiled threat, like your source at the hospital probably received. But they're not screwing around. They didn't want you scared into silence—they wanted you dead."

"So you've said." She gnawed on her inner cheek. "Where'd you leave it with Spence?"

"What do you mean?"

"I mean, how'd you get hold of his airline ticket? How'd you manage to elude him?"

He held her stare for a long time, wondering how much he should tell her. Finally, all he said was, "I didn't."

Chapter Fifteen

"Daily, this is Gray Bondurant. Gray, Daily Welsh."

Barrie loved Daily for not making an issue of their showing up on his doorstep at two o'clock in the morning. He didn't chastise or barrage them with questions. He merely grunted as he stepped aside and waved them in.

It was obvious they'd gotten him out of bed. Spikes of thinning gray hair radiated from his scalp like the points on the Statue of Liberty's crown. He was wearing a threadbare undershirt and a pair of boxer shorts that reached almost to his knobby knees. A pair of black socks did nothing to flatter his white, virtually hairless legs.

Upon leaving the coffee shop, they'd agreed that they needed a place to stay where they could rest, regroup, and decide what their next course of action would be. Gray had followed her directions to Daily's house. Now, she could tell what he was thinking: If this was the best they could do in terms of refuge, their future was indeed perilous.

Daily's little house was hardly a fortress, and, to a stranger's eye, he appeared to be a terribly ill man whose life depended upon his modest pension check and breathing apparatus—all of which was entirely, and unfortunately, correct.

"I know this is a terrible imposition, Daily," Barrie said as he went around the living room switching on lamps. "But there was nowhere else to go. . . . They killed Cronkite."

His hand froze on a light switch. "Killed Cronkite? Who did?"

"It's a long story."

"I've got all night."

The pain in his expression reflected what she was feeling. He opened his arms, and she walked into them. Customarily she was the one to hug him, while he acted the curmudgeon and spurned her displays of affection.

This time, he not only initiated the embrace but held her, patting her back, a bit awkwardly but earnestly. "Sick sons of bitches. What'd they do, poison his food? If I ever catch 'em . . . Who did it?"

Barrie stepped away from him and removed her glasses to dry her eyes. "There's a lot to tell."

Daily went automatically to his recliner, wheeling his canister of oxygen with him. She took her usual seat on his sofa. Gray remained standing. So far, Daily had shown no curiosity about why the retired national hero had emerged from seclusion and was standing in the center of his living room in the middle of the night.

Now, he nodded toward Gray. "What's he doing here?"

"My house was blown up tonight."

"Blown up? You mean like *ka-boom*?" He looked at her, then at Gray, then back at her.

"It's gone, Daily. Destroyed. Everything. Including my tape library," she said bitterly, thinking about the irreplaceable videos that had taken years to collect. "Bondurant thinks the back door was booby-trapped. Cronkite went in ahead of me, through his doggie door."

Daily was aghast. "Who would do such a thing?"

"The President."

"Excuse me? The President of the United States?"

"Bondurant thinks the explosion was meant to kill me because of the questions I've been asking about Vanessa's health and her baby's death," Barrie explained.

"Jesus." Daily looked up at Gray. "What makes you think—Sit down, for chrissake. You're making me crane my neck."

For the first time in hours, Barrie felt like smiling. Gray sat down on the only other available spot—beside her on the sofa.

"What makes you think Merritt would go this far to keep Barrie quiet?" Daily asked him.

"He dispatched Spencer Martin to handle me simply because I'd talked to her."

"Define 'handle.' "

"Assassinate."

"I thought you two were friends."

"We were. Nevertheless, he came to Wyoming to assassinate me because he was afraid that Barrie had told me her theory about the baby's death. That should give you some indication of how determined they are to put a lid on her story before it gets out."

Frowning, Daily smoothed down a few spikes of his crown. "You sure about this?" he asked skeptically.

"He's sure," Barrie said. "Tell him, Bondurant."

While he recounted for Daily the peculiarities of Spencer Martin's visit to Wyoming, she wondered how she could have failed to recognize Gray among the passengers on her flight back to Washington. She hadn't paid much attention to her fellow travelers, but wouldn't he have stood out? Obviously he'd made certain that he wouldn't. His talent for being a chameleon did not increase her confidence in him. In many ways it made her more mistrustful.

"So, as far as anybody knows, Spence Martin was never in Wyoming," Daily summarized.

"He didn't touch anything inside my house except the silverware he ate with, and I washed that. His avoidance of touching anything was one of the first warning signals I picked up."

"Where's Martin now?" Daily asked.

Gray was stone-faced. The awkward silence stretched out until Barrie was forced to answer. "Mr. Bondurant is disinclined to say how he managed to escape him."

She glanced at the rigid profile of the man seated beside her. She didn't doubt that he could kill someone, even a former friend. His cold eyes and that narrow slash of a mouth indicated he was capable of it. If he'd killed Spencer Martin in self-defense, that was excusable. But could she take his word for that?

Daily put into words a question that she'd been asking herself. "Wouldn't Spence Martin have checked in with the President by now?"

"Ordinarily, yes. He even excused himself from the room on the pretext of placing a call to the White House. But he wouldn't have called until he could give David a full report, including my extermination. David's probably pacing the floor tonight wondering why he hasn't heard from Spence, but he can't send anyone to Wyoming to look for him because Spence wasn't supposed to be there."

"Sooner or later somebody's bound to miss him and start looking," Barrie remarked.

"Spence never had family or close friends," Gray said. "David and his administration have been Spence's entire life. To understand that, you have to understand where Spence came from. He was a frail, nerdy kid, bullied in school, picked on for being small. But he was much smarter than the average kid.

"All those years of being the bullies' target made him determined to become the best bully of all. He achieved that goal—he came to be the most feared bully in Washington. It's understood that crossing Spence is tantamount to spitting on the Oval Office. Spence wouldn't have informed anyone where he was going. He accounted only to David."

"Even the President's top aide can't be that autonomous," Barrie argued. "The Department of Justice, Attorney General Yancey, the FBI, the—" She broke off when Gray began shaking his head.

"Bill Yancey's a good man," he said. "Almost too good to suit the administration. Yancey and David have locked horns several times since his appointment. But believe what I'm telling you. Spencer Martin's network of agents is as elite and ruthless as the Third Reich's SS. They operate like moles in every government agency, including the Secret Service. Spence's men are kept on standby at all times. If his orders countermanded ones they'd received through official channels, Spence's would be the ones these guys obeyed."

Barrie hugged her elbows. "You're scaring me."

"These are some scary characters. Most of them are specially trained troops who have retired and don't have a war to fight."

Barrie wondered if he was aware that he'd also described himself.

"If it's something really vital," Gray added, "Spence would do the job himself."

"Like assassinating a former recon buddy."

Gray acknowledged Daily's remark with a grim smile. "Right. Like that. Although most often he would assign the job to someone else. Usually it's done with Spence out of town, so he'd have an alibi if the actual perpetrator got caught or left traceable evidence. I'm sure he made an arrangement like that for Barrie's townhouse. It's not unusual for him to be away. It will be a while before anyone becomes curious enough to start asking questions."

"Merritt will be curious."

"Once David learns that I'm alive," he said in response to Barrie's statement, "he'll know that Spence failed to accomplish what he went to Wyoming to do."

That sobering comment silenced them for a time. Finally, Daily turned to Gray. "I admire what you did over there in the Middle East."

Gray acknowledged the compliment with a slight nod. "But?"

"But forgive me for saying that you could be feeding us a barrel of bullshit."

The insult seemed to have no effect on him. "You have every right to be suspicious. It's no secret that there was tension between David and me when I left Washington."

"Because of his wife."

Barrie couldn't believe Daily's temerity. He was saying the things, asking the questions, she hadn't dared.

"Vanessa was part of the final rift, yes."

"Then why should I believe anything you've told us?"

"In other words, I could be making all this up in the hope of crushing David Merritt's presidency."

"The thought crossed my mind," Daily admitted with his characteristic candor.

With more composure than Barrie would have expected, Gray said, "I didn't start this. I didn't seek out Miss Travis with a hot story. She came to me with questions about the baby's death, questions that mirrored my own suspicions."

That came as a surprise and made her angry. "Why didn't you tell me that? You led me to believe that you thought I was the worst kind of opportunist. You—"

"Let the man talk, Barrie," Daily said. He looked at Gray. "What aroused your suspicions?"

He rose and began to pace while he talked. "Vanessa can be charming and sweet. But she can also be the most exasperating, self-centered, manipulative creature God ever made. She's strongly influenced by her father and by David, but I've seen her turn their machinations to her advantage, and without them realizing it."

"You're not painting a very favorable picture of her. In fact, the woman you've just described fits my earlier impressions of her," Barrie admitted.

"My point is that, despite her problems, I know Vanessa wanted a baby more than she wanted anything," he said. "I know that with certainty. She was willing to go through anything to have a child, even though doctors discouraged pregnancy because of her illness."

"Illness?" Daily looked at them quizzically.

"She's manic-depressive," Barrie explained, then told him what Gray had told her.

"Son of a gun," Daily said, dumbfounded.

"It's a pity she hasn't made her condition public," Barrie remarked. "Thousands of people could have benefitted from knowing about it. Other patients would have been encouraged by her ability to live a full and rewarding life in spite of the illness."

"Until recently," Gray said.

"Right," Barrie agreed.

"She should not have been left alone that night."

"It was reported that the White House nanny had requested the night off to handle a family emergency," Daily reminded them.

"Her request was made in advance. The question is: Why wasn't there a stand-in nanny?" Gray said. "Why was Vanessa left alone to care for the baby, with only David and Spence as backups in case of emergency, when everyone concerned knew that Vanessa was often incapable of handling emergencies?"

"Being manic-depressive, Vanessa would have far more than the normal feelings a woman experiences following the birth of a child. Feelings of resentment, inadequacy, entrapment, and so on." Barrie looked at Gray. "That's why you didn't share your suspicions with anyone, isn't it? You wanted to protect her."

"I was protecting her with my silence, but not in the way you mean. You see, I don't agree with you. Vanessa did not smother her baby."

"I'm confused," Barrie said irritably. "You agree that he didn't die of SIDS."

"Correct."

"That makes no sense," she said softly. "If Vanessa didn't smother him, then who . . ."

The argument died abruptly on her lips. She glanced at Daily, who had been following the discussion. Their eyes connected, held, and she saw that his sudden realization matched hers.

She swung back to Gray. "Merritt?"

He nodded.

"But *why?*"

"What would make a man hate a three-month-old enough to kill it?"

She did not need to think about it. "If the baby wasn't his."

He nodded brusquely, then turned his back on her and walked to the window.

Of course. This explained so many prevalent questions.

Vanessa's distress and utter helplessness. The waiver of an autopsy. The violent attempts to stifle the story. Bondurant's involvement. Especially Bondurant's involvement.

Slowly her gaze moved to him. He was still standing with his back to the room, peering through the crack in the faded draperies.

Daily stood. "Well, I think accusing the President of the United States of baby killing is enough excitement for one night. At least it is for an old fart like me. I'm going back to bed. You two are welcome to stay here as long as need be."

The trolley carrying his oxygen tank had a squeaky wheel. It could be heard as he made his way down the hall and into his bedroom. When he closed the door behind him, a thick silence descended over the house.

Barrie said quietly, "The President gave me his hearty approval to interview her."

"To throw everybody off track. Which is more suspicious: publicly addressing an issue, or keeping it hush-hush?"

"I suppose you're right."

"I'd bet everything I own."

"You're afraid for Vanessa, aren't you?"

He turned around and looked at Barrie, but he said nothing.

"As long as she appeared well adjusted," Barrie said, organizing her thoughts as she spoke, "you dismissed your suspicions about the baby's death. But when you saw my interview with her, you realized that she wasn't herself, even considering her fluctuating moods and behavior. That caused you to entertain more doubts. Then I came to see you, and my theory echoed what you'd feared all along—that the baby's death wasn't caused by SIDS. Spencer Martin's visit clinched it for you.

"Now you believe that Vanessa's life is in jeopardy,

too. If David Merritt killed an infant, what compunction would he have against killing his wife to ensure that his first crime is kept secret?"

"None whatsoever," Gray said. "If you don't believe anything else I've told you, believe that. He'll do anything to protect his presidency and get a second term. Anything."

Barrie rubbed her arms to ward off a sudden chill.

"You look ready to drop," he remarked. "We'll take this up again in the morning. Get some sleep."

"Are you serious? I won't be able to sleep."

"Lie down and close your eyes. You'll sleep."

Too tired to argue, she gestured toward the back of the house. "The guest room, for lack of a better word, is at the end of the hall. There's a cot in there, but I don't recommend it. Cronkite was the last to sleep on it."

He looked toward Daily's closed bedroom door. "Do you trust him?"

"With my life."

"Then it's likely they'll know to look for you here."

"No one knows I come here."

"Care to explain that?"

"No, I don't." Her friendship with Daily was something she kept just between the two of them, and she didn't feel moved to share with Bondurant the reasons why. "No one will look for me here. For the time being, we're safe."

"Okay," he said, grudgingly. "I'll sleep out here. You take the cot."

She started down the hallway, almost too tired to place one foot in front of the other. She didn't remember ever feeling so physically and emotionally spent.

In the bureau in Daily's second bedroom, she found a pair of pajamas that were atrociously ugly even for Daily's nondiscriminating taste. She took the pajama top into the bathroom with her and filled the tub.

She'd gone almost twenty-four hours without sleep. Her eyes were gritty. Her joints and muscles ached. She had skinned her knees. She swallowed two aspirin tablets taken from Daily's medicine chest, then gratefully submerged herself, even her head, in the hot water. After soaping and shampooing, she reclined against the back of the tub and closed her eyes.

As her physical discomforts were eased by the bath, her emotional injuries began to hurt more. Her heartache was profound. Considering how many human lives were taken by natural disasters, disease, war, and murder, it seemed petty to mourn the demise of a mutt. Nevertheless, she felt a crushing sense of loss. Try as she might, she couldn't keep from sobbing.

Droplets of water leaked from the faucet into the tub, making soft little splashes that were oddly comforting. Tears rolled down her cheeks, off her chin, onto her chest, then followed the valleys of her body into the water. Each time she thought she had cried herself out, she would remember something else endearing about Cronkite and the cycle would begin again. Fresh tears would find their way through her closed eyelids and eventually into the bath.

It wasn't until she felt cool air against her skin that she realized she was no longer alone. She opened her eyes. Bondurant was standing in the doorway, one hand on the doorknob, the other on the jamb, eyes fixed on her.

Barrie didn't move. It would have been useless to reach for something to cover herself. He'd already seen everything there was to see. He'd already touched everything, too. Intimately. Her body began to respond similarly to the way it had that morning in his bedroom, with a fluttering heat.

"Are you okay?"

Unable to speak, she nodded.

"You've been crying."

She couldn't think of an appropriate response, so she said nothing and continued to hold his stare. It wavered only once, when his eyes flickered over her body before returning to her face.

Gruffly, he said, "Rocket, Tramp, and Doc."

Puzzled, she shook her head slightly.

"My horses. They do have names."

He stepped back into the hallway and pulled the door closed.

Chapter Sixteen

Senator Clete Armbruster arrived at the White House early the following morning, demanding to see the President immediately. He was informed that the President was awake but hadn't yet left his private quarters. Armbruster said he would wait. He was escorted into the Oval Office and offered coffee. He had almost finished his second cup when David Merritt strode in, looking as fit as always but somewhat irritable.

"Sorry to keep you waiting, Clete. What's so urgent? Thanks," he said to the secretary who'd passed him a cup of coffee. "You can leave us alone now."

Clete was impatient by nature. He'd been up since four. He'd dressed and read the *Post*, killing time until he could call on the President at what he considered a reasonable hour. The long wait had given him time to work up a full head of steam.

He wasted no time. "I want to see my daughter. Today."

"I was told you went to Highpoint yesterday."

"I'm sure you were also told by that quack who passes himself off as a doctor that he refused to let me see her."

"At her request, Clete. Are you taking your blood pressure medicine? Your face is beet red."

His son-in-law's unflappability raised his blood pressure even higher. "Listen here, David, I want to know what's wrong with Vanessa. Why the isolation? Why the full-time nurse? If she's that sick, she should be in a hospital."

"Calm down, Clete, before I have to take *you* to the hospital." Merritt led the senator to a sofa, then sat down beside him. "Vanessa's been drinking. Alcohol and her medication don't mix well. George and I confronted her about it, and she agreed to get treatment for her dependency."

"Dependency? It's gotten so bad as to classify it as that?"

"Clinically, I doubt it. That was Vanessa's term. But she realized that a few glasses of wine every day could develop into a more serious problem if she didn't stop it now."

"Why didn't she confide in me? Why didn't you?"

"I wanted to tell you," David said. "I wanted to ask your advice, but Vanessa insisted that you not be told."

"Why not?"

"She was ashamed, Clete." Merritt got up and poured himself another cup of coffee. "She didn't want you to be disappointed in her. She thinks the sun rises and sets in you."

"And vice versa. She's always come to me with her problems, and I've fixed them for her."

Vanessa had been only thirteen when her mother died, but Clete hadn't panicked at being left alone to raise his teenage daughter. Vanessa had always been Daddy's girl. He'd doted on her from the day she was born and had wielded more influence over her childhood than had his wife.

Maybe he had spoiled her a little, but he excused his excesses. Some people seemed naturally entitled to pampering, and Vanessa had always been one of them. In early adulthood, when her disorder was diagnosed, Clete regarded it as even more reason to coddle and protect her.

"Perhaps she felt it was time to start solving her problems herself," David said. "Or maybe she didn't want to worry you. In any event, she begged me not to tell you any more than we're telling the public, which of course is the truth. She's dealing with her bereavement in seclusion."

"For how long?"

"For as long as it takes George to get her stabilized. Vanessa feels the same. She wants to be the First Lady she was before she had the baby. Once her medication is regulated, there's no reason she can't be. Hold the thought," he said, forestalling Clete's next comment.

Merritt picked up the remote for the large-screen TV, which had been muted. During their conversation, Clete had noticed that David's attention was divided between him and the screen. He turned to see what had piqued the President's interest.

A reporter, standing against a backdrop of scorched trees, smoking rubble, and working firemen, announced, "The quick response of firefighters prevented the flames from spreading to other residences on this street near Dupont Circle. The fire was confined to only one townhouse." The camera panned the black, smoking remains of a building. "This morning, ATF agents and local fire officials are raking through the smoldering rubble, searching for clues as to the cause of the explosion."

He referred to his notes. "The townhouse was owned by Barrie Travis, a reporter for WVUE, a local, independent television station. Ms. Travis recently won acclaim for producing a feature series on SIDS. It's believed that Ms. Travis survived the explosion, but thus far she's been unavailable for comment."

He signed off and the anchorman in the studio came on. David muted the TV as his father-in-law stood up. "I intend to keep hounding her until she sees me."

"Barrie Travis?" David asked sharply.

"Why in hell would I want to see her? Shame about her house, but she's a pain in the butt. Been pestering my office for a statement about Vanessa's seclusion." He made a swatting motion with his hand, signaling his dismissal of the reporter.

"I want to see Vanessa," he stressed. "She should know I'm not going to scold her over a few glasses of wine. She can't help being sick."

"My sentiments exactly, Clete. I pleaded with her not to blame herself for any of this, but you know how Vanessa strives for perfection. She hates catering to the limitations that the manic-depression imposes on her."

Merritt clapped him on the shoulder and ushered him to the door. "I wish we could visit longer, but I've got a slew of appointments this morning. I'll be speaking with Vanessa by phone this afternoon. I'll give her your love."

"You do that."

The senator had allowed himself to be patted on the back and to be led like a child to the door. But if David Merritt, President of the United States, thought he could placate him with a few banal comments and then ease him out of the Oval Office with his glib talk and guileless smile, he was wrong.

A smiling David Merritt opened the door.

An unsmiling Clete Armbruster shut it.

Merritt looked at him, perplexed. "What is it, Clete?"

"You and me go back a long way, David. I recognize talent and potential when I see it, and in you I saw plenty of both. I didn't want to be president but I wanted to create one. You had the raw material necessary. You took coaching well. You were a fast study in politics. My instincts about you were right, and I couldn't be prouder of you."

"Thanks."

"But I remember one night eighteen years ago when you came to me, scared shitless and whimpering like a pup because you'd fucked up so bad. You remember that night, David my boy?"

"What's your point?" Merritt said tightly.

"The point is," Armbruster said, moving in closer, "that the incident to which I refer bears enough of a resemblance to this one to make me mighty uncomfortable."

"My God, Clete, you can't compare—"

The senator stopped the earnest appeal by thumping his fist into Merritt's chest. "I know your marriage to my daughter isn't perfect. No marriage is. I know you screw around. Hell, I've even covered for you, because I accept that you are a man first and my son-in-law second. I've tolerated your dalliances because, basically, you've made Vanessa happy." He lowered his voice to a deep growl. "But if you ever make her unhappy, I'm going to be pissed, David. You hear me, boy?"

"Careful, Clete. It sounds as though you're threatening the President of the United States."

"You're goddamn right I am," Armbruster said angrily. "You better remember who put you in this office. I made you, I can break you. I'm not afraid of that slick little shit Spence Martin or his secret army of thugs or anybody else. I have power in this town that you can't imagine. I've cultivated a lot of friends and an equal number of enemies, and I'm holding markers for every one of them."

He paused to give that time to sink in. "Now, son, I want you to tell me that Vanessa is going to be as right as rain when Dr. Allan gets finished with her up there in Highpoint."

"I swear it."

The senator gave him a long, level look. "You'd better not be lying to me, David. Or you can kiss your pecker and your presidency bye-bye."

~~

Merritt saw his father-in-law out, then wasted no time in booting up his computer and typing in the security code that accessed Spence's laptop.

Nothing. *Nothing!* Spence's unit was not responding. It had been programmed with several fail-safe backups. There was no explanation for a complete shutdown, unless the laptop had been destroyed. If that was the case, their private communiqués would have been destroyed with it, because such a contingency had been built into the program.

But Merritt's chief concern wasn't the computer system. Its inaccessibility was. It was a signal that something had gone drastically wrong. Spence wouldn't have let anything happen to their link-up unless he was out of commission, too. And the only way that was possible was if Gray—

"Gray."

Merritt spoke the name like a epithet. Saint Gray, the one mistake the President owned up to. He'd brought him on board because he'd mistaken Gray's reserve for ruthlessness. Who could have guessed that the man trained to kill instantly with his bare hands would turn out to be valorous? Gray and his code of ethics had been a squeaky cog in an otherwise well-greased wheel.

Gray Bondurant wasn't, however, without flaw. He'd loved another man's wife. *His* wife.

The probability that Gray was to blame for Spence's failure to report in filled Merritt with dread and rage. Furiously, he typed in a code that accessed a terminal in an innocuous office across town. When he received clearance, he typed a single entry: Bondurant.

The man on the other end, one of Spence's best secret soldiers, would know what to do. He would go immediately to check out the situation in Wyoming. There was nothing left for Merritt to do but sit back and wait for word.

No, actually there was more he could do. He asked his secretary to place a call to the office of the director of the Bureau of Alcohol, Tobacco and Firearms.

After exchanging pleasantries, Merritt asked, "What have your boys uncovered about that explosion in Dupont Circle last night?"

He could tell that the director was puzzled by his interest, but the man answered directly. "We've just begun our investigation, Mr. President. At this point, the cause is anybody's guess."

"Barrie Travis is a close friend of Mrs. Merritt's. This explosion has my wife feeling very anxious, and frankly, the First Lady doesn't need any more stress. I promised I would call and inquire. I hate to bother you, but you know how it is."

Sounding less guarded, the director said, "Of course, Mr. President, I understand. Please assure Mrs. Merritt that we're on top of the situation."

"And you'll have closure on it as soon as possible?"

"I'll make it a priority, Mr. President."

"Mrs. Merritt and I will appreciate that. By the way, has anyone spoken to Miss Travis this morning? What's her state of mind?"

"I'm sorry, sir, I don't know. No one's seen her since the explosion. Witnesses who saw her immediately afterward said she was extremely upset. Her dog was killed in the blast."

"Hmm. Terrible. Well, keep me posted."

"Of course, Mr. President."

Merritt hung up, but his mind was no more at ease than it had been before the call. Spence would have made certain that the explosion couldn't be traced to the White House. Even so, it would be best if the investigation was limited to a perfunctory level.

This was indeed a vexing morning.

Merritt wasn't worried about his father-in-law's threats. The senator wasn't nearly as fearsome as he prided himself on being. Most of the friends and enemies he'd boasted of were either retired, dead, or too deep into their dotage to rain destruction on a popular president.

Besides, the senator couldn't create a shit storm around the President without getting plenty slung onto himself. Clete shared the skeleton in his closet. Regardless of his threats, he wasn't about to open the door of that closet and start rattling bones.

But he would continue pestering him about Vanessa until he was satisfied that she was doing well. Something had to be done to assuage his concern. Later today, he would consult Spence—

He swore out loud. There were several items demanding Spence's attention. *Where the hell is he?*

Although in his gut he *knew*, David couldn't bring himself to accept the obvious.

Chapter
Seventeen

"*I*'ve never been thrilled with the guy, but I'm still having trouble believing he could do that."

"He could do it. Easily."

"Who could do what easily?" Barrie asked, entering Daily's kitchen, where he and Gray Bondurant were having coffee. She poured herself a cup and joined them at the table. She avoided looking Bondurant in the eye. As he'd predicted, she had slept well.

After exchanging good mornings, Daily answered, "Gray was convincing me that our president is capable of committing murder."

"I have no proof of what I'm about to tell you," Gray said. "You might think I'm delusional, or paranoid, or a downright liar."

"Or we might believe you," Barrie said. He turned his head and, for the first time that morning, their eyes met. Her tummy went weightless. Quickly, she returned her attention to stirring creamer into her coffee.

"Well, let's hear it," Daily said.

"David appointed me to organize and command the recons that rescued those hostages. There was a reason."

"You were eminently qualified?"

"So were a lot of other men. But he sent me over there to die."

"Because of the gossip linking Vanessa and you?" Barrie asked.

"Yes."

He paused for a few moments, as if collecting his memories. "I chose thirty men. The best recons the Marines had to offer. These young guys could creep up on you and pluck out an eyelash and you'd never know they were there.

"We were flown in by helicopter from a carrier in the Persian Gulf. A squadron of F-16s created a diversion and took heat so we could be dropped in. We walked three miles into the city. I can't describe the stench. There was raw sewage and rot everywhere. The country's entire national budget was appropriated for war; none to sanitation and quality of life.

"The place was a warren of ancient buildings and dead-end streets, but Intelligence had given us the prison's exact location, and we knew how we were going to penetrate it. We had a blueprint of the building and a detailed description of its security from a former prisoner. The security wasn't sophisticated or well organized, but the guards were part of the military and were heavily armed. We also knew the location of the cells where the hostages were being held. Needless to say, we had rehearsed and timed our every move.

"It went like clockwork. We took out the guards without them ever knowing what hit them. Once we reached the hostages, I was worried that they'd blow it, but they were quiet and obeyed our hand signals without question. A couple of them had injuries that had gone untreated. All of them were weak from malnutrition and sickness, but they could walk. We were halfway home.

"It was when we were on our way out that everything began to unravel. Several of the guards had dragged a young boy prisoner into a vacant cell and were taking turns with him. Since they weren't supposed to be there, and that part of the prison was supposed to be closed off, we walked right into the middle of it. All hell broke loose. Gunfire erupted from both sides. The first one I took out was the boy."

He fell silent. Neither Barrie nor Daily so much as blinked.

"He, uh . . . he couldn't have been more than nine or ten years old." He closed his eyes and massaged his eye sockets with his thumb and middle finger. "The backs of his legs were running red with blood. The floor was slick with it. I'm sure his bowel had ruptured. Those bastards had . . . Well, he was screaming. With that much blood loss, he wouldn't have made it. He was in agony. So I shot him."

Through the tears standing in her eyes, Barrie watched him reach for his coffee cup, but he didn't drink from it. He folded his strong hands around it and held on.

"We rained hell down on those goddamn perverts, but of course we were blown. We had—God, I don't know how many corridors still to get through. The hostages had lost their cool and were terrified.

"But we were determined not to die in that shit hole. Miraculously, we made it out of the prison, but by then the army had been alerted. We were surrounded by American-hating, gun-happy troops. Those crazy sons of bitches were shooting anything that moved—even their own men—in their bloodlust to kill us.

"We found some temporary cover. I radioed our air support to see if they could help us out. They did their part, but the choppers couldn't get in any closer than the designated place. If they got shot down, we'd all die.

"One of my men reconnoitered and found an alley that looked clear. We ran to it, although we had no idea where it would lead. Right then, getting away from the prison was all we cared about.

"But as soon as we entered the alley we started taking sniper fire from the rooftops. My guys took out the shooters one by one, but for five minutes or so we were pinned down with very little cover. That's when it happened."

He raised his head and made eye contact with both Barrie and Daily before continuing.

"We'd spotted sniper fire coming from the open window of what looked like an apartment building. Someone suggested firing a missile into it, but David had urged me to prevent civilian casualties if at all possible. He wanted this to be a rescue mission, not an aggressive action that would create ill will in the world community.

"Pinned down as we were, our only choice was to draw the sniper's fire and let one of our sharpshooters pop him. I volunteered to be the decoy. I made myself an open target. My guys blasted him. But during the exchange, one of my men turned his assault rifle on me.

"His name was Ray Garrett. He was a big, rawboned boy from Alabama. I grew up in Louisiana, so we had joked about being from the South. I had selected him, worked out strategies with him, ran the drills with him. But he was going to kill me. And would have, except that we made eye contact.

"He must have entertained an instant of doubt, and that saved my life. He hesitated a second too long to fire. That's all it took for an enemy shooter to pick him off."

Gray stared into space for a moment, then took a deep breath. "You know the rest, more or less. After six harrowing hours, we made it to the choppers. We even brought Garrett's body out with us, and he was given a hero's burial."

"Maybe you were wrong," Barrie ventured in a soft voice. "In the confusion—"

"There was no mistaking his intent. He was only ten feet away from me. No one else saw it, but I did."

"Remember the President's blunder?" Daily said. "When it was announced that the mission had cost one American life, Merritt eulogized *you*."

"I'd forgotten that," Barrie cut in. "The faux pas was forgotten during all the excitement of your victorious return, but I remember what an embarrassment it was for Dalton Neely. He'd called a press conference to announce the success of the mission and the safe return of the hostages. Then he read a brief statement from the President that commended you for making the ultimate sacrifice for your countrymen. He said there was never a better soldier and patriot than Gray Bondurant, never a better friend. There wasn't a dry eye in the crowd."

"When David heard there'd been a casualty, he assumed his assassin had succeeded in killing me. He made the statement before checking out the facts."

"How'd they know that young man was corruptible?" Daily asked.

"I don't believe he was," Gray said, surprising them both. "Garrett couldn't have been bribed with material gain. I'm sure that Spence, acting as the President's mouthpiece, approached him and made me out to be a traitor, a spy, a threat to democracy, something like that.

"Garrett was an excellent Marine, but he wasn't a whiz kid. When he aimed that rifle at me, he was carrying out a direct order from the Commander in Chief. Nothing less than that could have compelled him to betray me, not even the threat of death. I didn't blame him. He was a pawn for David and Spence. They killed him as surely as that enemy sniper."

"Did you confront Merritt about this?" Barrie asked.

"God knows I wanted to, but I couldn't without revealing my hand and leaving myself more vulnerable."

"But you got the hell out of Dodge."

"I didn't resign out of cowardice," he replied testily.

Daily, who'd made the remark, raised both hands in surrender. "Don't take offense. None was intended."

"I resigned my job at the White House because I didn't want to be in the service of David Merritt."

"But you're still an irritant to him. Suddenly Wyoming isn't far enough removed from the White House."

Gray nodded. "David knows I'm on to him. First about Garrett, now about Vanessa's baby. I'm a problem that never quite got resolved, so he sent Spence to resolve it once and for all."

"Because of me," Barrie said forlornly.

"It would have happened sooner or later. I'd been waiting for it for a long time. David couldn't very well eliminate me while I was in the limelight, being touted as a national hero. So he pretended to enjoy and share the accolades I received.

"Once public awareness had waned, he figured he could more easily dispose of me without drawing attention to it. With or without you, Barrie, it was only a matter of time."

"Now that we know the problem, how're we gonna solve it?" Daily asked. "I don't have long to live, but I'd rather not finish out my days in federal prison for threatening to destroy the President."

"Once the truth about the baby's death gets out, this administration will die a natural death," Gray assured him.

"I agree," Barrie said. "That will take care of itself. My primary concern is for Vanessa. Right now, she's the biggest threat to Merritt."

"I don't buy this 'seclusion' nonsense for a second. David's got her sequestered somewhere."

"For what purpose, Gray?" Daily asked.

"To intimidate her into keeping her mouth shut about how the baby died. I know how he thinks. To him, Vanessa got no worse than she deserved. He'll try and convince her that she brought this on herself by cheating on him. Depending on what method of persuasion he's using, she may or may not survive it."

" 'Method of persuasion'?"

"I can't bring myself even to think about it."

"What's with Armbruster? Has he rolled over and played dead?"

"I'd like to know that myself, Daily. But until I know more, I'd rather leave him out of it and work independently."

"What are you going to do?" Barrie asked.

"I've got some ideas."

Evidently he wasn't going to reveal those ideas.

Daily said, "You're welcome to make this house your base of operation."

"Thanks, but I don't want to put you in danger, too."

Daily laughed. "What've I got to lose? Besides, this is a safe place. Nobody will be looking for you here."

"So she said last night," Gray said, nodding toward Barrie.

"She doesn't let on that we're friends," Daily explained.

"Why?"

"That's a private matter between Daily and me," Barrie snapped.

Daily said, "But you can take my word for it, Gray. This is the safest place for you."

"What about your job?" Gray asked Barrie.

"She was already in trouble at work," Daily answered for her. "Feds went there asking questions about her."

Gray frowned. "Not regular feds—Spence's men, I'd bet. He would have covered all his bases. Barrie, how many people at the TV station know about the story?"

"I didn't discuss it with anybody."

"Friends?"

"No one except Daily."

"Lovers?"

Detecting the mockery behind his question, she gave him a terse no.

"Good," Gray said. "The fewer people who know about this, the better."

Daily said, "After last night, I think she should lay low, at least until we know what's going on with Mrs. Merritt."

"Absolutely." Gray turned to her. "Stay here with Daily and keep out of sight. Let me handle this. I promise, though, you'll get first crack at the story."

"You do? Why, thank you ever so much." She shot each of them a withering look. "You two have been talking about me as though I'm not here. You even went so far as to make my plans for me. Well, thanks, but no thanks. Here's how it's going to be."

~~~

"Sorry, miss, this area is off limits."

"That was my house. I lived here. I'm Barrie Travis."

As she'd known they would, the words worked like a magic wand. Within seconds, she was surrounded by reporters who'd been loitering about with their cameramen, waiting to get a statement from someone, anyone, official.

Interviews with neighbors and eyewitnesses had been exhaustive, but all had similar stories to tell. Every possible angle had been covered. There was nothing new to report. At this point, the authorities were reluctant to speculate on what had caused the explosion. The investigating ATF agents were particularly reticent. Nobody was talking.

Now, suddenly, the elusive Barrie Travis was. Microphones and video cameras were aimed at her. "As you can see, my home was totally destroyed. I was left with only this," she said, spreading her arms. "But the greatest loss to me was my dog, Cronkite, who died in the blast."

"Where have you been since the explosion?"

"Why haven't you come forward before now?"

"Do you know what caused it?"

She held up her hand to stop the barrage. "As to the cause, I'll leave those answers to the authorities."

"Do you think it was an accident?"

She looked quizzically at the reporter, as if his question were absurd. "Of course it was an accident. What else could it be? When the investigation is complete, I'm sure there'll be a logical explanation."

Gray had said that Spencer Martin would have made certain of that.

"Now, please, if you'll excuse me . . ."

They trailed her to her car, which was still parked where it had been when the explosion occurred. A few diehards even followed her to WVUE, but she dodged them in the parking lot, refusing any further comments. The rent-a-cop at the door barred them from following her inside.

An hour earlier, she had rejected Gray's and Daily's advice to keep out of sight. "I'm not about to go underground," she told them heatedly. "First of all because I don't think it would do any good. If Spencer Martin's intelligence system is as pervasive as you say, I'd be found anyway.

"Second, my job is reporting news. Ironically, I've made news. I'd be crazy to not to make the most of my present notoriety.

"Third, the more visible I am, the less likely it is that another fatal 'accident' will happen to me. Just as you said about yourself earlier, Gray, Merritt won't make a move as long as I'm in the limelight."

"Way to go, Bondurant," Daily had said sourly.

"Whatever else he is, Merritt is no fool," Barrie had continued. "He can't make a second attempt on my life without it looking awfully fishy to even the most naive mind. No, gentlemen," she'd declared, "as long as I'm seen, I'm safe."

Now word spread like wildfire that she was in the building. Howie made it to her cubicle faster than usual and shooed everybody else away. His opening line was, "Jesus, Barrie, we thought you might be charcoal."

"Sorry to disappoint you."

"I'm trying to be nice."

Maybe he was, because he looked truly crestfallen over her remark. "How would you like an exclusive for the evening news tonight?" she asked. "An interview with me, just as I am." She'd had to dress in the same clothes she'd worn the night before. "Looking pitiful and pathetic. I might even be able to eke out a tear or two for a close-up."

His little eyes lit up. "That'd be great!"

"Tomorrow, I'll do a follow-up story, something to do with near brushes with death, confronting one's mortality—something along those lines. I'll try and get sound bites from clerics and psychologists who deal with trauma victims. Maybe by the end of the week, the investigators will have determined the cause of the explosion."

"That soon?"

"I doubt it'll be a lengthy investigation," she said with a wryness that escaped him. "Anyway, once I get their ruling, I'll do a story on how they piece together the evidence to re-create the scene and find the cause."

"Jeez, you're hot. No pun intended." Taking a precautionary look over his shoulder, he whispered, "Any chance that it was intentional? Did somebody get wind of the exclusive you're working on? Could your story and the explosion be connected?"

"You've seen too many Sylvester Stallone movies, Howie. There couldn't possibly be a connection. That big story of mine?" she said with a deprecating laugh. "It was nothing compared to having my house explode in front of my eyes. So you and Jenkins can relax. I've looked death in the face. Believe me, that changes your perspective like that!" She snapped her fingers. "From now on, you'll see a very different Barrie Travis around here."

Gray had said she made a poor liar. She hoped he was wrong.

"Well, I'm mighty glad to hear that," Howie said, expanding his chest. "I knew if I stayed after you long enough, I'd whip your cute little butt into shape."

Behind her ingratiating smile, Barrie was grinding her teeth.

Chapter
Eighteen

$\mathcal{T}$he President was working out his frustration in his private gym inside the White House. He viewed the Stairmaster and other equipment as enemies that must be conquered. Sweat dripped from his nose, earlobes, chin, and fingertips. Well-toned muscles bulged as he pushed them to their limit.

The errand boy he'd dispatched to check out the situation in Wyoming had contacted him earlier that morning via computer. His report wasn't what Merritt wanted to hear. It appeared that Spence had never been to Gray Bondurant's place. When asked what Bondurant had to say about it, the gofer had dropped the second bomb—there had been no trace of Bondurant either.

Despite the report, Merritt was certain that Spence had been there. He'd just been careful to cover his tracks. He was also certain that Gray wouldn't have vanished without a compelling reason. From that, he deduced that Gray had snuffed Spence before Spence had a chance to snuff him.

If that deduction was correct, Gray was wise to them. The ramifications of that were so vast, so dismal, that Merritt had sought the seclusion of the gym. He needed time alone to think, to plot.

Gray wouldn't be afraid to joust with the presidency. Deterrents that would cause fear and trembling in anyone else who challenged the White House wouldn't faze him. Nor would he eventually give up and go away. When Gray thought he was right, he would stop at nothing to defend his point. His convictions were as solid as Gibraltar. That inflexibility was one reason why Merritt hated him.

When he took the oath of office, he had great plans for the three of them. He himself was gifted with enough charisma and political savvy to convince Congress and the nation of anything. Spence was the ruthless strong-arm of the trio. He didn't require justification, he merely performed, efficiently and expediently. Gray was an expert strategist. He viewed each situation from every possible angle and always chose the best approach to take. Together, they could have been the most powerful three men in the world.

If only Gray hadn't had a lech for Vanessa and developed a conscience.

"Damn fool," Merritt muttered as he levered himself off the padded bench and reached for a hand towel. As he wiped his face and the back of his neck, someone knocked on the door. "Come in."

A Secret Service agent opened the door. Standing beside him was Gray Bondurant.

"Mr. President," said the smiling agent, "I have a surprise for you."

Merritt broke a wide grin, which felt to his face like a crack opening up in a slab of concrete. "Gray! God, man, this is a surprise."

Gray too was smiling, though, as usual, it contributed no warmth to his eyes. "I took a chance that you'd be free long enough to say hello." He gave Merritt an approving once-over. "The nation should sleep well, Mr. President.

You look fit enough to defeat singlehandedly all its enemies, domestic and abroad."

Shaking hands and slapping each other on the back, they played out the charade. There was no reason for the Secret Service agent to doubt their cordiality. Rumors of a rift between them had been vehemently denied. When Gray had left the White House, their friendship was supposedly as strong as ever, perhaps even stronger because of the spectacular success of Gray's mission.

It required all of Merritt's acting skills to mask his rage. He'd been blindsided by a master. Hadn't he just been thinking about what an expert strategist Gray was? This was a well-planned ambush made to appear innocent. Gray had come straight to the mountain, unannounced and disarming. White House staff knew him well and wouldn't be suspicious. He'd come to see his pal the President, and how nice of him.

What galled Merritt most was that he had to continue Gray's game, at least until he figured out what he was up to. When they were alone, he moved to the juice bar. "What can I get you?"

"Whatever you're having."

Merritt poured two glasses of orange juice. "Goddamn, it's good to see you," he said, clinking their glasses in a toast.

"Don't let me interrupt your workout."

"I was about to quit. Can't take as much as I once could," he said with a self-effacing grimace.

"I doubt that."

"Mind if I get in the whirlpool?"

"Not at all."

Merritt slipped out of his shorts and stepped into the swirling, bubbling water from which a cloud of steam was rising. "Ahh, feels great. Want to join me?"

"No, thanks." Gray dragged a chair to the edge of the whirlpool and sat down.

"Your hair's gone grayer."

"Heredity," Gray replied. "Didn't I ever tell you that my dad was prematurely gray?"

Basically, Gray Bondurant was unchanged. His body was still hard and taut, his expression still resolute. Envy was a rare emotion for the man who'd brought himself all the way from a trailer park to the White House; but envy was the foundation for his hatred of Gray.

He was more handsome than Gray. Perhaps even more intelligent. Equally as strong, physically.

But Gray had a steely core of self-confidence and morality that allowed him to look any other man in the eye without flinching. Even in the good ol' days, when they were in the Corps together, long before their clash, Merritt had always been the first to look away from sustained eye contact with Gray. He resented how comfortably and well Gray wore honor and nobility and despised him for his principles, while secretly envying the additional strength they gave him.

"Your belly's still flat," he observed. "I'm glad to see that Wyoming hasn't turned you into a wuss."

"It's tough country, but if I hadn't earned my spurs in Washington, I couldn't have handled it."

Merritt chuckled. "I've missed your sense of humor. It's dry as dust, but you could always make me laugh." He spread his arms along the tile rim of the whirlpool. Thinking he already knew the answer, he asked, "What brings you to Washington?"

"A woman."

He hadn't seen that one coming. Gray had thrown him another curve ball. He covered by laughing. "A skirt? A woman has finally toppled the mighty Bang 'em Bondurant? Hard to believe."

"Sad, but true."

"Please," Merritt groaned. "Don't ruin my image of you by telling me you've acquired some sensitivity. You haven't turned into a 'nineties kind of guy,' I hope."

Gray offered his grim half-smile. "Never. That's why this one perfectly suits my needs. She's good to look at, has a voice straight out of a porno film, and, best of all, she's not too bright."

"Does this girl wonder have a name?"

"Barrie Travis."

Merritt winced. "You've got to be kidding. She's a royal pain in the ass. Granted, the voice is sexy. Face and figure definitely earn high marks. But, Gray, buddy, she's trouble. If she reads anything more than sex into the relationship, she'll latch on to you and you'll never be able to shake her. Are you sure you know what you're getting into?"

"Right now I'm getting into her."

The two shared a bawdy snicker. "That can't be all bad," Merritt conceded.

"It's good enough to get me off my ranch and back here."

"For how long?"

Gray shrugged. "Until I get my fill of her and go back."

Merritt finished his juice and set the glass on the tile, then eased himself out of the whirlpool. He wrapped a towel around his middle and took a chair near Gray's. Pursuing this conversation with his former friend might get him into hotter water than he'd just gotten out of, but he couldn't resist. If Gray could continue this parody of a friendly reunion, so could he. When it came to acting, his skills were far superior to Gray's. He'd had more practice.

"Where'd you two meet? I want all the juicy details."

"She tracked me down. Just showed up one day last week out of the blue."

"What for?"

"A story. Or rather a new angle on an old one. She wanted to do a follow-up piece about the hostage rescue mission."

"And you didn't tell her to take a hike? You never liked reporters."

"It's not her profession I'm fucking, David."

Merritt laughed. "See? There's that dry wit again." Then he drew his brows into a steep frown. "I just remembered. Her house burned to the ground last night."

"Yeah. It was the damnedest thing."

"I saw her on the news this morning, talking to reporters. She's one spunky chick."

"That's what makes her challenging."

"So, where are you two staying? Hotel?"

"No, with a friend."

Barrie Travis's friend was a retired newsman named Ted Welsh. Even in Spence's absence, his intelligence network had provided Merritt with pictures of Welsh in a bathrobe, retrieving his morning paper from a weed-infested front lawn. The old geezer was reported to have emphysema and looked about as dangerous as a housefly.

Quite a pair, Travis and Welsh, living in Welsh's ramshackle house, as they plotted the destruction of his presidency. It was laughable. In one swoop, he could be rid of them both.

Gray was the problem. With him as their ringleader, the trio reached a level of menace that wasn't so laughable.

"Speaking of friends," Gray said, "I'm surprised you don't already know the juicy details about Barrie and me. I thought Spence would have told you. He came to see me shortly after her visit to the ranch."

Merritt's smile slipped a fraction. Even the most accomplished actor couldn't have maintained one. "Spence is taking some vacation time. Practically had to force him to go, workaholic that he is. He said he might stop by your place, but I haven't heard from him since he left. Did he say where he was headed after Wyoming?"

"He didn't mention any plans. But you know Spence. He'll turn up when you least expect it. I certainly wasn't looking for him when he showed up at my place."

Merritt had clung to a thread of hope that Spence was still alive. He now knew with certainty that he wasn't. Spence was dead. Gray had killed him.

Merritt couldn't let himself get sentimental about it. He didn't need Spence anyway. He didn't need anybody. But then, Spence had been extremely handy to have around. Men with his talent and blind, unquestionable loyalty and obedience were rare. Even more rare were men with absolutely no conscience.

Gray had robbed him of this valuable asset and was sitting here cracking jokes about it, a guileless expression on his face. Merritt wanted to smash it. But he carefully schooled his anger. To reveal it would be self-incriminating.

Besides, he didn't want to waste energy on a situation that couldn't be reversed. Spence would be the first to agree that mourning was counterproductive and only the weak would indulge in it.

"I was wondering, is the First Lady around?"

Gray's question served as a cattle prod on Merritt's private musings. "Uh, no, she's still away."

"At this 'undisclosed location'?"

"That's right," Merritt replied. "And I'm sworn to secrecy."

Gray leaned forward, propped his forearms on his thighs, and assumed a confidential posture that Merritt frequently used himself. "David, I've been worried about her.

Is she okay? Level with me now. Don't give me the bullshit that Neely feeds to the media. How is Vanessa, *really?*"

"Are you trying to get a scoop for your new bedmate?"

"When we're in bed, she's got better things to do than interview me."

"Hard to talk with her mouth full, huh?"

Gray grunted the required laugh. Then his lined, lean face turned serious again. "Vanessa hasn't seemed herself since the baby died. Is she ill?"

Had Merritt had a choice at that moment, he would have gone for Gray's throat. This man had made him a cuckold. The gossip about him and Vanessa had been quelled, but not soon enough.

How many people had concluded that Gray, not he, was the father of Vanessa's baby? How dare the son of a bitch mention the brat without so much as a glimmer of apology in his arctic blue eyes?

By a force of will, the President of the United States reined in his fury. How could he have explained Gray's drowning death in the whirlpool of the White House gym? Even Spence wouldn't have been bold enough to try and sell that one to the attorney general and the American public.

Suppressing his murderous impulse, he bowed his head and plowed his fingers through his hair. "I don't mind telling you, Gray, it's been rough. She blames herself—her illness—for not being a perfect mother and saving the baby from crib death."

"I was afraid it was something like that. I understand George Allan is working with her. Is he qualified to deal with this?"

"Eminently. He's been her attending physician for years. He knows exactly what she needs to keep her functioning as normally as possible. Once she's over this crisis, she'll be fine."

"I hope so."

Merritt made a point of glancing at the wall clock, then rose to his feet. "It's been great seeing you, Gray. I hate to wind it up, but I've got a cabinet meeting in half an hour."

"I was lucky to get to see you for even this long." Gray stood and the two shook hands. "Please tell Vanessa that I asked about her. Any chance I could visit her?"

"Afraid not. She's getting better every day, but she won't even consent to see Clete. Convey my regrets to Barrie Travis about her townhouse."

"Yeah, I'll do that."

Secret Service agents were standing outside the door of the gym, waiting to escort the President back to his quarters. To one of them, he said, "Please see Mr. Bondurant back to his car."

"That's not necessary," Gray said easily. "I used to work here, remember? I know my way around."

"All the same," Merritt said, matching Gray's nonchalant tone, "we like to give old friends the red-carpet treatment."

Chapter
Nineteen

To say that the President was upset was quite an understatement.

By telephone, Merritt had just informed Dr. George Allan of his surprise visit from Gray Bondurant. He made it sound as though he'd been delighted to see his old friend, but George could read between the lines: David didn't want Gray lurking around Washington, looking too closely into the death of Robert Rushton Merritt.

George had convinced himself, as the nation had been convinced, that the infant had died of SIDS. When he'd rushed to the White House nursery that night after being summoned from home, he had accepted David's word that he and Vanessa had discovered the child dead in his bassinet.

Not wanting to know any different, George hadn't asked many questions. He'd facilitated the baby's burial, as instructed by the President. End of story.

Only it wasn't. Vanessa had gotten a nosy reporter involved, who, according to David, had approached Gray Bondurant. Obviously, David's purposes were better served by putting a slightly different spin on what had actually transpired in the nursery. He surely didn't want Gray Bondurant's curiosity aroused. Because if anyone could unmask David Merritt, it was Gray.

"What about the, uh, reporter?" George asked. "I heard on the news that her house was destroyed in an explosion."

"Yes, I heard that too. It's unfortunate, of course, but at least her personal crisis has diverted her attention away from us." After a moment's pause, he added, "This is all Vanessa's fault. She's responsible for Barrie Travis's tenacious interest. If she hadn't contacted her in the first place, we wouldn't have her pestering us now." Then he asked, "How's Vanessa today?"

That was the President's graceful transition into the real purpose of this call. George, keeping his panic in abeyance, gave him an update on his wife's condition.

Then David issued George his instructions.

He didn't spell them out, but he didn't need to. The message was clear to anyone who was listening for it, and George was.

Today was the day. The President was cashing in his marker.

George replaced the telephone receiver and covered his clammy face with his hands. He was trembling from the inside out. There was a loud roaring in his ears. He felt faint and nauseated.

He considered calling Amanda. Stalwart and serene, she was an island of calm in the chaos he'd made of his life. Sometimes just the sound of her voice gave him hope, even though the landscape of his future was a minefield leading to disaster. And that was reason enough not to call her. Why burden her with the consequences of his mistakes?

Instead of telephoning his wife, he took a Valium.

This was the kind of dirty work David usually assigned

to Spence. Spence wouldn't have the shakes. Spence wouldn't need a Valium. George wondered what David was holding over Spence to command such blind obedience. Or was it the other way around? Was Spence the puppeteer and David the puppet? Or—and this was most probable—Spence didn't need a reason for doing the things he did.

He thrived on cruelty. He had never loved a woman or known a woman's love. He'd never witnessed the birth of a child he'd created through love. He'd never held a squirming new life in his arms and looked down at it with tears in his eyes. He'd never experienced guilt or remorse, either.

George might be a coward, but he was a better man than Spence Martin.

But that point was moot. Spence, it seemed, had vanished. In carefully couched words, David had suggested that Gray was responsible for Spence's unexplainable absence. George hoped that if Gray had killed him, he'd made the heartless bastard suffer first.

Gray was smart for getting out when he had. George wished he had that kind of courage. Gray had said, "I'm outa here," and that was that. But then, Gray hadn't had a noose around his neck.

George did, and it had just gotten tighter.

He pinched the bridge of his nose until it hurt. Then he lowered his hand and looked across at the closed door of the small, paneled study. He could sit here another hour or two staring at that door, but eventually, he would have to carry out the presidential directive. The longer he put it off, the more he would think about it, and the more he thought about it, the more contemptible it became.

He came to his feet with all the alacrity of a ninety-year-old. His tread was leaden as he left the study and crossed the hall.

The sickroom was stifling.

Jayne Gaston was an attentive nurse. She conscientiously bathed her patient every morning and changed the linens on the bed. But a sickroom was a sickroom, and illness had an odor.

Dr. George Allan approached the bed. "How's she doing?"

"She's sleeping now." The nurse gazed sympathetically at her patient.

George gave Vanessa a cursory examination. He listened to her heartbeat, checked the chart for her blood pressure and temperature, all without looking at her face. Her eyes were closed, thank God. He couldn't have looked into her eyes. After this, he wondered, how would he ever be able to look into Amanda's, or his own.

"She became agitated a while ago and began crying," the nurse reported. "She begged me to let her get up. Dr. Allan, if she feels strong enough, I don't see—"

"Thank you, Mrs. Gaston."

"Doctor, I'm sure you know best, but—"

"I'm sure I do, too." He gave her a stern look. "I will no longer tolerate this second-guessing, Mrs. Gaston."

"I'm only considering what's best for the patient."

"You don't think I am?"

"Of course you are, Doctor. I wasn't implying that at all." She drew herself up straighter. "But I'm a well-trained nurse with years of experience."

"Which is why you were retained for this position. But you're overstepping your bounds."

"Mrs. Merritt is overly sedated. If you ask me—"

"I didn't!" George shouted.

"Furthermore, I think her lithium dosage is dangerously high."

"You see the lab reports. Her lithium blood level is exactly where it should be."

"Then I don't trust the lab, and I don't believe the reports."

George's heart was pounding against his ribs. His knees had turned to jelly, his pulse throbbed behind his eyes, and he knew his face was red.

Forcibly calming himself, he said stiffly, "Your services are no longer needed, Mrs. Gaston. Please pack your things immediately. I'll have someone return you to Washington tonight."

She splayed her hand over her chest. "You're firing me?"

"You no longer fit in to Mrs. Merritt's treatment program. Now, if you will—"

She shook her head stubbornly and reached for Vanessa's hand. "I won't go. She's my patient, too. I refuse to leave her in this condition. If you want my honest opinion, I think she's toxic and near comatose."

"If you won't go voluntarily, I'll have no choice but to have you physically removed."

He strode across the room, opened the door, and shouted for the Secret Service agents.

Chapter
Twenty

"*B*arrie Travis?"

"Speaking. Who's this?" Barrie plugged up her free ear with her fingertip to better hear the soft-spoken woman over the cacophony of the newsroom.

"Do you know about Highpoint?"

Barrie was instantly alert. "In what regard?"

"Something's happened."

"Can you be more specific?"

"No. I don't know. I can't say." Her distress was clear. "Someone needs to find out what's going on out there."

Then the caller hung up.

Barrie rang the switchboard operator. "Did the caller you just put through identify herself or say where she was calling from?"

"No, she just asked to speak to you. Another kook?"

"I'm not sure. Thanks."

She sprang from her chair and grabbed her satchel. She was finished for the day. Her story for the evening newscast was completed and on the producer's desk. No one would miss her if she left a little early.

Over the last several days, she'd done a passable job of convincing the viewing public—which she hoped included David Merritt—that she was carrying on business as usual following the loss of her townhouse.

The jury was still out on the cause of the explosion that had destroyed her house, but to all appearances, she hadn't made any connection between it and her forays into the private lives of the President and First Lady.

As she rushed through the newsroom, she considered snagging a cameraman and taking him along, just in case this tip proved to be valid. But she decided to exercise restraint. She would take a camcorder to Highpoint. If a story was brewing, she would at least have the unfolding events recorded on home video.

First, however, she had to devise a way to get into Highpoint without being shot.

~~

"You didn't recognize the voice?"

"Didn't I just say that?" Barrie said irritably. "No, Gray, I did not recognize her voice."

"Don't get riled at him," Daily said. "He just doesn't want you to go off half-cocked, is all."

It infuriated her that Daily took Gray's side. "I'm not asking anybody to go off half-cocked with me. Stay here. I couldn't care less. Myself, I'm following up this lead."

"Could've been that crank," Daily said. "That Charlene."

"It wasn't," she insisted. "I don't know who it was, but she didn't have the characteristics of your average crank caller. She sounded cultured and educated. And scared. I believe what she said."

Daily stayed on it. "You've got no verification that anything unusual is going on at Highpoint. This could be Justice Green all over again. You'll wind up with egg on your face and your ass in a sling."

"What about Justice Green?" Gray asked.

"Nothing," Barrie snapped. She glared at Daily, then sliced the air with her hands and said, "This discussion is over. I'm going."

She wouldn't have returned to Daily's house and informed them of her plans if she'd had the camcorder with her. Recently purchased to replace the one she'd lost in the explosion, it was still in its box in Daily's guest room. With batteries now installed, she checked it out, placed it in her satchel, and turned to her worried compatriots. "Well, wish me luck."

Daily was so distressed that he began to gasp for breath. He turned to Gray. "You're the Marine. Any ideas?"

"Short of hog-tying her, absolutely nothing. But I'll go with her, and she'll probably get us both shot." He said this as he stuffed a pistol into his waistband.

Just then Barrie's pager went off.

"One of your sources?" Daily asked.

"They're the only ones who have this number besides you."

She didn't recognize the telephone number on the digital readout, but she instantly identified the voice who answered what apparently was a pay phone. She could hear traffic noise in the background. The source wasted no time in imparting his message, then hung up immediately.

Thoughtfully, Barrie replaced the receiver and looked up at Gray. "Let's go if you're going."

"Who was that?" Daily asked, following them to the door, dragging his squeaky trolley along. "Was it about Highpoint?"

"No. It was nothing," Barrie replied, but her weak smile

belied that. "We'll call you as soon as we know something. Try and get some rest."

"Try and keep yourself in one piece. I'd like to be able to visit you in prison."

≈≈

"Where in Louisiana?"

"What?"

"You said you were from Louisiana. What town?"

"A wide spot in the road," Gray said. "You've never heard of it."

"I got good marks in geography."

"Grady."

"I've never heard of it."

Gray drove intently, both hands gripping the wheel. They were headed southwest, toward the Virginia countryside. The scenery was a panorama of rolling pastures, horse farms, and forests, but neither of them seemed to notice.

These were the first words they'd exchanged since leaving Daily's neighborhood. Unable to stand another mile of hostile silence, and her own troubled thoughts, Barrie had broached what she hoped would be a neutral topic.

"In terms of growing up there, how was it?"

"Fine."

"Good childhood?"

"It was okay."

"Bad?"

"Did I say bad?"

"Then it was good?"

"It was *okay*. Okay?"

"You don't have to bite my head off. I'm just curious about where a man like you comes from."

"A man like me?" he repeated sardonically. "What kind of man am I?"

It was a moment before she came up with a rejoinder she liked. "Tall."

He actually cracked a smile, albeit a fleeting one.

"Parents?" she asked.

"Two."

"Give me a break, Bondurant."

After a moment he said, "My mother and father were killed when a spin-off tornado from a hurricane struck their place of business."

"I'm sorry," she said sincerely. "How old were you?"

"Nine. Thereabouts."

She had a hard time grasping that—not that his parents had been casualties of a storm, but that he'd actually been a child. She couldn't imagine him as a carefree little boy, playing with other children, engaging in games at birthday parties, ripping open presents with family members gathered around the Christmas tree.

"That morning in Wyoming, you told me you learned ranching from your father."

"He always kept a herd of beef cattle. But he also ran a fix-it shop in town. Wasn't an engine in the state he couldn't fix. And Mother was almost as good with a wrench as he was."

Barrie noticed a rare softness about his stern mouth. "You loved them."

He shrugged. "I was a kid. Kids always love their parents."

Even when they aren't lovable, Barrie thought. "Who raised you after they died?"

"Alternately, both sets of grandparents. They were good people. They're all dead now."

"Siblings?" she asked.

"A sister. Still lives in Grady. Mother of four, married to a CPA who's president of the school board and a deacon in the Baptist church."

"That must be nice for you, having nieces and nephews to spoil."

"I don't see them."

"How come?"

"My brother-in-law thinks I'm dangerous."

"Are you?"

He turned his head. Laser-beam eyes seemed to spear straight through her. "Haven't you figured that out by now?"

"Yes." She lowered her gaze. "I think you might be very dangerous."

Staring through the windshield, she realized that without her noticing, dusk had deepened into full-blown night. The woods on both sides of the two-lane highway were dark. After several moments, she said, "That call I received before we left Daily's house was from my source in Justice."

"You have a source in the Justice Department?"

"Is that so surprising?"

"Who? Which division? How senior?"

"You know I can't tell you that."

"Well then, I guess we'll just have to hope he's not one of Spence's moles."

Ignoring the barb, Barrie said, "My source told me that you and Merritt were in a closed-door meeting today."

"That's right."

"Funny you didn't mention it to Daily or me."

"There was nothing to it."

"You had fifteen minutes alone with the President of the United States and there was nothing to it?"

"I just dropped in—"

"Dropped in? I could drop in, but David Merritt would never give me a private audience."

"I've got friends in the Secret Service. I showed up unannounced so I could gauge his reaction to seeing me."

"Which was?"

"He almost crapped in his shorts."

He recapped for her their conversation, then added, "I let him know that Spence had failed to carry out his last mission."

"And that's all there was to it?"

"That's all."

"Maybe."

He glanced at her, his eyes suspicious. "Why would your source contact you about my visit with David?"

"Out of concern for my safety. My source is a little edgy about the company I'm keeping. For instance, it was suggested to me that the President could be using you to lay a trap for a meddlesome reporter he wants kept quiet."

"I no longer work for the President."

"So you claim. But I wonder just how many layers there are to your relationship with the Merritts. You were Merritt's blood brother before you became his wife's lover. That could create a lot of ambiguity."

His hands curled tighter around the steering wheel. "Why don't you say what you're thinking."

"I'm thinking that perhaps your loyalties are hopelessly divided."

He shot her another fiery glare, but he neither confirmed nor denied the allegation.

"Was my name mentioned in the meeting?" she wanted to know.

He nodded.

"In what context?"

"I told him I was boinking you."

Barrie felt her cheeks turn scarlet. "I prefer that over your other word, although it's still crude."

"That's the way I remember it being. Crude."

"Did he happen to shed any light on Vanessa?" she asked, bringing him back to the subject.

"Nothing new."

"Would you tell me if he had?"

"Probably not."

"Why?"

"Because you're already in over your head."

"For an exclusive story that'll rock the world, I'm willing to take a few risks."

"Well, I'm not," he said shortly. "I'm not willing to risk my life, or Vanessa's, or even yours, just so you can negotiate an extra few thou on your next contract. I'm trying to get us through this alive, and I don't want my strategy compromised by an amateur with stars in her eyes."

That stung. "I'm a professional."

"Maybe in TV news," he said. "But at Highpoint, we're not going to be facing studio cameras. We're going to be facing armed men. You're not up to it."

"I'm tougher than you think."

"Oh, I know you're gutsy. I seem to recall exactly how far you'll go to get your story. Or have you forgotten?"

Since he seemed bound and determined to get a reaction from her, Barrie lowered her voice to a sultry pitch and said, "No, I haven't forgotten. I haven't forgotten a moment of it. More to the point, Bondurant, neither have you."

Her table-turning worked. A muscle in his jaw twitched. Smiling smugly, she returned her gaze to the road ahead.

Her complacency was short-lived. "Look out!" she screamed.

With the hair-trigger reaction of a trained commando, he swerved to avoid a collision. Coming around the bend were four motorcycle policemen, riding two abreast. Following them were a fire truck, an official-looking car, and an ambulance. All were traveling at high speed.

Gray hugged the ditch in the opposing lane until all the vehicles had streaked past, then he executed a hairpin U-turn and took off after them.

"You're going to follow them?"

"Damn straight."

"But why would—?"

"Overhead," Gray said, answering her question before it was completed. She pressed her cheek against the window and saw two helicopters bank steeply as they rose above the treetops. "Your anonymous source was right. Something's happened."

"But Highpoint is over there," she said, pointing in the opposite direction.

"The presidential retreat is on the other side of the lake, but this whole area is called Highpoint. Dr. George Allan's weekend home is on that ridge." He motioned with his chin toward the approximate spot in the forest from which the helicopters had taken off. "That's where they've been keeping Vanessa."

"How do you know?"

"I had a hunch, and it's just been confirmed. That car behind the fire truck was government issue, probably Secret Service."

His hands were still planted firmly on the steering wheel. He had the accelerator of Barrie's car on the floorboard to keep up with the taillights of the last vehicle in the emergency motorcade.

"What do you think this means?"

"What do you think?" he asked tightly.

She was reluctant to voice her thoughts. "Dr. Allan wouldn't harm her. Not deliberately. Not with the Secret Service guarding her."

"The White House was crawling with Secret Service the night the baby died. That didn't stop the doctor from claiming that the kid died of SIDS. If David's got George Allan's balls in a vise, he'll say and do just about anything."

They followed the motorcade into Shinlin, a picturesque, well-tended community of about fifteen thousand. Because of the town's proximity to the presidential retreat, the locals were accustomed to having motorcades disrupt the serenity of their tree-lined streets.

Gray maintained a discreet distance. He was two blocks behind the vehicles when they pulled into the emergency entrance of the hospital.

Barrie looked at Gray. "If Vanessa needs emergency medical attention, why wasn't she brought here by helicopter?"

Before either could speculate, the rear doors of the ambulance burst open, disgorging George Allan. The doctor was disheveled and overwrought. His shirtsleeves were rolled up to his elbows; his hair was standing on end, as though he'd been raking it with his fingers. He, the driver, and another paramedic lifted a gurney from the ambulance.

Strapped to the gurney was a sheet-draped form.

"Oh, my God, no!" Barrie cried.

The paramedics rolled the gurney toward the automatic glass doors. The two men in the government sedan got out and somberly fell into step behind the gurney as it was wheeled into the hospital.

Dr. George Allan bent from his waist and vomited onto the pavement.

Chapter
Twenty-One

*W*hen Clete Armbruster's telephone rang, waking him from a deep sleep, he rolled over and checked the clock on the nightstand. "Goddamn." A call at this hour portended an emergency of some sort. "Yeah?"

"Senator Armbruster?"

Expecting the clipped articulation of an aide, he wasn't prepared for the soft, husky, female voice more suited to sex than heralding bad news. Ironically, that caused him to panic. It had been a while since he'd retained the services of a professional, but the first thought that streaked through his mind was that one of his past companions had been instructed to notify all her former clients of a life-threatening virus.

"Who is this?"

"Barrie Travis. Vanessa's friend. The reporter."

The senator irritably kicked off the covers, swinging his thick feet and legs to the floor as he sat up. For Barrie Travis to call herself Vanessa's friend was a real stretch. It was even more of a stretch for her to call herself a reporter. For the life of him, he couldn't figure out why Vanessa had granted her the recent interview.

"What do you want?"

"I must talk to you. It's about Vanessa."

"Do you know what time it is? How'd you get my private number, anyhow? Didn't my office staff make it clear to you that I will not discuss my daughter with members of the press?"

"This isn't that kind of call, sir."

"Who do you think you're kidding? Good night."

"Senator! Please don't hang up!"

The anxiety in her voice caused him to reconsider. Taking the cordless phone into the bathroom with him, he stood over the toilet and relieved himself. "What's going on? Another explosion?"

"It's imperative that I see you."

"What for?"

"I can't tell you until I see you."

He chuckled as he flushed the commode. "I can hardly stand the suspense."

"I assure you, Senator Armbruster, that this is not a journalist's trick, nor is it anything to laugh about or to dismiss lightly. Please believe me when I say it's of the utmost importance. Will you meet me?"

He rubbed his head. "Ah, Christ. I'll probably live to regret it, but call my office tomorrow and make an appointment."

"You don't understand. I need to see you immediately. Right now."

"*Now?* It's the middle of the goddamn night."

"Please. I'm at a diner in Shinlin, corner of Lincoln Street and Paul's Meadow Road. I'll be waiting for you."

She hung up, and the senator blistered the walls of his bedroom with expletives. Slamming down the telephone, he lowered himself to the edge of the bed and splashed some Jack Daniel's into a glass. He drank the shot in one swallow and had every intention of ignoring the call and going back to sleep.

But again he hesitated. What the hell could that reporter know about Vanessa that couldn't wait until morning?

As though it were a mortal enemy, he stared balefully at the telephone. He wouldn't be able to return to sleep. Besides, there'd been an urgency in her voice that seemed genuine.

He got up and dressed. In ten minutes, he was in his car driving to Shinlin. He knew the town because he'd visited Highpoint so many times. It was mindless driving.

His memory drifted back to another night, eighteen years ago, when he'd been awakened in the middle of the night. He'd been taking a few days' vacation at his farm in rural Mississippi. The pace of life there was slow and virtually carefree. Except on that night.

He was awakened by an insistent ringing of his doorbell. The housekeeper came from her room behind the kitchen, pulling tight the belt of her robe, but Clete reached the front door first.

David Merritt stood on the threshold, dripping rainwater like a near-drowned cat and looking about as wretched. A lightning flash revealed long, bloody scratches along his cheek.

"What in hell happened to you?" Clete exclaimed.

"I'm sorry to get you up, but I had to see you immediately."

"What's wrong? Did you have an accident?"

David glanced apprehensively toward the housekeeper. Clete dismissed her and she returned to her room.

Clete then led David into his study, turned on the shaded desk lamp, and poured the young man a brandy. David sat on the windowseat, cupped the snifter with both hands, and downed the contents in one swallow.

"You usually don't drink like that," Clete observed, as he passed David a handkerchief to stanch the bleeding scratches on his face. "Whatever's eating you must be bad. So, let's have it."

Clete stretched out in his leather recliner and reached for a cigar. David rose and began to pace.

"There's this girl."

"I figured," Clete said, waving out the match he'd used to light his cigar.

"I met her when we were here last summer."

"Local girl? Where'd you meet her? What's her name? Who're her people?"

"Her name is Becky Sturgis, but you wouldn't know her. She's trash, a nobody. I picked her up at a redneck lounge out on the highway. She was drunk when I got there. We scoped each other out, wound up dancing. We flirted, started necking. It got hot and heavy real quick. She was all over me. We either had to go outside, or it was going to get embarrassing. We'd barely cleared the door of the place before she pulled me to her. We did it right there against the wall of the building."

It would have been hypocritical to chastise his protégé for a sexual indiscretion. When he was David's age, he'd had some pretty wild escapades himself. It was only with maturity that he had learned the value of discretion and good judgment. Nevertheless, he felt that some chastening was called for.

"Several great statesmen have been denied the White House because they got their brains and their peckers confused. They got it mixed up which one to screw with and which one to think with."

"I know that," David said tightly. "I honest to God thought she was harmless. She was pretty, sexy, and unencumbered. She lives alone, works at a dairy as a dispatcher for their delivery trucks, has no family to speak of."

Clete grunted skeptically. "If she's so harmless, what brings you to my door at this time of night, bloodied up and looking like you might lose your supper on my dearly departed wife's prized oriental rug?"

"I . . . I killed her."

Clete's lips went so slack that the lighted cigar almost fell into his lap. Gradually he recovered his wits enough to leave his recliner and pour another brandy, this one for himself. He quaffed it almost as greedily as David had drunk his. Clete could see his dreams for the young man dissolving like a sugar cube.

David Merritt had so distinguished himself as a volunteer in the Armbruster campaign that he was soon offered a paid position. When Clete first met him, David had only recently been discharged from the Marines. He was disciplined and intuitive. He required little or no supervision and executed every assignment with aplomb and expediency. It wasn't long before Clete vested him with more responsibility.

Following his election to the Senate, he invited David to join his staff in Washington. For the past two years David had proved himself a valuable asset and a quick study in politics. Clete had already laid big plans for him, because he saw that David had what it took to make an excellent politician.

He had a hands-on, working knowledge of economics because he'd had to make do with the meager resources available to him in his youth. In his spare time, he studied law and government procedure. He had a distinguished military service record. He was handsome and articulate and, until tonight, free of scandalous baggage.

It took every ounce of self-control Clete possessed not to walk over and slap the shit out of him for being so stupid. "I guess you had a good reason for killing her," he said harshly.

"I swear to God it was an accident."

"Don't swear it to God," Clete roared. "Swear it to me, boy."

"I swear it, Clete."

He studied David's face for a long time but saw no signs of dissembling in the shattered expression. He was one scared young man. "Okay," Clete said. "What happened?"

"First I've got to backtrack. After that first time, I began seeing her whenever we were here."

Clete rolled his cigar from one corner of his mouth to the other. "At Christmas?"

"Yes, sir."

"Easter?"

David nodded.

"While you were courting Vanessa? You've been playing us both for fools," he shouted.

"You've got it wrong, Clete," David said emotionally, his voice cracking. "You know how I feel about Vanessa. I love her and want to marry her, but . . ."

"But you felt the urge to dip your wick into some trashy girl who gets drunk and screws against the outside wall of a redneck beer joint. Is that your idea of how to conduct your love life?"

The outburst cleared Clete's head. He returned to his recliner and let his temper simmer as he puffed furiously on his cigar. David wisely gave him time to calm himself. Finally he snarled, "Give me the rest of it."

"On our last trip here, she called me to come see her out at her place. When I got there . . ." He paused, dragged his hand down his face. "I couldn't believe it. Her stomach was out to here."

Clete merely stared at him for several moments. "Hand me that brandy bottle." David complied, although Clete looked ready to clobber him with the crystal decanter. Clete took two swallows from it. "You're telling me she was pregnant?"

"She was then. She had the kid a few weeks ago. A boy."

"He's yours?"

"How the hell do I know?" David cried, raising his voice for the first time. "It's possible, but it's just as possible that he could belong to a dozen other men. She claimed he was mine."

"*Was?* Past tense?"

"She started bugging me to come see the baby, insisting he was mine. I was afraid that if I didn't do it, she'd do something really crazy.

"So I went over there tonight to give her some money. I thought that was the least I could do. But . . . but she was beyond reason, Clete. She threw the money in my face, said I couldn't buy my way out of my responsibility to her, said she'd settle for nothing less than marriage."

Every word was like another strike of the hammer, nailing shut the coffin of David Merritt's political future. Clete now feared he himself might lose his supper on his late wife's prized oriental rug.

"I told her straight out that marriage was not an option," David said. "I told her that I was already engaged to someone else, to a woman I love."

He paused and glanced at Clete. "I realize I haven't formally proposed to Vanessa, and I don't intend to until she's finished college, but she knows how much I love her. It's been more or less understood that—"

"Get on with it," Clete rudely interrupted. "What happened when you told this tramp there'd be no marriage?"

"She went berserk." David sat down again and covered his face with his hands for a few moments. Finally, he lowered his hands and clasped them loosely between his knees.

"She was using a dresser drawer for a crib. I guess her shouting had scared the baby. Anyway, he was screaming, and that seemed to drive her over the edge. She said she wasn't going to be stuck with a kid to raise alone, and then, she . . . she wrapped her hands around his neck and started choking him. I tried to pry her hands away, but I couldn't. She strangled him."

"Jesus Christ!" Clete gasped. "She killed him?"

David nodded. "I couldn't believe it. One minute he was crying, and the next, he was silent. Dead."

"Why didn't you call the police?"

"She didn't give me a chance," he cried. "The bitch attacked me. That's where I got all these scratches. She came at me like a wildcat. I had to protect myself. We scuffled. She lost her balance and fell against the corner of a built-in table. It must've fractured her skull. There's blood all over the place. She's dead."

He squeezed his eyes shut, but the tears couldn't be contained. He began to sob. Shoulders shaking, he cried like a baby. "One mistake. One mistake, and now all you've done for me, all we've worked toward, is ruined. And Vanessa. Jesus," he blubbered. "What will Vanessa think of me? How will this affect our future together?"

Clete had spent too much time and care cultivating David Merritt for the presidency to throw it away because of a girl who wouldn't be missed and a baby who never should have been born. If all they had to consider were the political consequences of David's misdeeds, Clete would have cleaned up the mess to protect his investment.

But by bringing Vanessa into it, David ensured Clete's swift intervention. He wasn't about to let his daughter's heart be broken by learning that the man she had adored for years and hoped to marry had impregnated some piece of white trash and then accidentally killed her.

In the grand scheme of things, Becky Sturgis and her baby didn't amount to much, while David Malcomb Merritt was destined for greatness. One of these days he would wield more power than any other individual in the world. Why should all his potential be sacrificed to one error? Why should Vanessa's hopes and dreams be denied when she was blameless? Innocent of any wrongdoing, she would be the one to suffer most.

No way in hell would Clete let that happen.

"Okay, boy, pull yourself together." He approached David and gave his back a hearty whack. "Get a shower. Have another brandy. Go to bed. Say nothing about this to anyone. Ever."

David looked up at him, his expression bleak. "You mean—"

"I'll take care of it," Clete said.

David rose unsteadily. "I can't ask you to do that, Clete. Two people are dead. How are you going to—"

"Let me worry about the particulars." He poked David in the chest with his stubby index finger. "My job is to make the problem disappear. Your job is to clean up your act. You understand, boy?"

"Yes, sir."

"No more indiscriminate screwing around. When you gotta get off, you go to a professional for a nice blow job and send me the bill."

"Yes, sir."

"We can't get you elected president, then have a bunch of sluts come crawling out of the woodwork waving paternity suits, now can we?" Clete smiled.

Timidly, David smiled back. "No, sir."

"Now, where's this girl's trailer?"

Clete took care of the problem that night. As David had said, it was one hell of a mess, but the word *impossible* wasn't in Clete's dictionary. In less than forty-eight hours, the entire Becky Sturgis incident was history.

David had never expressed any curiosity as to how Clete had made two bodies disappear with no questions asked. He never asked how Clete had managed to obliterate Becky Sturgis's entire existence. Taking his cue from Clete, David acted as though the incident had never occurred. In the eighteen years since, they had never mentioned it again. Not until a few mornings ago in the Oval Office, when Clete had subtly alluded to it.

The death of his own grandchild had been a disturbing reminder of another young woman and her newborn son. The two incidents were dissimilar, but they bore enough of a resemblance to trouble him.

With vexing frequency a thought flitted through the senator's mind:

Had David Merritt, and not the mother, killed that baby eighteen years ago? And if so, had he killed again?

Chapter
Twenty-Two

$\mathcal{B}$arrie kept a close watch on the door of the diner, eager for, yet dreading, Senator Armbruster's arrival.

In a region where Georgian architecture was prevalent, the eatery was a misfit. Its shiny, gaudy 1950s motif was achieved with gleaming chrome and turquoise vinyl. The floor was checkered with black and white tiles. At this time of night, business was limited to a few hospital employees and a teenage couple who were slurping alternately on melting milk shakes and on each other.

Nursing their coffee, Barrie and Gray occupied a booth in front of a wide picture window that afforded a view of the emergency room entrance. After his attack of nausea, Dr. Allan had taken a moment to collect himself, then had followed the grim cortege into the hospital. He hadn't reappeared, and there'd been no further activity.

Gray had said little. His eyes remained fixed on the doors through which Vanessa's body had been carted. He was seated with his forearms resting on the flamingo-pink tabletop. Occasionally he would flex his fingers into a fist, then straighten them rigidly. He looked tenuously tethered and extremely dangerous.

Barrie cleared her throat. "They'll probably try and pass her death off as a suicide."

"Not if I have anything to do with it. Vanessa wouldn't have killed her baby, and she wouldn't have killed herself."

Impulsively, Barrie reached across the table and laid her hand on his arm. Startled by her touch, he looked down at her hand, then up at her face.

"I'm sorry, Gray," she said. "I know you loved Vanessa. The baby . . ." She hesitated. "He was yours, wasn't he?"

"What difference does it make?" he snapped, shaking her hand off his arm. "He's dead and so is she."

Barrie took the rejection hard. Even her father, on the rare occasions when he had bothered to come home, had never physically rebuffed her or been intentionally mean to her.

"You go to hell, Mr. Bondurant."

She slid from the booth, wanting to walk out and leave him there alone to rot in his misery. If not for Senator Armbruster's imminent arrival, she would have. Instead she went into the ladies' room. Placing her hands on either side of the sink, she leaned upon it until she had worked up enough courage to raise her head and face herself in the mirror. Maybe she wasn't as aggravated with Gray as she was with herself. His pain was raw, his emotions honest. Hers were conflicting. A struggle between her professional interests and her conscience was creating a moral dilemma for her.

She was an eyewitness to an event that would make history. The career-making potential of the story boggled her mind. She became giddy at the thought of being the first and only reporter on the scene to break the story.

But a woman's wrongful death was hardly cause for celebration, especially when one was as personally involved as Barrie was. If she had ceased to probe the mystery surrounding the child's death, would Vanessa still have been killed? In pursuit of a hot story, had she gone too far? Was she in any way responsible for the course of events that had resulted in this tragedy, or had Vanessa's fate been sealed long before she invited Barrie to coffee?

The hell of it was, she would never know. For the rest of her life, she would be plagued by those haunting questions.

She washed her hands, thoroughly, then pressed a damp paper towel to her face. When she came out of the rest room, she saw Clete Armbruster approaching the entrance. She met him at the door.

"Senator Armbruster." It suddenly occurred to her that she hadn't rehearsed what she would say. He was an intimidating man under any circumstances. She certainly didn't welcome being the one to tell him that his daughter was dead. "Thank you for coming," she said lamely.

"Young lady, you'd better have a damn good reason for getting me up in the middle of the night," he said, following her to the booth. "I wouldn't be here except—" He came to an abrupt halt when he saw Gray Bondurant.

Gray stood up. "Clete, it's been a while."

The senator was not pleased to see him. Obviously he didn't hold Gray in the highest esteem, and it was easy to guess why. A father would naturally resent a man who had damaged his daughter's honor, especially if she also happened to be the First Lady of the United States, where more than personal virtue was at stake.

"Bondurant." He ignored the hand that Gray extended. "What are you doing here?" He turned to Barrie. "Is this the big surprise you hinted at, the 'matter of utmost importance'?"

"Please sit down, Senator. Give us a chance to explain. Would you like some coffee?"

"No." He took one side of the booth; Barrie and Gray shared the bench across from him. Drawing a bead on Gray, he remarked, "You're a long way from Montana."

"It's Wyoming, and I'm not here because I want to be."

"I've never known you to do anything you didn't want to."

"He's here because he believes lives are at risk," Barrie said. "As do I."

Armbruster's eyebrows shot up comically. "Really? Whose? Justice Green's?"

His ridicule stung, but she kept her cool. "You may not have much confidence in my credibility," she said, "but what I'm about to tell you is the unvarnished truth. You can draw your own conclusions. Agreed?"

"I'm interested in what you have to say only to the extent that it involves my daughter."

Barrie took a moment to arrange her thoughts. "Senator, I don't think your grandson's death was accidental. I believe he was murdered, probably smothered so his breathing would be interrupted and it would look like SIDS."

Armbruster looked at her incredulously. "What are you implying, young lady? If you're suggesting that Vanessa—"

"David killed him," Gray interrupted, cutting to the chase.

Remaining perfectly still, only the senator's eyes moved, springing back and forth between them. After a moment, he leaned forward across the table and hissed, "Are you insane?"

"No," Gray replied calmly. "David killed Vanessa's baby because he didn't father him."

"That's a goddamn lie!" Armbruster protested, but keeping his voice low. "You're the last one to make moral judgments against my daughter, Bondurant. You slandering son of a bitch, I ought to shoot you right here, right now."

Gray's face grew taut. "David did not father Vanessa's baby. He couldn't have. He had a vasectomy. Years ago."

Barrie was as astonished as the senator by that piece of news. Gray disregarded her soft exclamation and concentrated solely on Armbruster. "Nobody knew about it, Clete. Not even Vanessa. Especially Vanessa. For years she tried everything to conceive, and the bastard let her, knowing full well that it would never happen. He took a perverse pleasure in watching her unravel every month when she got her period."

Barrie stared at Gray's profile. She had already determined that he was a complex individual, but she was beginning to wonder exactly how many facets there were to him. Just when she thought she'd seen all of them, another was turned to the light.

"David Merritt never underwent a vasectomy or I would have known about it," the senator said. "You're lying."

"I don't care whether you believe me or not, Clete. I'm telling you the way it is. David couldn't father a child, but Vanessa didn't know that until after she got pregnant and told him."

Clete continued to glare mistrustfully, but Barrie detected a chink in his hostility. "How do you know all this?" he asked.

"Vanessa called and told me."

That news flash took Barrie aback. She had assumed that once Gray retired to Wyoming, he'd had no further contact with Vanessa. Apparently the senator also had been under that impression. He appeared as surprised as she.

"She called me crying," Gray continued. "She asked me what she should do."

"So the baby was yours," Armbruster said.

"That isn't the issue."

"The hell it isn't!"

The two men glared at each other, Armbruster with accusation, Gray with defiance. Finally he said, "Do you want to hear the rest of this or not?"

Armbruster made an impatient motion with his hand.

"Despite everything you saw in the media," Gray said, casting a glance in Barrie's direction, "David went ballistic when Vanessa told him she was pregnant, because that confirmed the gossip of an affair with me. You know how David takes offense at the merest slight, so you can imagine what that scene must have been like for Vanessa.

"Jesus." Gray sighed, shaking his head. "He put her through sheer hell every day of those nine months. David had no choice except to go along with all the fanfare, but he was only biding his time."

The senator's wide shoulders had slumped forward. Apparently he was giving Gray's story some credibility.

Barrie was the first to break the sudden, heavy silence. "Why didn't the President have George Allan perform an abortion?"

"I was wondering that myself," Armbruster said.

"Because an abortion wouldn't have been painful enough for her," Gray replied without hesitation. "I think David wanted to punish her for her infidelity. I think the worst punishment he could devise was to let her carry the child, give birth to it, come to love it, perhaps even relax her vigilance over it. When she did, he meted out his punishment, in spades. And since Vanessa witnessed the murder, he . . ."

Barrie realized that he couldn't bring himself to tell the senator what must be told. She turned to the older man. "Mrs. Merritt contacted me for a reason. I believe she was trying to signal danger."

"Danger?"

"For herself. Because she knows of the President's crime." Barrie looked at him sympathetically. "I called you tonight, Senator, because we believe that the President has . . . has made it impossible for her to testify to his criminal act."

"Made it impossible?" he repeated. "What do you mean?"

Barrie inclined her head toward the hospital. Armbruster looked through the plate glass. It reflected the interior of the diner, including their somber images. "She was taken there by ambulance about two hours ago," she said.

"From George Allan's house?"

She nodded. "We followed them."

Armbruster no longer looked like the powerful, brash, authority-wielding statesman he was. He looked like a father who'd just heard terrible news about his only child. In the last few moments, his face seemed to have lost its battle with gravity. Lines appeared more deeply etched, folds of flesh sagged more heavily. His voice was weak, laden with denial. "I was in that house only a few days ago."

"Did you actually see Vanessa?" Gray asked.

When the senator shook his head, the loose skin beneath his chin wobbled. "George told me she was resting and didn't want to be disturbed, even by me. He assured me that rest is all she needs."

"Clete," Gray said patiently, "George will do anything David tells him to, just as he did the night David killed the baby."

"But the Secret Service is there to protect her."

"They couldn't protect your grandson. Believe me, David has planned this meticulously—with Spence's help, I'm sure. Vanessa takes a lot of medication. He'll probably use that. If she succumbed—"

"Succumbed?" Armbruster repeated. "Are you saying . . ." His eyes darted from Gray to Barrie.

Later, Barrie couldn't remember leaving the diner and jogging the short distance to the emergency room entrance. The Secret Service agents were nowhere in sight. The nurse on duty at the reception desk asked pleasantly if she could help them.

The senator didn't even glance in her direction. He marched through a pair of automatic doors, with Barrie and Gray close on his heels. Dr. George Allan was leaning against the wall at the far end of the corridor. He looked no calmer than he had when he'd accompanied Vanessa's body into the hospital. When he glanced up and saw Armbruster, Barrie, and Gray bearing down on him, his face turned the color of putty.

"Senator Armbruster, what . . . what are you doing here?"

"Where's my daughter?" He looked at the door behind the doctor. "Is she in there?"

"No."

"You lying bastard." He pushed the doctor aside, but George Allan grabbed his sleeve.

"Senator, please. I can't let you go in. Not until the medical examiner sees her."

Armbruster made a choking sound like a sob. Gray grabbed the doctor's lapels and shoved him against the wall. "You weasel shit. They'll fry you for this—if I don't kill you first."

Alerted to a crisis situation, hospital personnel had collected at the end of the corridor, but not even the chief security guard was brave enough to intervene.

Armbruster opened the door that Dr. Allan had been guarding, but he drew up short on the threshold, then he fell back against the doorjamb, grasping on to it for support.

Across the room, against the wall, was the gurney. The security straps had been removed. The still form had been draped in a blue sheet.

"Oh, Jesus." His voice sounded like rending cloth.

He pushed himself away from the door and trudged across the tile floor. Barrie and Gray were on either side of him, ready to lend support. George Allan came into the room. His vehement protests went unheeded.

When they reached the gurney, the senator simply stood there gazing down at the blue sheet, his large hands hanging heavily at his sides.

"Clete?" Gray said.

The senator nodded. Gray picked up two corners of the sheet and pulled it back.

A gasp went up as they stared down into the face of the cadaver, into the face of Jayne Gaston, R.N.

Chapter
Twenty-Three

"Jayne Gaston was the private nurse hired by George Allan to care for Vanessa while she was in seclusion at Highpoint." Barrie lay on her back on the cot on which Cronkite had taken his naps when she'd brought him to Daily's house. She was bringing Daily current on last night's events. "By the way, thanks for not turning me out," she said.

"Where else would you go?"

"Exactly my point. I'm a pariah. If I were a leper, I couldn't be more aggressively avoided. Maybe I should tie a bell around my neck to warn people that I'm coming down the street."

"That's not very funny," Daily said sourly.

"I didn't think so either." Her voice was thick with unshed tears. "Anyway, back to last night. Apparently Jayne Gaston suffered cardiac arrest yesterday afternoon at Dr. Allan's Highpoint home. He attempted to revive her, but to no avail."

For a time, Daily's wheezing was the only sound in the small, cluttered room. Scattered about were the few purchases Barrie had made since the demolition of her home.

Most of the clothing was still in shopping bags. Daily sat at the end of the cot, Barrie's stocking feet resting on his thighs. He was giving her an uninspired foot massage.

"If the nurse died in the afternoon, why'd they wait till after dark to remove the body?" he asked.

"Dr. Allan had to arrange for Vanessa's transport back to Washington. He wanted to shield her from the trauma of Mrs. Gaston's death. A helicopter was dispatched to return her to the White House, but by then she'd learned about Mrs. Gaston. She was inconsolable. According to the doctor, the two had formed quite an attachment.

"Then, Mrs. Gaston's next of kin, a son who lives here in the city, couldn't be located immediately. Dr. Allan didn't want to arrive at the hospital with her body before the son was notified."

"But that happens all the time."

"But not when the deceased is the First Lady's private nurse. Dr. Allan was afraid the story would be leaked and get out over the airwaves before the son could be reached. He wasn't too far off."

"I guess that makes sense," Daily muttered. "Seems a thin excuse, though, if you ask me."

"Well, anyway, Dr. Allan waited to call the ambulance until he felt he couldn't wait any longer. Gray and I happened to see the motorcade on the road. We followed it. When we saw the dead body . . ." She sighed.

"You drew a conclusion based on supposition instead of fact."

"Rub it in, why don't you?"

"I can't believe you actually called Armbruster to the scene."

"Believe it. Armbruster, and a WVUE cameraman whose timing was excellent. He showed up seconds after my dreadful mistake was discovered. He recorded for posterity my astonishment and Gray's, Armbruster's near-collapse, and the arrival of Ralph Gaston, Jr., the deceased's son, who not only was dealt the blow of his mother's death but was plunged into the tumultuous aftermath of my snafu.

"Some sadistic individual on the hospital staff notified the local press, which in turn . . . Well, you know the denouement. We created headlines. Thank God the story was killed before the networks got there. I absconded with the only videotape of the event."

She paused to blot her eyes and blow her nose. She'd been weepy ever since the tongue-lashing she'd received from Senator Armbruster. Impervious to eavesdroppers, he'd lambasted her for making a goddamn fool of herself and, worse, of him. She ought to be horsewhipped for scaring him like that, he'd said, and warned that she was going to pay for her unforgivable, inexcusable, and unprofessional behavior. Having no doubt that he meant every word, Barrie had taken his warning to heart.

His threat hung over her like the glittering blade of the guillotine. She was doomed; she just didn't know when or how the blade was going to fall. In the long run, she might not have to fear the senator's reprisal: The suspense of not knowing what form it would take might be her undoing.

"Lord, Daily," she groaned, laying her forearm across her eyes, "how could I have been so wrong? Everything led me to conclude that the President of the United States had committed one, possibly two, murders. Logic should have demanded that I rethink it."

"Frankly, I don't think logic is all it's cracked up to be," he said sympathetically. "Thinking back through history, name me one great mind who didn't spit in the face of logic."

"Stop trying to make me feel better. Let me wallow in this misery. I've earned it."

He massaged the ball of her foot. "You screwed up pretty bad, all right. This is even worse than the Justice Green incident."

"I couldn't believe it," she said, almost in a whisper. "When Gray pulled back that sheet, I was prepared to see Vanessa's lovely chestnut hair and creamy complexion. Instead, there lay a stranger. I was stunned. And then of course Armbruster erupted like Mount St. Helens. And Gray . . ."

"Gray?" he prompted.

"He pulled a David Copperfield and disappeared."

Her foolhardiness would have severe consequences, but, of all of them, Gray's vanishing act was perhaps the hardest to take. She was resigned to being the target of Armbruster's vengeance. The senator would make her suffer for those few minutes that he'd believed his daughter was dead. For years to come, she would be the laughingstock of the Washington press corps. Whatever crumbs of credibility she had scraped together since the Justice Green debacle were now for naught. It would be years, if ever, before she regained a modicum of respect in journalistic circles.

Even if she hadn't notified her own TV station, word would have gotten out eventually. Pennsylvania Avenue was like Main Street in any small town in America. Gossip and bad news were telegraphed with lightning speed. A fiasco with such a high-profile cast of characters couldn't have been kept under wraps.

So she was braced for the ridicule. It would hurt. But not as badly as Gray's desertion.

She had looked from Jayne Gaston's death mask into his face, and one was about as animated as the other. Oddly, she'd been concerned more with Gray's reaction than with Senator Armbruster's. Of the two, the senator had been the more vocal and vituperative. His tirade had distracted her, and by the time he'd finished reviling her, Gray had vanished.

"I searched the hospital, then the parking area," she told Daily. "No one remembered seeing him leave. My car was where we'd left it, so I don't know what he used for transportation. He simply vanished."

She picked at a loose thumb cuticle. "I guess he was mortified that a man of his experience had been drawn into the fantasy of an idiot like me."

"Please," Daily groaned. "Self-pity makes me want to puke."

"I'm not—"

"You didn't convince Bondurant of anything, and you flatter yourself if you think you could. You confirmed suspicions he'd already had, remember?"

"But based on what I told him, he killed Spencer Martin."

"In self-defense."

"Are we sure of that?"

"You doubt it?"

"Well, if Merritt didn't have anything to hide, why would he have sent Spencer Martin to Wyoming to get rid of Bondurant? Because I had told him my wild theory, Gray must've misread the purpose of Spencer Martin's visit, the timing of which was probably nothing more than coincidence. Merritt isn't going to let his top adviser disappear without conducting an exhaustive search and investigation. Gray will be charged with murder."

"He covered Martin's tracks and probably disposed of the body so well that it will never be found," Daily speculated. "No body, no murder."

"That's a technicality."

"He didn't seem overly concerned."

"No, he was more concerned about Vanessa. When he thought she was dead, he looked like death himself."

Gray Bondurant loved Vanessa Merritt. Not lusted after, loved. He loved her enough to sacrifice his career for her. He had resigned so that neither her marriage nor her public status would be jeopardized by a scandalous affair. He loved her enough to relinquish any claim to his son. It must have been torture for him not to be there when the child was born, and then to mourn his death alone, in virtual exile.

Barrie would never receive that kind of love, and peevishly felt that such devotion was wasted on a woman as shallow and selfish as Vanessa Armbruster Merritt. She was ill, true. But did that excuse her for being grossly manipulative? Why had Vanessa involved her at all? Why had she tossed out those red herrings for her to follow?

"He's quite a stud," Daily observed.

"Hmm. What? Who? Bondurant?" Barrie quickly retracted her foot and sat up. "I wouldn't know."

"You two didn't . . ." He raised his eyebrows.

"Of course not."

"But you would've liked to."

"Give me a break. Our Mr. Bondurant has some admirable traits, but he's about as far removed from my ideal man as one could get. He's the strong, silent type, which, as far as I'm concerned, translates into asshole with an attitude.

"He killed a friend in what he claims was self-defense, but we have only his word on that. He's hung up on a woman he can never, ever have. He lives like a hermit out in the boonies, which is weird and sort of spooky.

"Even if he lived around the corner and was Mr. Upstanding/Involved Citizen of the Year, he's made no secret of his opinion of me, which is that I'm a walking calamity, a disaster waiting to happen. Anyway, this entire conversation is pointless because I'm not interested in him, and anyway he's disappeared, too. Okay?"

"So how long after you met him were you in bed together?"

"About ninety seconds."

"Jesus, Barrie."

"Yeah. A real professional approach, but only if you're a hooker." She sighed. "Since my career as a journalist is over, perhaps I ought to consider going into the purveyance of personal pleasure."

"You, a hooker?" Daily chuckled. "That I'd like to see."

"I'd have to charge extra for watching." She swung her legs over the edge of the cot. "This conversation, which I began in the hope of boosting my spirits, has made me feel even more depressed. I'm going to take a shower."

"A shower won't cure what ails you."

"Well, I'm going to shower anyway." She dug into a shopping bag for a new set of underwear. As she clipped off the tags, she said, "If I could be granted one wish, Daily, it would be to pick up my life the day Vanessa Merritt called to invite me for coffee. I would decline."

"Meaning that now you're convinced the Merritt baby died of SIDS, and that the rest of it was just a product of your bad judgment and active imagination?"

She looked up at him sharply. "Aren't you?"

~ ~

"You look radiant!" Senator Armbruster smothered his daughter in a bear hug. "I can't tell you how good it is to see you."

"It's good to see you too, Daddy." She returned his hug, but he sensed her restlessness and released her. Her smile was as bright as a ten-dollar diamond ring and much more counterfeit. "I saw myself in the mirror this morning. I don't think *radiant* is the word I'd use to describe me."

"You just got up from weeks in a sickbed. What do you expect? You'll get the color back in your cheeks in no time."

"I think she looks gorgeous." This from David Merritt, who was buttering a blueberry muffin.

The three were sharing a continental breakfast in Vanessa's chambers. In Clete's opinion, the last thing Vanessa needed was caffeine, and she was on her second cup of coffee. "Maybe you should spend a few weeks at home," he suggested. "You could lie in the sun, sleep late every day, eat fattening southern cooking. What do you think, David? Should we pack her off to Mississippi?"

His son-in-law's best campaign smile was in place. He must have been practicing it. "I just got her back, Clete. I'd hate to have her leave again right away. Besides, she's definitely on the mend. George has worked wonders for her."

The senator didn't share his son-in-law's opinion of Dr. Allan. "Night before last, he looked to be hanging on to his ass with both hands."

Vanessa was at her vanity table, trying on earrings. "Which should I wear?" she asked, turning to face them and holding a different earring to each ear. "I think the pearls are best, don't you, Daddy?"

"The pearls are fine."

"They were Mother's."

"Yes, I know."

"My junior year in high school, you let me wear them to a dance, remember, Daddy? I lost one, and you were upset. But I went back to the gym the next day and searched until I found it. My dress was pink. You had a fit because you thought the seamstress had hemmed it too short. My date was that Smith boy, the one who went to Princeton and then flunked out. I forget what happened to him after that."

Before Vanessa was diagnosed as manic-depressive, Clete had been confused and saddened by the violent mood swings he witnessed. She could be abysmally depressed, agitated, anxious, or hyper. But he'd rarely seen her as hopped up as she was now. She was either in the throes of a manic episode or high on an antidepressant drug. The symptoms were so similar that it was difficult to tell. But she wasn't stabilized, which had been the point of her seclusion.

David must have noticed her behavior, but he was making a concerted effort to ignore it. He interrupted Vanessa's chatter to address her father's comment about the doctor. "George wasn't at his best the other night, Clete. And can you blame him? First he had the nurse die on him, then he couldn't locate her next of kin. To top it all off, Barrie Travis showed up at the hospital with you and Gray in tow, creating a hell of a ruckus and a media event that we all could have done without." Chuckling, he shook his head. "Tell me she didn't seriously think that the corpse was Vanessa."

"That little gal got an earful from me, I can tell you that," Clete said, jabbing the air with his blunt index finger. "And I'm not finished with her yet."

"I don't want to talk about it anymore," Vanessa said, leaving the vanity. "Look at my arms. Chill bumps. It's horrible to hear rumors about your own death."

"I'll never forgive that woman for what she put me through," Clete said. "I've known some irresponsible reporters, but she tops the heap. How in hell did she come up with that notion? What's your version of the story, sweetheart?"

"What story? Oh, you mean about what happened at Highpoint? It's foggy. I really don't remember leaving. When I woke up, I was in my bed here, and George was telling me that I was going to feel much better soon."

"And so you are." David moved toward her, took her hand, and kissed her cheek. But Clete noticed that Vanessa quickly put space between them.

"George told me that my nurse had had a fatal heart attack. I felt sorry about that, although I hadn't actually met her." She readjusted a heavy charm bracelet on her slender wrist. "This thing's bugging me."

"What do you mean, you never met Mrs. Gaston?" Clete asked.

"Just what I said, Daddy. I can vaguely remember her voice, but I couldn't pick her out of a crowd. I don't remember anything about what she looked like. Maybe I'll take this off." She slid the bracelet off her wrist and dropped it onto the table with a clatter.

"George Allan led me to believe that the two of you had grown very close," Clete said.

"George is right," David said. "You just don't remember, dear."

"I never met her, David," she insisted. "I ought to know if I did or I didn't, and I didn't. Why are you always correcting me? You always do that, and I hate it. It makes me feel stupid."

"You're not stupid."

"You treat me like I am."

"You were on medication, darling," he said smoothly. "You became very attached to Mrs. Gaston, but because of the sedatives you were taking to help you rest, you don't remember."

"Okay, okay, whatever." She waved her hands. "Jesus, I can't believe she died right there at the foot of my bed. That grosses me out." She replaced the bracelet on her wrist and shook it. "I love wearing this bracelet. I like the way the charms jangle. Like sleigh bells at Christmas."

"Christmas will be here before we know it," David

said, smile in place again. "Then we'll be ringing in the New Year. Election year. Let's forget about Barrie Travis and the nurse and all the unhappy events of this year and concentrate on next." He rubbed his hands together vigorously. "We've got a lot of campaign plans to make."

"I don't want to think about that yet."

Taking the cue from his daughter, Clete said, "I agree, David. I think you're jumping the gun a little. Let's get Vanessa hale and hearty first. There's plenty of time to make campaign plans."

"It's never too early to plan."

Vanessa began wringing her hands. "Just the thought of it . . . Listen, David, I feel much better than I have in a long time, but I don't think I'm up to appearing at the press conference this morning."

Clete had been shocked to learn that a press conference was scheduled for eleven o'clock in the East Room. Vanessa was expected to attend. Her stylist had been summoned to the White House. She'd done wonders with Vanessa's hair and makeup, but her skilled efforts hadn't completely hidden the dark circles beneath Vanessa's eyes, or the gauntness of her cheeks.

"Why do I have to be there?" she asked anxiously.

"It'll only last a few minutes," David said.

"That's no answer," Clete said. "Why's it necessary that she be there?"

Tightly, David replied, "Because Vanessa dragged Barrie Travis into our lives, that's why. That's when all this started, and it culminated with that debacle in the emergency room. Rumors are flying fast and furious. The only way we can quell them is to address Mrs. Gaston's death and explain exactly what happened.

"Besides, the people have missed seeing their First Lady. You've received thousands of cards and letters wishing you a speedy recovery. They can't go unacknowledged, Vanessa."

"Of course I'll acknowledge them. I'll get my staff on it right away. But can't we delay the press conference? Just for a few days?"

"It's already scheduled," David snapped. "Dalton would have a fit. Besides, if we cancel now, it'll only generate more speculation on why you were at Highpoint under the care of a private nurse. I can't afford any more negative press. Haven't you already cost me enough?"

"David!" Clete bellowed. "For God's sake."

He sighed. "I'm sorry. That was a terrible thing to say. I didn't mean it." He approached his wife, this time placing his hands on her shoulders. Clete could have sworn that she actually recoiled. "We've all been under a tremendous strain, but you more than anyone," he said gently. "Skip the press conference today if you want. It isn't that important. I shouldn't have insisted that you appear if you don't feel up to it."

Vanessa looked quickly toward her father, who saw in his daughter's eyes panic and helplessness. But she said, "No, David, I'll be there. It's my duty as First Lady."

He pressed her shoulders. "That's my girl. I wouldn't have scheduled the conference if I thought it would cause you a setback. George has assured me that you're strong enough. In fact, he told me that the sooner you get back into the swing of things, the better you'll feel."

"What do I have to do?"

"Nothing. Dalton will deliver a brief eulogy to Mrs. Gaston. He'll credit you with writing it, but he'll read it. All you have to do is stand there and look pretty for the cameras. You can handle that, can't you?"

"Of course she can," Clete said expansively. "What time does she need to be downstairs?"

"Shortly before eleven. If you could stay with her until then, Clete, I've got some matters to attend to." With that, David left the room.

"You should eat something, Vanessa."

"I'm not hungry. I drank some orange juice earlier." She crossed to the window and parted the drapes. "Daddy, I didn't want to bring it up in front of David, but did I hear him mention Gray?"

"Unfortunately," he grumbled. He had decided not to tell her about Bondurant's reappearance on the scene and wasn't at all happy that David had let it slip. "I hoped we'd seen the last of Rambo."

"He's here in Washington?"

"He was. By now, he's probably tucked tail and gone slinking back to Wyoming."

"You always hated him. You shouldn't have. He was nice to me. I wish I could see him."

"Let's not argue about him, Vanessa."

"What was he doing here? What brought him back?"

"It's a long story."

"I'd like to hear it."

"It can wait for another time. You've got plenty to deal with already."

"I want to hear about Gray," she demanded in a shrill voice.

Her composure was so tenuous, Clete obliged her. But only to a point. "I don't know what brought him back," he lied. "All I know is that he was in the company of Barrie Travis. I can't think of a more hazardous combination. On the other hand, the two of them richly deserve each other."

"How did Gray link up with her?"

"Who knows? What difference does it make? She's as unethical as they come. Bondurant is . . . Why go into it, Vanessa? You know what a low opinion I have of him."

"He's not like you think, Daddy. Not at all. He—"

Clete laid his thick index finger vertically against her lips. "I don't want to know, Vanessa."

"But you have to know. I have to talk about it." There were fractures in the beautiful mask the stylist had created for the press conference. Her blue eyes were riddled with emotional turmoil.

"Not now," he said softly. "Later."

"Things are so messed up. *I'm* messed up, aren't I? David's just pretending I'm well. But I'm not. You know it too, don't you? I'm . . . cracked on the inside, aren't I? I can feel it."

"Shh, shh," he said, drawing her close. Pressing her face into his lapel, he placed his lips close to her ear and whispered, "Listen to me, Vanessa. You've always trusted me to take care of things, haven't you? Well, I'm still taking care of things. You've got to trust me. I'll handle it. All of it. I promise. Okay?"

She pulled away. He gazed deeply into her eyes, hoping that his message would penetrate her confusion and the drugs in her system. Finally she nodded.

"Good. Now, go powder your nose," he said cheerfully. "The First Lady of the U.S. of A. can't appear on TV with a shiny honker!"

She headed to the bathroom, then turned back. "Will Spence be there this morning?"

"I suppose so. Why?"

"Nothing. I haven't seen him since I got back, that's all."

The senator's heavy brows pulled together above the bridge of his nose. "Come to think of it, I haven't seen him around in a while, either."

Chapter Twenty-Four

"You're as dry as a cornstalk in August."

David poked and probed, but, although it was uncomfortable, Vanessa didn't protest. Her pleasure was derived from his futile attempts to penetrate her. "All my juices are gone, David. You dried them up."

"No, you used them up creaming for Bondurant."

Wedging his hand between their bodies, he separated the tender folds of flesh and rammed into her. She bit her lip to keep from crying out and giving him the satisfaction of knowing he'd hurt her. This travesty of making love wasn't even sex. It was domination. He was exercising his power over her, wanting to leave no doubt of his supreme authority.

His insults had lost the impact they'd once had. Repetition had weakened their effect. With another guttural litany of obscenities, he climaxed. As he rolled off of her, he was gloating.

"Before congratulating yourself, David, keep in mind that there's no life in you." She plucked a tissue from the box on the nightstand and wiped away the semen between her thighs. "You're sterile, remember?"

"Shut up."

"Even if I'd known about your secret vasectomy, I probably would have taken a lover just for the experience of making love with a man who's capable of giving life."

"If you say that again, I'll—"

"You'll what, David?"

"I don't think you want to know."

"Are you threatening me? You want threats? Okay. What about the night Robert Rushton died?"

"Why do you keep dredging that up, Vanessa? It serves us both best to bury it, just like we did the kid."

She came off the bed but remained at its side, confronting him. Naked, the physical effects of her recent ordeal were startling. She had lost so much weight that her pelvic bone protruded grotesquely from her concave abdomen. Her skin had lost its elasticity and hung in loose pouches where toned muscles had been.

Ordinarily, she would have been frantic over such unsightly changes in her form. But she was unmindful of everything except her consummate loathing for the man lying supine on the bed.

She'd been semiconscious when they transported her from Highpoint to Washington. This morning, she'd been as taut as a highwire. Drug juggling. That's what George was doing for David. He was playing with her medication, keeping her high or low to suit her husband's purposes. How much could her system stand?

More stabilized now, and able to assess her situation clearly, she wasn't certain that she preferred this soundness of mind. Cognizance bore a shocking reality—namely, that Nurse Gaston's untimely death had halted David's plans for her.

She had endured the press conference like the well-bred politician she was. Standing between her husband and her father, facing the lights and cameras and microphones which had been part of her life for as long as she could remember, she wondered if anyone watching was aware of the terror that gripped her. Or if anyone had noticed the jewelry she was wearing. More to the point, had anyone noticed the piece of jewelry she *wasn't* wearing?

David hadn't noticed. Emboldened by that small success, she said, "You think you're so smart to have everybody believing that little Robert died of SIDS."

"Which is preferable to everybody knowing the truth about him, isn't it? Wouldn't you rather everyone believe the lie? You like being First Lady. What would happen to you if the world learned the truth?"

"You're not thinking of what would happen to me," she said scornfully. "You're thinking of what would happen to *you*. To make damn sure the truth never comes to light, Dr. Allan was going to kill me with my medication, wasn't he?"

"You're delusional, Vanessa."

"No, tonight I'm seeing things with frightening clarity." She laughed mirthlessly. "Too bad, David. You *failed. You* failed. I'm still here. Weaker, maybe, but with every intention of making your life a living hell, just as you've made mine."

"Yes, anyone can see how hellish your life is." He sat up and gazed around at the luxurious surroundings. "You live in the most prestigious house in the nation. You're married to the most important man in the world. You have so many people granting your every whim, you can't possibly keep track of them all. You don't even know the names of the people who make your life so comfortable and seamless.

"Clothing designers line up, begging for the opportunity to outfit you. You travel on *Air Force One,* and have access to several yachts. A fleet of chauffeured limousines is at your disposal. An entire nation and half the rest of the world adores you." He reached out to stroke her thigh. "It's no wonder you're so miserable, Vanessa."

She slapped his hand away. "Why didn't you just break my heart years ago, David? When I was young and helplessly in love, why didn't you abuse my love then and be done with it?"

"Because it's been fun to be the monster in your fairytale life. You think you're miserable, Vanessa, but you don't know what misery is. Misery is being poor, and helpless to do anything about it. Misery is living with two stinking drunks who make no secret of despising you just for being born, and knock you around for amusement.

"You grew up rich. Every goddamn thing you ever wanted was handed to you on a silver platter. You never had to beg or scrape or even wish for a single thing in your whole fucking life."

"Is that why you're punishing me?" she cried incredulously. "Because as a child I had more advantages than you?"

"No," he said evenly, "I'm punishing you because you spread your legs for a man I trusted and called my friend. That," he said scornfully, pointing toward the vee between her thighs, "caused him to betray *me*." His voice had risen and his face had become congested with rage.

"You betrayed me first," she shouted. "With dozens of other women. Hundreds, maybe. God knows how many." Her hands formed tight fists of anger and despair. "I worshiped you, David. I was sixteen when you joined Daddy's campaign. I couldn't wait to grow up so I could marry you. I've always loved you. The only reason I broke my marriage vows was to hurt you.

"Despite the other women, I wanted our marriage to last. Even after I learned about your vasectomy and realized that the baby wasn't yours, I was willing to make a clean start. I wanted us to be in love again."

David began to laugh, shaking his head sadly, indulgently. "Vanessa, I was never in love with you. Do you really think that if your name had been anything other than Armbruster I would have shackled myself for life to a stupid, shallow, sick bitch like you?"

She took in a quick breath and expelled it on a broken sob. Seeing his cold, implacable heartlessness, she wondered how she had ever been suckered in. What an amazing talent he had for charming people—her, her father, a nation of voters.

"You're evil," she said.

"And you're crazy. Anybody who knows you knows that." He brushed her aside as he rose from the bed and reached for his robe.

Vanessa gripped the back of a chair. "I'm not as stupid and shallow as you seem to think. I won't let you get away with trying to murder me."

"Careful, Vanessa," he said softly. "Threatening the President of the United States is a serious crime."

"I don't care what they do to me. I'm going to destroy you."

"Is that so?"

When he came toward her, it was difficult not to cower, but she stood her ground.

Until he backhanded her across the face.

She fell against the wall, holding her hand to her cheekbone, which felt like it was dismantling beneath her skin.

"Never threaten me again, Vanessa. You'll do *nothing* except continue being the vapid, obedient nonentity you've always been, first for your father, then for me.

"And speaking of Clete, don't imagine that you can topple me without dragging him down, too. He's been in on every crooked deal in Washington since the Johnson administration. You can't destroy me without destroying Daddy dear in the bargain. So call all the goddamn reporters you want, and drop hints about malcontent in the White House, but be prepared to see the end of Senator Clete Armbruster."

He strode to the door, but got in a parting shot. "At one time you were a pretty good piece of ass. Now, you're not even that."

He walked quickly across the corridor to his own bedroom, giving cursory nods to the Secret Service agents who wished him a good night. Even though he'd won the round with Vanessa—and it hadn't even been a close contest—he'd come away from it angry. The problem of what to do about her was still unresolved.

God damn that nurse!

His bed had been turned down. The nightstand lamp was low. The chamber looked intimate and inviting. He thought about summoning one of his regulars, the syndicated columnist who was a strong advocate of women's rights in print but whose blow jobs were legendary. She thought that being sneaked into the White House was a big turn-on and usually rewarded him well for the thrill. But Vanessa's whining had squelched his desire. Which only gave him more justification to be steamed.

He poured himself a glass of water, added a dash of whiskey to it, and carried the glass into the bathroom. He brushed his teeth, rinsed, and spat into the sink. When he reached for his whiskey-spiked water, he caught movement behind him in the mirror.

As he spun around, the glass slipped from his hand and shattered onto the floor. Clutching his chest, he fell back against the sink.

"Mr. President. You look like you've just seen a ghost."

"Jesus." David sank down onto the commode. He was trembling. "I thought you were dead."

Spencer Martin leaned negligently against the door-jamb. For all his nonchalance, he looked worse for wear. His clothes were Kmart stock and appeared new, but he was unshaven, and it looked as though he hadn't showered or washed his hair in weeks.

Having recovered from his initial shock, David said, "Where in hell have you been? You look like shit. Smell like it too."

"Before making good my escape, I lay in my own waste for several days."

"Your escape from what?"

"I think the pioneers quaintly referred to it as a root cellar. Actually it's a hole in the ground—in this case, beneath the barn of your friend and mine, Gray Bondurant." Spence sneered. "Can you believe it? That motherfucker shot me."

David listened as Spence described the casual breakfast they'd shared. "He admitted Barrie Travis had been to see him, but apparently he was on to me from the beginning. He got off a shot before I could fire." His lips narrowed to a thin, bitter line. "He's going to regret not killing me when he had the chance. Being the Boy Scout he is, he didn't aim to kill."

"What happened then?"

"He packed my shoulder wound, stripped me naked, trussed me up like a Thanksgiving turkey, and placed me in the cellar. My hands were tied, but I could reach the food and water with my mouth. If I rationed it well, it was enough to last for several weeks. Just before he closed the door on me, he reminded me that I had aced survival training. 'So survive, you son of a bitch,' he said.

"The gunshot wound was painful, but I knew that if it didn't get infected, it wasn't life-threatening. It took me twenty-four hours—I'm guessing—to get my hands free. He knew I would eventually, but he also knew it would take me a while, if ever, to get out.

"The area was about eight feet square. The ceiling was about four inches above my head, and from the ceiling to the barn floor was a foot of hardpacked earth supported by lodgepoles. Of course, I didn't know that until I got out."

"What about the door?"

"Wood. But he'd placed two steel I-beams over it. I suppose they were leftovers from the construction of the house. He'd drilled three holes into the door for ventilation. The beams were placed parallel, about an inch and a half apart, just the diameter of the air holes, lengthwise along the door. Then he'd scattered hay over them. A casual observer would never have noticed."

"I sent a man out there."

"One of mine?" When David nodded, Spence said, "Then he's dead meat. He should have gone over every square inch of that place."

"How'd you get out?"

"I clawed my way. The food—dry pasta and bread mostly, some cereal—didn't provide me anything to work with."

"What about the water containers?"

"Styrofoam. No lids, no straws. I had nothing but these," he said, holding up his hands. "Eventually I was able to create a hole, outside the perimeter of the door and away from the beams, large enough for me to wiggle through. If the ceiling of the cellar had been any higher, I couldn't have reached it. There was nothing to stand on except my bare feet."

"Lucky for you the barn floor wasn't concrete."

"Gray built that place on the site of a pioneer home, and probably wanted to preserve some of its character." Spence grinned, but it was a chilling expression. "He's always been stupidly sentimental."

"He's here, you know."

"I figured."

David told Spence about his unannounced visit from Gray Bondurant, then filled him in on the events that had taken place during his absence. "It was damn rotten luck," he said of Jayne Gaston's death. "George was gradually increasing Vanessa's dosage of lithium, but recording what it should have been. When he ordered a stronger sedative, the nurse staged a revolt. He tried to have her forcibly removed. She went into cardiac arrest and died. Then your favorite reporter, and mine—"

"I know," Spence said. "I read the article in the *Post* and couldn't believe she was still among the living. Nobody could have walked away from that explosion, David."

"Her dog went into the town house ahead of her."

"Talk about rotten luck."

"After the incident in Shinlin, Clete is on her case. She's been publicly humiliated and professionally trashed. Hopefully, she's learned her lesson."

"Hopefully, but she's a slow learner."

"You're right." David nodded solemnly. "What about Gray?"

"For now, I think my return should be kept our secret, don't you?"

"But surely you were seen coming in tonight."

"I'll have the guards told that keeping my return confidential is a matter of national security. My men will circulate the rumor that there've been threats made on the life of the First Lady—something to that effect."

"That's good. It'll serve our purpose."

Spence looked at him. "Then you're still committed to it?"

David, thinking back on the recent scene with Vanessa, said, "More than ever. I've been with her tonight. She's still obsessed with the baby's death. Our problem hasn't gone away."

Spence, looking directly into his own reflection in the mirror above the sink, said, "Then we have a lot of work to do."

"First things first." David rose. "I can't tell you how much I missed you, or how glad I am to have you back. Now please, for God's sake, take a bath."

Chapter Twenty-Five

"*M*s. Travis, your conduct is inexcusable."

"I'm well aware of the magnitude of my mistake, Mr. Jenkins. It's been a humiliating experience for me."

Frowning sternly, WVUE's general manager continued. "Senator Armbruster called—personally—to give me his version of what happened. His account was even more detailed than the news stories. I listened with increasing dismay over your rank unprofessionalism, and I'm flabbergasted to know that an employee of this station could behave in such a manner."

"I regret causing you and WVUE any embarrassment. If I could undo it, I would."

It was in her best interest to appear penitent, and she was, for the mistake she'd made. But she resented Armbruster going behind her back and tattling as though she were a wayward child. If he'd had more to say to her, he should have said it to her face.

"Compared to the enormity of your error, the consequences were minimal. Thank God. The President's press conference helped to put the incident in perspective."

"Yes, sir, it did."

"All's well that ends well."

This chirping comment came from Howie Fripp, who'd been called in on the carpet with her. Up till now he'd been gnawing on a hangnail and sweating rings into the underarms of his dingy white shirt. Barrie knew that his anxiety wasn't for her. He cared only about his own hide and how intact it would be when the general manager was finished.

Jenkins pounced. "It was you who actually dispatched the cameraman, wasn't it, Fripp?"

"Uh, yeah, but only because Barrie called and told me to. She said she was sitting on the story of the century."

"God forbid," Jenkins said.

It stuck in her craw, but she felt obligated to defend Howie. "Howie can't be held responsible, Mr. Jenkins. I called him at home and asked him to dispatch a photographer." Her cheeks grew hot beneath the general manager's baleful stare. "One of the many decisions I've come to regret."

She regretted it because having the media there had turned a bad situation into a disaster. But that call also twinged her conscience because it had been made out of spite. She'd been miffed at Gray for rejecting her expression of sympathy. She'd never been a Clete Armbruster fan. As to Vanessa, until Barrie had been swept up into a phantom intrigue that threatened her life, she had looked upon the First Lady with barely concealed derision. And, as long as she was being honest with herself, she confessed to feeling jealous of Vanessa because Gray was still in love with her.

So when Barrie dialed Howie and delivered her urgent message that night, she hadn't been feeling charitable toward any of them. Exit objectivity.

Oh, the call had been justified. Selfish, maybe, but justified. Given that set of circumstances, no reporter in the history of journalism would have failed to call for backup. It could have been the story that launched her career into superstardom.

In retrospect, however, it made her appear as insensitive as a dyspeptic vulture. She supposed she was getting her just deserts.

Jenkins said, "Armbruster could sue our ass nine ways from Sunday over this, and frankly, I couldn't blame him if he did."

"Senator Armbruster had good reason to be upset," Barrie said meekly. "I put him through several minutes of hell, for which I apologized profusely. I've also called the White House numerous times, hoping to personally make amends to the President and First Lady. They refuse to take my calls."

"I can't imagine why," Howie muttered.

Jenkins shot him a dirty look.

Barrie continued, "I wish to let President and Mrs. Merritt know how grievously I regret my mistake and to apologize for any distress I might have caused them."

"Very noble of you, Ms. Travis. But if and when they accept your call, do not represent yourself as an employee of WVUE." He clasped his hands together on his desktop and looked at her levelly. "As of now, your association with this television station is terminated."

She had fervently feared this. Just as fervently, she had denied that it could actually happen. While dealing with the more immediate repercussions of her blunder, she'd managed to hold off her dread of dismissal. Now, she was forced to confront the reality of it.

"I'm fired?"

"You have one hour to clear out your desk and leave the building."

"Please reconsider, Mr. Jenkins. I've learned my lesson. From now on, I'll be scrupulously careful. I'll check out every fact."

"It's too late, Ms. Travis. Nothing you say will change my mind."

She threw herself on his mercy. "You know about my town house."

"Yes. Bad timing."

"I need my job."

"I'm sorry. The decision has been made."

Her mind in chaos, she began grasping at straws. "Okay, take me off the street and keep me in the newsroom."

"Ms. Travis—"

"I'll write copy. I'll edit scripts. I'll answer the telephone, run the teleprompter, deliver the mail, go for sandwiches. It'll be like probation. Then in a few months you can reevaluate me."

"Please, don't embarrass yourself further," he said in the firm but kindly voice one reserves for the hopelessly doomed. "You no longer fit in with our program."

"What does that mean?"

"It means that your standards don't meet ours. It means that you haven't lived up to our expectations of you. It means that I'm terminating you for an accumulation of offenses, not just for this one in particular."

"Bullshit."

Howie winced.

Jenkins looked rather taken aback himself. "I beg your pardon?"

"Why don't you try being a man about it, Jenkins? Admit the real reason you're firing me—because Armbruster demanded my head on a platter."

Jenkins's face turned red, letting her know she'd hit the nail on the head. She stood up and pulled herself to her full height. "You've got it backward, Jenkins. This piddling TV station with its second-rate reputation and chickenshit management no longer fits in with *my* program."

"Want fries with that?"

Barrie considered the fat and calorie content of the french fries against her craving for them. "Sure. Why not? Large."

She paid for the take-out cheeseburger and fries and returned to her car. She was dining alone tonight. After months of encouraging Daily to get out more, he had chosen tonight to heed her advice, and had accepted the invitation of an old newsroom crony to go to a Brigitte Bardot film festival.

"Is he driving you?" Anytime he went out alone, especially after dark, she worried about him.

"Yes, *Mother*. He's picking me up and bringing me home. And before you ask, I'll check my oxygen tank and make sure it's full, although if I pant over the young Bardot as much as I hope to, I might run out of air before I get home. And if I jerk off, I'll die gasping, but happy."

He'd added that last just to irritate her. She hadn't told him that she'd been fired, because she knew he would insist on staying home to console her. No sense in both of them being miserable.

Following the meeting in Jenkins's office, one of the station's rent-a-cops had escorted her back to her cubicle and hovered over her as she cleaned out her desk. She was so infuriated at being treated like a criminal that she said snidely to the guard, "What does this dump have that I could possibly want to steal?"

"Nothing personal, Ms. Travis. Company policy."

"Yeah, yeah."

Having already removed everything from her hard drive and stored it on diskettes, she emptied her desk drawers of files, notes, and scripts dating back almost to the day she was employed. She unceremoniously dumped everything into crates, which the station had provided, then the guard helped her carry the boxes to her car and load them into the trunk.

Disinclined to spend the evening alone in Daily's depressing house, she debated where to take her picnic supper. The Lincoln Memorial? The Jefferson? Both looked beautiful by night. Still undecided, she pulled out into traffic.

"Barrie?"

She screamed and stomped on the brake.

"Don't look back and don't stop."

The car behind her screeched to a halt, missing her rear bumper by a hair. The furious driver leaned on his horn, then whipped his Honda Civic around her and shot her the finger.

"Take a right at the next intersection," Gray instructed from the corner of the backseat. He was slouched so low, his head wasn't visible in the rearview mirror.

"You scared the hell out of me," she shouted angrily, but she followed his instructions.

"It's really stupid for a woman alone not to check the backseat before she gets into her car."

"The car was locked."

"*I* got in."

His reasonable remark infuriated her. "I figured you were back in Wyoming playing cowboy by now. Why'd you leave me the other night to face the music alone? That was damned cowardly of you. And what are you doing in my car anyway? How'd you know where I was?"

"Go left up ahead, then immediately get into the right-hand lane and take the first street. Is there a green sedan about three cars back?"

"Am I being followed?"

"Check your rearview mirror, but don't make it obvious."

"Uh, no . . . yeah. There's a green car half a block back."

"Lose them, Barrie."

"Lose them? You've lost me. How do you know that car's following me?"

"You've had a tail all day."

"How do you know?"

"Because I've been tailing the tail."

"Pray tell, Mr. Incredible Vanishing Man, why I should believe you."

"Lose the tail and lose the attitude, okay? Try not to let them know you're dodging them."

Although she had a hundred questions to ask him, she concentrated on her driving. "This is fun," she said when she managed to speed through a light that trapped the green sedan.

"Oh yeah, lots," Gray grumbled from the backseat.

After about ten minutes of erratic driving, she told him that the green sedan was no longer in sight.

"Get on a straightaway. Head out of the city. Make sure another car hasn't taken up where the other left off."

She kept a close watch on her mirror. After a while, she told him she was almost certain no one was following them.

"Okay. First chance you get, turn around and go back the way we came."

"What for?"

"I've got a room."

❦

In the motel room registered to him under an assumed name, Barrie shared her cheeseburger and fries. There was a small end table and one chair near the window, but they dined sitting cross-legged in the center of the double bed.

"I got fired," she told him as she stuffed the used napkins and wrappers back into the sack. "My sincere apologies weren't enough for Senator Armbruster. He called the station manager this morning and got me canned."

"You can't be surprised."

"I guess not. Armbruster hasn't survived this long in politics by fighting fair, and serious ass-kissing is part of Jenkins's job. So, no, I'm not all that surprised. Then, to make a lousy day even lousier, I learned that Cronkite died as a result of my own carelessness."

"How's that?"

"That was the ATF's ruling on the explosion. My dog tripped over an electrical cord when he entered the kitchen through his trapdoor. The socket sparked and ignited natural gas from the oven, which I'd left on when I went to Wyoming. Without any ventilation, the gas had compressed. It wouldn't have taken much of a spark to ignite it, they said. Luckily, my homeowner's insurance will cover the full loss." With a sad smile, she added, "Of course, Cronkite wasn't covered."

"Your house was torched and your dog was killed, but don't worry, ma'am, it's covered by insurance," he said bitterly.

"Didn't you hear me, Gray? It was an accident."

"Like hell. When did you last use your oven?"

"I don't remember."

"Have you ever turned off the pilot light?"

"No."

"Have you ever stretched an electrical cord across the path of the back door?"

He was voicing questions she'd already asked herself. Hearing them from him only made her more determined to deny the obvious answers. "But the investigation—"

"Was right on. That's exactly how the explosion

occurred because somebody set it up to happen like that. Spence wouldn't have had his guy plant a sophisticated bomb. Anything elaborate would have created complications in the cover-up.

"He arranged it before leaving for Wyoming, and he opted for simplicity. Actually it was a no-brainer. Duck soup. You lived alone, so a lover or elderly parent or roommate wasn't going to be an obstacle. You were out of town, so there was time for the gas to accumulate. The explosion was planned and executed to look like an accident due to your oversight. It was a fluke that Cronkite went in ahead of you. They couldn't have foreseen that."

"They?"

"David Merritt sanctioned it."

She shook her head. "Baloney. You're basing that on the assumption that he had a big bad secret, and I was getting too close to uncovering it," she said. "We know better now. I was wrong about Vanessa and the baby's death and . . . everything. So were you. We were wrong. Right?"

"Why'd you have someone tailing you all day today? Even if there is nothing to your story—and I still contend there is—David never forgives a slight. Whether or not the allegation is true, your implied accusation pissed him off enough to have you killed."

Her bravado collapsed. "Do you think he'll try again?"

"That's a safe assumption."

"Good thing I've already had my supper," she murmured. "I just lost my appetite."

"There's one last french fry."

"I'll split it with you." She broke the cold french fry in two, put one half in her mouth, and extended the other to him. He surprised her by nibbling it straight from her fingers.

At the touch of his lips against his fingers, delicious sensations spiraled through her. Her limbs suddenly felt heavy, but her tummy floated weightlessly. She began to tingle, even to the tips of her toes.

Toes that she set firmly on the floor as she stood up. "I'm not going to sleep with you, Bondurant. In case that's what you have in mind, I want to save you the embarrassment and the physical discomfort of getting all worked up for nothing."

"I don't embarrass, and I'm very comfortable, thanks. Am I to assume that you used the word *sleep* euphemistically?"

"You know what I meant."

He looked at her for a moment. "I know what you meant, but I don't recall asking."

"That's right, you didn't. You don't. You didn't ask the first time."

"I didn't have to."

There was no point in arguing that. He hadn't needed to woo her that morning in Wyoming, so why had she presumed that he planned a fancy seduction tonight?

"I'm going to take a shower," she mumbled. She picked up her satchel, carrying it and her smarting pride into the tiny bathroom and closing the door.

Chapter
Twenty-Six

"A man painted me once."

"Painted you?"

She'd come out of the bathroom wearing only her sweater and panties. She smelled like soap and damp skin, some of which he'd glimpsed when she quickly pulled her sweater over her head before sliding between the sheets. He'd taken up a sentry post in the chair near the window, where he took periodic peeks through the blinds and was doing his damnedest not to think about a clean-smelling, seminaked Barrie Travis only a few yards away.

"I don't mean he painted my body," she clarified. "He painted me on canvas. I posed nude for him."

"How come? Need the money?"

"No, it wasn't that. I was in college, feeling frisky and rebellious and wanting to do something outrageous and that my parents would definitely disapprove of. He asked, and I thought, what the hell. As long as he kept his studio warm."

"How'd it go?" Gray asked.

"His studio turned out to be a ratty attic apartment that

smelled of turpentine and unwashed artist. He smoked a lot of pot, drank a lot of cheap wine, and was very morose and moody."

"What about the painting?"

"It was a disaster. A few of my body parts got lost in the translation. He felt he'd been betrayed by his own labor of love. He was in the throes of an artistic tirade when I collected my clothes and sneaked out. But he did hold to his promise to keep the place warm."

Gray's snuffle could have passed for a laugh. "Was he the one who taught you how to give head?" After a moment, when it became obvious that she wasn't going to reply, he turned toward her.

She was lying on her side, facing him, knees drawn to her waist. Her hair was tumbling around her face and over her bare shoulders, childlike. Which had been one of the first things he'd found intriguing about her—that irresistible combination of womanly allure and childish vulnerability. Of course now, weeks later, when the snug heat of her was still vivid in his memory, there was no question that she was more woman than child.

Her expressive eyes showed a mix of innocent perplexity and hurt. "Why do you do that, Bondurant?"

"What?" he asked.

"Why do you say things intentionally crude, insulting and hurtful?"

"It wasn't meant that way. I was trying to tease you. I guess I'm not very good at it."

"I'd say you're pretty lousy at it."

"Character flaw."

A long moment passed before she said in a whisper, "The artist taught me nothing except to keep away from artists. As for learning how to . . . I sort of, hmm, developed my technique as I went along." After a significant pause, she added in an even softer voice, "That morning at your ranch house."

His body responded to the erotic memory, making the damned uncomfortable chair even more uncomfortable. Nor could he comfortably look into her eyes. He didn't want to be her virgin voyage on any sexual adventure. That gave him significance. With significance came a responsibility he wasn't certain he could handle. Changing the subject, he asked, "What brought that story to mind? About the painter."

She gave a shrug. "I don't know. I guess I didn't know what else to say."

"That's a real thing with you."

"What?"

"Always feeling the need to *say* something."

"That's not true."

"See?"

She made a face. "Very funny."

"Yeah, I'm a regular comedian. People tell me that all the time. That I'm a comedian and a tease."

He didn't even crack a smile, but she laughed. Giggled actually, rolling onto her back and flinging her arms over her head. He hadn't been around laughter much, not since he'd been an adult. Her laughter was as enticing as her voice, genuine and spontaneous. He liked the sound of it.

"Thanks, Bondurant," she said. "After the day I've had, I needed a good laugh. Although I should be used to it by now."

"What?" he asked.

"Getting sacked. This isn't the first time."

"Was Daily the first to fire you?"

She cocked her head inquisitively.

"He told me."

"Oh, well, that was good of him," she said, meaning exactly the opposite.

"Idle conversation."

"Yeah, right. While enlightening you on my turbulent professional history, did he happen to mention why he had fired me?"

He shook his head. He was lying. Daily had told him the story with a great deal of elaboration. But he couldn't get enough of her voice, even though a steady diet of it was jeopardizing his resolve to keep his hands off her. When running for your life, a romantic interlude isn't in the program.

"Well," she began, smiling at the memory, "Daily and I didn't start out as friends. He gave me my first job in TV news. Of course, I thought I knew everything there was to know about broadcast journalism, so from the get-go I resented even constructive criticism. Daily thought I was an airhead who had nothing to contribute to the profession.

"Not long after he hired me, he started looking for reasons to fire me. But he was shackled by FCC, and EEO, and a whole alphabet soup of hiring and firing regulations. But Daily got a break. I self-destructed."

She'd been first on the scene at a county courthouse where a gunman had opened fire inside a courtroom. Based on the testimony of a woman who'd narrowly escaped a hail of bullets, Barrie reported that dozens of people had been wounded.

"In the 'bloody melee.' I think that was my exact wording."

Then, on live television, she reported that the shooting was taking place in Judge Green's court. "That made it even more of a story because it was rumored that he was under consideration for a seat on the Supreme Court. On camera I speculated on whether the shooting was politically motivated. Was Judge Green the target of an opposing radical, or was this retribution for an unpopular ruling? Had he survived, or was he wounded?"

As it turned out, Judge Green was on the golf course when a caddie came to tell him of the unfolding story. The incident had occurred in another court, and the only thing wounded was the ceiling light fixture, which had been shot out during the struggle between the bailiff and a man who'd brought his deer rifle to court to use as evidence in a civil suit involving poaching.

"My eyewitness was later identified as the mentally challenged woman who refilled iced tea and water glasses in the basement cafeteria. As far as anyone knew, she had never been above the first floor of the building.

"Sealing my fate was the fact that my special report had interrupted *The Young and the Restless*. Judge Green's wife never missed an episode. When she heard my report, she ran from the house, fell over a sprinkler head in their yard, and broke her right wrist. Other viewers were incensed over the program interruption, especially when they learned that there had been no drama at the courthouse, certainly none to rival the soap opera script. They melted the switchboard with irate calls.

"My credibility was shot to hell. The station's as well. The newsroom suffered the scorn of our competitors. And just in case somebody missed it, the TV critics in the local newspapers used it as fodder for days. Daily was taken to the woodshed and thrashed by the station's management for hiring me. It's a wonder he kept his job. He fired me in a heartbeat. The only one who benefitted was Judge Green, who is now a Supreme Court justice."

"An unpopular one."

"Which is another point in my loss column. More than one pundit editorialized that if not for the sympathy Judge Green garnered as a result of my fiasco, his nomination would never have been approved. The American people have me to thank for sticking them with an ineffectual

Supreme Court justice. Daily holds to that theory, by the way."

"With all that between you, how'd you get to be friends?"

"A few years ago I heard through the press corps grapevine that he'd been forced to retire because of his emphysema. I felt duty-bound to pay him a courtesy call." She gave a small Mona Lisa smile, and Gray asked what the secret was.

"Daily admitted that he'd been unusually hard on me because what I lacked wasn't talent, but maturity and common sense. He was willing to help me if I'd shut up and listen. He's been my best friend ever since."

"Why do you keep your friendship a secret?"

"Mainly because it's personal, and I've always been a stickler for keeping my personal and professional lives separate. Second, because . . ."

"Because if it got around that you'd kissed and made up with your former enemy, you'd lose the respect of your colleagues."

"Very perceptive, Mr. Bondurant. When you burn a bridge in broadcasting, it's usually a conflagration, and usually for keeps. If anyone knew I was friends with Daily now, I'd be regarded as softie trying to hack it in a cutthroat career."

Her smile was so ingenuous, he hated to be the one to ruin it. "Your secret's out, Barrie. I've been following them following you. They know where you're staying." At her anguished groan, he added quickly, "I don't think they'll bother Daily. But we should advise him first thing tomorrow."

"Why are they following me?"

"Most of the Secret Service agents assigned to David, Vanessa, and the White House are Spence's men. They went through the recruitment program and met all the standards, but they're his."

"How can they flout the regulations?"

"That's the beauty of it. They don't flout them. They maneuver with the adaptability of quicksilver. If anyone questions them, they can say that you fall into the category of an emotionally disturbed person who merits watching."

"To say the least," she muttered.

"Try and get some sleep."

He got up and turned off the lamp, then returned to the window and peeked through the blinds. For five minutes he watched the parking lot for any suspicious cars or movement.

Satisfied that they had eluded the surveillance, he glanced at the bed and was disconcerted to find Barrie watching him. "I thought you'd gone to sleep."

Again, she was lying on her side, but now her hands were stacked palm to palm beneath her cheek. "Who are you, Gray Bondurant?"

"Me? I'm nobody."

"Not true," she said sleepily. "You're somebody."

"Go to sleep."

"You need rest too. The bed is wide enough for both of us."

No way in hell could he crawl in with her and not partake of that skin, that voice. "I'm going to sit up for a while."

"What for?"

"So I can think."

"About what?"

"Go to sleep, Barrie."

"One more question?"

"Okay," he sighed.

"That morning at your house, that was no-strings-attached sex, right?"

"Right."

She lowered her eyes for several seconds, then looked up at him again. "Pretty terrific sex, though."

He smiled in the darkness. "Pretty terrific."

"But you didn't kiss me. Not on the lips. What have you got against mouth-to-mouth kissing?"

"That's two questions. Good night."

"George?"

His wife's voice seemed to come to him from a distant shore across an ocean of scotch. Dr. Allan raised his head and saw Amanda silhouetted in the open doorway of his home office. She looked lovely, desirable, and strong. He couldn't stand the sight of her. Her strength accentuated his weakness.

She came into the room. When she reached the desk, she picked up the liquor bottle and checked the amount remaining in the bottom of it. Even in his inebriated state, the silent rebuke didn't escape him.

Querulously he said, "What is it, Amanda?"

"So you do remember me. I'm glad to know that. Do you by any chance recall that you also have two sons?"

"Is this a riddle?"

"Your older son is withdrawing a little deeper into himself each day. I've begged him to tell me what's troubling him, but he becomes sullen and silent. His teachers at school have had similar experiences lately. He bottles up his problems inside himself, and no one can pry them out. He's so like you, it frightens me.

"I've just come from your younger son's bedside, where I listened to his prayers. He asked God to help Daddy, then he started crying, and I had to hold him until he fell asleep."

George rubbed his tired, bloodshot eyes. "I'll go in and kiss them good night later."

"You're missing the point. I don't want you to kiss them good night. Not in your present condition. They're not stupid, you know. They know that something is terribly wrong with you, and it goes beyond the drinking."

" 'The Drinking'? Like it's a proper noun?"

"It's become one. What's the matter with you?"

"Nothing."

"Oh really? Would you call the last forty-eight hours typical? You came home yesterday morning looking like something out of a fright film. God knows how long it had been since you slept. You didn't offer me a single word of explanation for your lengthy absence or how you looked. You didn't ask after my well-being or the children's. You came straight up to this room and sequestered yourself and haven't come out since."

For emphasis, she slammed the bottle back onto the desk. "You're stinking drunk, and I've heard you crying. The first makes me angry, and the second breaks my heart. George," she said imploringly, "how can I help you if you won't tell me what's wrong?"

"Nothing's wrong."

"Dammit, George, when did your definition of marriage change?"

"Whaddaya mean?"

"If you won't confide in me, then we don't have a marriage, not the kind we pledged to each other. But on paper at least I'm still you're wife, and I demand to know what the hell is going on."

"Christ, are you deaf?" he shouted. "*Nothing's wrong.*"

She didn't back away from his mounting anger. Coldly, she said, "Don't lie to me. You're coming apart before my eyes."

"Leave me alone."

"No, I won't," she said, giving her smooth bob a hard shake. "You're my husband. I love you. I'll defend you with my dying breath. But first I have to know what has turned you from a fine physician, husband, and father, into a blubbering drunk."

He glared at her, but she didn't back down. Amanda had a merciless stubborn streak. "Your problem has something to do with David, doesn't it? Don't bother to lie. I know he's at the root of your personal crisis. What brought it about?"

"Drop it, Amanda."

"What did he ask you to do?"

"I said to drop it."

"What kind of control does he have over you?"

"He doesn't!"

"He does!" she shouted right back. "And if you don't break that control, he's going to destroy you."

He lunged to his feet, banging the desktop with his fists. "The woman died, okay?"

"What?"

"There, I've said it. I've confided my problem to you. Are you happy now? Satisfied?"

"You're talking about the nurse."

"Yeah, the nurse. The one who died in our lake house three days ago. Sudden cardiac death." He bowed his head and clasped it between his hands. "I tried to get her back, but I failed. I failed and she died." His shoulders heaved on a sob.

"Were you drunk?"

"I'd taken one Valium, that's all."

"Did you do everything you could?"

He nodded. "I tried for half an hour to resuscitate her. Finally the Secret Service agents pulled me off her and said it was no use, that I was wasting my time."

Amanda drew a staggering little breath and laid her hand on his shoulder. "I'm sorry, George," she said gently.

He longed to accept her sympathy. He knew her arms would welcome him in spite of the angry words they'd exchanged. Her breasts would be soft, her voice soothing, her embrace a haven he could crawl into and perhaps hide from his demons for a while.

But he didn't deserve her consolation or her forgiveness. His rank unworthiness caused him to resent her for extending such unconditional love. So he rebuffed it and shrugged off her hand. "What could you have done?" he asked belligerently. "What miracle would you have worked to make the problem disappear?"

He turned his back on her and lurched to the liquor cabinet. Opening another bottle of scotch seemed to require more dexterity than his fingers were capable of, but he managed to get it open and pour himself another drink.

"Oh, no, wait," he said, turning back to Amanda. "You can solve any problem, right? You can do everything you set out to do. Achievement is your middle name. No, make that Excel. Excel is your middle name."

He knew that the scathing words hurt her deeply, but he couldn't stop himself from saying them. He wanted somebody to feel as rotten as he did, and Amanda was the only one around. But she refused to be provoked. She maintained her composure.

"I couldn't have solved your problem, George, but I could have sympathized."

"Lot of good that would have done."

"You've lost patients before. Because you're a healer, you naturally take it hard when nothing you do can save a patient. But you've never been this disconsolate."

Tilting her head, she peered into his eyes. He was drunk, but not so far gone that he didn't fear she would read more in them than he wanted her to know. He looked away. Not soon enough.

"I'm getting the expurgated version of this story, aren't I?" she said. "What else happened at the lake house?"

"Who says something else happened?"

She gave him a retiring look. "I know you, George. You're omitting some crucial element of the story."

"The nurse bought it. That's it."

"It concerns Vanessa, doesn't it?"

"No."

"Then what made this woman's death—"

"What do you want from me?" he bellowed. "You asked what was bothering me, and I told you. Now get the fuck out of here and leave me the fuck alone!"

He'd never used that kind of vituperative language with her. He couldn't believe he had now, although the words seemed to reverberate off the paneled walls, echoing their vulgarity. Had he stooped so low as to verbally abuse his wife? The thought was like an anchor that dragged him deeper into an abyss of depression and self-disgust. He downed his drink quickly.

Amanda, her own disgust apparent, walked away from him. At the door, she turned around. "Yell and curse at me, George, if it makes you feel any better. I'm tough. I can take it."

She raised her left fist so he'd be certain to see her wedding ring. "David Merritt took an oath of office, but so did I, at the altar on our wedding day. I pledged that nothing short of death would part us, and I meant it. You're my husband, and I love you. I'm not going to surrender you without a fight. I'll do everything within my power to prevent this man from destroying you, even if he happens to be the President of the United States."

Chapter
Twenty-Seven

"Not that again," Daily groused.

Barrie had tuned his television to VH-1 and set the volume at a deafening level. "Gray thinks your house is under surveillance."

"Bugged, too?"

"They don't need to bug it to eavesdrop," Gray told him. "The equipment is so sophisticated, they can listen to conversations from blocks away."

" 'They'?"

"Spence's men."

"Bastards," Daily muttered. Then he nodded toward Gray and said to Barrie, "I thought he split."

"So did I. He, uh, surprised me last night."

"I got home from the Bardot film festival late," he said. "You weren't here. I worried all night."

Meekly, she said, "I forgot to call."

Daily indicated that they should take their usual seats on the sofa. "Am I to assume that the story's not over yet? You still think the baby's death was no accident?"

"I think that's a given," Gray replied. "This whole thing

started with that, and now it's escalated into something even bigger. David's trying to keep a cap on it, but he's having a hard time of it. Spence failed to take me out. Things at George Allan's lake house went awry when the nurse died.

"Her death left Dr. Allan exposed at a time when neither he nor David wanted exposure," he conjectured. "It brought a halt to whatever witch-doctoring he was practicing on Vanessa."

Barrie picked it up from there. "Because the nurse's death would eventually come to light and focus attention on Vanessa's health, he had to . . . *revive* her, for lack of a better word, and hustle her back to Washington."

"On the morning of the press conference they made her visible to the whole world," Gray said. "To anyone who doesn't know her well, she appeared normal. I think she's still in danger."

"What makes you think so?" Daily asked. "It all seemed very pat to me. Neely read the First Lady's eulogy to the nurse. The Merritts' thoughts and prayers are with her family. Blah, blah, blah."

"Vanessa was sending a distress signal," Gray said. "She wasn't wearing her mother's wedding ring," he explained. "It's been on the ring finger of her right hand since Clete placed it there the day her mother died. That morning, it was notably absent. She kept bringing her hand into view, especially when she knew the cameras were on her. I think she wanted someone to notice that she wasn't wearing it."

Daily said, "You really think she was signaling for help?"

"Yes."

"The ring could have been misplaced," Barrie argued. "Maybe it wouldn't stay on because of all the weight she lost. Or she might simply have grown tired of it. It could have been at the jeweler's being resized or cleaned. There are dozens of plausible reasons for her not wearing it."

"That's right, there are," Gray said. "If I were back in Wyoming watching her on TV and saw that she wasn't wearing it, I might be mildly curious, but not necessarily alarmed.

"However," he continued, coming to his feet, "since Spence was sent to ice me, since I witnessed your house being vaporized, and since I know that surveillance teams are following you, I'm inclined to be more than mildly curious."

"And I think you're right," Barrie admitted grudgingly. "That press conference was Vanessa's only public appearance since her 'seclusion.' If she's as healthy as the White House claims, she would have launched back into her schedule, right?" On impulse, she picked up Daily's phone and dialed a number she had committed to memory.

"Who're you calling?" Gray asked.

"Vanessa's office."

"Remember, everything you say is probably being monitored."

"They'll just assume I'm up to my old tricks. Turn down the TV."

The sudden silence was as jarring as the racket had been. "Good morning," Barrie said pleasantly when her call was answered. "My name is Sally May Henderson. I represent the Daughters of the American Revolution. We would very much like to present the First Lady with one of our distinguished service awards in recognition of her ongoing campaign to feed and shelter the homeless."

She emphasized that the organization wished to present the award in person. "The publicity would bring to the nation's attention the continued need for the shelters and soup kitchens the First Lady has been so instrumental in organizing." Politely, but firmly, she was told that a meeting wasn't possible in the near future. The First Lady was still recovering from her recent indisposition.

"I see. Well, please extend to her our warmest regards. We'll be in touch again." She hung up and turned to Daily and Gray. "Her staff has been instructed not to schedule any appointments for her until they get the go-ahead from Dr. Allan."

Gray turned up the volume on the TV again, then said, "David is going for broke."

"It seems so."

Daily was rubbing his jaw, looking worried. "Are you suggesting what I think you are?"

Bondurant said, "Vanessa has become less of an asset and more of a liability. David eliminates liabilities."

"You're guessing," Daily stressed.

"Uh-uh. I know." Gray returned to the sofa and sat down. For a moment no one said anything.

Finally, Barrie spoke up. "My career has been a joke. I've screwed up more often than not. God knows, my gut instinct is anything but reliable. But this time I *know* I'm right. Our president is a criminal." She looked up at Gray. "I may distrust my instincts, but I trust yours."

"Thanks." He glanced at Daily, then back at her. "Look, you two should take an extended vacation, somewhere out of the country. If David is convinced that you've given up, that you're no longer a threat, he'll relax his vigilance. I'll take it from here, and hopefully save Vanessa before David can implement plan B."

"Not bloody likely," Barrie said heatedly. "We're talking about the attempted murder of the First Lady. As a citizen, I can't turn my back on that. Not only that, but I was the first one Vanessa approached for help. If I hadn't misread the signs, she might be safely with her father now. Because I dropped the ball, she's still under her husband's tyranny.

"And it's because of his treachery that I've lost everything that was important to me. Cronkite, my home, my job. I've got a vendetta against that son of a bitch in the Oval Office. And God help him. Because I'm the worst kind of enemy to have. One who has nothing left to lose."

"Except your hide," Daily said, wheezing.

"No," she said softly, "except *you,* Daily."

"Don't turn those teary eyes on me, missy. You've got shit for brains. Both of you," he said, cutting his eyes between her and Gray.

"How can we *not* expose Merritt for what he is?" she asked gently.

"You're talking crazy. Have you two listened to yourselves? He's the freaking President of the United States. The highest office in the land and the most powerful individual in the world. You fuck with him, you'll wind up dead."

Barrie looked at Gray and saw in his eyes a commitment that matched her own. Ironically, the very thing that had kept them apart now bound them together.

Turning back to Daily, she said, "If Merritt plans to have me killed, I at least want to put up a fight. But I refuse to place you in danger. Take the long vacation."

"You should leave this afternoon, as soon as arrangements can be made," Gray urged.

"Where would you like to go, Daily? Mexico?"

"And get the trots? Hell no."

"The Bahamas?"

"There's a hurricane in the Caribbean. Don't you watch the news?"

"Australia?"

"I'm not going anywhere," he said firmly. "Why would I leave and let you two have all the fun?"

"It's not going to be fun, Daily," Gray said with the manner of an undertaker. "You can't fuck around with these guys. When it comes to carrying out an assignment, they mean business. So we must mean business too. At the risk of sounding melodramatic, this could easily become a life-or-death situation."

"I'm already in a life-or-death situation," Daily retorted. He spread his arms to encompass the shabby room. "I've got less to lose than Barrie. I have an incurable disease. I've got no wife, no kids, nothing. The way I figure it, if I can help you, I won't die forgotten."

Barrie crossed the room, leaned down, and kissed the top of his head. "You're decrepit and ugly, but I love you dearly."

"Cut that out. I hate that mushy shit." He waved her off. "Okay, Bondurant, what do we do first?"

Chapter
Twenty-Eight

$\mathcal{B}$arrie smiled at Jayne Gaston's son across the threshold of his home. "Hello, Mr. Gaston. Barrie Travis. Do you remember me?"

"All too well. What do you want?"

"I brought you this," she said, holding out a potted blue hydrangea. "May I come in?"

He hesitated, deciding whether he would speak with her. Finally, he stepped aside. "For a few minutes."

Ralph Gaston, Jr., was a mild-mannered man in his midthirties who had gone soft around the middle. He lived in a neat brick house in the middle of the block in a middle-class suburb of D.C. Barrie had located him through the telephone directory.

She was led through rooms that were clean but littered with toys. "My wife took the kids to the mall," he explained as he stepped over a Playskool lawn mower.

"I'm sorry I missed them. I wanted to convey my condolences to them as well."

She followed him onto a screened back porch, where it appeared he'd been watching an NCAA football game on a portable TV. He turned down the volume and took a sip of the beer on the end table. He did not offer her anything to drink. She took a seat in the aluminum lawn chair he indicated.

Barrie began by clarifying that anything they said was strictly off the record. "I'm not here as a reporter. It might actually make you feel better to know that I was fired from WVUE."

"In fact it does make me feel better," he said bluntly. "You got no less than you deserved, Ms. Travis. My mother was a lady. She had dignity, and rarely called attention to herself. You made a black comedy out of her death. After the media circus you created at the hospital, I find it difficult to be civil to you."

"I don't blame you. More than anything, I regret that your bereavement was made so public."

"Are you trying to apologize?"

"Very much so."

"Apology accepted." He started to get up. "Now if you'll excuse—"

"Your mother must have been enormously excited when Dr. Allan hired her," Barrie said, forestalling him.

"What makes you say that?" His voice cracked like a whip, surprising her.

"Uh, well, because he placed so much trust in her."

"Oh," he said, visibly relaxing. "Yeah, she felt really fortunate to get such a good job. She said it was particularly gratifying to have such an important patient."

Barrie's journalistic instinct was sizzling like bacon in a hot skillet. What had she stumbled upon here? Her initial motive had been sincere: She had wished to apologize for her gaffe and its effect on the Gaston family.

But this meeting with Ralph Gaston was also part of her and Gray's strategy to protect Vanessa. They could hardly report the President's alleged crimes to the local police.

They had nothing substantive to take to the Justice Department. They couldn't assault the White House with guns blazing. Their attack had to be much more subtle.

Gray's view, with which Barrie and Daily concurred, was that the administration must be destroyed from within. It must collapse upon itself like a dying star. The energy of Merritt's presidency must, paradoxically, cause its own extinction.

Information was the only weapon available to them. They needed to know exactly what had happened in George Allan's lake house. Barrie had volunteered to start with Jayne Gaston's son. She hadn't really expected to learn anything of monumental importance, but maybe she had underestimated the potential of this interview.

Ralph had used words like *fortunate* and *gratifying* to describe his mother's feelings about her job as the First Lady's private nurse, which implied that she had felt unworthy of the post. Why? Barrie wondered.

"Did your mother have a history of heart problems?"

"Only for the past couple of years," Ralph said, somewhat defensively. "But she stayed on top of it. She got regular checkups, took her medication religiously. You couldn't keep Mom down if you tried. She loved her work. She was an excellent nurse."

"That's what I've heard. Dr. Allan raved about her. So did the President."

"He sent flowers to the funeral."

"Really? He sent me flowers once." In another lifetime. Before she knew that he was a killer. "Had your mother suffered a previous heart attack?"

"It was mild," he replied, resuming his defensive posture. "She recovered quickly. It never affected her work."

"No one has questioned her skills or her performance, Mr. Gaston."

He rubbed his hands over the tops of this thighs. Barrie recognized it as a nervous gesture. The middle-class suburbanite with the soft middle was no longer quite so mild-mannered. He said, "If Mom was good enough to attend the First Lady, she was good enough to attend anybody."

"Precisely."

"She was eminently qualified."

"I'm sure she was. How did she like working for Dr. Allan?"

"What do you mean?"

Barrie flashed him an insider's smile. "Just curious. You know how egotistical doctors can be. Some of them think they walk on water. I just wondered if that had been your mother's experience with Dr. Allan."

"She never said."

Barrie knew immediately that he was lying. "I take it your mother was satisfied that the First Lady was getting the proper treatment for her illness?"

"Mrs. Merritt didn't have an illness. She just needed a long rest."

"Of course. That's what I meant."

"No," he said, shaking his head, "you meant to imply that my mother would deliberately overlook it if a patient was receiving improper treatment."

"I implied no such thing, Mr. Gaston. The President has gone on record praising your mother and Dr. Allan for the excellent care they provided Mrs. Merritt."

"So what's your point?"

What *was* her point? "It's just a shame that for all his healing talent, Dr. Allan couldn't save your mother's life."

"He said he did everything he could."

"And you believe him?"

"Why wouldn't I? He's a great doctor and a decent man. He gave Mom a chance when no one else would."

"A chance?"

"To work." Suddenly he shot to his feet. "I don't want to talk about this anymore. My mother died only a few days ago. I'm still very upset."

"Of course. I'm sorry."

Barrie did not pressure him. She was coming away with much more than she had hoped to gain. Actually, she was leaving with more questions than answers and was eager to do some further investigating.

"It was awfully kind of you to see me." At the front door, she clasped his hand warmly. She believed that, like the rest of the nation, he had been conned by the men in power. So, although he had been borderline rude to her, she felt only pity for him. "Please convey my sympathy to the rest of your family, and, again, I apologize for any heartache I contributed."

~~

Ralph Gaston, Jr., watched as Barrie Travis made her way down the sidewalk and got into a car parked at the curb. He waited until she had driven away before moving hastily to the telephone.

His call was answered on the second ring.

Ralph had spoken with a federal agent only twice in his life—the day before yesterday, when one had appeared at his mother's wake, asking to speak with him alone, and now. Both times, his mouth had gone dry and his palms had grown wet.

"You told me to call if that reporter showed up. Well, she just left my house."

"You spoke with her?"

"Yes, sir. I wanted to slam the door in her face, but I did as you told me and tried to act casual."

"What did she want?"

"To apologize." He recounted their conversation, then answered all the man's questions with the crisp precision of a new recruit. "Mostly she asked leading questions about my mother's medical history and the treatment Mrs. Merritt received from Dr. Allan."

After a tense silence, the government man said, "You did well, Mr. Gaston. President Merritt will appreciate your assistance."

Ralph swallowed a lump of pride. His orders had come directly from the Commander in Chief. He'd been told that Barrie Travis's desire to malign the administration was fueled by an unnatural jealousy of the First Lady.

Barrie Travis was intensely antagonistic toward the White House, ergo she was an enemy of the nation. It was still undetermined how far her subversive tendencies would go, but after the incident in Shinlin they were operating on the side of caution. That's why the President had asked to be notified immediately if she called on the Gaston family seeking information, which she then might use to further her destructive purposes.

"I'll pass this information along to the President immediately," Gaston was told. "You executed your duty well."

"Thank you, sir. Glad to be of service. Is there anything else I can do?"

"Please notify me if she comes around again."

"I don't think she will," Gaston said. "She's been fired from the TV station. She wasn't here today as a reporter, just as a person."

"I seriously doubt that."

Spence replaced the telephone and turned to the President. "That was Gaston. He still thinks he's talking to an FBI agent. Guess who just paid him a courtesy call?"

"Dammit!"

When was this problem going to disappear? He had more important things to think about. He was on his way now to attend a meeting with the Joint Chiefs. Some disturbing Intelligence reports had been coming out of Libya. In a few weeks he'd receive the reconciliation bill on next year's budget. The cuts worked out by both houses of Congress would evoke the ire of special interest groups, and it would fall to him to pacify them. At the crux of every decision, of course, was how it might affect the outcome of next year's election.

These administrative matters required his concentration, but of necessity they were taking a back seat to this persistent problem. "She's worse than a stubborn dose of the clap," he grumbled. "She won't go away."

"She can. And so can Gray. We can pop them."

"Too risky, Spence. They've made too much news lately."

"But mostly with Clete. He's gone on record lambasting them. If they met with a violent end, the senator would be the first to fall under suspicion."

Merritt chewed on that. It was an appealing idea. One stone, two birds. Three, counting Clete. Spence's surveillance team was keeping them informed of every move made by Gray and Barrie Travis and that old man they were shacked up with. Wiping them out in one fell swoop was tempting. It would be expedient and neat. It was an enticing proposal, but . . . Too dicey.

"No, Spence."

"I've got people who could handle it. It would be so far removed from the White House that—"

Merritt held up his hand. "Bill Yancey is too much of a wild card," he said of the attorney general. "I can't chance it. Besides," he added, "your idea is self-serving. You want a shot at Bondurant."

"True. But it would also solve your problem."

"I want to solve the problem, but we've got to play it smart. They can't do too much harm as long as they don't get to Vanessa."

"Be reasonable, David. We can't keep her prisoner inside the White House indefinitely."

He looked at his aide. "No, we can't. Not when her condition is worsening again."

Their telepathy worked again to communicate Merritt's message. Spence nodded his understanding and reached for the telephone. "I'll call Dr. Allan to come immediately."

Merritt took the receiver from him. "And have another heart attack victim on our hands? George assumes you're dead. Better let me make this call."

Chapter
Twenty-Nine

"Where the hell have you been?" Gray demanded as soon as Barrie came through the front door. "You were due back two hours ago."

"I've been uncovering some very interesting information," she said. "Relax. I'm okay. I had my tail for company all afternoon. He peeled off at the last corner. I'm starving." She pitched her car keys to him. "Go get supper while I take a shower, then we'll talk."

An hour later, all three were clustered around the table in Daily's kitchen, the remains of their carryout meal congealing in white pasteboard containers. The radio was blaring from the corner.

Barrie apologized for worrying them. "I didn't call because I couldn't have said anything significant. You'll forgive me when I tell you what I found out."

"From Ralph Gaston, Jr.?"

"Indirectly." Keeping her voice well below the level of the radio, she described her meeting with the late nurse's son. "What was strange, he kept insisting that his mother was an excellent nurse."

"So?"

"So, nobody that I know of ever suggested otherwise. Why would he argue a point that hadn't been raised? That struck me as odd, so after I left him I did some investigating, including a call to one of my sources in the criminal justice building, who fed her name into the NCIC. Voilà! An arrest record and an a.k.a. turned up."

The two men quickly looked at each other, then back at Barrie. "For years following her marriage to Ralph Gaston, the nurse continued to use her maiden name professionally. Jayne Heisellman."

"That rings a bell," Daily said. "How come?"

"Because, a few years ago, a terminally ill patient died while in Heisellman's care. Euthanasia was suspected. She adamantly denied the allegation, but the devout Roman Catholic family of the patient went to the D.A. and demanded an investigation. The grand jury no-billed her for lack of evidence. The patient's death was ruled a consequence of pancreatic cancer and Heisellman was cleared of all suspicion."

"I remember now," Daily said.

"I should have," Barrie replied with chagrin. "It was one of the first stories I covered for WVUE. I didn't recognize her in the morgue. She had aged, and, well, the situation there wasn't conducive to instant recollection.

"Even though she was cleared of any criminal activity, the accusation brought on enough stress to cause her a heart attack. This too was documented in the press. She recovered, and after six months was given the green light to return to work. But not so easily done.

"The investigation left an indelible blot on her previously flawless record. She had been forced to leave the health care facility where the incident had occurred, and even after switching to her married name she was turned down for job after job."

"Let me guess," Gray said. "Until she was hired by Dr. Allan."

Barrie formed a pistol with her fingers and fired it at him. "Right on, sport."

"They hired a nurse who had been suspected of mercy killing—"

"In the event that Vanessa died *mercifully*. Or, if she died by other means and the nurse intended to talk, she could conveniently succumb to a heart attack."

"Which would've been feasible because of her history of cardiac complications."

Their thoughts were so in tune that they could complete each other's sentences. She finished by saying, "However it went down, they had an ideal scapegoat."

"Good work," Daily told her.

"Thanks," she said, basking in his compliment.

"Do you think Dr. Allan killed the nurse and passed it off as another heart attack?" he asked.

Gray absently scratched his cheek. "Possibly, but I don't think so. George is . . . I don't know, weak. He doesn't strike me as ruthless, as a man who could snuff someone in cold blood. He's not like Spence. Or David."

"I think the heart attack caught them all off guard. At the hospital, the doctor didn't act so much guilty as flustered." Turning to Barrie, he asked, "What about Gaston? Is he a player?"

"No. His only concern was for his mother's reputation."

"So where does all this leave us?" Daily wanted to know.

"I haven't the vaguest," Barrie replied with deflating honesty.

After a few moments of silent reflection, Daily said, "Well, I'm beat. Besides, that damn thing's driving me nuts." He shot the radio a murderous glare.

"Just don't let your frustration get the best of you again."

Too late, Barrie realized her mistake. She'd spoken without thinking. Daily gave her a fulminating look, which Gray's radarlike perception intercepted.

"What's going on?"

Daily said defensively, "See here, Bondurant, this is my house, and I do in it what I like, when I like."

Gray's expression was growing darker by the second. "If something happened that I need to know about—"

"Oh, for heaven's sake," Barrie cut in. "Let's not make a federal case of it. Daily got a little upset this morning. While you were out, a sedan kept driving past the house. He lost his temper, went out on the porch, and gave it the finger. That's all there was to it."

"Except that now they know we've marked them," Gray said, his displeasure clear.

"Daily didn't mean to—"

"I'll thank you not to defend me," Daily said curtly. Then he turned to Gray with as much defiance as he could muster. "Who are you to order me around in my own house?"

"This isn't a pissing contest between us, Daily." Gray's voice was softer and kinder than Barrie would have expected. "Anything I advise you to do is for your own safety. And Barrie's. I can't impress upon you enough how dangerous these men are. They're spoiling for a fight. Please don't give them one. I don't want your death on my conscience."

Daily looked like a child who'd been unfairly reprimanded. With a brief nod, he yielded to Gray's expertise. "Hell," he grumbled as he stood. "I'm going to bed."

Barrie volunteered to clear the kitchen and bade him good night. Gray followed him from the room. Since their treasonous conversation for the night was concluded, she turned off the radio and blessed the silence. When the kitchen was tidy, she turned out the light and went into the living room.

Gray was slumped in the far corner of the sofa, his head resting on the back cushions, his legs and feet stretched out in front of him. Barrie could barely make out his form in the darkness, which was unrelieved except for the jaundiced glow of the streetlight through the draperies.

For the first eighteen years of her life, she'd been overlooked by two people more intent on making each other unhappy than on the happiness of the child they'd conceived in a rare second of marital harmony. Perhaps that's why she'd chosen a profession where she was constantly seen and heard. Broadcast journalism wasn't for anyone who wished to keep a low profile. Once a neglected child, she now had high visibility. She'd been ridiculed and rebuked, but rarely was she ignored.

Except by Gray Bondurant. It was galling that he could so easily ignore her. Not her specifically, but the intimacy they'd shared. Since the morning they met, there had been little personal exchange between them.

True, that morning in Wyoming had been a chemical reaction, an *accident*, certainly not an act of love or even affection. She didn't expect him to blow a trumpet every time she entered a room, but wasn't some acknowledgment called for? It was as though it hadn't happened. When he'd had the opportunity to get into bed with her in the motel, he hadn't even tried. That was the worst possible insult.

Tonight, he seemed withdrawn and particularly self-absorbed. She debated the wisdom of walking into this lion's den. But cautious approaches had never been her style.

She crossed the room and planted herself directly in front of him. Without preamble, she said, "You can't just act like it never took place."

"Why not?" At least he didn't play dumb. "I thought we agreed that it was no-strings-attached sex."

"We did."

He shrugged as though to say, *So, case closed.*

"Even if it was casual sex," she said, "can't we still acknowledge that it happened?"

"What purpose would that serve?"

"Well, it would . . . it would . . ." She sighed with exasperation. "I don't know. I just feel that we shouldn't ignore it."

"Because of your father?"

If he had started speaking in tongues, she couldn't have been caught more off guard. "What do you know about him?"

"That he was never there for your mother or for you. That he was a habitual adulterer who died among satin sheets with a lover, and that your mother killed herself over it."

"Daily certainly was thorough, wasn't he?" she said bitterly. "He had no business discussing my personal life with you."

"I held a gun to his head. Figuratively speaking."

"Why so interested, Bondurant?"

"Why so testy?"

"You've been testy whenever I approached the subject of your past."

She couldn't see his eyes in the darkness, but she felt their lingering, thoughtful appraisal. "You're a contradiction, Barrie, and I was trained to study and analyze contradictions because they're usually very significant."

"Okay, I'll bite. In what way am I a contradiction?"

"For instance, the more grim the situation, the more jokes you crack. With men, you send mixed signals. One second you're fending off anything remotely sexual, the next . . ." He let the sentence trail. "Chivalry demands I stop there."

"You're a real prince."

"I wanted to know why you run so hot and cold. After what Daily told me, I have a better understanding of you. Your father's rejection is what made you so ambitious."

She threw her hip out and rested her hand on it. "You don't say?"

"You work hard to win Daddy's notice and approval. You seek affection, but you're also afraid of it. You assume a feminist air, rejecting a man before he can reject you, but that hard-core posture conflicts with your natural tendencies, which are altogether feminine. Your father made you wary of men."

"I'm not wary, Bondurant. I'm smart. And I'm not mistrustful of all men, just some."

"Most."

"Most are untrustworthy. Unlike my mother, I'll never let a man treat me as though I'm invisible. Which brings us around to you and the purpose of this conversation. I don't expect chocolates and roses from you. Just don't look through me and pretend that I don't matter."

"Fair enough."

"Good. Fine. Good night."

"Good night."

Alone in the cramped bedroom, lying on the narrow cot, Barrie realized that she'd made her point. But it was a very empty victory.

Chapter
Thirty

$\mathcal{V}$anessa Merritt was having breakfast in bed. She hadn't been out of her bedroom in three days, ever since the night David had struck her. He hadn't been to see her, either.

Propped against a mound of pillows, she watched Katie Couric interview the defense secretary, who'd recently returned from North Africa. There had been reports of a military buildup in Libya and air strikes against Israel. The Libyan government denied responsibility for the bombings. The secretary had advised President Merritt not to take any drastic measures, either political or military, until intelligence networks had substantiated the reports.

David would be furious if he was forced to take aggressive action. That kind of executive decision invariably provoked strong bipartisan responses and public outcries. Engaging in even a skirmish with hostile forces could cost votes.

Vanessa smiled at the thought of the dilemma this might cause him.

Her smile disappeared when an assistant tapped on the door and announced that Dr. Allan wished to see her. "What do you want, George?" she asked ungraciously as he approached her bed.

"Is that any kind of greeting?" he asked, his bedside manner impeccable. "I came to check on you."

"Did David order it?"

He pretended not to see the unsightly bruise and swelling beneath her eye. "He left this morning for the Caribbean to check on the hurricane damage."

She nodded toward the TV. "The news covered his farewell wave as he boarded the plane at Andrews. He looked very resolved. I'm sure that singlehandedly he'll slay the hurricane like a dragon. Sir David the Dauntless."

"Sarcasm doesn't flatter you, Vanessa." He slipped a blood pressure cuff on her arm.

"Neither does this bruise on my cheek, which you've so admirably tried to ignore. Was David afraid I might need reconstructive surgery on my cheekbone? Is that why he sent for you—to assess the damage and give him an estimate on repairing it?"

"I came because it's time for another blood-level check." He removed the blood pressure cuff and replaced it with a strip of rubber, which he wrapped tightly around her biceps to form a tourniquet. "And David thought that perhaps more rest might be required before you're fully recovered."

" 'Rest'? You mean seclusion?"

God, no! she screamed. Silently. What good would it do her to scream out loud?

The Secret Service agents would come running. She would accuse George of trying to kill her a second time. Her guards and the assistant who'd shown George in—she looked like the kindliest of grandmothers in her baggy sweaters and SAS shoes but was undoubtedly one of David's well-placed spies—would look upon her with pity for being so far gone. She would be drugged and carted off anyway.

There was no one to help her. She was trapped. During the press conference she had tried signaling for someone to come to her rescue. Hadn't anyone who knew her well noticed that she wasn't wearing her mother's wedding ring?

Apparently not. Not Gray, anyway. Spence had disappeared, but his loyalty was strictly to David anyway. She remembered her father's whispered promise that he had everything under control, but where was he this morning?

"I want to call my father," she said as George swabbed the inside of her elbow with icy alcohol.

"I'll phone him for you later. Make a fist for me so I can draw some blood."

"I want to call him now," she said in a voice made shrill with fear.

She threw off the covers and swung her legs over the side of the bed. Unmindful of her nakedness, she reached for the telephone on her nightstand. Nervously, she juggled the receiver and wound up dropping it. She dropped to the floor on all fours and scrambled to pick up the telephone.

"Vanessa, for God's sake!" George placed his hands around her waist and tried to pull her up.

"Let go of me, you son of a bitch!"

She fought him, but he knocked the phone from her hand and hauled her to her feet. She flailed her arms. Curling her fingers, she tried to rake his face with her nails. "I won't let you do this to me again."

"I'm only trying to help you."

"You lying hypocrite," she hissed. "Stop pretending. We both know why you're here. You've been ordered to put me out of commission again, right? At least until the evidence of my husband's abuse has healed. Bad press for the First Lady to be sporting a shiner after a domestic quarrel, huh?"

Again she struggled, but his arms held her fast. "Don't work yourself up, Vanessa, or I'll have to sedate you."

"If he asked you to, would you kill me, George?"

"Jesus, no!"

"Liar. You tried up at Highpoint. What's he got on you?"

"I don't know what you mean."

"You're covering a murder for him, so he must have a secret on you. What is it, George?"

"I don't know anything about a murder."

"Oh yes you do. But you won't tell because David's got you, doesn't he? I know him, you see. That's the way he operates. What ax is he holding over your head? Something to do with Amanda? That would get you where you hurt most, wouldn't it? You've always been so fond of that insipid wife of yours. Or has David threatened the lives of your children? He's good at that too. Take it from me, he's—Ow!"

Without her noticing, he'd reached for a prepared syringe and driven the needle into her thigh, depressing the plunger before she could stop him. "I'm sorry, Vanessa. You gave me no choice."

"You had a choice, George. We all have choices. Damn you!" she cried, her voice cracking. "Damn you and David to hell."

❧

That evening, Dr. Allan pulled his car into the driveway of his home but made no effort to get out and go inside. He sat staring without seeing through the windshield, his hands lying listlessly in his lap. He was exhausted, lacking the initiative even to open the car door.

Lights were on inside the house, and he took comfort in that. Each time he returned, he feared he would find all the windows dark, the rooms deserted, the closets and bureau drawers empty. He lived in dread of Amanda moving out and taking the boys with her.

She had sworn she would fight for him, but at what point would she give up? When would she come to the realization that he might not be worth saving? He saw the disgust in her expression every morning when he appeared at the breakfast table, trembling and bleary-eyed, hungover from drink and guilt.

He loved Amanda for still caring enough to ask where he'd been and what he'd been doing, but he also resented her keen perception. She possessed an innate lie detector that was more accurate than any available to law enforcement agencies. Plausible explanations were increasingly harder to come by.

Guilt made him defensive and verbally abusive. After several nasty scenes, she had stopped asking him about the medical duties he was performing at David Merritt's behest. Probably she'd stopped prying because she was sick of his lies, and possibly to spare their sons the trauma of overhearing the vicious quarrels.

Her eyes conveyed censure and contempt. He felt her patience wearing thin, her tolerance diminishing, her love dwindling. Any day now, she might leave him. Then he would die of shame and despair.

He took a hefty swig from the liquor bottle he'd kept tucked between his thighs on the drive home. He almost wished that a traffic cop had stopped him and arrested him for DUI. He would gladly have pleaded guilty to the charge. Jail time served for drunk driving would be preferable to the life sentence he was serving for David. If he were in jail, David would have to find another doctor to solve his problem. George would be more than happy to relinquish the duty.

He'd waited in the Oval Office until David returned from his hasty trip to the Caribbean, where his goodwill mission had been well documented by the media. The young, handsome, vital President Merritt was photographed sifting through storm damage and consoling islanders who'd lost homes and loved ones to a fierce force of nature.

If they only knew, George had thought, *how much more destructive the man dispensing the platitudes is.*

In spite of his long day, it seemed the trip had invigorated him. He sailed into the Oval Office looking robust and slightly suntanned. "George! What's up?"

As if he didn't know. "I regret to inform you that your wife has become ill again. This morning, I took it upon myself to move her to a private facility where she'll be well cared for."

The son of a bitch actually pretended to take the news badly. Subdued, he asked if his father-in-law had been notified.

"I thought you might wish to tell Senator Armbruster personally."

David asked George to speak with Dalton Neely about the proper wording for a press release, and George agreed to do so first thing tomorrow morning.

If he noticed Dr. Allan's haunted expression and lack of enthusiasm for his current project, he gave no sign of it. He was confident that his instructions would be carried out to the letter no matter how George felt about them.

What ax is he holding over your head?

George rued the day he'd met David Merritt. What had seemed at the time an auspicious occasion had turned out to be the most ill-omened event in his life. Quite by accident— or had it been as random as David made it seem?—the promising young resident had met the up-and-coming young congressman on a racquetball court. When the two shook hands, George experienced a power surge in his arm. It was as though he'd received an injection of David's charisma and energy. That infusion forged a friendship.

They began meeting to play racquetball or to have a drink or a quick lunch. The Allans, newlyweds on a tight budget, couldn't entertain lavishly, but David seemed perfectly at ease having hamburger dinners on the patio of their modest apartment. When he married, his bride was less enthusiastic about these casual evenings with the Allans. Vanessa and Amanda hadn't bonded as their husbands had. George guessed it was because Amanda was so intellectually superior to Vanessa. The two women couldn't have had more dissimilar personalities and interests. But their indifference to each other hadn't hampered the friendship between him and David.

It wasn't long before George considered David his best and most trusted friend. So naturally, when his life seemed on the verge of disaster, David was the person to whom he ran for help.

The patient admitted to the emergency room, a young black male, had collapsed during a neighborhood basketball game. Judging by the age and appearance of the patient and his friends, George immediately suspected a drug overdose. He asked the gang what drugs their friend had been doing that day.

"He wants to play in the fuckin' NBA," one of the boys informed him. "He don't do no heavy drugs."

George wasn't convinced. Every symptom screamed barbiturate OD combined with alcohol. He ordered a gastric lavage and ipecac.

What George didn't know, but was told by the patient's mother when she arrived, was that he'd had rheumatic fever as a child, which had left him with a damaged aortic valve. He was suffering heart failure brought on by a vigorous game of basketball.

Before George could take the necessary measures to correct his mistake, the ipecac took effect. The boy aspirated into his lungs and literally drowned in his own vomit.

Stricken with guilt and panic, George ran to David, who listened while he blubbered out his story. "He was disoriented and couldn't tell me. He could've made it if I hadn't jumped to the wrong conclusion. A more thorough pulmonary examination would have—"

"Did the other kids tell you he had a weak heart?"

"The mother said he never wanted any of his friends to know, or they'd think he was a sissy. Jesus," he sobbed, burying his face in his hands, "the mother could sue the hospital and me for malpractice."

He saw his career being grounded before it ever got off the ground. He was only months away from completing his residency. His and Amanda's dreams were dashed.

"Don't be so hard on yourself," David said calmly. "What were you supposed to think? He was a black street kid, for crying out loud."

"It never occurred to me that it was his heart."

"Of course not."

"But it should have," George insisted. "I shouldn't have dismissed other possibilities just because one diagnosis seemed so obvious."

"Look," David said, "if you think I'm going to let my friend suffer for an honest mistake for the rest of his life, you've got another thing coming. Do you trust me?"

Mesmerized by David's composure, George nodded.

"Did anyone overhear the boy's mother telling you about his heart defect?"

"I don't think so. We were alone."

"Good."

"But it'll be in his records. She brought them to the hospital with her."

"Where are they now?" David asked smoothly.

George produced the incriminating folder and gave it to David. "You never saw it, understand?" David said as he locked the folder in his safe. When he turned back around, he laughed at George's expression. "Relax. You're the only one making a federal case out of this. Patients die in the emergency room all the time. I promise you, no one will investigate it too closely."

"What about his mother?"

"She probably expected him to drop dead suddenly. She'll figure it had to happen sooner or later, and she'll trust that you did everything you could to save him."

George gnawed on his lower lip. "Because he died in the ER of obvious causes, there probably won't be an autopsy."

David clapped him on the back. "So stop sweating it."

As David predicted, no one questioned the cause of death that George signed off on. After the funeral home claimed the boy's body, the mother was never heard from again.

Their guilty secret strengthened their bond. David introduced George to his congressional colleagues and other influential people. He touted him as the finest medical man in Washington, and since he did it in the same earnest, persuasive manner in which he introduced bills to the House of Representatives, people believed him.

By the time George entered private practice, he was well established with the movers and shakers in Washington. Years later, when he was appointed the official White House physician, he sold his lucrative practice for an incredible sum and bought a house around the corner from the residence of the vice president.

Things couldn't have been better.

Then he was called to the White House in the middle of the night to pronounce three-month-old Robert Rushton Merritt dead, and Dr. George Allan's charmed life began its descent.

David had called in the favor granted years earlier. George had never asked, but he'd assumed that David still had the boy's medical history in his possession. Misdiagnosing the boy's ailment had been an honest mistake, and a deadly one, but George could have survived it if he'd only owned up to it at the time. It was the coverup, the lie, that the medical community would be hard-pressed to forgive at this late date. David's solution, which had seemed George's salvation, had actually been his undoing.

Because of his present celebrity, an investigation into that long-forgotten episode in the ER would make headlines. It wouldn't matter how many patients died because of doctors' mistakes. Everyone's attention would be focused on that boy, his hapless mother, and the doctor who'd committed the fatal screw-up.

He had to protect his family against a scandal like that. The nest egg from the sale of his practice would support Amanda and the boys for the rest of their lives. She wouldn't be left with a paltry life insurance policy or an enormous debt to pay.

Left?

It suddenly occurred to George that he was thinking of his life in the past tense. Which was just as well. If he carried out David's latest edict, he was as good as dead.

After a moment of taut silence, Gray said, "You really pissed her off."

Daily's sigh rattled deep in his chest. "Yeah, I was pretty hard on her. After all she's been through lately, I should've cut her some slack, I guess. I'd better go and talk to her."

"Don't bother. Let her sulk. Chalk it up to PMS. She'll cool off after a while. I'll talk her down."

"You're fucking her, aren't you?"

"Once."

"That's it?"

"You keeping records?"

"What're your plans for her?"

"I don't make plans with women."

Daily didn't let Gray's intimidating blue gaze deter him from speaking his mind. "Sometimes I could choke her, but I love that girl like she was my own blood. I don't want her to get hurt. Not by you and not by this. Maybe it's time we cut bait and stop this nonsense."

"You didn't think it was nonsense a week ago."

"I've got the right to change my mind. This all started with Barrie's thirst for a hot story. I'm beginning to think her ambition was contagious. It rubbed off on me, and I should have known better.

"Then she went to Wyoming and got you riled up too. And it didn't take much, did it, Bondurant? One whiff of Vanessa-in-trouble, and her hero comes running. Hell, you get right down to it, the three of us are pathetic."

"You okay, Daily?"

"Do I sound okay?" he gasped. "I'm too old and sick for this shit. I'd like my declining days to be a little more peaceful. I don't particularly want the word *traitor* engraved on my tombstone, either. It takes a strong person to admit when he's been wrong. I'd like to think I have that much strength of character left."

He came to his feet and shuffled toward the door, dragging his squeaky oxygen trolley after him. "Don't forget to turn out the light. You two aren't paying rent and electricity's not free, you know."

Gray rinsed their coffee cups in the sink, went to the door, and switched off the kitchen light. Then he, Barrie, and Daily huddled there in the darkness for several minutes.

Barrie pinched Gray's earlobe and pulled his head down so it was level with hers. "What was that crack about PMS?" she whispered directly into his ear.

"Sorry," he mouthed.

Daily was doing his best to breathe silently. "Are you sure this is going to work?"

"No," Gray whispered with sobering honesty. "You're clear on how to use that?" Earlier, he'd given Daily a crash course on how to read the infrared detector.

"Sweep the area," Daily said, his voice barely audible. "If there's somebody lurking in the dark watching the house, this LED will let me know."

"Good," Gray said. "If you see something, whisper to me. I'll hear you." He put the wireless earphone into his ear. It worked with the portable two-way radio in the pocket of his jacket.

"These're neat toys." Even in the darkness Barrie could see the sparkle in Daily's eyes.

"Only problem is," Gray said, "the pros have neater ones. Okay, let's go."

When Daily gave them the thumbs-up, they slipped out through the back door. There was no moon, so it would be difficult for the surveillance team to see them, unless night-vision binoculars and infrared detectors were being used. As Gray had said, the pros had neat toys too. He'd marked the surveillance vehicles—a van today, a service truck yesterday, an RV the day before—parked on Daily's street one block away. Although a week had passed without any overt activity, Spence's secret police force was living up to his standards, even in his absence.

Daily's car and Barrie's were parked in plain sight out front, so Gray hoped that the back of the house wasn't being monitored. He also hoped that their scripted little scenario in the kitchen had worked to delude the surveillance team into believing that there was dissension within the ranks. Gray didn't trust the noise generator to cover their conversations completely, so they had been careful to let their eavesdroppers hear only what they wanted them to hear.

Soundlessly, they left the tiny square of crumbling concrete that served as Daily's rear porch and ran across his patch of backyard at a crouch. As he had on the night her house went up in smoke, Gray led her through several residential blocks via backyards and alleyways. Two dogs barked at them, but nothing else untoward happened, like G-men emerging from the shadows, automatic weapons aimed.

Gray had left a car parked behind a single-story office complex. When they reached it, he said into the radio's tiny microphone, "How's it looking, Daily?"

"Not even a mole fart. Good luck."

"Over and out."

Barrie was out of breath, as much from tension as exertion. They got into the car, but she waited until they were under way before she asked, "Do you think they're on to us?"

"We'll know in a few minutes."

He drove away from Daily's neighborhood, speeding up occasionally, then slowing to a crawl, weaving an intricate pattern through the residential streets. Finally he said, "Unless a helicopter shows up soon, I'd say we're clear." He removed the earpiece and set the two-way radio system on the seat between them.

"You and Daily were certainly convincing," she said wryly. "To anyone who might've been listening, I came across as an ambitious, seditious, slutty nitwit with PMS."

"That about sums it up."

She shot him a dirty look. "Where'd you get the car?"

"Parking lot of a shopping mall."

"You stole it?"

"No, I identified myself to the owner as someone trying to overthrow the President and asked if he would mind lending me his car."

"Not funny. The car will be reported stolen by now. We could be stopped."

"I switched license plates with a Chevy Blazer. There are thousands of these Tauruses in the metropolitan area. Besides, I'll ditch it tomorrow and get something else."

"You certainly treat crime with a cavalier attitude."

"Compared to the crimes we might have to commit before this is finished, grand theft auto is minor. Now, what's his address?"

~~

Howie Fripp lived alone in a four-room apartment on the third floor of a walk-up. Each year the stairs seemed to get a little creakier, as did his knees. They were aching by the time he unlocked the door and went in. He switched on lights as he made his way into the minuscule kitchen and set the sack of Chinese carryout on the table.

"Hello, Howie."

"*Jesus H!*" He spun around in time to see Barrie stepping from his dark bedroom into the kitchen.

"Did I startle you, Howie? Gee, I'm sorry. I know how annoying it can be to have someone sneak up on you like that."

"You scared the hell out of me! What are you—"

He saw the tall, slim man standing in the shadows behind Barrie. "Who's that?"

"Gray Bondurant, meet Howie Fripp." She stepped aside to afford Howie a better look at the commando with the fierce blue eyes, graying hair, and mean mouth.

"You're Gray Bondurant?"

"I see you've heard of him," Barrie said.

Howie swallowed a knot of apprehension. "A pleasure, Mr. Bondurant."

"I wish I could say the same."

Even his voice sounded tough. It reminded Howie of the man he'd once played billiards with—the one he had hoped would become his friend. The one who had never returned to the bar.

Howie's eyes darted back and forth between his uninvited guests. He didn't like the expression on Bondurant's face. Not one bit. He wore the confident, fearless air of a predator who'd just spotted his next meal and knew that it was going to be an easy kill. "What are you doing in my apartment?"

"We came for information." With the toe of his boot— *Whaddaya know? Some guys really do wear cowboy boots*—Bondurant dragged a chair from beneath the table. "Sit down, Howie. Don't let us interrupt your supper. We can talk while you eat."

Howie dropped into the chair, but he shook his head when Bondurant pushed the sack of Chinese food across the table toward him. The thought of sweet and sour pork and shrimp chow mein made his stomach heave. His attempts to hide his queasiness failed.

"What's the matter, Howie?" Barrie asked. "You look sort of green. Aren't you glad to see us?"

"I'm not supposed to talk to you, Barrie. Not under any circumstances. Jenkins threatened to fire me if I gave you the time of day."

"Then you're in luck, Howie, because we already know the time of day," Gray Bondurant said.

"It's not that I don't want to talk to you, Barrie, it's just, you know—jeez, I gotta protect my interests. It's nothing personal, I swear. We parted friends, didn't we? No hard feelings. At least none on my side."

His armpits were leaking like a ten-year-old garden hose. "I . . . I . . . Hey, wait, I have a message for you. Just a minute, I jotted it down on a slip." He patted his pockets until he found it.

"Here," he said, extending her the note. "This call came in just as I was on my way out tonight. Said she was a friend of yours. Demanded to speak to you, so the operator put her through to me."

"Charlene Walters," Barrie read.

"That's right. She said it was urgent and gave me her phone number. See, I wrote it down right there."

"She's not a friend. She's a nutcase who's always calling me."

"Oh." That was disappointing. Howie had hoped this Charlene might be somebody important, somebody Barrie wanted badly to speak to. He was trying his best to be helpful, but he didn't think Bondurant was impressed. His granite expression hadn't softened.

Howie watched fearfully as the tall, imposing hero pulled out the remaining chair at the table and sat down, straddling it backward. His movements were sinuous and silent. His eyes would give anybody the creeps. Howie thought they seemed to drill straight through his skull. A sane person wouldn't mess with this hombre.

Barrie leaned against the kitchen counter and folded her arms. She looked relaxed and was smiling a smile that Howie knew was artificial. "You're sweating like a pig, Howie."

"I want to know why you're here."

"Gray and I just dropped by for a friendly little chat."

"About what?"

"Oh, things. The weather. The Redskins' season. Do they have a snowball's chance in hell of getting into the playoffs? The new Harrison Ford movie. What's going on at the White House. Things like that."

"*I* don't know what's going on at the White House."

"Of course you do, Howie. You work in a newsroom."

"Barrie, please, give it up. You're only going to get into more trouble."

"I'm touched by your concern. Truly. But I'm more interested in what you've heard about the First Lady recently."

"Nothing."

"You must have."

"Swear to God."

"Since I'm no longer there, who's covering the beat?"

"Grant. He says it's tighter than a rich man's asshole over there. Nothing's leaking."

"There's always something leaking. Rumor. Gossip. Reportedly Mrs. Merritt has gone away again. Why? Where? Has anyone seen her? Is her health that poor? Is her condition life-threatening?"

"I swear," he whined, "I don't know anything. Jeez, you've become obsessed, you know that? You've turned into a total wacko over this. How come you've got nothing on the brain except Mrs. Merritt? It isn't natural, Barrie. I think you've flipped out, is what I think."

Barrie pulled in a deep breath, then expelled it on a sigh. She looked at Gray and shook her head. "I told you he wouldn't cooperate. We might just as well go."

She headed for the door, but Gray stopped her. "We can't leave him to tell the feds we were here asking questions."

"Hmm, I suppose you're right." She looked down at Howie with a dubious frown.

He was distinctly uneasy with the tone their conversation had taken. "I'm not going to tell anybody you were here."

"I'm afraid we can't take that chance." Bondurant reached inside his jacket and withdrew a pistol from the waistband of his pants.

Howie began chanting, "Oh shit, oh fuck, oh Jesus, oh shit, oh God. I don't want to die. I don't. I don't. Don't kill me. Please."

With a terrifying *click*, Gray pulled back the hammer on his Magnum revolver.

Howie squeezed his eyes shut and he began to sputter. "B . . . Barrie, p . . . please, you can't let him kill me. We were friends."

"Friends? Friends, Howie? You can't be serious." She laughed. "Friends don't sell each other out, which is what you always did to me with Jenkins. You treated me like crap every day I worked with you. Besides, I don't make Gray's decisions. If he's made up his mind not to leave you to rat on us, there's really nothing I can do about it. But I'd rather not watch. I'd never eat Chinese food again. Gray, do you mind waiting till I get into the other room?"

"Pleeeeeze," Howie begged with a sustained sob. "For God's sake, Barrie."

"Sorry. It really is out of my control." She pushed away from the counter. On her way out, she paused to press his shoulder in a final farewell.

Bondurant stretched his arm across the table and pressed the bore of the pistol against the center of Howie's forehead.

"I did hear something but I don't know if it's true or not." The words rolled out so fast, they tumbled over one another like circus acrobats.

Barrie stopped, turned. She was frowning skeptically. "You'd tell us anything now. You'd make something up just to keep Gray from shooting you."

"No, no, I swear. I swear, Mr. Bondurant." He drew an invisible X over his heart.

"What have you heard?"

"There's a rumor that Mrs. Merritt has been checked into a hospital for substance abuse."

"Old story," Barrie said. "There was speculation on that before."

"This time it's serious," Howie said nervously. Bondurant was still scowling.

"What hospital?"

"I don't know. No one knows. And it could be just gossip."

Bondurant looked across at Barrie. Barrie shook her head. Bondurant shrugged and bumped Howie's forehead with the pistol again.

"D . . . Dr. Allan takes a helicopter from the White House lawn every day," he rushed on. "He's usually back in an hour, hour and a half. But nobody knows where he's going or even if these quick trips have anything to do with the First Lady. And there's talk that he has trouble at home."

"The Allans' marriage is solid," Bondurant said. "I've been around them. They're crazy about each other."

"He and the missus aren't getting along. That's the gossip. So maybe he's flying off to visit some skirt, who knows?"

Howie turned his head, looking hopefully at Barrie, then at Bondurant. "I swear to God that's it. That's all I've heard. Jenkins said he'd shove the Washington Monument up my ass if I even talked to you. So, if you do anything with this info, you can't let him know I told you. Promise, Barrie, okay?"

"What do you think?" Bondurant asked her. "Is he lying?"

"I'm not!" Howie cried.

"I'm not sure," she said, gnawing the inside of her cheek. "He could be, just to save himself. On the other hand, he knows that if he's feeding us bullshit, you'll only come back for him."

"I'm not. You won't," Howie said hastily.

Bondurant fixed a blue-hot gaze on him. Howie's entire life flashed before his eyes at least three times before Bondurant uncocked the hammer and withdrew the pistol. "Tell you what, Howie. I won't kill you tonight if you give us a reason to come back tomorrow."

"What for?"

"The name of the hospital. That's not asking too much, is it? The name of a hospital in exchange for a nice takeout Chinese meal like you've got yourself there, and a chance to eat it."

"I don't . . . How am I gonna find out the name of the—"

"That's your problem. But I bet you come through."

"Don't count on it," Barrie said. "He'll agree to anything to save his sorry butt. Then he'll probably double-cross us."

"No I won't!" Howie squealed. "Swear to God I won't, Mr. Bondurant."

"Do what you want, Gray," Barrie said. "But I don't trust him. He's a maggot."

"Thanks for reminding me." Bondurant's voice sent chills up Howie's clammy spine. "She tells me that you used to give her a hard time at work, Howie."

"That's not true."

"He's not only a sexist sleazoid, he's a lying sexist sleazoid," she said.

The dangerous blue eyes narrowed another fraction of an inch.

Howie squirmed in his seat. "Okay, maybe . . . maybe I did joke with her some, but I never meant anything by it."

"You look like the kind of guy who would make lewd comments to a woman because you can't get her attention any other way."

"That's exactly what he did," Barrie said.

"That's right, I did." Howie's enthusiastic nod of agreement made his head wobble on his neck. "Whatever Barrie says, I'm guilty as charged."

"Did you make snide comments about her sex drive, her love life, her figure, her sex in general?"

"Sometimes."

"You stared at her legs, ogled her breasts, said and did things that diminish a woman's dignity."

"Yeah, I did that. Sure did. I'm sorry as hell about it too."

"Really?" Gray said dryly.

"Really. Yes, sir. If I don't regret it, may I be struck blind for lying."

Bondurant thoughtfully tapped the barrel of the pistol against the back of the chair. "If I ever hear of you insulting or mistreating her again, I'm going to be pissed, Howie. You'll pray to be struck blind rather than have me after you."

"I . . . I understand."

"What about tomorrow?"

"I'll try to find out what you want."

"I hope you come through for us."

Relaxing, Howie smiled. "'Cause you'd hate to kill me, right?"

"No. Because I'd hate to waste a perfectly good bullet making mush of your brain."

Abruptly Bondurant rose, stuffing the pistol back into his waistband. He then disappeared into the bedroom. Without a word, Barrie followed.

"Where are you going?" Howie called after them. "Hey! What time tomorrow? Where?"

He was answered only by a malevolent silence. When he finally worked up enough courage to leave the kitchen and venture into his bedroom, it was empty. His guests seemed to have vaporized. If not for the wet stain on the front of his trousers, he might have imagined the whole terrifying episode.

Chapter
Thirty-Two

"*I* felt sorry for him."

"Don't. When you compared him to a maggot, you insulted maggots everywhere."

They had left Howie's apartment via the fire escape and bedroom window through which they'd entered, and were on their way back to Daily's house. Barrie was staring pensively through the windshield of the car that Gray had stolen without a qualm. "You're a scary guy, Bondurant. You really frightened him."

"Fear's a good motivator."

"I wonder if it's the most effective one, though."

"We'll know tomorrow night."

"He was trying to be helpful." She fished the note Howie had given her from her pocket. "Good ol' Charlene," she said with a light laugh. "Apparently she hasn't learned that I'm no longer employed at WVUE. I never actually spoke to her, but she was a faithful caller." On impulse, Barrie asked Gray to pull over to the curb and park in front of a pharmacy.

He did as she asked and got out of the car with her. "Drugstore's closed," he remarked.

"I don't need the drugstore. I want to use the pay phone."

He glanced around. "Not a great neighborhood to be loitering on a street corner."

"I feel reasonably safe, what with the security lights inside the store and you with that portable cannon inside your pants." He gave her an arch look. "You flatter yourself, Bondurant. Got any change?"

The number Howie had written was in an area code unfamiliar to her. To avoid phone records, she didn't use her calling card, but fed coins into the slots. After much pinging and panging, the call went through. It rang several times. She was about to hang up when someone finally answered.

"Yo!"

"Excuse me?" She raised her hand, indicating to Gray that her call had been answered.

"Who gave y'all this numbah?"

"Uh, Charlene Walters," Barrie replied. "May I speak with her please?"

The only response to her request was a phlegmy laugh punctuated by nasal snorts.

"Is Ms. Walters there?"

"Yeah, she's here. But this phone is off limits after lockdown."

"Lockdown?" Barrie looked up at Gray, who registered the same surprise as she. "Exactly where are you?" she asked.

"Central Corrections. Pearl, Miss'ippi."

"Is Ms. Walters an inmate there?"

"She is that—for a helluva long time too. How come y'all're calling her?"

"Who am I speaking with, please?"

The man identified himself as a guard who just happened to be passing by the pay phone when it rang. She asked if it was possible for her to speak with the warden. "This time o' night? You a lawyer or what?"

She finessed her way around a direct answer and conveyed to him how vitally important it was for her to speak with a prison official, stressing that the matter could not wait until morning. "Okay," the guard grumbled. "Gimme the numbah where you're at. If he sees fit, he can call you back."

Barrie would rather have had the warden's number, but she settled on giving the guard the number of the pay phone. When she hung up, Gray asked how an inmate in a Mississippi prison would know about her.

"The SIDS series was fed to a satellite. It could have been aired on any TV station in the country. Apparently a station that goes into the prison ran it. Prisoners frequently get fixated on celebrities. Although I know it's a stretch to think of me as a celebrity."

"Why is it 'vitally important' that you speak to her tonight?"

"It isn't," she admitted. "Most of her messages consisted of calling me an idiot. I'm just curious to know why she thought so." Gray's eyes were narrowed in concentration. "What?" she asked.

"I was just thinking. Both David and Vanessa are from Mississippi."

"You're right, they are," Barrie said, grabbing the telephone receiver on the first ring. "Hello, this is Barrie Travis."

"Deputy Warden Foote Graham."

"Thank you very much for calling me back, Warden."

"No problem, ma'am. How can I he'p you?"

She identified herself as a broadcast journalist in Washington, D.C., and told him about the repeated calls from Charlene Walters.

"She pesterin' y'all?"

"No, it's not that. I just wondered why Ms. Walters would be calling me."

"There's no tellin' what Crazy Charlene might do."

Barrie looked up at Gray, who was intently gauging her facial expressions. She frowned, shook her head, and rolled her eyes. "Crazy Charlene?" she repeated for his benefit.

"Yes, ma'am. Seventy-seven years old, but Charlene's still full of piss 'n' vinegar."

"Seventy-seven? Good Lord, how long has she been in prison?"

"She's a lifer. No parole. Been here since I came, and that's going on eighteen years. I think she's outlasted everybody. Nobody remembers when ol' Charlene wasn't here. She's sort of like a . . . what do you call it? A mascot. She's a leader. Well liked by the other inmates. And quite a character, too. She'll give you her opinion on any subject whether you ask for it or not."

"Then it comes as no surprise to you that she saw my story on TV and decided to call."

"Doesn't surprise me a'tall. What was the story about?"

"Sudden Infant Death Syndrome."

"Hmm. I thought you might've touched on a subject dearer to her heart. She's pretty outspoken about corruption in the government, police brutality, legalizing dope, issues like that."

"What was her crime?"

"She and her husband held up a liquor store. For less than fifty bucks, he shot a sixteen-year-old clerk and three customers in the head. The state executed him a while back. Because Charlene didn't actually pull the trigger, and she swore her old man made her go along or else, she wasn't given the death penalty."

"None of that relates to SIDS, does it?"

"Not that I can figger."

"Well, thank you very much for your time. I apologize again for calling you at this hour, Mr. Foote."

"Graham, Foote Graham. No problem. Glad to've been of service."

Barrie was about to say goodbye when Gray nudged her, triggering her memory. "Oh, Warden Graham, one last question. I don't suppose Charlene has any ties, no matter how remote, to Senator Armbruster or President Merritt?"

"The President? Well, why didn't you say so in the first place?"

Her heart seemed to stop. Everything in the universe shrank small enough to be concentrated into the grimy telephone receiver she was gripping with fingers that had turned as white as chalk.

"What'd he say?" Gray asked, inching closer.

She motioned for him to be quiet. The warden was saying, "It's entirely possible that Charlene has some connection to both our senator and President Merritt."

"How so?" Barrie asked huskily.

"Any number of ways. You see, Charlene gets around."

"I thought you said she was a lifer."

"That's true. But if you're to believe Charlene, she led a colorful life before her incarceration. For starters, she was Robert Redford's college sweetheart. That came on the heels of her fling with Richard Nixon. Somewhere in there she had Elvis's love child, and engaged in one of those French threesomes with Marilyn Monroe and Joe DiMaggio while they were married. Charlene takes credit for inspiring him to invent the Mr. Coffee."

Barrie slumped against the wall of the phone booth. "I get the picture. She's a loony tune."

"As loony as they come," he said, filling her ear with laughter that was much more melodious than the guard's.

After a moment, he said, "I'm sorry to be laughing at your expense, Miz Travis. Was this real important to you?"

"Yes."

"Awful sorry, ma'am. Guess you've wasted your time."

"Not altogether," she said with chagrin. "I've never met anyone named Foote before."

Once she and Gray were in the car again, she ripped the slip of paper bearing Charlene's name and number into tiny pieces and let them flutter from her hand to the floor. "Responding to a crank caller," she said with self-derision. "That ought to be some indication of how desperate I am. I'd hate for Howie or Jenkins to know that I'd sunk that low."

"It could've turned out different."

"Don't patronize me," she said crossly. "It was a stupid impulse, and I'm ashamed I acted on it. Problem is, I'm fresh out of ideas. If Howie doesn't produce, what then?"

"What about your sources?"

"You haven't heard my pager beeping, have you?"

"Checked the batteries?"

She scowled at him. "The pager isn't malfunctioning, Bondurant, I am. As far as journalism goes, I'm washed up in Washington."

"You still have a way with words."

The more he tried to boost her spirits, the more recalcitrant she became. "Nobody, not even the most secret unidentified source, wants to be associated with me. I couldn't get a job cleaning toilets in any news facility in this city, maybe in the country."

Leaning her head back, she sighed. "I meant about ninety percent of what I said tonight before we set out. I do wish I had my life back. I miss Cronkite. I miss my house. It was no palace, but it was my home. I miss my work, the deadlines, the rush I get when I'm on the scene of an event, the gratification I feel when I put together a good piece. God forbid, I think I even miss Howie, because it was almost good to see him tonight."

Gray looked at her askance. "You must be suffering a severe case of self-pity."

"Aren't you, just a little? Don't you miss your ranch and your horses, your precious solitude? Don't you sometimes wish I'd never come calling?"

"But you did come calling. So what difference would wishes make now? For the past year I've been retired, but I knew I'd see action of some sort again. Subconsciously I was waiting to see what form it would take. The catalyst turned out to be Robert Rushton Merritt's death. Who could have predicted that? Nobody. Ultimately, we can never know what's going to happen to us next." He raised one shoulder in an indifferent shrug. "I take things as they come and try not to look back."

"God, don't you ever crack? Don't you ever let one human emotion pierce that damn armor of yours? Can't you ever just let go and *feel?*"

When her voice cracked, she shut up so he wouldn't know that she was on the verge of tears. Yes, she felt like a fool for tracking down a crank caller. Yes, she was frustrated because they hadn't penetrated the wall of secrecy surrounding Vanessa. For all they knew, she might already be dead. Barrie was more convinced than ever that making himself a widower was Merritt's ultimate goal. Each day that Barrie failed to expose him, he moved closer to succeeding.

Yes, she was worried about Daily, because he looked and sounded increasingly bad. He put up a good front, but she knew he was declining. His specialist had said there was nothing more to be done. The disease had progressed to a stage where even the most aggressive and innovative treatments wouldn't benefit him and would only diminish the quality of the life he had left.

Yes, yes, yes. All those concerns were troubling her tonight. But the number-one, champion tear maker was the man beside her. Gray Bondurant remained an enigma. They'd been intimate, but she didn't know him. Despite all the time they'd spent together, he was as much a stranger as he'd been that first morning, maybe even more of one.

That's why she felt like crying. She'd caressed his body, but she hadn't touched *him*.

Throwing down her caution, she said, "How can you not care about anything or anyone? What made you such an unfeeling bastard?"

A full minute of hostile silence passed before he said, "My folks died on the same day. Zap. They were gone. I was a kid. It hurt. But I got over it and came to rely on my grandparents. Then, one by one, they died. My sister and I were close, but her husband didn't take to me. He and her kids came first with her, so she more or less shut me out of their lives.

"I formed strong friendships with two men I trusted. I could read their thoughts before they thought them, and vice versa. We were as close as three heterosexual men can be. Then they betrayed me and have tried twice to kill me." He shrugged. "I guess I don't see any advantage to forming relationships."

It was more of himself than he'd revealed before. Yet, something was noticeably absent from his soul-baring monologue. "You left out the part about Vanessa and the baby," Barrie said. "You failed to mention that the love of your life was another man's wife."

Tersely, he said, "Yeah. I left that part out."

"Senator?"

Clete addressed the speakerphone on his desk. "What is it, Carol?"

"Gray Bondurant wishes to speak to you."

Clete rubbed his chin thoughtfully. "Tell him I'm not here."

"This is the third time he's called in two days."

"I don't care how many times he's called, I'm not going to talk to him. What about Dr. Allan?"

"I'm still trying to reach him, but I'm told he's unavailable."

"What the hell does that mean?"

"The White House staff hasn't been more specific than that, sir."

George Allan had called to inform him that Vanessa hadn't responded well to the adjustment he'd made on her medication. He'd also hinted that she was drinking heavily again. The upshot of the conversation had been to tell the senator that he was placing her in a private hospital for observation. Until she was stabilized, it was best that she not have visitors. In fact, prohibition of visitors was hospital policy.

It was goddamn Highpoint all over again. Vanessa had been shuttled off without so much as a goodbye to him, and she was unreachable. Allan had ended by saying he didn't expect her to be confined for a more than a few days.

As chairman of the Senate Finance Committee, Clete had been buried in meetings over the reconciliation budget. His presence was mandatory, but he had difficulty concentrating on the country's finances when worrying about his daughter. The doctor was dodging his calls. David hadn't deigned even to call and speak with him personally. It was beginning to stink. To high heaven. And part of the stench was Clete's own rising panic.

"Do they know it's me who's calling?"

"Of course, sir."

"Then I wish to speak to the President immediately."

While she was putting the call through, Clete left his desk and moved to the large window. He'd had the same view for more than thirty years, but he never tired of it. The automobiles on Washington's broad avenues changed. Clothing styles came and went. Seasons rotated. But the stalwart edifices of the United States government endured.

The emotional surge he derived from gazing at them couldn't be described as patriotism. It was more base than a love for his country. It was a passion for the power circulating within those buildings that gave him a rush of excitement not unlike an erection. He adhered to the adage that power was the strongest aphrodisiac. There was nothing to equal it. Nothing else even came close.

Any man worth his salt struggled to attain power. Then, once he had it, he fought like hell to keep it. It was inevitable that someone younger than he would seize the power he now wielded in Washington. But not today, and not tomorrow. He would choose the time to pass the baton.

And it wasn't going to go to David Merritt.

His secretary buzzed him again. "I'm sorry, Senator. The President's calendar is completely full today, and tonight he's scheduled to fly to Atlanta. He's not due back until midafternoon tomorrow."

Clete mulled that over for several seconds. "Thanks, Carol. Keep trying to reach that quack Allan. And get rid of Bondurant."

"Yes, sir."

Returning to his desk, he placed his feet up on it and swiveled back and forth in his well-worn leather chair as he contemplated his next move. David had acted faster than Clete had expected. He had figured David would let the heat cool down before trying again to eliminate the only witness to his child-killing.

Yes, Clete believed everything Bondurant and Barrie Travis had told him that night in the coffee shop. He'd taken whacks at Travis's credibility, but what choice had she given him? He'd been forced to create a ruckus over her gaffe in the hospital, or risk looking like a damn fool himself. He'd railed at her, but his wrath had been directed to his treacherous son-in-law.

Barrie Travis was a flake, but Bondurant wasn't. Clete might have doubted their story had she been the only one telling it, but he didn't doubt Bondurant. He'd never particularly liked the former Marine-cum-presidential aide. The man was taciturn to a fault. He wore his integrity on his sleeve. Clete mistrusted anybody that honest and straightforward.

Clete had never known Bondurant to lie. He'd evaded questions about his affair with Vanessa, which could be construed as lying by omission, but Clete regarded his silence as a gallant attempt to protect Vanessa from scandal, not to shield himself.

Knowing David's personality as he did, knowing of the incident involving a young woman named Becky Sturgis, Clete had no doubt that David could smother a child he knew wasn't his.

Clete chastened himself for not suspecting it earlier. The son of a bitch had tricked both him and Vanessa into believing that he wanted children. For years, she had tried all the remedies for infertility. David had refused to seek medical advice. Now Clete knew why. The bastard was firing blanks and didn't want anyone to know. Furthermore, he had subtly laid the blame of their childlessness on Vanessa, feeding her sense of inadequacy, which was a fundamental symptom of her illness.

Of course, Clete's conscience wasn't entirely clear. He had to assume partial responsibility for the spousal abuse his daughter had suffered. Where had he been all those years? Why hadn't he seen what was now so glaringly apparent? He'd been too busy putting David in the White House to see that David had cruelly rejected Vanessa's love.

As long as she did as she was told, didn't cross him, and appeared to be everything she was supposed to be, David was content. He had a long-suffering, beautiful wife who tolerated his casual affairs. But when Vanessa turned the tables and became pregnant with another man's child, David felt the death penalty was justified.

Yes, Barrie Travis and Gray Bondurant were telling the truth. They had forced him to open his eyes to what he hadn't wanted to see: David Merritt had put his daughter through hell; David Merritt had murdered his grandson; David Merritt had betrayed him; David Merritt must be destroyed.

But slinging unsubstantiated accusations at him on the evening news wasn't the way to go about it. Clete would have to defeat David surreptitiously, not by advertising that he was plotting against him. Anything other than a covert approach would result in failure.

Bondurant might have a chance of succeeding and getting away with it, but not while he was in cahoots with a journalist, any journalist, but particularly Barrie Travis. Clete knew that he had to operate independent of them, and he had to act quickly because David apparently had.

First, he had to find Vanessa. Second, he had to get her away from David. Third, he had to annihilate the bastard.

There were obstacles. One of them was Clete's own conflicting emotions. He felt his son-in-law's betrayal like a stake through his heart, but he couldn't afford to be sentimental about what might—and should—have been.

He also had to be extremely careful. While exposing David, he couldn't leave himself vulnerable to close scrutiny. Destroying an administration completely but cleanly would take deft maneuvering.

The problem with maneuvering was that it required time, and that, Clete feared, was in short supply.

～～

"Howie, isn't it?"

Howie nearly choked on his salted beer. He wiped his mouth with the back of his hand before extending it to the mustachioed man wearing a baseball cap over his ponytail. "Hey! I'd about given up on you coming back."

The man gave a thin, stiff smile. "I've been tied up."

"Well, it's good to see you. Can I buy you a beer?"

Although Howie was glad to see the return of the man he hoped to call friend, his invitation to a beer was issued halfheartedly. Tonight wasn't convenient. He'd stopped in at the bar only for a quick drink, not to socialize. All day, he'd been as nervous as a whore in church, wondering when Bondurant would pop up, demanding to know what he'd been able to ferret out regarding the First Lady's where-abouts. He had feared that either he or Barrie would show up at the WVUE studios.

But seven o'clock had come, the hour when he relin-quished his position to the overnight assignments editor, and there'd been no word from either Barrie or her menacing con-federate. He'd tried tricking himself into thinking they'd for-gotten about him, or had found what they wanted from some other source, but the attempted self-deception hadn't worked. The longer the day stretched out, the more anxious he became.

He doubted they would believe that he'd been unable to weasel anything from anyone at the White House, even though he'd tried his damnedest. Either everybody in town was lying, or nobody, but *nobody*, knew where Mrs. Merritt was hospitalized. That wasn't what Barrie and Bondurant wanted to hear.

So Howie had decided that even if he had to invent a medical facility, he would give Bondurant *something*. He figured the former Marine was as good as his word. If he didn't produce, Bondurant would just as soon kill him as not.

"Thanks, a beer sounds great."

"What?" Howie asked, jostled out of his grim musings.

"A beer?" His newfound friend was regarding him with puzzlement.

"Oh, sure, sure. It's been a hard day," Howie said, apol-ogizing for his momentary lapse. "Be right back."

When he returned with the beer, the man, a real cool customer, was chalking up a pool cue. "Watch yourself tonight. I've been practicing."

His grin reminded Howie of a carnivore with shifty eyes and very small, pointed teeth. "Uh, actually, I don't, uh, have time tonight." The only thing more disturbing than the man's smile was his frown. It quickly changed Howie's mind. "Well, maybe one quick game."

"Great. It'll give me a chance to salvage my pride."

Between shots, they made idle chitchat. Howie played poorly. He couldn't concentrate for thinking about who or what would be waiting to ambush him when he got home. Or did Bondurant have him in his sights now? Was he watching from the Laundromat across the street?

". . . about your friend?"

"Pardon?"

"I asked about your co-worker. The broad. Say, you seem preoccupied. If you've got something better to do tonight—"

"No, no," Howie said hastily. "Sorry."

Snap out of it, you idiot, he admonished himself. What the hell was the matter with him? Here was a cool guy practically begging to be his buddy, and what was he doing? Behaving like an asshole, that's what.

It was all Barrie's fault. It was *always* Barrie's fault. Hers and now Bondurant's. Who were they to be breaking into his apartment and pushing him around, anyway? They had no muscle. At least Barrie didn't. And Bondurant had been run out of town 'cause he couldn't keep out of the First Lady's pants. Screw 'em. If they came around tonight with their veiled threats, he'd call the cops on them.

Imbued with a new self-confidence, he hiked up his slipping waistband and took a swig of brew. "I canned her."

"No shit?"

"I felt bad about it," he said, his lips forming a moue of regret, "but she kept screwing up, gave me no choice."

"What else could you do, man?"

"Right." Howie sank his best shot of the evening. His friend hoisted his beer mug in a salute to his success. "I'm giving her a break, though."

"Oh?" The man lined up his next shot. The balls clacked solidly, but he failed to sink one. "Are you writing her a letter of recommendation?"

"No, I'm helping her on some undercover work."

As Howie had hoped, the man's eyebrows rose. He was impressed by the adventurous sound of that. "What kind of undercover work?"

Stung by the humiliation he'd suffered from Bondurant, Howie was pleased to be flexing his muscles. So what if he stretched the truth a little? His buddy here would never know the difference. Besides, even best friends bullshitted each other. It was all part of the guy thing.

"She's working freelance now, still digging into that big story I told you about. When she ran up against a brick wall, who'd she come to for information? Yours truly."

"Information about what?"

Howie winked. "White House insider stuff."

"And you got it for her?"

"Don't think it came easy," Howie said, puffing out his chest. "It didn't. I had to do some investigative work myself, tap in to my real hush-hush sources, but I found the creamy nougat center that Barrie's after."

"Must have made her happy."

"She will be."

"You haven't told her yet?" The man's eyes brightened and the mustache lifted in a grin. He cuffed Howie on the shoulder. "Ah, I get it. You're holding out until you get something from her in return, huh?"

Howie chuckled. He had his new pal right where he wanted him, believing that he was a lady-killer, a man of the world, a force to be reckoned with, and nobody's fool. "I'm seeing her later tonight. For what I've got to tell her, I think she'll be willing to swap favors, don't you?"

❦

Tonight Barrie was driving a Volvo, stolen that afternoon from the parking lot of a medical complex. When she reached Howie's building, she slowed to a crawl. "Where should I park?" she asked Gray.

"Down the block. Stop and let me out here. I'll go up first."

"Through the front door?"

"Last night's theatrics intimidated him, so I feel safe in making a more straightforward approach tonight."

"What if he couldn't find out anything?"

"I'll know if he's lying. See you up there," he said, stepping onto the pavement and closing the door.

"Be gentle," she called, but he either didn't hear her, or he chose to ignore her.

Howie's courage was short-lived. Soon after he parted company with his new friend and left the bar, his anxiety returned. On the drive home, his palms became so slippery that he could barely keep them on the steering wheel.

Bondurant was going to kick his ass if he didn't have something useful to report. And if he made something up and Bondurant found out, which he would surely do within a matter of hours, he'd probably come back and kill him. Either way, Howie was screwed. Unless he begged Barrie for mercy. She'd been pretty harsh last night, but he didn't think she could stand by and let Bondurant shoot him in cold blood.

"No, she'd go into the other room so she wouldn't lose her appetite," he muttered as he parked in his designated spot at the rear of the building and took the stairs. With shaky hands he unlocked his door and swung it open. He hesitated, straining to hear the slightest sound. Finally, he stepped into his living room and closed the door behind him.

He was fairly certain that he was alone in the apartment and that nobody had entered it since he'd left that morning.

Even so, he scurried through the small rooms, moving quickly from lamp to wall switch, flooding the place with bright light. He looked through his bedroom window at the fire escape, having determined that his callers last night had used it to get into and out of his apartment. There was no one on the metal stairs zigzagging down the side of the building.

He went to the kitchen. Nerves had turned the beer in his belly sour. He belched as he opened the refrigerator, looking for something to soak up the excess acid.

"This is nuts," he muttered around a mouthful of cold spaghetti of indeterminate age.

He wasn't a kid. He was a man. Yet he was creeping around his own home, scared of his own shadow. Ever since Barrie got this harebrained notion about the First Lady, Howie's life hadn't been worth shit. He'd had trouble at work, with Jenkins. Trouble in his leisure time, too. How could you cultivate a friendship when you were worried about a Marine recon making hash of your head? Now, the trouble had invaded his home.

Well, he was mad as hell and he wasn't going to take it anymore!

As soon as Barrie arrived, he intended to—

There was a knock on his door.

Reflexively, his gut constricted.

Then his bravery reasserted itself, and he strode belligerently to the door and yanked it open, prepared to give Barrie and Bondurant a piece of his mind. But only one guest had come to call, and he was smiling.

"Hello, Howie. May I come in?"

Barrie stepped out of the Volvo and conscientiously locked the door behind her. As she walked briskly down the sidewalk, she smiled over the irony of protecting the stolen car against car theft. She glanced up at the third floor of the corner building. The shades were down, but lights were on in all the windows of Howie's apartment. That was reassuring. If Gray was going to do something really ugly, he would do it in the dark, she thought.

She went through the vestibule and started up the staircase. It had the musty smell of antiques stores. She tapped on the door of Howie's apartment. And waited. No one came to answer. Pressing her ear close to the wood, she listened, but couldn't hear any conversation coming from the other side. She turned the knob; the door was unlocked.

"Howie? Gray?"

She went in.

The lights went out.

The brightly lit rooms were suddenly plunged into penetrating darkness. The situation called for a scream, but she was too terrified to utter a sound. She felt the vibration of the floor as someone moved quickly toward her across the living room. Spinning around, she groped for the doorknob, found it, but before she could turn it, a hand closed over hers.

"Don't make a sound."

Recognizing Gray's voice, she nearly collapsed with relief. She turned to him. "What's going on?"

"We're getting out of here. Now."

"Wait," she said, resisting as he tried to open the door. "Where's Howie? Is he here?"

"Yeah, he's here."

"Where? What'd he say?"

He didn't answer. She couldn't see him, but she sensed that he was standing rigidly, looking down at her with that unrelenting stare of his. She could feel his breath on her upturned face. "Where's Howie?"

"Shh."

Her voice rising along with her panic, she said, "What have you done to him?"

"Be quiet."

Pushing him aside, she stumbled across the living room. "Barrie, no!"

She felt air against her arm as he reached for her but missed in the darkness. In Howie's kitchen, her thigh painfully caught the corner of the dining table. She located the light switch and flipped it several times, but nothing happened. Someone had tampered with the main breaker in the fuse box.

Gray seized her arm. "Come on, Barrie. Now."

"Let go of me!" she cried, trying to wrench her arm free.

Outwrestling him was hopeless, especially in the dark. She couldn't get her bearings, but she was at least as well acquainted with Howie's kitchen as Gray was. She remembered the general layout, and as they struggled, she worked her way toward the window. When she was within reaching distance, she grabbed the bottom of the shade and gave it a hard tug. The old-fashioned shade whooshed up and spun onto the roll with the flapping sound of a million bat wings. The streetlight illuminated the kitchen.

"Dammit!" Gray growled.

With a herculean shove, Barrie pushed him aside. "Howie?" she called out.

And then she saw him, lying in the doorway between his kitchen and his bedroom. He was staring up at her. His mouth was slack and gaping wide. So was the gash that extended from ear to ear across his throat. In the pale bluish light, the blood pooling beneath him looked black.

Before she could scream, Gray covered her mouth with his hand. His lips were directly against her ear. He whispered a single word.

"Spence."

Chapter
Thirty-Four

"Spencer Martin?" Daily's confusion was plain. "You said you'd killed him."

"No, *she* said I'd killed him." He glanced at Barrie.

She was cradling a cup of scalding tea between her hands, mindlessly rocking back and forth as she sat on the edge of Daily's sofa. His house was dark. They'd managed to sneak back in undetected. At least that's what Gray hoped. With Spence a factor, the risks had suddenly become much greater.

"I only incapacitated him," he explained. "But I should have killed him."

He then described how he'd wounded Spence with a gunshot and placed him in the root cellar beneath his barn. "I wanted him to survive, but not to escape. I thought I'd come here and, with Clete's help, get Vanessa safely away from David within a matter of days. A week at most."

He glanced at Barrie, who was still staring vacantly into space. "It hasn't worked out that way. I should have known Spence would get free, although damned if I know how he managed. He probably clawed his way out."

"You're that sure it was him who killed Fripp?" Daily asked.

"I'm that sure. I know his style."

"If Howie had ever met Spencer Martin, he would have boasted about it," Barrie said, speaking for the first time in five minutes.

"They could have met for the first time seconds before Spence sliced his throat."

She shook her head. "The police said there was no sign of forced entry. Howie recognized his killer and invited him into the apartment."

Daily leaned forward. "What are you saying, Barrie?"

Gray spoke for her. "She's saying that Howie was expecting me and that I killed him."

A split second after making eye contact with him, she averted her head. He didn't let her off lightly. "Well, isn't that what you're thinking?"

"I don't know what to think," she cried, setting her cup of tea aside. "I can't think." She came to her feet and began rubbing her arms vigorously. "I can't think of anything except how gruesomely Howie died. He wasn't my favorite person," she said in an uneven voice, "and I won't pretend that he was. He was a loathsome individual, but he was a human being, harmless and innocent where this matter is concerned. I dragged him into it. I got him killed. His murder will be on my conscience for the rest of my life."

She sat down and began to cry.

Neither of the men said anything until Daily asked, "What'd the police say?"

Gray had wanted only to get the hell away from the scene, fearing that Spence might return to finish them off. But Barrie had insisted on doing what was right and called 911. Short of knocking her unconscious and carrying her from the apartment, there was nothing Gray could have done but stay with her during the questioning by homicide detectives.

They admitted to the investigators that they'd had an appointment to visit Howie that evening. When they arrived, his apartment was dark, but the door was unlocked. They'd found him dead. They had touched nothing except the doorknob, a couple of light switches, and the hem of the window shade. Gray had remembered to wipe down the fuse box before the first squad car arrived. It would have been difficult to explain why he'd wanted to flee the apartment in darkness.

"The detectives theorized that Howie had been jumped outside his apartment door and forced inside. His pockets had been rifled, so robbery was the suspected motive. It could have been a mugger, they said, or a gang initiation."

"Any suspicion cast in your direction?" Daily asked.

"There might have been, except for a footprint in the blood. It was a man's sport shoe, the kind sold by the thousands every day all over the country. Apparently the killer realized his mistake, because there was only that one imprint. The detectives figure he took off the shoe to keep from leaving a bloody trail out of the apartment.

"My guess is that Spence left the imprint on purpose so the police would surmise exactly what they did—that somebody randomly spotted Howie as he entered the building, followed him up the stairs, and did him for a few lousy bucks. It happens several times a week in that neighborhood. The police will go through a few routine procedures, then write up all the paperwork, it'll be filed, and the murder will remain unsolved."

"How can you be so damn casual about this?"

Once again Barrie was on her feet, glaring at him, causing his temper to snap. "What do you want me to do, confess?" he asked angrily, bearing down on her.

"I want you to explain why you went into Howie's apartment ahead of me."

"I wanted to make an impact."

"That's an understatement."

"That doesn't mean I killed him."

"Why'd you cut the lights when I came in?"

"To spare you from seeing him."

"After I saw him anyway, why did you try to hustle me out?"

"If Spence was lurking around, it wasn't safe."

"Spence. Spence, who's miraculously been resurrected." She waved her arms in the air. "Praise the Lord."

Gray felt his jaw tightening. "Would it make you feel better if I said, 'Okay, I confess. I sliced open the toady's throat'?"

"You're disgusting."

"What are you bellyaching about anyway? You should be hopping up and down with glee. I'm surprised you didn't call for video as soon as you hung up from 911. You were the first reporter on the scene of a grisly murder. That's right up your alley, isn't it? Isn't that what turns you on? That, and jumping into the sack with any man who might give you a juicy story in exchange."

"That's enough, Bondurant," Daily interjected.

Gray paid no attention to the reprimand. He was focused exclusively on Barrie. "I don't have to defend myself, to you or to anybody. Believe what you want. I really don't give a shit."

He turned his back to her, but had taken only a few steps when she charged after him, much as she had that first morning in his house. "If Spence is alive, why would he seek out Howie and kill him?"

"Hell if I know," he said, shaking off her hand. "Maybe he knew Howie was leaking us information he didn't want leaked."

"How would he know?"

He gave a cynical snort. "You've got to stop assuming these men play by any rules. They don't. There are no restrictions placed on them. Not moral, political, or emotional. They see something that needs doing, they do it, and they don't care how. They have no conscience. Until that sinks in, they've got you whipped, because you do play by the rules."

Having said that, he looked at Daily. "You want me to leave now, I'll leave."

Sighing heavily, Daily came to his feet. "Every time the two of you get me out of bed in the middle of the night, it's bad news." That's all he said before shuffling off to his bedroom.

Gray gave Barrie a hard, challenging look, but she said nothing, just turned away and followed Daily down the hall.

Cursing beneath his breath, Gray removed his boots and shirt and lay down on the sofa. It was too short for him; he had to prop his feet on the armrest. He could sleep just about anywhere, under any circumstances. He'd trained himself to fall asleep at will. He'd learned how to drop off instantly and sleep deeply, while leaving one portion of his subconscious awake and alert to danger.

But tonight his training failed him. He was too angry to sleep. Angry and . . . Hurt? Was that the word? "Christ." He placed his forearm across his eyes. Hurt? Over what? Her inane accusation? Over her suspicion that he was a murderer? What an asinine, sophomoric emotion to be nursing.

Believe what you want. I really don't give a shit. Hell of it was, he did. He didn't know exactly how he wanted Barrie to think of him, but it sure as hell wasn't as a cold-blooded killer. He couldn't think of a single reason why her opinion should matter to him, but it did.

She was a smart-ass. Too impulsive for her own good. She had a stinging, sarcastic sense of humor that she used to cover fear and disappointment. But she wasn't a coward, and courage was a trait that Gray admired. Her mind was razor sharp. Perhaps she was too inventive to be an objective journalist, but that creative bent only enhanced her intelligence. She'd suffered rejection, and he could sympathize, even empathize to some degree.

She also had a hell of a lot of integrity. It was a cheap shot to accuse her of using seduction to get a sound bite. He hadn't meant it that morning in Jackson Hole, and he didn't now. He didn't even believe it.

She probably couldn't explain that predawn orgy at his house any more than he could, and he couldn't even come close to explaining it. He'd chalked it up to spontaneous, all-consuming, inexplicable lust, and let it go at that. It was safer not to overanalyze such intense sexual encounters. Best to blame it on the animalistic aspects of man, and forget it. Or try to.

Despite his snide comments to the contrary, he'd known the minute he touched her that morning that she was no femme fatale. Her reactions were too honest, her responses too undisciplined.

He didn't want to think about her undisciplined responses. Not tonight, when he was furious with her. But recollections crept from their hiding places at the edges of his mind and taunted him. Thoughts crowded his otherwise compartmentalized mind, thoughts of breasts that were small but full, of nipples that seemed never to be completely relaxed, of her whispers in the darkness in that voice that alone could arouse him.

"Gray?"

He lowered his arm and sprang into a sitting position in one sudden motion. He hadn't heard her approach, so he was

surprised to see her standing only a few feet from the sofa.
He cleared his throat. "Yeah?"

"Were you asleep?"

"Getting there," he lied.

"I've figured out what we should do next."

"What?" he asked, thinking hopefully, *Screw ourselves blind?*

That wasn't at all what she suggested.

∽∾

Barrie knew of the area. It was a well-kept Washington
secret because a number of prominent people lived on these
twisting, heavily wooded streets near Embassy Row. They
were in shouting distance of the well-traveled Massachusetts
Avenue, but unless you were looking for them specifically,
you would miss them. They weren't on many maps.

The houses were set well away from the street, screened
by tall hedges or brick walls. Many had electric gates for
additional security. Barrie was jittery when Gray pulled the
car to a stop in the driveway of an estate that was for sale.

"We could get shot," she said.

"We could."

"What do you think she'll do when we come traipsing
through her backyard?"

"We won't know until we do it."

This had been Barrie's idea. Last night, it had seemed
like a good one. Now, she was less sure. "You say you've
met her before?"

"A couple of times, at official functions. But we've
never engaged in any private conversation. She may not
even remember me."

"I doubt that." They shared a taut look for several
moments, then she added softly, "You do make an impression on people, Mr. Bondurant."

"Yeah. Take for instance the impression I've made on you."

Barrie looked down at her clasped hands. "I'm sorry about that. Last night, I mean. I never really believed that you could . . ." She bit down on her lower lip. "I was upset. And frightened."

"Forget it." He opened the car door.

"No, please." She laid a restraining hand on his arm. "I don't want this to fester."

"Okay. Say whatever is on your mind."

"I thought about it all night and tried to look at it from every angle. If Spence did escape and return to Washington, if he somehow tracked down Howie and discerned that he was feeding us information, and if he did get to Howie's apartment minutes before we did and killed him, why did he plant a clue that would divert the investigation away from us?

"Spence could have made it look like we killed Howie, say out of spite for getting me fired. Safely behind bars and trying to prove our innocence, we'd be out of his and Merritt's hair. So why would he purposely get us off the hook with local police?"

Without having to think it over, Gray replied, "Because he has something larger in store for us."

"Like what?"

"I don't know yet. That's why we must tread very carefully." He looked past the vacant colonial mansion to the woods behind it. "Let's go."

Although she was even more shaken now than before their conversation, Barrie got out of the car. She'd been careful to bring with them the newspaper ad for the sale of the estate. The ad might provide a plausible excuse if anyone stopped and asked them why they were snooping around.

She followed Gray's lead as he moved along the high iron picket fence that demarcated the property. It took them five minutes to reach the rear boundary. "That's theirs," he said, pointing ahead.

On the far side of the greenbelt between the two properties, she saw the roof of the house. "Lead on."

The leaves on the hardwoods were just beginning to turn, providing a colorful palette of contrast to the evergreens. Fallen leaves crunched underfoot as they picked their way through the woods. At any other time, under any other circumstances, this would have been a pleasant outing.

They held back when they reached the wide, carefully tended lawn fanning out behind the red brick Georgian house. Bright chrysanthemums bloomed in the gardens. The hedges were as perfectly manicured as a debutante on the night of her coming-out ball.

"Since I met you, Bondurant, I've seen a lot of backyards. This is by far the prettiest."

He came close to smiling, but it never fully developed because just then a woman came out the back door. She was carrying an armful of what appeared to be rolled-up posters secured with rubber bands.

"That's her," Gray said. He stepped from the sheltering trees and started across the lawn. Barrie followed with trepidation.

The woman was slim and attractive. After placing the posters in the backseat of her Jeep Cherokee, she straightened up. That's when she spotted them. To her credit, she didn't turn and run or demonstrate apprehension of any kind. She stood her ground.

As they came closer, Barrie saw that her expressive dark eyes seemed troubled. They shifted from Barrie to Gray, then back to Barrie. Before either she or Gray could begin to explain why they were there, Amanda Allan said, "Thank God you've come."

Chapter
Thirty-Five

She led Barrie and Gray through the large, homey kitchen, past a gracious dining room, and into a cozy living room. A low fire was burning in the grate. The room smelled faintly of apples and cinnamon. Framed photographs of two young boys, Dr. George Allan, and Amanda were scattered around the room, documenting their family history and the children's growth. The furnishings were tasteful and beautiful, but comfortable. The atmosphere was inviting.

Barrie envied the other woman the beautiful room, the children, and the home she'd made. Not so enviable was the tension in Amanda Allan's face and carriage, which portended doom.

It had occurred to Barrie last night that Mrs. Allan might be agreeable to discussing her husband's work, especially if there was disharmony between the couple, as Howie had said. She'd thought of it as a long shot but worth a try. Never would she have expected Amanda to appear so relieved to see her and Gray. Nor would she have expected this woman, who seemed to have everything one could desire, to look so miserably unhappy and stressed.

When they were seated, Amanda addressed Gray first. "How are you? A lot has happened since we last saw each other." He nodded, then introduced her to Barrie. "I know who you are, Ms. Travis."

"And I know who you are," Barrie said. "At least I do now. You called me at WVUE and alerted me to what was going on at Highpoint." The moment Amanda had spoken to her outside, Barrie had recognized the voice and identified her as the anonymous tipster.

"I apologize for being so mysterious. I felt I had to do something, tell someone, but wasn't sure how to go about it. You came to mind because of your interview with Vanessa."

"You knew something untoward was going on at your lake house?"

"I sensed something was wrong, but I didn't know what. George . . ." She rolled her lips inward. Amanda wasn't the kind of woman who would weep in front of strangers. She didn't continue until she had regained her composure. "George doesn't confide in me anymore. But I believe if that nurse hadn't suffered a fatal heart attack when she did, Vanessa would also be dead."

"I'm afraid you're right," Gray confirmed.

She looked at Barrie with barely controlled desperation. "Once you left the TV station, I didn't know how to contact you."

"Why were you trying to reach me?"

"To tell you something you obviously already know. David Merritt isn't the man that everyone's been duped into believing. He's an unconscionable villain. He must be stopped." She fixed her dark eyes intently on Barrie. "May I ask you something?" Barrie nodded. "You burst into the morgue at Shinlin Hospital because you believed it was Vanessa's body under the sheet, right?"

"Right."

"And you also believed that my husband brought about her death?"

Barrie looked at her sadly. "I'm sorry. That's precisely what I thought. And so did Gray."

Amanda folded her hands together in her lap. "I see."

"Vanessa's manic-depression and the medications required to keep her mood swings under control offer a physician lots of room to maneuver. Wouldn't you agree?"

"Yes," Amanda replied thickly. "I would imagine so."

"We have several good reasons to believe that Vanessa is still in grave danger," Gray said.

"From George?"

"From David."

"But *through* George."

He didn't need to answer. His expression made it clear.

Barrie knew they weren't telling Amanda anything she hadn't already figured out. Still, having her worst fears confirmed couldn't be easy. But she retained her dignity, which won Barrie's admiration.

"I realize how extremely difficult this must be for you, Mrs. Allan," she said. "I've never met him, but based on what I know of your husband, I don't believe he's acting maliciously."

"I know him," Gray said. "I think he's as much David's victim as Vanessa is."

"We didn't come here to accuse Dr. Allan of anything," Barrie said. "We're only seeking information."

"You don't have to defend yourselves to me," Amanda said with a bitter laugh. "Ever since David assumed office and appointed George the White House physician, he has put my husband through pure hell."

"David's gifted that way," Gray remarked.

He and Amanda exchanged a look of shared understanding that momentarily excluded Barrie. Finally breaking the eye contact, Amanda focused on a recent family portrait on an end table. "George is caught up in something terrible. Whatever it is, he's powerless to extricate himself from it. It's wreaking havoc on our personal life. It's having an adverse effect on our children. It's put George at war with himself. He's tormented. He's disintegrating right before my eyes, and I can't seem to reach him, not even with pleading or with threats of leaving him. Whatever this *something* is, it's more powerful than I." She looked at Barrie. "Do you have an inkling?"

"David Merritt killed Vanessa's baby. It wasn't SIDS."

Amanda pressed her thin, white fingers against her lips to keep them from trembling.

"Your husband was trapped into complying with something that goes against his nature as a healer and his personal moral code," Barrie said softly. "That's why he's tormented."

What she couldn't bring herself to say was that Dr. Allan had covered the murder for the President and was now assisting in the elimination of the only witness to the crime.

But Amanda was an intelligent woman. She didn't need it spelled out for her. Finally, she lowered her hand. Her lips were pale, but no longer trembling. "I loathe that man for what he's done to my husband. Even if it means implicating George in a crime, I'll do whatever I can to help you expose David Merritt for what he is. I prefer having George alive and serving time in prison to having him dead. If this nightmare doesn't end for him soon, it's going to kill him by one means or another."

"Barrie and I were hoping you would agree to help," Gray said.

Amanda turned to him. "Plainly speaking, you believe that David has commissioned George to eliminate Vanessa?"

"Yes, we do."

"What about her father? Clete Armbruster would kill anyone, including his son-in-law, if one hair on her head was harmed. Have you asked him for help?"

"We've tried," Barrie told her. "But since the debacle in Shinlin, he won't even speak to us."

"There could be another reason he's avoiding you," Amanda said. "The senator isn't altogether innocent. He plays high-stakes politics. George has alluded to some of his shenanigans."

"My theory exactly," Gray said. "If Clete starts firing accusations at the White House, chances are good they'll ricochet and he'll wind up shooting himself. David's M.O. is to get the goods on the people surrounding him. Dirty secrets instill blind loyalty. No one is exempt. Not even the father-in-law who got him elected."

"I have no such loyalty to David Merritt," Amanda said. "What do you need from me?"

"The name of the facility where George is keeping Vanessa."

"I don't know. He hasn't told me. But I presume it's Tabor House."

Barrie looked across at Gray. He appeared as puzzled as she.

"A private detox hospital," Amanda added.

"I never heard of it."

"You wouldn't," she explained. "Tabor House is kept very hush-hush. It's available only to high-ranking government officials and their immediate families. Substance abuse among high-profile Washington personnel occurs more often than anyone would guess. The facility was founded about twenty years ago so that the government could save face when someone in power needed to be detoxed."

"Where is it?"

"Virginia. By car, about an hour and a half."

"That explains George's helicopter trips from the White House lawn every day," Gray said. "Can you give us directions?"

She frowned with consternation. "I've never been there. Visitors aren't allowed. But I know the name of the nearest town."

They followed her into the kitchen, where she sat at a built-in desk and wrote down for them what she knew. Finding the exact location of Tabor House would be left to them. Gray read over the information she'd provided, then pocketed the paper. "This is more than we had," he said. "Thank you, Amanda."

"Gray." She laid a hand on his arm. "I trust you to be careful. With George, I mean. I'm doing this to save his life. *Our* life. But by helping you, I also feel that I'm betraying him."

"I understand the conflict. I've been experiencing a similar one. Remember, I once served under David, as his aide and his friend." He paused. "I won't do anything to physically harm George. You have my word," he reassured her.

She pressed his arm, then dropped her hand. "This is so terribly dangerous for you. I'm surprised you took a chance on coming here."

Barrie told her about the surveillance they'd been under since the incident in Shinlin. "We were followed when we left my friend's house. Gray was able to lose the other car in traffic. But I must warn you that someone else we talked to was murdered last night."

"My God."

"Why don't you and the children go away for a while. Until all this is cleared up," Gray suggested.

She considered it, but only briefly. "If I took the children out of school and fled, that would make us look all the more suspicious. Besides, I won't leave George."

Barrie's admiration for the woman increased again.

"We took every precaution to protect you, but don't trust anyone," Gray warned her. "Not even someone you ordinarily would. Like Spence Martin."

Amanda cocked her head. "But . . . you took care of that viper. Didn't you? I assumed . . ."

"What do you mean?"

Amanda indicated the small TV built in to the kitchen cabinetry. "It was on earlier. A news bulletin."

"What was the news?" Barrie asked.

"Gray. Gray Bondurant was the news."

Chapter
Thirty-Six

Gray Bondurant, hero of the hostage rescue mission, was being sought by the FBI for questioning into the disappearance of Spencer Martin, presidential aide.

David Merritt heard of this at the same time as the rest of the country did.

He and Spence were holding a confidential meeting in the President's private quarters. Only a handful of people at the White House knew that Spence was in residence. He had moved into an extra bedroom on the third floor. Here, they could talk freely. The room was both soundproof and impossible to bug.

"The guy was a moron," Spence said of Howie Fripp. "He was actually glad to see me. Invited me in. Didn't even stop to wonder how I knew where he lived."

"You're sure he didn't have time to contact Travis and Gray between the time he left the bar and when you showed up at his door?"

"I had him in sight the whole time." Spence took a sip of Pepsi. "But it wouldn't have mattered if he had contacted them. He didn't know anything. He was only boasting that he did, to impress me. He couldn't—"

"What the hell is that?"

Turning to see what had captured David's attention, Spence was as alarmed to see his face on the television screen as the President was. It was an old picture, probably the only one of him on file. Nevertheless, he was recognizable. He picked up the remote control and disengaged the mute button.

". . . has been reported missing."

David and Spence looked at each other with complete bafflement, which only increased as the network's Capitol Hill correspondent went on. "It is believed that Gray Bondurant, who came to national fame following a daring hostage rescue mission, was the last person to see Spencer Martin, when he recently entertained the President's adviser at his ranch in Wyoming. A full-scale investigation to locate Mr. Martin is under way."

"Jesus!" Spence surged to his feet. "Who's responsible for this?"

"I don't know. But I'm going to find out." He reached for the telephone and demanded that a call be placed to the attorney general.

"Use the speakerphone," Spence said.

Attorney General William Yancey was out, so one of his subordinates got a good taste of wrath, presidential style. "What the fuck is going on? Where is Mr. Yancey? I want to speak with him immediately."

"He and Mrs. Yancey are out to dinner, Mr. President."

"Well, track him down. Now. In the meantime, I want to know who authorized this investigation into Spencer Martin's disappearance."

"Mr. Yancey himself, sir. As I understand it, he received a tip."

"A tip? He got a tip? And he's authorized a full-scale investigation on that basis alone?"

"The tip came from a very reliable source, Mr. President."

"Who?"

"Senator Armbruster."

David swung his gaze toward Spence, who launched into a vicious, albeit silent, spate of obscenities. Lowering himself into a chair and massaging his temples, David imposed a rigid calm over his voice. "I see. Senator Armbruster probably just forgot to discuss it with me beforehand."

"The senator said that Mr. Martin has been missing for almost two weeks." After an uneasy pause, he added, "Mr. President, Mr. Yancey assumed that Senator Armbruster was acting on your behalf."

"Well of course he was," David said smoothly. "I too have become increasingly disturbed by Mr. Martin's absence. What I don't understand is why Mr. Yancey is looking for Mr. Bondurant."

"Sir, Bondurant recently told Senator Armbruster that Mr. Martin had been to his place in Wyoming. As far as anyone can tell, that was the last report on Mr. Martin's whereabouts."

"Has Mr. Bondurant been apprehended?"

"Not yet, sir."

"Keep me posted."

"Of course, Mr. President."

"And track down Mr. Yancey. I wish to speak to him immediately."

"Certainly, sir. I'll convey the message right away."

David disconnected. "Well, do you want to suddenly reappear and put a stop to this nonsense?"

Spence paced for a moment. "No. I can operate better if I'm not visible. But I'll order my men to look the other way if they spot Gray. We sure as hell don't want him questioned by the FBI or Yancey."

"Yancey," David repeated with rank dislike.

William Yancey had seemed the perfect man for the position of attorney general in the Merritt administration. Ten years David's junior, he was as young and aggressive as Robert Kennedy had been when his older brother appointed him to that job. Like Kennedy, Yancey had distinguished himself in criminal prosecution, both in state and federal jurisdictions. He was charismatic, attractive, and articulate. So David had asked him to sign on, and he'd regretted it ever since. Yancey was too sharp, too industrious, too honest. Yancey and Bondurant would be a dangerous pairing of like minds.

"As soon as Gray sees this news story, what's to stop him from strolling into Yancey's office and volunteering that you're buried in his root cellar?"

"He won't do that."

"Why not?"

"First, because it would put him out of commission. At least temporarily. He'd have to explain why he shot me and imprisoned me in his cellar. It would take time to get to the bottom of that, time that Gray doesn't want to spend. Second, when he saw Howie Fripp's body, it was a good as a calling card. Gray knows I'm no longer in that cellar."

David frowned. "Timing's suddenly become critical, hasn't it?"

"Very."

"Dammit, we don't need this," he said angrily. "What the hell was Clete thinking?"

Spence indicated the telephone. "I suggest you ask him."

"I really don't understand why you're so upset, David,"

Clete said, flicking his cigar ashes into a china ashtray bearing the presidential seal.

The senator had responded immediately to the President's summons. With the complete understanding that an enraged David Merritt was waiting for him, he'd approached the meeting in an upbeat frame of mind. Pulling off a tricky double-cross always put him in a good mood.

David was shitting bricks over this matter of Spence and Bondurant, just as Clete had known he would. David certainly didn't want Bondurant to go on record as saying that Spence had been dispatched to assassinate him. Naturally, he would deny any such claims and turn the tables on Bondurant by calling him a traitor and a murderer.

But the damage would already be done, and it would be irreparable. Seeds of doubt would already have been planted in the public's mind. Prior to an election year, this was sticky business for an incumbent. The opposition party would have a field day pointing out to an impressionable public the shady kind of characters their president surrounded himself with.

By betraying Gray Bondurant, Clete had made an enemy, but the man was expendable. Barrie Travis certainly was. He'd sliced-and-diced her credibility all to hell after that scene in the hospital morgue.

Even though they had David Merritt dead to rights, Clete had no qualms about stymieing their efforts. He couldn't have those two loose cannons running around causing mishaps, jeopardizing his own plans to destroy David.

There was also the outside chance that, in their bumbling fashion, they would stumble across the Becky Sturgis affair. That would unquestionably ruin the President. But it would also ruin Clete Armbruster. In the line-up of his priorities, self-preservation was second only to power.

So, to keep Bondurant and the reporter occupied, he'd clued Attorney General Yancey to the fact that the former recon was the last person known to have seen Spencer Martin alive. Now that they'd been derailed, Clete's aim was straight. He had to get Vanessa healthy and away from David permanently, then destroy him.

Meanwhile, David was on a verbal rampage. "Without discussing it with me first—"

"I've been trying for days to discuss it with you," Clete interrupted. "You haven't taken my calls. You were in Georgia yesterday. This afternoon you had that meeting—"

"I know what my agenda was, Clete. You could have waited until I was free before calling Yancey."

"On the contrary, David. I did not feel that this could wait any longer. People have been asking about Spence."

"What people?"

"People on your own staff. People to whom his absence is noticeable. You've been distracted, so they've come to me."

"Why you?"

"Because you and I are so close." Clete let the statement lie there like a gauntlet, daring David to pick it up. "Everyone assumes that you share your thoughts and concerns with me. If you discussed Spence's unexplained absence with anyone, it would be with me." He puffed contentedly on his cigar.

"Gray told you that Spence had come to see him?"

"That's right. The night I met him and the Travis broad in Shinlin."

"There was so much going on that night, how did Spence's name even enter into the conversation?"

Clete frowned as though trying to remember. "I can't exactly recall. Best as I remember, it was a casual reference. I probably wouldn't have thought of it again if Spence had reappeared. But he hasn't, and it doesn't look like he's going to. I did some snooping. His mail's backed up. Nobody in his apartment building has seen him in weeks. He hasn't returned phone calls. Looks like he went to Wyoming and got swallowed by a Teton, doesn't it? Appears that Bondurant was the last person to see him."

David laughed. "That language has such sinister overtones, Clete. Are you suggesting that Gray killed Spence?"

"Do you have another explanation?"

"That's ridiculous."

"Is it?"

"Yes," David replied testily.

"Yancey doesn't seem to think so."

"*Yancey*. I had reservations about appointing him. I wish now I'd heeded them."

Clete chuckled. "Because he's much like Bondurant. Always in your face over something. He doesn't kowtow like the rest of them. In any event, he talked to somebody over in the FBI criminal division, who agreed that a little chat with Mr. Bondurant is in order."

Clete stuck the cigar in the corner of his mouth, moved to the liquor cabinet, and poured himself a straight scotch. He held the cut crystal tumbler in front of a lamp and studied the play of light through the facets. "When they question Bondurant, I wonder how much he'll tell them about Spence's visit to Wyoming."

He turned and looked pointedly at his son-in-law. The two men exchanged a long stare. David was the first to smile, in grudging respect for his shrewd mentor. "So you know. Gray told you."

"That you sent Spence there to kill him? Yes, he told me. Makes one wonder what else he knows—or thinks he knows—that you'd rather keep quiet."

David sat down on a divan and crossed one ankle over the opposite knee. Clete wasn't fooled by David's seeming insouciance. He wasn't nearly as relaxed as he wished to appear.

"What do you want, Clete? I know you too well. You didn't orchestrate this bullshit FBI investigation on a whim. You for damn sure didn't do it out of concern for Spence. Then why? What is it you want?"

"My daughter."

"My *wife*, you mean."

"You're ruining Vanessa's life. I won't let it happen."

"Where Vanessa is concerned, my wishes as her husband take precedence over yours, Clete. Let me assure you that she is in excellent hands."

"Where? Allan's lake house again?"

"Her condition became much too serious to be treated there. She flipped out one morning. George had no choice. He had to remove her to a nursing facility."

"Which facility?"

"Tabor House."

"The detox hospital?"

"He knew her privacy would be guaranteed there." David got up, crossed to his desk, and retrieved a slip of paper from the middle drawer. "Here's the number. Call it if you don't believe me."

Clete snatched the paper from him and asked the White House operator to place the call. While he waited, he slammed back the scotch. Finally a mellifluous voice answered. "Tabor House."

"This is Senator Clete Armbruster. Let me speak to whoever's in charge."

"One moment, please."

Soft music played in his ear as he waited for the call to be directed. He wondered if this really was a telephone line to the exclusive substance-abuse hospital or if David was tricking him.

"Clete? I've been expecting to hear from you. The President told me you'd be calling."

He recognized the voice. Dr. Dexter Leopold, former surgeon general, now administrator of Tabor House. "Hello, Dex. How's my daughter?"

"I'll be perfectly honest with you, Clete. She was in bad shape when Dr. Allan brought her here. Her medication wasn't working because she was drinking so heavily. But we've got it stabilized now, and she's much improved."

"Give her the best treatment available, Dex."

"That goes without saying."

"I want other doctors on her case, not just Allan."

There was a slight pause on the other end. "That would be awkward, Clete."

"I don't care how awkward it is."

"Dr. Allan is her physician of record. Until Mrs. Merritt herself—or President Merritt if she's incapable of making the decision—replaces him, I must recognize him as the physician in charge of her case."

Dex Leopold was reputed to be an honorable man, but David could have gotten to him somehow. If George Allan was slowly killing Vanessa, would Dr. Leopold look the other way? "Exactly where is Tabor House?" Clete asked. "I'd like to come see her tomorrow."

"I'm afraid I can't allow that, Clete," the doctor said gently. "You know the policy here. Absolutely no one except the patients and the staff are allowed on the premises. That's the only way we can protect our patients' privacy and maintain the hospital's integrity. Seeing family can cause a setback, especially once the patient is medically healed and we're working on the psychological phase of recovery."

"But surely, Dex—"

"I'm sorry, Clete, no exceptions. Not even the President has been allowed to visit Mrs. Merritt, although he's asked to each time he's called. If I turn him down, I must say no to you too. It's what's best for Mrs. Merritt, I assure you."

Clete's eyes cut to David, who was watching him, his expression unperturbed.

"All right," Clete conceded. "I want Vanessa to be well again. She's had it rough ever since the baby died."

"So President Merritt informed me. He regrets not getting her into therapy following the baby's death. If she'd had counseling then, this crisis might have been avoided. But don't worry. We'll return her to you fully restored."

"You will if you know what's good for you," Clete said just before hanging up.

"Satisfied?" David asked.

"Not by a long shot." Clete strode to the door of the Oval Office. "Be very careful, David. I don't care how many people you've lined up to lie for you and do your dirty work, I'll have my daughter back, or else. A few weeks ago I reminded you that I put you here, and I can take you out." He snapped his fingers an inch from the President's nose. "Like that."

Chapter Thirty-Seven

*W*ell before daylight, Clete headed downstairs to pour himself a cup of coffee. Before going to bed each night, he set the timer on the coffeemaker.

That first steaming cup always brought back cherished memories of his boyhood, before he knew how to spell *politics* or even what the word meant, before he learned that some men placed ambition and greed above honor, before he had become one of those men.

His father had been a tall, strong, quiet man to whom committing one crime to cover another would have been unthinkable. He'd had only a third-grade education, but he knew all the constellations and could calculate in record time the number of dots on the dominoes just played. He was slow to anger, but quick to defend an underdog in a fight.

He had served under General Patton in Germany. That's where he'd been killed and buried. But before the war he'd lived and worked as a wrangler on a cattle ranch in south Texas. During spring roundups, he would sometimes let young Clete ride along with him and the other cowboys.

The most dangerous animals on the range weren't other men from whom you had to protect your back, but rattlers, spooked horses, and cranky longhorns. The days in the saddle were long, hard, and dusty. The nights were star-studded. At dawn every morning, before the workday began, the cowboys gathered around the campfire and drank cups of scalding, stout coffee.

After the war, his widowed mother moved them to Mississippi to live with her family. Clete had spent the remainder of his youth far from the cattle ranch, and the majority of his adult life in Washington, but sixty years later, he could still recapture the mingled smells of frying pork, and manure, and leather, and his father's cigarettes, handrolled as he hunkered down over breakfast under the sky. No coffee in the world had tasted as rotten as that camp coffee. None since had tasted as good.

Clete had loved those mornings. He'd loved his father too. He remembered how glad he'd been to ride along beside him, and how the other men, no matter how tough, had treated his father with earned respect. How proud Clete-the-boy had been to be his father's son.

On this morning, as on all others, Clete avoided thinking about whether his father would be proud of Clete-the-man.

He switched on the kitchen light.

Gray Bondurant was sitting at the table. He had helped himself to a cup of coffee. "Morning, Clete."

His voice was level. His slouch was hardly a confrontational posture. But Clete knew that to Gray Bondurant, betrayal was the ultimate offense. And Bondurant was a dangerous man.

Clete wondered if his reminiscences of his father and campfires and roundups had been harbingers of his imminent death at the hands of a man he had sorely wronged. He was ashamed of the fear that fissured through him.

Of course, he let none of his apprehension show as he poured himself some coffee and joined his uninvited guest at the kitchen table. It would have been a waste of breath to ask Bondurant how he'd gotten inside the house. The sophisticated alarm system had been armed, but it wouldn't have deterred the recon who'd penetrated the walls of a Middle Eastern prison.

Holding Bondurant's chilly, implacable stare, Clete took a fortifying sip of caffeine. "I guess saying I'm sorry won't cut it."

"Not hardly, Clete. Call off the dogs."

"I can't. It's gone too far. It's out of my hands."

"Bullshit. You started the ball rolling. You can stop it. Or are all your boasts about the power you wield just so much hot air?"

Bondurant was a worthy adversary. He wasn't going to be put off with verbiage. Clete decided to cut to the chase. "What do you want?"

"I want to find Vanessa and return her to you. But I can't have the FBI breathing down my neck while I go about it."

"Vanessa's no longer in danger."

"You believe that?"

"She's at Tabor House."

"I know where she is."

Clete wondered how Bondurant had come by that information, but he knew it was pointless to ask. "Last night I talked to Dex Leopold. He's the ramrod there now. I've put him on notice that she better come back to me safe and sound."

Bondurant snuffled with scorn, then leaned across the table. "Did you believe anything that Barrie and I told you about Vanessa's pregnancy and the baby's so-called SIDS?"

Being the politician he was, Clete held his silence.

"If you think there's any truth to what we told you, do

you believe David will let it go now? You know him better
than anyone, Clete, so what do you think? If he did in fact
smother Vanessa's baby, do you think there's a ghost of a
chance that he's going to let her live to tell about it?"

Clete mentally debated the question, although the
answer was terrifyingly simple. "What do you want?" he
repeated brusquely.

"Freedom to move around without fear of being apprehended. I don't care how you do it, get me out of hock with
the FBI."

"How do you propose I—"

"Don't pull that shit with me. You'll think of something, and you'll be convincing. Tell them you were grossly
misunderstood, misquoted, misled. Make something up, but
make it believable. Get them off my tail. In return, you'll get
Vanessa back."

"I'll get her back anyway."

"The question is whether you'll get her back alive."

"David wouldn't dare go that far. I've put him on
notice too."

"All the more reason for us to act quickly."

"I'll do my own acting, thank you."

"Okay, have it your way. But there's one more thing
you should know. Spence hasn't mysteriously disappeared.
He's alive and well and in Washington."

"The hell you say! I thought you killed him."

"Well, I didn't, although I might live just long enough
to regret it. He's back. I've seen his handiwork. Do you think
he and David will allow the FBI boys to interrogate me?
Never. They'll try and kill me first."

"So it's your own skin you're bargaining for, not
Vanessa's."

That shot caused a glint of anger to appear in the other
man's eyes, but he kept his cool. "Spence won't stay invisi-

ble forever. He'll materialize. When he does, they'll publicize it and have a good laugh at your expense. You'll look like a doddering old fool for raising a false alarm. Yancey and the FBI will denounce you for meddling and dragging them into a farce.

"After that, who's going to believe you when you blame David for whatever misfortune befalls Vanessa? No one. You'll be written off as delusional and senile. David will have won on all accounts."

"You're lying." Bondurant didn't honor the accusation with a denial, merely stared at Clete with those cold blue eyes. "I told David last night why I called Yancey and got the investigation going. If Spence was still alive, he would have told me."

"Would he? Or is he setting you up?" Bondurant leaned slightly forward again. "Cagey as you are, Clete, I'm sure you've cooked up a delicious plan to destroy David for killing your grandson, but your way will take time, and time is something we don't have."

The man was making sense, but Clete wasn't ready to concede. "What if I don't do as you ask?"

"Then good luck. You're on your own."

"I've been doing things on my own for a damn long time. I have a pretty good track record."

"Then why isn't Vanessa here with you now instead of locked away in some hospital, incommunicado, under the watch and care of David's lap-puppy George Allan?"

It was a good question. Clete had no answer for it. Still, it was hard for him to back down. Retraction wasn't in his nature.

"You're bluffing. You want Vanessa safely back as much as I do. With or without my intervention, you would fight off the FBI and anybody else to storm the castle and rescue her."

"Maybe once. Not anymore."

"Got another girl, huh? Barrie Travis?"

Clete didn't expect him to rise to the bait, and he didn't. "In many ways, Vanessa is a delightful woman. But she's selfish."

"Listen here," Clete said, shaking his index finger in Bondurant's face. "I won't have you or anyone criticizing my daughter."

Ignoring him, Bondurant continued. "She learned early on to cover her own ass, and she had a damned good teacher in you. Vanessa always gives herself top priority, and never so much as when I resigned my White House post. She let me bear the brunt of the gossip about us, never uttering a single word in my defense, never interceding with David on my behalf."

"So why are you offering to help her now?"

"Patriotism."

Clete snorted. "Self-aggrandizement is more like it. You're a hero. Saving the First Lady is an irresistible challenge."

"Nothing as romantic as that, Clete. An innocent baby is dead. Shouldn't his killer be punished? I also want closure on my association with David's presidency. I want it to be over with once and for all, and that'll never happen until his administration is upended and the ugly underbelly is exposed. And while Vanessa no longer holds my affection, she certainly doesn't deserve to die."

"Saint Gray," Clete said snidely.

Bondurant came to his feet, signaling that he'd done all the haggling he intended to do. He seemed exceptionally strong as he stood over the table. Clete suffered by comparison. The younger man's sinewy strength made him feel old and soft and weak.

"What's it going to be, Clete? Do I implement a rescue?"

"I'll think about it."

"Not good enough. Call Bill Yancey—now—or I disappear, and Vanessa's life rests in your hands alone. You're mean and cunning enough, you might defeat David and survive. She won't."

Clete never surrendered. Never. But he knew from his football days at Ole Miss when it was prudent to fall back and punt.

As she was making her way from the fresh grave back to her car, two men fell into step with her, one on each side. "Miss Travis?"

"Yes?"

They showed her their FBI badges. "We'd like to ask you a few questions."

"Now?" she asked incredulously. "In case you haven't noticed, this is a funeral."

"We noticed," one said. "We're sorry about Mr. Fripp. We've had a problem locating you and figured you'd be here."

"Your insensitivity is unforgivable," she said.

Pathetically few people had attended the brief, secular service at Howie Fripp's interment, which was a sad commentary on his life. Almost exclusively, those in attendance were co-workers from WVUE, most of whom had used the funeral as an excuse to take an extra hour at lunch. In chatty groups, they were hurrying back to their cars, having upheld their moral responsibility and now free to socialize on company time.

Barrie's tears were real. She genuinely felt sad, not only for the horrible way in which Howie had died but because there would be no atonement for the crime and because no one really cared anyway.

One of the agents nudged her from her lament. "Even

though this is an inconvenient time, Miss Travis, we'd still like to talk to you."

"Since you've got me surrounded, what choice do I have? But do you mind if we move a little farther from the grave?"

"Not at all."

When they reached her car, she blotted her eyes one last time and turned to face them. "I told the police everything I know about Mr. Fripp's murder. They took my statement at the scene."

"That's not why we're here," one of the agents said.

"No?" she said, pretending to be taken aback and puzzled. "Then what's this about?"

"Gray Bondurant."

"Oh, him," she said in a drop-dead voice. Folding her arms across her chest, she assumed a bored but disgruntled pose. "What do you gentlemen wish to know about our nation's erstwhile hero?"

"For starters, where he is."

"I don't know. I don't want to know. He's a creep."

The agents exchanged a look. One said, "It's our understanding, Miss Travis, that the two of you have been spending a great deal of time together."

"That's right, we have. *Had*, rather. Until yesterday, when he turned up as one of America's Most Wanted. As if I didn't have enough problems," she said, rolling her eyes. "First my house blew up, killing my dog. Then I had a shouting match with Senator Armbruster, during which he did all the shouting. That incident got me fired from my job.

"Then I indulged in a . . . well, you know," she said demurely. "I got involved in a *thing* with this guy. But what woman wouldn't be attracted to him? He's a national hero, for heaven's sake. The strong, silent type. Very sexy. And he has these eyes that just . . ." She shivered in mock delight.

"Well, anyway, we were getting along pretty well, then yesterday his mug shows up on a news bulletin. Scared the hell out of me. I told him to get lost and he did." She sighed wistfully. "I should have known he was too good to be true."

"When did you last see him?"

"Just as I said, yesterday."

"What time?"

"Hmm, let's see. Midafternoon."

"Can you be more specific?"

"No. Up until I saw the news flash, I wasn't watching the time."

"What were you doing?"

She shot him a telling look.

"I see. You were having an . . . assignation?"

She giggled. "How quaintly put."

"Where did it take place?"

"Some motel. I don't remember the name."

"Location?"

"You got me. It was along a freeway, I remember that. I didn't pay any attention to where we were going."

"You don't have any idea what part of town you were in?"

Bowing her head, she pulled her lower lip through her teeth, looking distressed. "I, uh . . . God, this is *so* embarrassing. Gray, Mr. Bondurant, was driving, see. And I . . . Oh, jeez! Can I just say that on the way to this motel I wasn't exactly sitting up straight in the seat and that my head was below the dashboard?"

The agents exchanged another look. One's eyebrows were encroaching on his receding hairline.

"I'm not even sure the motel had a name," she continued. "He picked the place. Between you and me, it was kind of sleazy. You know the type of place. Rooms rented by the hour. Clean sheets optional. On top of being wanted for questioning by the feebs—Oh, sorry, guys. I meant no disrespect. Anyway, Bondurant was cheap. Our first date, he took me to an I-HOP. Can you believe it? If he hadn't been so good in bed, and those blue eyes and all, I would have ended it right there."

One of the agents cleared his throat. "Uh, did Mr. Bondurant ever talk to you about Spencer Martin?"

"Sure. All the time. They were buddies. The two of them and the President are like this," she said, crossing two fingers.

"Did he say anything about Mr. Martin going to Wyoming to see him?"

"Yes. In fact, I think I was there just a day or two ahead of Mr. Martin. I went out there, thinking I'd do a piece on Bondurant, a what's-he-doing-now type story. Right away, we sort of hit it off, you know? He followed me back to Washington. But before I could produce the story on him, I got canned. Now I find out he might be more dangerous than I thought."

"You thought he was dangerous?"

She flashed the agent an angelic smile. "To my libido."

"Oh."

"Did he ever exhibit any hostility toward Mr. Martin or the President?"

"No. Matter of fact, he saw the President recently." She winked. "But I bet you guys already know that, don't you?"

"You haven't heard from Bondurant since yesterday afternoon?"

"No. Sorry. Can I go now? Funerals aren't my favorite thing." She reached toward her car door. "Besides, there's really nothing more I can tell you. Getting involved with Mr. Bondurant, even to a limited extent, was just one of several bad choices I've made recently. I'm sure you're aware of some of my more public blunders. This is one I'd like to forget. The sooner the better."

"If you hear from him—"

"I won't. When I told him to take a hike, he launched into that male thing. You know, that 'how dare you walk out on me, I'm God's greatest gift' speech."

"If he does contact you, please give us a call."

"I certainly will." She took the card the agent handed her and placed it in her handbag. "I don't want to get into trouble on account of him. If he contacts me, I'll be sure to let you know."

They thanked her for her time and walked back to their sedan. Barrie watched them go, feeling no animosity toward them. These two were among the good guys. They were doing their job as ordered by their superiors. They were performing by the book.

Not so the surveillance team set up on Daily's block. They hadn't yet stormed the house in search of Gray, which confirmed what they had suspected—those "agents" belonged to Merritt's personal army within the FBI, commanded by Spence Martin, who didn't want Gray to be found and questioned.

At any time, the President or his aide could command those men to move in and eliminate the pesky band of saboteurs living in Daily's house. Why hadn't they?

It was a question that plagued them all. Gray seemed to think they hadn't made a move because they had something larger in mind, a grander scheme in which he, Barrie, and Daily would trap themselves.

She feared he was right.

Chapter
Thirty-Eight

Daily signaled to the hippie selling roses at the busy intersection. In under five seconds he was lying on the floor of the backseat, and Daily went through the green light.

"Good going, Daily," Gray said, slipping off his head-band and wig. "They're three cars back and there's a bus between you."

"I'm getting good at this," Daily replied from behind the steering wheel. "How's the flower business?"

"Lucrative. I hate to give it up. Who's that?" he asked, referring to Daily's passenger.

"I've named her Dolly."

Dolly was a wide-eyed inflatable doll. She was wearing a jacket that belonged to Barrie and an auburn wig even more matted than Gray's hippie braid. The shoulder harness and seatbelt held her in place in the passenger seat.

"She's supposed to be me," Barrie said, crouched in the other corner of the backseat.

Without raising his head too high, Gray took a closer look at the doll. "Pretty good resemblance."

"I'm glad you said that," Barrie declared, unperturbed. "Now I don't feel so bad about trashing you to the FBI." She told him about being detained after Howie's funeral.

"That was before Armbruster owned up to his mistake and you were removed from the Most Wanted list. Whatever you said to him worked. He was all over the news this evening, claiming that there'd been a total breakdown in communications. He hinted that the error rested on the shoulders of his office staff, the efficiency of which is being reevaluated. Through the senator, Merritt assured the nation that Spencer Martin is handling a 'delicate personal matter.'

"Which covers everything from a hemorrhoidectomy to high treason."

"Right. And that he will resume his duties at the White House when the matter is resolved. Clete received some mild criticism from his colleagues, but he took it on the chin and was good-natured about it."

"Tell him about your call from Justice." As prearranged, Daily had been driving aimlessly, trying to shake their surveillance, but he'd also been following their conversation.

"From your source?"

She nodded. "I was paged and returned the call, but instead of giving me information I already had, which was that the search for you had been called off, my source was after information."

"Like what?"

"Like, 'What the hell is going on?' End quote. Because of this snafu with Armbruster and Yancey and the criminal division of the FBI, everybody's a little fractious this afternoon. Frankly, it does my heart good." She smiled at him cheekily. "So, honey, that's about it for me. How was your day?"

"I found Tabor House."

Just in case Gray had located the hospital, Barrie and Daily had come prepared.

"Do you think you've lost our tail, Daily?"

"About five minutes ago."

"But there may be an electronic tracker on the car," Gray said. "I haven't found a transmitter, but that doesn't mean it's clean. We have to make this switch in a hurry."

Following Gray's directions, Daily drove to a multilayered parking garage, where, on the second level, Gray had another vehicle waiting. Barrie and Gray alighted. Daily also stepped out, letting his car idle. "Take care of yourselves," he told them.

"I'm more worried about you than us," Barrie told him. "You're sure your tank has enough oxygen?"

"Yes."

"Drive around, have supper, act as natural as possible," Gray told him. "Keep them busy for several hours, but don't take any chances. Don't take *any* chances."

"I know, I know," Daily said cantankerously. "We've gone over this a dozen times. I know what to do."

"You'll do fine," Gray told him. "Come on, Barrie."

She hung back, wishing Daily didn't look so frail. Counter-intelligence maneuvers and breathing apparatus seemed hugely incompatible. "Whatever happens, we'll be back before dawn. I'll check on you as soon as I can. Promise me you'll be careful."

"I'll be careful."

"And that you won't be cross with Dolly."

"She's an easy broad. She doesn't nag."

"And that if you start feeling bad, you'll go home."

"I promise."

"You promise, but you *won't*," she said with mounting consternation. "I know you won't."

"Barrie!" Gray called from the front seat of the other car. "Haul it."

"Get going or you're gonna screw up Gray's plan," Daily told her.

He tried to get back into his car, but she placed her arms around him and hugged him tightly. "You're my best friend, Daily," she whispered. "For life."

"Yeah, yeah," he said crossly. This time she let him push her away, but she wasn't fooled by his brusqueness. His reluctance to say goodbye matched hers, piercing her with a cold splinter of foreboding.

"Daily—"

"It'll be okay." He slid behind the wheel.

Nodding, she closed his car door. She tried to catch his eye, but he wouldn't look at her as he dropped the car into gear. She stepped back as he drove away. She watched his taillights until they disappeared around the sharp curve at the end of the row.

"Barrie?"

"I'm coming." She got into the car with Gray. On the front seat beside him was a shopping bag. "What's that?"

"Supplies. What's that?" he asked, pointing to her leather satchel.

"Camcorder," she said absently. "Do you truly think Daily will be all right, or were you just saying what he and I wanted to hear?"

He braked the car and turned toward her. "You don't have to go," he said. "It might be a better idea if you stay with Daily, protect him, and let me do this alone."

The ease with which he could dismiss any contribution she would make infuriated her. "Go to hell, Bondurant."

"I think that's where we're headed."

They drove to a middle-class suburban neighborhood, where he parked the car at the curb in the middle of the block. "Keep a look out," he told her as he got out of the front seat and into the back. "I'm going to change."

"Change what?"

"My clothes."

He swapped the hippie-style faded jeans and tie-dyed T-shirt for a charcoal-gray suit, white shirt, and dark tie. "You should have told me," she remarked. "I'm underdressed."

"Didn't your mother tell you it was better to be over-dressed than under?"

"Probably. I didn't listen very well to anything she told me."

"Well, listen up now," he said, opening the car door. "Don't make a sound and do exactly what I tell you."

Keeping to the shadows, they walked to the house on the corner. Lights shone in nearly every window. A TV set in the front room threw dancing bluish light on the walls, seen through the open blinds.

In the driveway were a car and a pickup with a camper mounted over the bed. Gray signaled Barrie to wait beside the evergreen hedge dividing the property from the neighbor's. Leaving the shopping bag with her, he approached the camper from the rear. The door was locked, but Gray picked the lock within seconds and waved her forward. She scampered from her hiding place to the back of the camper. When they were both inside, he closed the door and relocked it from the inside.

"Have a seat." He indicated a padded bench running along one wall. He took off his jacket and folded it over his thigh as he sat down.

She spread her arms wide. "What are we doing?"

"Waiting."

"I hate to be the one to clue you, Captain Marvel, but this isn't Tabor House."

"The guy who lives here works there. I found the hospital early this morning when the night shift was getting off. I followed him home."

"How do you know this isn't his night off?"

"I don't."

"How do you know this will work?"

"I don't."

"What if it doesn't?"

"I'll try something else. Now will you give the questions a rest? Somebody might hear us in here. Sit."

She sat and lapsed into a moody silence. Soon the padded bench no longer felt padded. After about an hour, she said, "Being a commando isn't all it's cracked up to be. It's boring."

"Shh." He held up his hand, signaling for quiet.

Through the walls of the camper, she heard what sounded like a screen door slam. Then she distinguished two voices, one male, the other female. "Drive carefully," the woman was saying.

"I will."

"Are you working a double?"

"No. I'll be home around eight."

"I'll have breakfast for you."

The man's voice grew louder as he came closer to the pickup. "Sleep tight. 'Bye."

They heard his footsteps on the concrete, then the metallic click as he opened the driver's door. The camper rocked slightly when he got in. Gray noticed that Barrie was about to speak and laid his finger against his lips.

The motor sputtered a few times, then came to life. They felt a slight jolt when the parking brake was released. As soon as they were under way, country music started blaring from the truck's souped-up speakers.

"The music's a bonus," Gray said. "Now we can talk freely without being overheard."

"He works at Tabor House?"

"Judging from the overalls he wears, I would guess the engineering or janitorial department."

"What's it like?"

"The hospital? A converted mansion. Georgian design. Lush grounds surrounded by a high wall. Very secluded. It's at least ten miles off the state highway. You'd have to be looking for it to find it. There's a gated entrance with an armed guard. One road in. Same road out."

"He's going to drive us in," Barrie said, catching on to Gray's plan.

"That's the idea."

"What if the guard checks the camper?"

"There's a decal on the windshield of every employee's car."

"Pretty ingenious."

"Save that for when we make it out of there in one piece."

The thought was so sobering, she changed the subject. "What happened with Armbruster?" After he'd recounted their conversation, she asked, "Do you trust him?"

"I can piss farther. But so far he's held up his end of the bargain. I'm going to do my best to uphold mine."

"I can't believe they bought his story about incompetence on his staff."

"Clete can twist anybody's arm."

"Even at that—"

"And when twisting it doesn't work, he breaks it off. He talked to the right people and made himself understood, that's all. He wants his daughter back, no matter what. So he was willing to make a bargain with the devil—namely, me—if I can save Vanessa's life."

Gray's motivation was love. Barrie hadn't allowed herself to think too much about that. Nor had she allowed herself to consider the depth of Vanessa's gratitude, and what form it might take, once this was over.

Best case scenario: Vanessa would survive. Her marriage to David Merritt would not. She would be free to live happily ever after with the hero who'd rescued her from her murderous husband.

And Barrie would have what she wanted—the long-awaited exclusive that would finally launch her career and take it to heights that she'd never before thought possible. That *was* what she wanted more than anything, right?

Irritated by the thought, she said sullenly, "I don't suppose you brought along a deck of cards, something to pass the time."

"If you're bored, you can change." He nodded at the shopping bag. "That's your costume for the evening."

Inside the bag was a nurse's uniform—pants and a tunic in matching coral polyester—along with a pair of white walking shoes and a navy jumpsuit.

Gray said, "The nurses don't wear matching uniforms, so you won't stand out."

Barrie dumped the contents onto the carpeted floor of the camper. "What's with the jumpsuit?"

"That's mine."

"Dashing." She stood up and reached for her belt buckle. "Aren't you going to turn your back?"

"No, but you can turn yours."

If he wasn't going to make a big deal of it, then neither would she. She could act just as blasé as he, she told herself as she stepped out of her shoes and pulled her shirttail from her waistband. At least the camper was dark, with only a little light coming from the curtained windows on each side.

After unbuckling her belt, she unzipped her slacks and pushed them down her legs. When they were off, she folded them and placed them in the bottom of the shopping bag. Next she unbuttoned her blouse and removed it, leaving her in panties and bra. At least they were a matched set. At least they were new, fresh from Victoria's Secret.

But she was no lingerie model. She was no Vanessa Armbruster Merritt, either. Maybe the semidarkness would be kind and soften the comparison.

Simultaneously she and Gray noticed that the truck was slowing down. Barrie looked across at him. He checked his wristwatch. "We haven't had time to get there. Why's he stopping?"

"For gasoline, maybe?"

"I don't know," he said, peeking through a crack in the curtains. "I don't see anything."

The truck continued to slow and then rolled to a stop. The radio went off when the driver cut the engine. His door creaked open. The cab rocked when he stepped out.

"Hey, sugar," they heard him say. "Been waiting long?"

Chapter
Thirty-Nine

*D*aily took seriously his job as a decoy.

Shortly after separating from Barrie and Gray in the parking garage, he spotted a gray sedan that, for several blocks, maintained a safe distance behind him. After some calculated wending through city streets, Daily was sure he was once again being tailed.

Maybe Gray had been right, and his car had an electronic tracker planted on it. Or maybe the bastards were just lucky to have picked him up again. Or maybe Merritt's secret police were more pervasive than even Gray knew. That was a scary possibility. However, it was unlikely that his thugs would accost a sick old emphysemic on a busy street. Daily felt relatively safe.

For the first hour, the game of chase was fun, but eventually the monotony overcame him. After his third yawn in five minutes, he tuned his radio to a station that played rap music, for the simple reason that he hated it with a passion. If that obnoxious racket couldn't keep him alert and edgy, nothing could.

When his stomach began to growl, he pulled into the

drive-through at McDonald's and ordered Big Macs for him and Dolly. The youngster manning the window noticed that Daily's date was an inflatable doll, but he didn't comment and Daily offered no explanation. Better to let the kid think he was a pervert rather than a subversive.

He parked his car in front of the dining room and absently watched other customers come and go while he ate his burger and fries. He didn't have much appetite, so he finished only half his meal. He could swear that Dolly looked at him reprovingly when he disposed of their leftovers.

Disinclined to begin driving again, he sat with his hands resting listlessly in his lap and continued to monitor the McDonald's clientele. He was particularly interested in the couples with young children. These seemingly happy families were living proof that the ideal wasn't entirely unattainable. Rather than deriving any pleasure from this testament, however, the kids with the Happy Meals made Daily feel incredibly sad.

Not for the first time, he acknowledged that he'd missed out on what was really important in life. He should have married that sweet little schoolteacher who'd been so crazy about him. He'd been just as crazy about her. He'd fallen head over heels for her soft brown eyes and gentle mannerisms the first night they met. One of her smiles could make him feel like a million bucks.

But he'd taken her for granted and treated her badly, opting too often to work overtime rather than keep a dinner date. She had always run a distant second to his pursuit of a good story. Between taking her to the movies and following a hot lead, there was no competition.

She'd been a sweetheart, truly, putting up with him longer than she should have. But he'd stretched her patience too far. She'd given up on him and married someone else, a

man more stable and attentive, one who wasn't so dedicated
to his work and his freedom.

*Funny how the freedom of youth turns to loneliness in
old age.*

More and more lately, he thought about her and contemplated what could have been.

Catching himself in the poignant thought, he scorned
his self-pity. *Somewhere along the line, I've become a pitiful
old fool.*

Impatient with his maudlin reverie, he started his car
and backed out of the parking lot. The sedan was across the
street at a Taco Bell. It pulled out behind him. He took 66 out
of the city until it intersected with 495, then he doubled
back, heading northwest. It was amusing to watch the sedan
in his rearview mirror as it tried not to lose him in traffic,
although he wasn't so naive as to believe that the gray sedan
was his only tail.

He reentered D.C. via Chevy Chase, Maryland, and
drove back downtown. He made a drag down Wisconsin
Avenue, where eclectic crowds seeking the nightlife of
Georgetown vied for tables in crowded bars and restaurants.

Letting his nose lead him, he continued driving through
the city until he once again reached the outskirts. He was
getting bored, and sleepy, and weary from sitting behind the
wheel for so long.

His mind drifted back to the schoolteacher. He'd been a
damn fool to let her get away. She would have made a loving
wife. They could have had kids, grandkids by now. These
autumnal years wouldn't be so lonely, and he wouldn't be
depending solely on Barrie for company. She was a great
kid, and he loved her like she was his own flesh and blood,
but she wasn't a life partner. There was a difference.

Maybe, if he had married that sweet lady way back
then, he wouldn't be so afraid of dying now. "Some life for

her," he muttered. "Having to take care of a gasping old fart like me."

His own voice snapped him out of his daydream. Where the hell was he? Unaware, he'd driven himself into an industrial park with row upon row of warehouses, one barely distinguishable from the next. All were closed at this hour. At loading docks, empty trailer trucks stood open like behemoths with their maws spread wide.

Daily's car, and the one following it, were the only moving vehicles on these deserted streets. Becoming more disoriented with each turn, he wound his way deeper into the concrete maze until he entered a street that came to a dead end.

"Damn!" He glanced quickly at his rearview mirror. The sedan was right behind him in the cul-de-sac.

Acting on instinct, Daily hooked a sharp U-turn and was just about to pull up even with the sedan when the driver spun the wheel hard to the left. Daily had to stand on his brake pedal to keep from hitting the sedan broadside.

It would have been better if he had. He might have stood a chance of fleeing the scene of an accident. He feared there would be no escaping the three angry men who got out of the car and came toward him.

"You're ten minutes late." The woman's whining could be heard through the walls of the camper.

"*Shit!*" Gray hissed.

"What's going on?"

"I picked a Romeo with a bedroom on wheels. Hurry!"

He tossed her shoes, clothes, shopping bag, and satchel up onto the bunk that jutted into the cabin of the camper and extended over the cab of the pickup. "Get up there. Quick."

"No way. It's like a coffin."

Having no time to argue, he grabbed one of her bare ankles. With the other hand splayed over her bottom, he launched her up onto the bunk, where there was less than a foot of space between the mattress and the ceiling. When not in use, the bunk served as storage space for extra bedding and pillows. Gray chinned himself up and crawled in among the pillows, blankets, and sleeping bags.

"Get way back in there," he said to Barrie, who, for once, did as she was told without question. She made herself as small as possible in one of the forward corners.

The couple could be heard approaching the rear of the camper.

"I'm getting tired of this stupid thing," the woman complained. "Why can't we go to a motel?"

"Because this is more private."

"And free."

"It's not a matter of money. Honest, baby. Motels keep records. You don't want my old lady finding out about us, do you?"

During this spat, Gray worked frantically to reposition the rolled-up sleeping bags and pillows at the end of the bunk. With luck, they would shield them when the couple entered the rear of the camper. Then he scrunched Barrie even farther into the corner. With only seconds to spare, he pulled a quilt over them, heads and all.

"When they join us up here, it's going to be awfully crowded," she whispered.

"Do you have a better idea?"

If she did, she had no time to say so. The rear door opened and the dome light came on. The camper rocked with the man's weight as he stepped inside. "Here we go, baby." He gave a low whistle. "You look like dynamite tonight. Is that a new blouse?"

"Like it?"

"I like it a lot. How quick can we get you out of it?"

"You're such an animal!"

The door was closed and the light went out. Laughter. Sighs. The wet, sucking sounds of passionate kissing. The whisper of clothing being removed. The rasp of a zipper. A low moan.

"You're a handful," the woman said.

"You better believe it, baby. Tighter."

More sighs and smacking sounds, then: "I'm about to bust already," the man panted. "Come on, let's—"

"Do we have to get up there?" she asked in her nasal whine. "I hate it up there. I banged my head on the ceiling last time."

"Okay, okay, just . . ."

"Wait a minute!" she screeched. "Don't tear them. I'll take them off if you'll wait half a second."

Apparently the poor bastard was beyond the point of no return. From below came the sounds of bodies knocking against the wall or the floor. Gray couldn't be sure. He didn't want to be sure, because knowing for sure what was going on below would conjure up mental images that he was sure he couldn't handle right now. He tried to think of something, anything, to buffer the unmistakable sounds of sex. He squeezed his eyes shut, wishing he could shut his ears as effectively, wishing he could suspend all his involuntary responses, one in particular.

Barrie was lying perfectly still, hardly breathing, as tense as he. He knew because he was aware of her stillness, and her breathlessness, and her tension. He was aware of every damn thing about her, from the fragrance of her shampoo to the feel of her toes nestled against his knees.

What was happening on the floor of the camper was a scene straight out of a stag film, the kind of movie a bunch of guys get together and watch while polishing off a few six-packs. It was the kind of rendezvous recounted in graphic language in hard-core porno magazines. It was a fantasy with no artistic value. It wasn't even elegantly erotic. It was juvenile, base, and . . .

To hell with it. He was burning hotter than a furnace.

He realized that he wasn't turned on so much by what was going on below as he was from lying entwined with Barrie. She was seminude; he was fully clothed. A turn-on in itself. The danger of discovery was as enticing as it had been when he was six, sneaking off with the eight-year-old preacher's daughter to play Adam and Eve in her daddy's peach orchard. And it was one of Nature's mischievous tricks played on Man that the more helpless he was to satiate his arousal, the more aroused he became.

The man below brayed like a jackass. A moment later, he grunted, "Was it good for you, baby?"

"No, and I'll be damned before I fake it."

"Don't worry, I'm gonna take care of you. I've got plenty of rubbers and forty-five minutes before I have to leave for work."

Forty-five minutes!

Gray couldn't stand it that long. What about Barrie? Was this having any effect on her? He could feel her breath against his neck. It was rapid and hot. Agitation or arousal?

Seeming to read his mind, she moved slightly. Very slightly. Her knees, which were bent almost to her chest, began to straighten, but so gradually that at first he thought he was imagining it. Eventually they came even with his belt buckle, then moved past it. He held his breath as she painstakingly, moving only a fraction of an inch at a time, eased her knees over his erection. Then her shins slid along his thighs, past his knees, until her legs were aligned with his and they lay belly to belly, male to female.

She tilted her head back slightly. Then a little more. It couldn't be his imagination because he could no longer feel her breath against his neck, but against his lips. And, although it was dark beneath the quilt, he knew she was looking at him, at his mouth.

You're a fool if you do, he thought a heartbeat before bending his face closer to hers and kissing her.

Her lips parted beneath his, only slightly, but enough to make him reckless with lust.

Don't do this, Bondurant.

But no sooner had he thought the words than his tongue was making love to her mouth, her sweet, silky, sassy mouth. Soundlessly, his hand slid down her back until he was palming her bottom, planting her middle solidly against his. Only one ply of silk separated her from the distended fly of his trousers. Without any overt motion, only a subtle undulation of her hips, she rubbed against it.

A guttural sound, more a vibration than an actual noise, issued from his throat. She tensed. He tensed. He pressed his cheek against hers and tried to breathe silently, though it was almost impossible to do since his heart was racing.

But they went unheard and unnoticed, because the couple below was engaged in silly, flirtatious, verbal foreplay, punctuated by her shrill giggles. They could have been revealing the location of Jimmy Hoffa's body for all Gray cared.

He was focused solely on kissing Barrie, mouth to mouth, wetly and wantonly. He lost count of the number of times he kissed her, of how many times his tongue made forays into her mouth. He never broke contact with her lips, not even when they had to pause to breathe or risk suffocation. But even then, she angled her head up and the tip of her tongue flirted with his upper lip. He indulged her, letting her play and tease and tantalize until he couldn't take it anymore.

He pressed his tongue deeply into her mouth. He held

her tighter, angling himself against the cleft of her thighs. And he stayed there. And stayed. Fucking her in his mind. Sweet heaven and holy hell.

It was the most sustained, most intense, most intimate, most satisfying, most frustrating sexual encounter he had ever experienced. In turns, he wanted it to end with an explosive climax, and to continue into eternity.

The denouement wasn't left to him, or to Barrie, however, but to the two strangers.

Not until the camper door was opened and the light came on, was Gray jolted back to reality. Then the door was closed and locked from the outside. The couple lingered just beyond the door, planning their next rendezvous. The girl won the argument. He grudgingly agreed to meet her at a motel.

Barrie and Gray lay still, unwitting eavesdroppers to the sad parting of the illicit lovers. Finally the interlude ended when the man climbed into the cab of his truck and drove away.

Once they were in motion and the radio was blaring again, Gray yanked the quilt from over their heads. He avoided looking at Barrie. Now that it—whatever *it* had been—was over, he felt exactly as he had when the preacher caught his daughter and him beneath a peach tree, comparing the two best ideas God had ever had.

He lowered himself out of the loft. "Get down and get dressed."

He knew he sounded brusque, but he also knew that he couldn't afford to sound any other way. She'd made him forget all his training. He knew how to withstand enemy torture, to disassociate his mind from physical pain. The Marines hadn't trained him to withstand Barrie Travis.

She managed to climb down from the bunk on her own. Garth Brooks was singing through the speakers about drinking whiskey and beer with friends in low places. Gray was grateful for the noise. It helped relieve the awkward silence between them as Barrie put on the nurse's uniform. Gray put his suit coat back on, then stepped into the overalls, zipped them up, and put a cap on his head.

When Barrie finished dressing, she sat down on the bench. He passed her the satchel he'd retrieved from the bunk. In the semidarkness, he saw that her eyes were wide and watchful. "That's the first time you've kissed me."

"So?"

"So aren't we going to talk about it?"

"No."

"Why not?"

"Because we're about to attempt the kidnapping of the First Lady of the United States. We should be thinking about the operation."

"The operation? I'm a woman, Gray. Not one of your recons."

"You insisted on coming along. If you don't like the way I command the mission, you can stay behind. But I need to concentrate, so—"

"One question? Please?"

"What is it?"

"Was it good for you, baby?"

He tried not to smile, but couldn't help it. He even uttered a passable laugh. "Shut up, Barrie."

"I thought so." Then she gave him that soft, smug, knowing smile that a woman gives a man when she knows she's got him where she wants him.

After that she obediently remained quiet. Not another word was spoken until the pickup began to slow down. The driver turned off the radio as he came to a stop at the guard gate.

Gray looked across at her and whispered, "Well, we're here."

Chapter Forty

$\mathcal{T}$wo of the three men approached the driver's side of Daily's car. The other moved around to the passenger door. They were opened simultaneously. "Mr. Welsh?"

"Who wants to know?"

He was taken by the arm and pulled from the front seat. He heard a pop and a swish of air and realized that Dolly was history, stabbed in the chest with a pocket knife.

"Hey!" Daily shouted. "Was that necessary? Who the hell do you think you are?" It was hard to sound tough when breathing was an exertion. He sounded so goddamn weak, he could have laughed at himself.

The three men weren't laughing, however. In fact, they were the grimmest trio he'd ever had the displeasure of meeting. One more and they'd have reminded him of that merry band, the four horsemen of the apocalypse.

"We think we're the FBI." They flashed badges at him.

"Yeah, right," he said sarcastically, knowing them to be Spencer Martin's heavies.

"We've been following you all evening, Mr. Welsh," said the one who was obviously in charge. "Did you really think we'd fall for that stupid-looking doll? We're not idiots, you know. A woman who never speaks, never moves?"

"Is that a legitimate question or a commentary on your sex life?"

His quip didn't amuse the man, who spun him around, flattened him against the fender, and pulled his hands together behind his back, securing them with a plastic cable tie as he Mirandized him.

"What are you arresting me for? I haven't done anything. Unless inflatable dolls have become illegal. What do you want with me?"

"We want to talk to you about your houseguests."

"What houseguests?"

"I bet he'll cooperate if you yank that tube out of his nose," one of the others suggested to the leader.

Daily fought off panic. If they disconnected him from his oxygen tank, he'd be dead in no time.

"I don't think that'll be necessary," the leader said. "Not yet." Daily's knees went weak with relief, but his next words indicated that Daily's reprieve was only short term. "Our boss is real pissed off at you and your cronies."

"As if I give a damn. Isn't Spencer Martin man enough to come pick me up himself? Or is he scared of Bondurant?"

"Spencer Martin?" the man repeated, playing dumb. "Don't you watch the news? Mr. Martin is taking a brief leave of absence from his duties at the White House."

"Yeah, yeah. He's really scraping the bottom of the barrel if you're the best he can recruit for his nasty little army."

The three men shared a look among them.

Daily guffawed. "What? Surprised that I know? You thought it was a secret? Guess again."

The leader said, "Old man, you're way out of your

league. You'd be wise to cooperate with us. Where are Barrie Travis and Gray Bondurant tonight, and what are they up to?"

"Suck my dick, asshole."

The man took an angry step forward, but one of the others held him back. "Where are they, Welsh?" he shouted.

Daily knew that he was up shit creek. Even if he told them what they wanted to know, he wasn't going to see another sunrise. These guys weren't just his interrogators, but his executioners.

His assignment had been to keep the bad guys busy, providing Gray and Barrie time to liberate Vanessa Merritt from Tabor House. As long as he had breath, that's what he would do. It wasn't exactly like going out in a blaze of glory, but it was a spark, anyway.

Belligerence wasn't working very well, so he took another tack and faked a swoon. "I don't feel so good."

"Tell us where they are, and we'll see that you get some rest."

Yeah, permanent rest. "Some motel," he mumbled.

"What motel? Where?"

"I don't know."

"*Where?*"

"Something with Washington in the name."

"Do you know how many motels there are around here with Washington in the name?"

"No," Daily replied innocently. "How many?"

The man grabbed him by his lapels and lifted him until the tips of his toes were barely touching the pavement. "If you want to see Miss Travis and Mr. Bondurant alive, you'd better get your memory back real quick."

"It . . . it's out toward Andrews," Daily stammered. "I went there with them once. I can't remember exactly where it is, but I'll know it when I see it."

"Okay, let's go." The man shoved Daily forward with such impetus, the cannula was jerked out of his nostrils.

"My oxygen!" he cried. "I've gotta have it." He frantically and futilely struggled against the hand restraints.

"Relax, Mr. Welsh. We don't intend to let you suffocate. Not until we know what your friends have planned for tonight."

The tubing was reinserted into his nostrils. His oxygen tank was taken from his car and transported, along with him, to the gray sedan. When they pushed him into the backseat, Daily was comforted to see that Dolly's remains also had been brought along.

At least he wouldn't die entirely alone.

"If anyone stops you and asks, you're filling in for someone who's sick."

Gray had been giving Barrie instructions for ten minutes, ever since their adulterous driver had left his pickup to report for work. As anticipated, the guard at the gate had waved the truck through without checking the camper. They were on the grounds, but not yet inside the hospital.

Gray had produced clip-on photo IDs with phony names for them to wear. "They won't pass muster on close inspection, but at a glance they look authentic."

"Dolly Madison?" she said, reading her name. "Speaking of Dolly, I hope she and Daily are all right."

"He'll do okay. Remember, there will probably be monitored security cameras, so even when no one's around, someone could be watching. Walk naturally and—"

"Purposefully. I know, I know. You've told me at least a dozen times."

"I just don't want us blown before we locate Vanessa."

"Will there be security guards on the inside?"

"I don't know."

"If there are, will they be armed?"

"Possibly. The Secret Service, definitely. But I'll take care of them."

"One more thing. Once we have Vanessa, how do you plan on getting out of here?"

"Plan A, I'll hotwire this truck. You and Vanessa can ride back here."

"What's plan B?"

"Hell if I know."

"Great," she muttered. But it was she who opened the camper door and stepped out first.

Tabor House was more extravagant than Gray's description of it. Built in a U shape around a center garden, the house had three floors. Avoiding the grandiose front entrance, they went to the employee side entrance, which Gray had spotted during his reconnaissance the day before. Shifts were changing. Doctors, nurses, and other personnel were leaving as others were reporting in for the graveyard shift.

"I'll go first," Gray said as they approached. "Wait a few minutes and then follow me."

"Follow you where?"

He shrugged. "Don't worry. I'll find you." He started off, then turned back. "Barrie, if something happens to me, get the hell out. Understand? Hide in somebody's car and ride out the same way we rode in. Okay?"

She nodded.

"You won't, will you?"

"No."

With a frown of disgust, he turned and disappeared through the employee entrance door. Trying to appear casual, she opened her satchel and, without taking out the video camera, checked all the mechanisms to make certain they were working properly. She also checked the tape deck to make sure she had remembered to load a cassette. It would be just like her to make history but forget to put a tape in the camera.

As she headed for the entrance, she was assailed by a thousand misgivings. But only one certainty. If she didn't do this, Vanessa Merritt would die in this building. So she kept her eyes focused on the floodlight above the entrance, letting it guide her as a lighthouse guides a sailor through a perilous reef.

She entered through what had probably been a mud room when Tabor House was a private residence. That ante-room led into a large, well-lighted, well-equipped commissary/lounge where the staff took their breaks. There were various vending machines for food and drinks, a commercial coffeemaker, an industrial icemaker, several microwave ovens, tables and chairs, and two doors designating rest rooms. A bank of metal lockers took up one wall. A roster of telephone extensions had been made into a poster, large enough to be read from any point in the room.

The shift change was almost complete, so the crowd had thinned out. One man, who was dressed like an orderly, was waiting for his meal to heat in the microwave. A nurse was talking into a pay telephone. Another was fiddling with something inside her locker. Two men wearing jumpsuits like the one Gray had on were seated at a table drinking coffee and talking about turbine engines.

No one paid her any attention. She walked through the room as though she did it every night at eleven o'clock.

Beyond that room, the hospital underwent a drastic personality change. Outside the bright sterility of the commissary was a corridor suggestive of hushed voices and stiff formality. The walls had a wainscot, embossed pastel paper above, paneling below. Brass wall sconces provided subdued lighting. The floor was carpeted. Barrie followed that hall to another that intersected it.

Left or right? Left or right? *Don't look covert, look purposeful.* Eeny-meeny, miney-moe. Okay, *right!*

The corridor she'd selected led toward the front of the building. Along it she saw offices, dark now, a formal reception/parlor area with a baby grand piano, and a solarium filled with tropical plants and ferns among cushioned rattan furniture. All very fancy, absent anything that looked clinical.

The atrium entry was quite impressive, with its sweeping staircase and a skylight fifty feet above the marble floor. In the center of this rotunda was a round foyer table on which stood an enormous floral arrangement, the gladiolus stems upward of four feet tall.

There was no one around except a janitor who was kneeling in front of a wall socket, tinkering with a screwdriver. Barrie went around the table to speak to him. "I might become a coke-head just to have the privilege of staying here."

"You can't afford it," the janitor said as he came to his feet. "There's nothing on the first floor except offices and meeting rooms."

"A records office?"

"Undoubtedly. But I'm sure the files are locked, and I didn't bring the tools for picking them. Besides, it would take too much time."

"Then what do you suggest?"

"A computer terminal," he said. "There's bound to be a patient roster that's constantly updated."

"Good idea. Onward and upward?"

"You take the elevator. I'll use the stairs."

"Meet you on two."

The elevator was an iron cage that had more aesthetic properties than mechanical. Barrie was grateful that it made it up one flight. She stepped through the wrought iron doors, turned to her left, and came face to face with a nurse, who was as shocked to see Barrie as Barrie was to see her.

"What are you doing in that thing? It's a deathtrap."

"Uh, I'm new," Barrie said, laughing nervously, which under the circumstances wasn't hard to fake. "Next time, I'll take the express. Dolly Madison," she said, sticking out her hand. "Please, no jokes about my name. Believe me, I've heard them all."

"Linda Arnold."

"Pleased to meet you."

Barrie caught a peripheral glimpse of Gray as he reached the top of the staircase. Taking advantage of the diversion she'd created, he slipped behind the charge nurse's desk. There was no one else in sight.

"When did you start working here?" the nurse asked.

"This is my first night. I'm assisting Dr. Hadley," she said, recalling one of the names she'd seen on the telephone roster in the commissary.

"I thought Dr. Hadley was on a six-month sabbatical."

"Yes, he is."

"You mean she."

"I said she." Barrie placed her hand on Linda Arnold's arm and leaned in close. "Between you and me, it's not going as the doctor planned. She's supposed to be working on a book, although I doubt she'll ever pull it together."

"Really? That's surprising. She's already so widely published."

"True, true," Barrie said, wishing writer's block upon Dr. Hadley, whoever the hell she was. "But this time, she's struggling."

"I'm sorry to hear that. She has so much to share, and she's such a gifted doctor."

"She is a dear, isn't she?" Barrie gushed. She had a

view of Gray's back. He was hunched over a desk. Had he found a computer terminal?

"What's all that?" The nurse indicated Barrie's heavy shoulder bag.

"Research materials I'm gathering for Dr. Hadley."

"All that?"

"Uh, yeah, and, well, I can't go anywhere without my, uh, Slim-Fast. I never leave the house with less than two cans, just in case. Always an extra pair of shoes. I have awful bunions. Magazines. You know, stuff. My husband teases me about my *stuff* all the time."

"Weren't you assigned a locker downstairs?"

"Yeah, but the gizmo thing . . ." She pantomimed working a combination lock. "I couldn't get it to work. Until I get the hang of it, I thought I'd better cart this crap around with me."

Nurse Linda Arnold tilted her head. "You look familiar to me, but I can't quite place you."

She recognizes me from TV!

"Where did you work before you became Dr. Hadley's assistant?"

"Oh, a zillion places. I get bored with the same old job, so I sort of, you know, go with the flow." Behind the nurse, Gray was giving her a thumbs-up. "Well, if you'll excuse me, I'm going to meander around and try to get my bearings."

"Can I help you—"

"No, no, I do better when I learn my way alone." She laughed. "I already know not to take that creaky old elevator again."

"Excuse me?"

Gray had approached them and tapped Linda Arnold on the shoulder. She turned to him. "Are you the one who called for the light bulb to be changed?"

"No. It wasn't me."

"Must've been the third floor. I thought she said second. Sorry." He doffed his cap and headed back to the staircase.

By the time Nurse Linda Arnold turned back around, Barrie had slipped out of sight.

⌒⌒

"They're not there."

The report came back to the main man via one of his dour sidekicks, the one who'd so viciously ended Dolly's brief life. It had taken them an hour and a half to "find" the motel.

"This is it," Daily said, wheezing hard. "I'm sure of it. The Washington Inn. Room one-twenty-two."

"There's a teamster in there, mad as hell 'cause I woke him up," the agent said, glaring at Daily.

"I don't get it," he said, looking helplessly from one to the other. "She said she was meeting Bondurant here tonight."

"You dropped her in a parking garage, didn't you?"

"How'd you guys know that?"

"Where was she going?"

"Here! That's what she told me, anyway. Swear to God. I was supposed to drive around with the dummy and be her decoy."

"This is bullshit," one of them said. "He's been jerking us around all this time."

To make his act more convincing, Daily began to beg. "Don't hurt me. Please. I had to do it. I'm scared shitless of him."

"Who?"

"Bondurant. He told me that if I fucked up, he'd kill me. And he will, too. Have you ever looked into his eyes? They're spooky as hell. The man's a natural born killer. If he finds out I brought you here, he'll kill me."

"Knock it off!" the leader snapped.

"Please, take me home," Daily pleaded. "If they're not here, I don't know where they are. Bondurant probably lied to me. Maybe he lied to Barrie, too. He could've been setting a trap for her. Have you thought of that? But what do I know? I'm just an old man. I don't know anything."

"He's lying," one of the agents said.

"Hell, yes, he's lying," said the leader. "Let's go."

In the car, the leader used his cellular telephone. "Welsh was lying about the motel. They weren't there." He listened for a moment, then said, "Yes, sir. I'm sure you can get more out of him than we've been able to."

Daily didn't like the sound of that. He liked even less what the gauge on his oxygen tank indicated. "I haven't got much air left," he said as soon as the man was off the phone.

"Sounds like a personal problem to me."

The other two didn't even bother to respond. From the floorboard, Dolly stared up at him with wide, dead eyes.

It was a long drive back to the city. Their destination turned out to be an innocuous-looking office building. As they escorted Daily to an emergency exit door at the rear of the building, he looked up at the sky. No stars could be seen, of course, because of the city lights. But there was a pretty moon.

That was nice.

They took a service elevator to the seventh floor. Their heels echoed along the deserted corridor as they marched Daily to the door at the end of it. The wheel on his oxygen trolley was squeaking. He never had gotten around to oiling the damn thing.

One of the men moved out in front and knocked on the door. A voice ordered him to come in. He opened the door, then stood aside. As Daily crossed the threshold into the room, he had a fleeting thought as to what form his torture and death might take.

His ominous host was backlit by the single lamp in the room, but Daily recognized him by his silhouette. "Mr. Welsh," he said in a voice that was almost friendly. "You've been awfully busy tonight. Aren't you almost out of oxygen by now?"

And Daily thought, *Oh, shit*.

Chapter
Forty-One

𝒯he broken water pipe in the storage room on the third floor of Tabor House produced the desired effect. Nurses and aides congregated as near as they could get to the door of the flooding closet. For as many staff as were involved, there were that many suggestions on how best to solve the problem. A nurse said she'd seen a janitor working in the storage room a few minutes before the geyser erupted, but he couldn't be found to assist in the containment and cleanup.

Barrie hadn't known what Gray intended when he left her in the stairwell, telling her to wait for him there and to "look busy" if anyone came by. When he returned several minutes later, his overalls and cap had been discarded, and he was once again in suit and tie. A water pipe had mysteriously burst. It wasn't too difficult to figure out what he'd been doing.

"Come on," was all he said. She followed his lead through the door to the third floor.

Because of the commotion in the south wing, nobody noticed them as they headed for the north wing. But when they rounded a corner, they saw two Secret Service agents standing guard outside room 300.

This is when we get shot, Barrie thought.

But Gray was cool. "Evening, gentlemen," he said crisply, walking right up to them.

They recognized him immediately. "Mr. Bondurant?" one said.

"How are you?" Gray flashed his grim smile.

"I thought you had retired. When did you—"

"I'll be glad to tell you all about it later. But we've got to move Mrs. Merritt immediately. There's been a small accident in the other wing. I don't think it's serious. This is strictly a precautionary measure. The President doesn't want to take any chances."

He held up his hand as though for silence, and pressed his fingers against the portable earpiece he was wearing. "They're ready downstairs," he said. "Nurse?" He nodded Barrie toward the door of the room.

"Yes, sir." She slipped past the two agents.

"Excuse me, sir, but nobody except Dr. Allan—"

The edge of Gray's hand connected solidly with the guy's larynx. Another swift blow, and he was down. The other had turned to detain Barrie. Gray gave him a karate chop on the back of the neck. He went down. Barrie held the door open while Gray dragged them inside.

It had taken no more than a few seconds. Gray hastily switched his phony earpiece for the Secret Service agent's.

He listened for a moment, then bent down and spoke into the tiny microphone the unconscious agent was wearing under his lapel. "Some excitement in the other wing, that's all." He paused to cough and clear his throat. "Leaking water pipe."

He listened again.

"No, we're under control."

He clicked off the transmitter. To Barrie he said, "There's another agent on the roof."

"Won't he notice the voice change?"

"I hope not."

Working quickly, Gray divested one of the agents of his two-way radio kit, so that he would be clued to the actions of the agent on the roof, and any others who might be in the area. Then he taped shut the agents' mouths and trussed them like turkeys, binding their hands and feet behind their backs with duct tape. For the time being, they were out of commission. But how long would it be before someone noticed they weren't at their post and came to check?

Barrie had no time to entertain that concern. Gray had already moved across the dim room where Vanessa lay motionless on a hospital bed. Her slight form created barely any valleys and hills beneath the covers.

Barrie moved to the opposite side of the bed. "Mrs. Merritt?"

"Vanessa? Can you hear us?" Gray said with more force, shaking her shoulder. *"Vanessa?"*

Her eyes fluttered open. When she saw Gray, there was a catch in her thready breath. "You've come?"

"I'm going to get you out of here."

"Gray." When her eyes drifted closed again, she was smiling faintly, assured that now she was safe. She was so sedated that she didn't even flinch when he ripped the tape off her arm and slipped the IV catheter from her vein.

Barrie didn't have to look very closely to see that Vanessa was seriously ill. Her eye sockets looked like dark craters in her skull. Her lips were colorless. Gray slid his arms beneath her, catching her behind her knees and shoulders, and lifted her from the bed. She looked like a child in his arms.

"Barrie," he ordered, "take the pistol."

He'd laid it on the bed when he picked up Vanessa. Barrie stared at the weapon, loath to touch it. The long silencer attached to the barrel made it look even more menacing. But Gray's expression looked more dangerous and deadly than the gun, so she did as he'd instructed. The weapon felt heavy and awkward in her hand.

"Careful with it," he said. "It's ready to fire. The service elevator is at the end of the hall. We'll use that to get to the ground floor." He glanced toward the two unconscious agents. "If you're legit, I'm sorry," he muttered. "If you're Spence's men, fuck you."

As they moved toward the door, Barrie asked, "What about security cameras?"

"I haven't seen any, have you?"

She shook her head. "What if somebody tries to stop us?"

"Shoot them," he said matter-of-factly. He motioned her with his head. "Check the hall."

She opened the door and looked around. The corridor was empty, although from around the corner she heard laughing and chatter about the flooded storage room. Apparently the absence of the Secret Service agents had not yet been noticed.

"Clear," she told Gray.

"Get the elevator."

She stepped out into the hallway and punched the button on the wall. Lighted numbers on the panel indicated that it was on the first floor. Barrie was sure it had never taken it longer to rise those two floors. She kept her eye on the corner, but no one appeared.

At last the elevator arrived, and it was empty. She stepped into it and pushed the Open Door button. Gray carried Vanessa across the hall in two long strides. Barrie pushed the Close Door button.

Nothing happened.

Not for several interminable moments.

Finally the door slid closed and they began their descent.

Barrie stared at the crack where the two doors met. When they reached the first floor and those doors opened, and someone was standing there demanding to know just what the hell they thought they were doing, could she shoot that person?

She was thankful that her mettle wasn't tested. There was no one waiting for the elevator when it reached the ground floor. She stepped out and checked the corridor. "A lot of people are in the commissary," she told Gray. There were sounds of conversation coming from that area. "It must be break time."

"Go the other way," he said. "That can't be the only exit. We'll go out through another door and circle around."

"I noticed French doors in the solarium."

They threaded their way back through the first-floor corridors. The French doors in the solarium were locked, but the latch was on the inside. She hesitated. "It could be wired to a security system."

"We'll take our chances."

She undid the latch and pushed open the door. The ensuring screech was earsplitting. Barrie turned in the direction from which it came and reflexively fired the pistol.

A tropical bird in a tall white cage sent up a terrible racket, although her shot had wounded only a Boston fern. The bird's ruff was standing on end, his multicolored wings were extended and flapping, and he was still screeching. "Shit!" she said.

They left the building at a dead run, although hospital personnel were obviously accustomed to the bird's temper tantrums because no one was pursuing them. Keeping to the shadowed perimeter, they skirted the well-tended yard until they reached the parking area.

"Hold it," Gray said.

She stopped, turned. She was breathing heavily. He seemed barely winded as he listened to the voice in his earpiece. He clicked on his transmitter. "Something in the employee parking lot?" he said into the microphone.

The other Secret Service agent! Barrie had almost forgotten him.

Her eyes automatically swung up to the roof, but she couldn't see him. Gray motioned her forward with his chin. She turned and began running again. Gray was right behind her, but she heard him say with feigned puzzlement, "No, she hasn't been disturbed." Then he shouted, "Damn! He's on to us, Barrie."

She ran full out the rest of the way to the pickup. When they reached it, she opened the rear door of the camper and clambered inside, then assisted Gray as he stepped in and laid Vanessa on the bench along the wall.

"Hold on!" he said as he leaped out the door and slammed it behind him. Moments later, the pickup was gunned to life and they began to move. Seconds after that, a shrill alarm pierced the peaceful countryside surrounding Tabor House.

༒

"Delicious pie, Amanda. Thank you."

David smiled up at her as she picked up his empty dessert plate and placed it on a serving tray. "Thank you, David. I'm glad you enjoyed it. Would you care for more?"

"No, thanks." He patted his belt. "Every calorie counts."

Unsmiling, she asked if he would like more coffee. He accepted, watching her closely as she refilled his cup. Then she excused herself, taking the serving tray with her and leaving him and George alone in the Allans' comfortable living room.

"Amanda never has warmed to me, has she?" David said.

"Want something in that?" George was at the liquor cabinet, adding a liberal amount of B & B to his coffee.

"No, thanks."

The President had invited himself over for the evening. George's two sons had reacted with predictable excitement. President Merritt had asked to see their homework and had written each a note to take to school the next day to share with their classmates.

After taking them away to bed, Amanda had offered to serve him and George pie and coffee in the living room. Her manner bordered on hostility, but David was used to her cold shoulder and, as he had for years, ignored it and pitied poor George for being married to such an icicle.

George returned to the sofa with his spiked coffee. David noticed that the doctor's hands were shaking enough to rattle the delicate china. "Why so nervous, George? If I didn't know better, I'd think you had a guilty conscience."

In a desperate undertone, George asked, "Why'd you come here tonight?"

"Aren't I welcome in the home of one of my closest and dearest friends?"

"I didn't mean to imply that."

"Good. I'm glad to hear it." David gave his fresh coffee a languid stir. "Now that we're alone, I'll get down to business."

"Which is . . . ?"

"I'd like your opinion of the health care bill Congress has submitted. I value your viewpoint as a physician."

Taken completely off guard, George stammered, "I . . . I'm only familiar with the major points."

"Which should give you a basis for an opinion. What do you think of it?"

When the telephone rang, George practically leaped from the sofa to answer it. "Hello. Dr. Allan speaking." He listened. "Yes, he's here."

He turned and extended the telephone to David. "It's urgent," he whispered.

"Put it on speakerphone."

George gave him a puzzled look, but did as requested. "This is the President," David said.

He listened as the caller informed him that the First Lady had been taken from Tabor House.

"What do you mean, *taken?*"

"Abducted, Mr. President. Kidnapped."

David came slowly to his feet. "What?" he said tightly. The hapless messenger repeated the message.

"Where was the goddamn Secret Service?" he barked.

"The agents were overpowered, Mr. President. Mrs. Merritt was carried from her room, placed in a vehicle, and driven away. The operation was well rehearsed and executed, sir. The hospital security force and Secret Service agents did their best to stop the abductors at the gate. However, they couldn't risk shooting at the vehicle and wounding the First Lady. The pickup truck failed to stop despite the warning shots fired. It crashed through the barrier and, unfortunately, escaped."

The loud conversation had drawn Amanda from another part of the house. David noticed that she didn't appear unduly surprised by the news.

"Has anyone claimed responsibility? A terrorist group?"

"Gray Bondurant and Barrie Travis have been identified as the suspects, Mr. President."

Upon hearing that, David's breath left his body in a rush. "Christ Almighty!" He plowed his fingers through his hair. "Has Bondurant gone completely around the bend?"

"He boldly approached the Secret Service agents guarding Mrs. Merritt's room, sir, and pretended to be acting on your behalf."

"Well, he wasn't!" David shouted, outraged by the suggestion. "He's to be treated like any other criminal. Is that understood?"

"Absolutely, Mr. President. The FBI's been notified. Local law enforcement has already located the vehicle. It was left parked at a truck stop several miles from the hospital. There was no sign of the First Lady or her kidnappers. Apparently they switched vehicles, sir."

More collected now, David said, "I'm returning to the White House immediately. I can be reached in the car."

"Certainly, Mr. President."

When the call was disconnected, David rounded on George. "How could you let this happen?"

"It wasn't my fault!" the doctor cried. "I wasn't even there. There must have been a breach in security."

"To say the very least," David shouted. "It seems that every time I place Vanessa under your care, something dreadful happens."

From the doorway, Amanda said, "If anyone is to blame for this, it's you, David."

"Amanda!" George exclaimed.

David wanted to strangle the snooty bitch for speaking to him like that, but he had to admire the guts it took. "Forget it, George," he said brusquely. "I've got to get back to the White House immediately. Are you coming with me?"

"Certainly."

They went down the front walkway, flanked by Secret Service agents who obviously had been alerted to the latest emergency. The limo awaited at the curb, one car behind it, one in front, four motorcycle policemen leading the motorcade.

Speeding through the streets toward Pennsylvania Avenue, David checked to see that the tinted glass behind the driver was raised, then turned to George and began laughing.

"I told you he would do it. Didn't I tell you that Gray was noble enough, *crazy* enough, to stage a dramatic rescue?"

George Allan stared into space. "Yes, David. That's what you told me."

"I knew he'd try to get her out of there. And when Spence's men reported that the old man, Welsh, was being used as a decoy tonight, I figured the escape was on."

"It seems you were correct on all counts."

"Did you do your part, George?"

"Yes. Just before I left her tonight."

"And it'll work?"

"It'll work. She'll die from a toxic level of lithium."

This would, of course, be determined in the post-mortem, but neither the doctor nor the president would ever be suspected because they were having pie and coffee together when Vanessa fell into the hands of Gray Bondurant and his accomplice, Barrie Travis. They would be charged with kidnapping and murder.

As an intimate friend, Gray would know that Vanessa's medication had to be carefully monitored and administered. Too small a dosage of lithium and her mood disorder couldn't be controlled. Too much could cause seizures, coma, or death, especially when combined with the sedatives she was being given at the hospital to ensure the rest that she needed.

"They'll want to know where Gray obtained the drug," George observed.

"A man of his resourcefulness?" David said, dismissing that as a problem. "A good prosecutor will have no trouble convincing a jury that he's clever enough to have obtained and destroyed all evidence of it."

"I'm unclear on their motive," George said. "If they went to all that trouble to rescue Vanessa, why would they kill her?"

George was so dense, sometimes David wondered how he'd ever earned a medical degree. He also had an irritating tendency to make simple things difficult.

"Gray was Vanessa's spurned lover. He wore his heart on his sleeve for the whole damn country to see. At first he was content to leave Washington and nurse his wounded pride in seclusion. But his antagonism festered. Finally, his ego couldn't be assuaged until Vanessa was dead."

"And Barrie Travis?"

"Is in love with Gray. She was happy to eliminate her competition. After the Shinlin incident, they're public enemy number one and number two. People will be ready to believe them capable of this heinous crime."

The President leaned his head back and smiled. "It's such a brilliant plan, George. So damn perfect. Spence always said it's better not to destroy your enemies but to let them destroy themselves. Too bad he isn't here to see this. He would have loved it."

Chapter
Forty-Two

Senator Armbruster was waiting for Barrie and Gray at the prearranged spot. The rotors on the helicopter were already whirling.

"Thank God you made it," he said as Gray bounded out of the car. "How is she?"

"Alive."

The senator had handpicked a team of medical personnel, ready to administer whatever emergency treatment Vanessa might require on the flight back to Washington. As she was lifted from the car and laid on a gurney, the doctor in charge began issuing orders to those assisting him.

"Sweetheart, what have they done to you?" Armbruster clasped his daughter's cold hand as he ran alongside the gurney toward the helicopter.

Gray detained the doctor long enough to shout, "It was awfully easy to get her out of there. Too easy. The damage might already be done."

Nodding that he understood, the doctor didn't wait to hear more. He jumped into the chopper, and within seconds it was airborne, leaving Barrie and Gray in the windy cross-currents on the empty shopping mall parking lot.

Barrie had recorded the transfer on video. Although the quality wouldn't be up to normal broadcast standards, it would be invaluable. They watched as the helicopter banked and headed back toward D.C.

"What'd you mean by that?" she asked Gray as she replaced the camera in her satchel. "What you said to the doctor."

"I've got a feeling that the folks at Tabor House knew we were coming."

She looked at him sharply.

"Think about it," he said. "Except for a token show of force there at the end, we essentially walked in and walked out with the First Lady of the United States." His face set and tense, he stared after the chopper. "We might have been too late to save her life."

"Freeze! FBI!"

The shout came out of the darkness behind them. Reflexively, they spun around. Four men were coming toward them at a run, handguns extended and aimed. Headlights flashed on. Two cars roared onto the parking lot and screeched to a halt only yards from them.

"Hands on your head, Bondurant."

Apparently he saw the advisability of complying. One of the agents came forward, found the pistol in his waistband, and took it. Another agent seized Barrie's satchel and patted her down. "I'm not armed."

"Don't say anything," Gray told her as he was being handcuffed and read his rights.

Following his lead, Barrie submitted to the arrest without a struggle. The story she had to tell, along with the video, would surely absolve her and Gray of any crimes committed during the rescue of the First Lady. But telling it now would be a waste of breath. She would wait until Senator Armbruster and Vanessa herself could corroborate the allegation that the President had killed his son and had planned his wife's death.

Barrie was escorted to one of the cars, Gray to the other. The agent held the door for her and assisted her into the backseat.

What she saw there, lying on the seat, filled her with such terror that she screamed and tried to back out of the open car door. *"Gray!"* But the agent had his hand on her back, pushing her inside.

Through the car window, she saw Gray. He'd heard her scream, sensed her alarm, and was struggling with the agents who were trying to force him into the other car. But with his hands cuffed behind him, he couldn't fight back. He was shoved into the backseat. Doors were slammed shut. With a squeal of tires, both cars sped away.

Barrie sobbed as she gazed at the other passenger in the backseat of the gray sedan, who stared back at her with sightless eyes, an obscenely vacant expression on her face, matted wig askew. Dolly.

⌒⌒

George Allan looked down at his two sleeping sons, their heads barely visible above the covers. His younger son, in the bottom bunk, was the rascal, the athlete, the destined-to-be heartbreaker. His charm would glide him easily through life.

The older boy had inherited Amanda's seriousness. Even in sleep, he seemed to be sorting through a problem. Of the two, he was the smarter, the overachiever. His intellect and self-discipline would guarantee his success in whatever field he chose. George hoped it would be medicine.

He kissed each of them softly, then closed the door behind him as he tiptoed from their room. The door to the master bedroom suite was ajar. Amanda had left the night-light on for him. No matter how bitter their quarrel, how estranged they felt, they shared the same bed every night. It was as though she left the light on so that he could always find his way back to her.

He gazed at her sleeping face. Strands of silky dark hair painted stripes across her pillow. Her breathing was slow and even. She looked lovely. He wanted to touch her, to kiss her, but he didn't for fear of waking her.

He backed out of the room, went down the hall to his office, and quietly closed the door. In desperate need of a drink, he poured himself one, carried it to his desk, and settled gratefully into the chair.

It had been a long night. He had waited with David until they'd received word that Vanessa was safely with Clete in the hospital.

George was very tired. He savored the drink, sipping it slowly, tracing the warmth it spread through his system. Its intoxicating properties were hampered by the sobering thoughts that haunted him—namely, what David had instructed him to do, as opposed to what he had done.

He finished his drink and unlocked his lower desk drawer. It wasn't a high-caliber gun, but when fired into the roof of one's mouth, it was sufficient to do the job painlessly. He checked the chambers of the revolver and saw that each one was loaded; then snapped the cylinder back into place and laid the gun on his desk pad.

Then he fished into his breast pocket and withdrew a small plastic bottle. The tamperproof seal was intact, and the lithium was still inside, not flowing lethally through Vanessa's system as David believed.

At the final showdown, George had defeated David by

stopping short of cold-blooded murder. He hoped that Amanda would view this as a victory. Perhaps this swan song of defiance would make up for his years of weakness. She might even love him for it. At least a little.

He set the vial on his desk pad, picked up the gun, and placed the barrel in his mouth.

During the long drive, Barrie tried to get news of Daily from the men who'd abducted her, but her screams, pleas, sobs, and threats didn't budge them from their resolute silence. Gray was as much in the dark as she when they reached their destination, an office building in downtown D.C. They were hustled into the service elevator, then led to the office at the end of the hallway on the seventh floor.

Because Gray was giving them a fight every step of the way, they pushed him inside first. His blasphemous exclamation didn't bode well for what awaited Barrie.

What she expected to see was Daily's bruised, battered, and possibly bloody body. Instead, he was semireclining on a sofa, looking fatigued. She was so grateful to see him, she stumbled across the dimly lighted office and knelt beside the sofa, not knowing whether to laugh or cry. "Daily, are you all right?"

"I am now," he gasped. "Seeing that you're okay and didn't get yourself shot."

"They had Dolly in their car. I feared . . ."

"They brought me a fresh tank of oxygen, so, for the time being, I'll live. Never mind me. Did you get Mrs. Merritt out?"

"We did. She's in good hands now, although she looked very sick. We're not sure whether she'll survive."

With the assistance of the agent who was removing her handcuffs, Barrie came to her feet and turned to face their host. Angrily she thrust her wrists out in front of her to show him the red rings around them. "Was the rough stuff necessary, Bill?"

Attorney General William Yancey looked abashed. "Hello, Barrie. Mr. Bondurant."

Gray looked incredulous. "You two know each other?"

"Since college," Yancey replied. "Barrie worked on the campus radio station as a reporter. I was president of the student political coalition. On slow days, she would come to me looking for a story."

"I still do sometimes. He's my source over at Justice."

"*He's* your source?"

"I don't impart anything confidential," Yancey explained. "Mostly I just confirm or deny information she's received elsewhere. I keep her from going astray, which is sometimes tough to do," he added, glowering at her.

"Bill, was this necessary?" Barrie repeated.

"We had to make a formal arrest. You and Bondurant are wanted for kidnapping." He glanced at Daily. "Mr. Welsh has confessed that he was an accomplice."

"Daily was instrumental, but it wasn't a kidnapping. We rescued Vanessa Merritt."

"From what, from whom?"

"From her husband."

Yancey looked gravely at Barrie, then at Gray. "I was afraid you'd say that."

"You don't seem terribly surprised," she remarked.

"I've been getting some very strange phone calls lately. From Armbruster. From Merritt. It seems Mr. Bondurant's reappearance in Washington has made everybody nervous. First I was urged to apprehend him, then I was urged not to. Turns out, Bondurant has been keeping company with, guess who, you. By the way," he added dryly, "you gave my men quite an earful at Howie Fripp's funeral. Imagine them recounting for me the one about the freeway blow job."

"The *what?*" Gray asked.

"Long story," Barrie mumbled. To Yancey she said, "I laid it on pretty thick because I wasn't sure they were good guys."

"They were FBI agents."

"I know, but I thought they might be . . ." She looked at Gray with consternation, wondering how much she should reveal.

From his position on the sofa, Daily relieved her of the decision. "She thought they were working for Spencer Martin."

"Spencer Martin," Yancey repeated thoughtfully. "Someone else had you under surveillance. My team intercepted them more than once. We wondered who it was."

"It was Spence," Gray said tightly.

Yancey turned to him. "And I'm supposed to take your word for that?"

"You're supposed to be the chief law officer in the country. That means going after the bad guys."

"It also means protecting the rights of guys that people *allege* are bad. For whatever reason."

Sensing the hostility rising between them, Barrie quickly interceded. "Bill, once the facts become clear to you, I'm sure you'll agree that Spencer Martin is a dangerous individual."

"I'm all ears. What *are* the facts, Barrie? Your name has been connected with the First Lady's since your series on SIDS, and the First Lady has been mysteriously absent. Dalton Neely's blather is an insult to my intelligence. Dr. George Allan strikes me as incompetent. The Secret Service is respectfully mute. We knew you were up to something tonight when you pulled that switch in the parking garage. We picked up the old man—"

"Hey!" The interjection came from an insulted Daily.

"—so he wouldn't get hurt or killed by persons you tell me were working for Spencer Martin." Opening his suit jacket, he placed his hands on his waist. "I want to know just what in hell is going on, and I've got to have the full story. That's why you were brought here instead of being taken straight to jail and booked on felony charges."

"I appreciate your trust, Bill," Barrie said. "But before I talk to you, shouldn't I have a lawyer present?"

"You may. If you want to go that route. Or you can simply level with me."

"Off the record?"

"Off the record."

For years she'd known him to be a man of honor. More than once his integrity had gotten in her way of a good story. She'd been angry with him for withholding information from her when it was a matter of national security, but he'd never steered her wrong, either. She had no reason to mistrust him.

"All right," she said. "But there's so much to tell, I don't know where to start."

"Let's start with Spencer Martin."

"How much do you know about him? He's—"

"Careful, Barrie." Gray nodded toward Yancey. "He might be your former classmate, and maybe he's proved to be a reliable and fair source, but before you spill your guts, remember who appointed him and who he works for."

Affronted, Yancey replied, "*I* remember who appointed me, Mr. Bondurant. But I work for the people of the United States, and I take my job and the responsibility that goes with it very seriously.

"True, I owe my job to David Merritt, but I'm not immune to the stink emanating from the White House these days. As for Spencer Martin, I know about his personal army. He's got informers and operatives planted in just about every department of the federal government, including, I'm ashamed to admit, those that fall under the auspices of the Department of Justice.

"More dangerous than that, however, is the influence he wields over the President. I want to know why and to what extent Merritt relies on him. Frankly, Bondurant, I was afraid for Barrie to be spending so much time with you. That's why I tipped her on your recent visit to the White House. I figured you were one of Martin's facilitators."

"You figured wrong."

"Probably. You got out because of Mrs. Merritt, I think."

Gray nodded. "She's also why I got dragged back in."

The attorney general looked steadily at Gray for several moments, then turned back to Barrie. "You started all this with that piece about SIDS, didn't you?"

"Actually, Vanessa Merritt started it by inviting me to coffee. It's a long story, and by telling it I'll be accusing the President of unspeakable crimes."

"That's why you were brought here," Yancey said. "No matter how long and involved the story is, no matter who's implicated, I want to hear it all."

Chapter
Forty-Three

"Shit! This whole thing is falling apart. Barrie and Gray haven't been caught yet. Vanessa's in the goddamn hospital. *In the hospital!* I was supposed to be receiving the horrible news that she'd died. Instead I get the happy news that she's being treated at GWU hospital."

"Calm down, David."

He rounded on Spence, his eyes as hard as diamonds. "Don't patronize me, Spence. If I'm fucked, then so are you. Remember that when you give me those smug platitudes of yours."

"I wasn't being patronizing or smug. I'm as concerned as you. But losing our heads will only make the situation worse."

"I don't think it could get any worse."

"Of course it could."

David slammed his fist into his opposite palm. "How could this happen?"

"I don't know. Everything at Tabor House went according to plan. My men swallowed their pride and let Bondurant overcome them. But how could we have known that Clete had a helicopter standing by only a few miles from there?"

"Well, you should have known. That's what I pay you for. And where the hell is George? He sneaked out and must have gone home. Call him there. Ask him if the doctors at the hospital will be able to undo what he's done."

"I've called his house several times. The line's been busy, and he hasn't responded to my page."

"He's Vanessa's doctor of record. Maybe he's been summoned to the hospital," David said hopefully.

"That's highly unlikely, David. After this, Clete won't let him within a mile of her."

"Christ! If this doesn't work—"

"We'll think of something else," Spence said smoothly. "What we mustn't lose sight of is that Vanessa has become a threat to the administration. She, you, and I are the only ones who know what happened in the nursery that night. George must suspect, but there's no way he can be sure. One way or another, we must guarantee Vanessa's silence. Then no one will know."

"Except," David said, thoughtfully regarding Spence, "me and you."

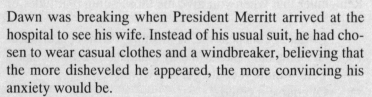

Dawn was breaking when President Merritt arrived at the hospital to see his wife. Instead of his usual suit, he had chosen to wear casual clothes and a windbreaker, believing that the more disheveled he appeared, the more convincing his anxiety would be.

Secret Service had appeared in advance of his arrival. The hospital was in a state of barely controlled chaos. The media was out in full force, vying for the latest news in the ongoing saga of the First Lady's health. The President entered the hospital through the kitchen and, using an elevator reserved for staff, was escorted up to her room.

When he went in, his father-in-law was standing at her bedside. "How is she, Clete?" he asked worriedly.

"Why don't you ask her?"

Vanessa appeared to be sleeping, but when David lifted her hand, her eyes came open. He beamed a smile on her. "Hello, darling. Thank God you're all right."

"Hello, David. How good of you to come," she said, her voice dripping sarcasm.

"Mr. President, this is Dr. Murphy."

He absently acknowledged Clete's introduction to the attending physician. "What's the matter with my wife, Doctor?"

"In my opinion, Mr. President, she was receiving an inappropriately high dosage of lithium, especially since it was combined with Haldol and other sedatives."

"I thought her blood levels were constantly being monitored."

The doctor shrugged. "Dr. Leopold has faxed me her chart from Tabor House. The levels recorded are what they should be, but they're inconsistent with what our lab here has found to be the case."

"How could Dex Leopold's staff make such an error?" No one ventured a guess. In fact there was an embarrassed silence coming from Dr. Murphy's side of the patient's bed. "What's her prognosis?" David asked briskly.

"She's toxic. I've got IVs flushing out her system. That will take several days. Then I'll readjust the dosages of her medication to an effective but safe level. She shouldn't be reduced to a zombie, as she was when she arrived."

"But she'll be all right?"

"Yes, Mr. President."

"Thank God." David squeezed Vanessa's hand and pressed it to his lips, then bent down and kissed her softly. Her lips were no warmer and no more responsive than those of a mannequin.

The doctor excused himself, leaving the three of them alone. Before Clete had an opportunity to launch an attack, David went on the offensive. "I'll have Dex Leopold's ass for this."

Clete said, "Before you get too involved with some- body else's ass, I suggest you start thinking about covering your own."

David feigned surprise. "What do you mean?"

There was a knock at the door. Spencer Martin walked in.

Vanessa drew a quick breath, showing more animation than she had up to this point. Clete said, "Well, well. The bad penny has finally come around again."

Spence seemed impervious to the insult. He looked past Clete to speak to Vanessa. "I'm glad to hear that you're on the mend." Then to David, he said, "Dalton Neely is having a difficult time convincing the media that Mrs. Merritt's prognosis is positive. I think you should address them your- self, sir, and assure the nation that the First Lady will soon be back in commission."

"That's a good idea," David agreed. "Clete, why don't you come with me? Your presence there will underscore the good news."

Clete looked down at Vanessa. "Is that okay with you, sweetheart? Do you mind being left alone?"

"I'm not alone any longer, Daddy," she said softly.

"You're surely not." He leaned down and kissed her forehead. When he straightened, he swept his arm toward the door. "After you, Mr. President."

David didn't like the senator's complacency. Not at all. He liked even less the pure loathing with which his wife looked at him. Nevertheless, he told her goodbye, promised that he would return for another visit later in the day, and kissed her hand tenderly before releasing it.

~~~

From the beginning, David Merritt had been a hands-on president, eager to press the flesh of the people who had elected him. His friendliness challenged the men sworn to protect him. Today was no exception.

To the dismay of the Secret Service, the impromptu press conference was held on the ground floor of the hospital, with media and hospital personnel crowding against the nylon rope that provided a tenuous barricade.

A harried Dalton Neely gratefully stood aside for the President, whose arrival had whipped the media into a frenzy. He was immediately bombarded with shouted questions. He held up his hands for quiet. When the clamor subsided, he announced that he and Senator Armbruster had just come from Mrs. Merritt's room.

"We've both spoken with her. She's lucid, she's doing well, and she's in very good spirits. Senator Armbruster and I have every confidence in the care she's receiving from this excellent staff of doctors, nurses, and medical technicians."

It was amazing to Clete that David could handle himself with such aplomb, no matter what the situation. Objectively, he could stand back and admire the president he'd cultivated almost singlehandedly. But he'd also created a monster. And, like in Mary Shelley's classic story, it fell to the creator to destroy his creation.

The President dodged a question about Dr. George Allan by saying that Dr. Allan was presently unavailable. To questions about Mrs. Merritt's so-called kidnapping from Tabor House, he answered that he would have no comment until he'd been fully briefed on the incident. "Reports have been conflicting," he said.

Then he begged their understanding for the brevity of the press conference, thanked them profusely for their concern, and made his way toward the exit. Clete declined to answer the questions flung at him, but he did ask David for a lift to his house.

David was nonplussed by the request, but he consented and informed the chauffeur that they would be making the unscheduled stop before returning to the White House.

"Take another one," Clete said brusquely to Spence when he tried to join them in the President's limo.

Spence looked to David for instruction. "Please, Spence," he said. Clete could tell that Spence didn't like it, but he went along to save face.

"When did he resurface?" Clete asked as the motorcade filed out of the hospital parking lot.

"When you made up that ridiculous story about a . . . what was it? A 'delicate personal matter'?"

"Something to that effect." Clete chuckled. "Frankly, I regret that Bondurant didn't kill the son of a bitch when he had a chance."

"Is that why you asked me for a ride? So you could once again give me your unsolicited negative opinion of my adviser?"

"No. What I have to say is much more important than him."

"Out with it, Clete. You've been dropping juicy little hints that I'm on the brink of doom and only you can save me."

"Actually, that's not too far off the mark, David. I'm the only thing standing between you and a shit hole so deep you'll never find bottom."

David whistled. "That does sound serious."

"Mocking me, David? Try this on for size." Clete cranked up his intimidating gaze to full throttle. "Vanessa's baby wasn't yours, so you killed it, and you've tried at least twice to kill her."

As Clete had known they would, the statements wiped the smile off David's face. "If Vanessa told you that, she's sicker even than we thought, and we both know she's a fruitcake."

Clete controlled his temper, not wishing to give David even that much advantage. "I'm not going to waste a lot of time on this, David. For every accusation I make, you'll have a dozen lying denials, explanations, or justifications. I know how you operate because I'm the one who taught you. So let's make this easy on both of us. I can guarantee you something you want and need."

"What's that?"

"My silence. And Vanessa's."

"In exchange for what?"

"Uncontested divorce."

David didn't bat an eye. "You must be going senile, Clete."

"I promise you I'm not."

"You've suggested a quick, uncontested divorce from Vanessa?"

"Not suggested. Mandated. Or else."

David Merritt's derisive smile returned. "Or else what?"

Clete reached for his briefcase and withdrew a sealed mailing envelope. "Or else I call up Bill Yancey and surrender this to him."

He passed the envelope to his son-in-law, who opened it and removed several color photographs. David dropped them as though they were live cobras.

"Turns your stomach, doesn't it? She bled like hell. But one thing Becky Sturgis did not do was die accidentally. She didn't fall backward during a scuffle with you and hit her head on the corner of a table, as you told me that night. You beat her to death, David. As these photographs of her will attest."

David recovered his shock with remarkable ease. "This is a bluff, Clete. One unworthy of you. *I'm* not in the photographs. These could be the pictures of any corpse. For that matter, you could have beaten this girl to death yourself."

"I could have, but I didn't. There's more in that envelope than the pictures." David shook it, and an audio cassette fell into his lap. "You killed her, David. You admitted as much in a tearful confession. Remember? If not, it's all there on the tape."

Softly Clete added, "I record everything, David. I later erase what's inconsequential, and keep anything that might someday prove useful. After I saw what you did to that poor defenseless girl and her baby, I decided to keep this particular tape."

It was gratifying to see beads of sweat forming on David's forehead. He said, "You'd never use this, Clete, because you're just as guilty as I am."

"I wouldn't want to," he conceded. "My life of public service would end in disgrace. Instead, I would much rather leave you to the devil, and live out the rest of my days revered as an effective statesman, with my daughter at my side. This nasty incident from your past," he said, nodding down at the photographs, "can vanish, *poof,* like that. All you have to do is let Vanessa go without a hassle and without any undue explanations to the media."

"How do you propose I do that?"

Clete shrugged. "The two of you have irreconcilable differences, period. The death of the child put a strain on the marriage. Millions of couples in America will empathize.

The honesty with which you approach the divorce might even win you a few sympathy votes."

David clenched his jaw. "Do you think I'm an idiot? A divorce before an election year would be political suicide. The party probably wouldn't even put me on the ticket."

"You don't know that. Divorce isn't a crime. However, double murder is, and there's no statute of limitations." He gave his son-in-law time to reflect on the ghastly repercussions should the Becky Sturgis story come to light. After a time, he said, "I'm offering you a generous deal, David. Even if I didn't have a vested interest, I'd advise you to accept it."

"Those pictures don't prove a goddamn thing, and neither does the tape."

"Doesn't matter whether it's proved," Clete said blandly. "The mere hint of a scandal of this magnitude would eliminate your chance for a second term. In fact, you'd become a pariah. No matter what you tried to do, this would haunt you for the rest of your life."

David looked on the verge of imploding, but Clete knew he'd won this first round. He would win plenty more rounds before David was on the mat, pleading for mercy. This was the big granddaddy scandal, but there were others, a whole bagful of them. One by one, he would draw them out and expose them. There were enough to last for years, enough to last long after Clete Armbruster was moldering in his grave. But he would die happy, knowing that David Merritt would never know another minute's peace.

But for the time being, Clete was satisfied. It was enough for one morning.

"You may keep those copies, David. I have others. By the way, in case you're thinking of sending Spence or one of his thugs after me, my attorney also has copies of the photos and the tape. He's been instructed to release them to the media in the event of my death by anything other than natural causes."

The chauffeur pulled the limo to a stop at the curb in front of the senator's home. "Wait a minute," David said, grabbing Clete's arm as he was about to alight. "You've guaranteed your silence, but what about Barrie Travis and Gray Bondurant? Aren't you in with them?"

Clete bristled at the thought. "With the airhead journalist and the man who seduced my daughter? Hardly. Leave them to me." He patted David on the knee. "Think over everything I said and get back to me. I'm sure you'll come around to my way of thinking."

$\mathcal{T}$he attorney general stood at the window, his fists pressing against the small of his back, stretching. Barrie wished she knew what he was thinking. Did he believe her? During the telling of her story, he'd interrupted occasionally to ask her to clarify a point, but when she finished, he'd stood up and begun to pace the room, without giving any indication of whether he thought she was telling the truth.

Gray had separated himself from them and was now watching the TV, on which the big news story of the day was being documented. He cursed beneath his breath when the President made his brief statement to the media at the hospital, but when a doctor reiterated that the First Lady would enjoy a full recovery, Gray couldn't hide his profound relief.

Naturally, Barrie shared it. But she wouldn't be human if she hadn't felt a twinge of jealousy.

At some point during Barrie's monologue, Daily had fallen asleep. She was glad he was able to rest. He looked completely done in.

"What I don't understand," said the attorney general,

turning to face the room, "is why Mrs. Merritt didn't blow the whistle on him herself."

Barrie replied without a moment's thought. "Fear. She was afraid of him, Bill. The day we met for coffee, she was about to jump out of her skin. I don't think all her jitters could be attributed to her manic-depression. That's when she first began to suspect that her days were numbered and that he would try something like this. Making that appointment with me was the first smoke signal she sent up."

Yancey looked over at Gray. "What about George Allan?"

"He's David's puppet. He hasn't got the balls to be anything else. David's got him by the short and curlies. Mrs. Allan admitted as much to us."

"That's right, Bill," Barrie said. "I'm sure she would substantiate your case."

"Case?" he repeated, snorting. "I don't have a *case*. I've got nothing except the word of two fugitives who are being sought for kidnapping."

"But you believe us," she said. "I know you do, or you wouldn't have brought us here in the first place." She joined him at the window. "Is it so hard to believe that a chief executive is capable of murder? Look out there." In the early morning sun, they could see the tip of the Washington Monument.

"Monuments to presidents. Some were scoundrels, some were good and honorable men. Tall, short, warriors, statesmen. But their one common denominator, besides the office to which they were elected, is that they were *human*. History has exalted them, made them larger than life, in some instances elevated them to demigods, but they weren't.

"They were men, mortals with character flaws. They laughed, cried, got mad, got constipated. They had no immunity from pride or pain or heartache or . . ." She looked at Gray. "Or jealousy. David Merritt knew that his wife had cheated. She bore another man's child. He couldn't tolerate that. So he did something about it."

He's done it before.

The thought struck her so hard, she shuddered. The words were so clear, she thought someone had spoken out loud. "What?"

Yancey looked at her. "I didn't say anything."

Gray said, "You were saying that—"

"Wait." She held up her hand for quiet.

The sudden revelation had so much impact it was almost biblical. Its power brought her to her knees. Literally. She sank to the floor.

"Barrie." Gray shoved Yancey aside and knelt down in front of her. He took her by the shoulders and looked worriedly into her eyes. "Barrie, what is it?" His voice seemed to come from a great distance, barely heard above the roaring inside her head.

He's done it before.

Where had she heard those words? Or had she read them? Why had they popped into her head now? Why did they seem vitally important?

Then, in a blinding moment of clarity, she remembered where she'd read them, and she knew the answers to those questions, and the back of her neck began to itch.

"Barrie, are you all right?" Bill Yancey was crouched beside Gray, his concern evident.

"Say something, dammit!" Gray said.

"What's happening?" Daily sat up and scratched his scruffy head. "What's going on? What's the matter with her?"

Daily. God bless him, hadn't he told her a thousand times that a good reporter dug *deep*, that there was *always* another layer to unfold, that you should never discount anything, no matter how seemingly unimportant and valueless?

The best leads—the ones that made a story sensational,

that elevated a so-so story into one that rocked the world—
were the ones found in the most unlikely places, places
you'd never think to look for them.

It had been there all the time. *All the damn time!*
Among the scraps of paper and notes that she'd taken from
her desk at WVUE. She had checked out the lead, but only
superficially. She hadn't dug deep enough.

She cautioned herself against getting too excited now.
She could be wrong. This could still prove to be a blind
alley, but gut instinct was telling her otherwise. In any case,
she had to find out.

Pushing the men aside, she surged to her feet. "I've
gotta go."

"Go where?"

"I . . . I'd rather not say. Not until I know."

"You want to leave, but you don't know where you're
going?"

"Of course I know where I'm going," she said impatiently. "I don't know what I'll find when I get there. Maybe
nothing. Maybe something. But I've got to go."

Bill Yancey said, "Barrie, I can't let you walk out of
here—"

"Please, Bill. Send someone with me. A U.S. marshal.
Let him handcuff me, I don't care. Just, please, let me do
this. It could bust this thing wide open."

"What could?"

"That's what I can't say."

"Why can't you tell me?"

"Because I don't want to look like a fool if I'm wrong!"

A long silence followed her shout.

Then: "Let her go."

It was Gray who'd spoken, and when Barrie turned to him
with surprise, his eyes were on her, communicating a thousand things, not the least of which was absolute faith in her.

In that instant, she knew she loved him. Dammit. She loved him very much.

"Let her go," he repeated, holding her stare. "She knows what she's doing."

 ≈≈

"Could've knocked me over with a feather when you showed up with a letter of introduction from the attorney general."

Deputy Warden Foote Graham was as disarming as his name. He belied the bully stereotype portrayed in prison movies. He was mild-mannered, slender as a reed, and wore wire-rimmed glasses. He was sensitive enough not to express any curiosity about the soiled nurse's uniform she was wearing. She hadn't taken time to change.

Barrie thanked him for seeing her without an appointment. "I left Washington in such a hurry, there wasn't time to notify you that I was coming."

Bill Yancey had greased the skids. After agreeing to the trip to Mississippi, he'd placed a private jet at her disposal. At the Jackson airport, there'd been a car and escort waiting to drive her to the prison in Pearl. Foote Graham was in awe of his well-connected guest and had readily agreed to assist in any way he could.

"I assume your interview with Charlene Walters is of an urgent nature?" he asked.

"I'm sorry, Warden Graham. That's confidential."

"I can't figure it," he said, shaking his head in bafflement. "But if you and Attorney General Yancey say it's a matter of national security, who'm I to question it."

He ushered her through a door that was opened for them by a uniformed female guard. "She's waiting for you," the guard said. "And mad as a hornet to be pulled away from rec time."

The prisoner was drinking a can of Dr. Pepper and did indeed look put out when Warden Graham and Barrie Travis approached her. Charlene Walters was a tiny woman, with a bony, concave chest and spindly arms and legs. Her white, overpermed hair formed a frizzy halo around her small head. Her snapping black eyes and the quick, abrupt manner in which she moved reminded Barrie of a sparrow.

Giving Barrie a once-over, she snorted with disdain. "Well, it certainly took you long enough."

Barrie extended her right hand. "I'm pleased to meet you, Mrs. Walters."

Crazy Charlene shook hands with her, then addressed the warden condescendingly. "We got private things to discuss. Do you mind?"

Although she had challenged his authority, Foote Graham smiled. "Of course not. I'll make myself scarce."

He joined the female guard who was standing at a discreet distance. Barrie and Charlene took chairs on either side of a small table. "I understand I'm interrupting your recreation time. I apologize."

"You got any cigarettes?"

Barrie dug into her satchel and produced the same pack she had offered to Vanessa Merritt a few weeks ago. Charlene shook one from the pack and placed it between her thin lips. Barrie lighted it for her, then asked if Charlene had any objections to her recording the interview.

"Not if you'll leave the cigarettes."

Barrie smiled in agreement. Once she'd checked the cassette recorder, she began. "You left several intriguing messages on my voice mail at WVUE."

"You thought I was a kook."

"Well, I—"

"Otherwise you would have called me back."

Charlene was going to be an exacting dance partner who wouldn't tolerate a single misstep. Barrie took another tack. "You're absolutely right, Mrs. Walters. I thought you were a kook. In fact, I still think you might be."

Leaning forward, Charlene winked mischievously. "I got them believing I am. Loony, I mean. I found Jesus right after I got here, but it was getting crazy that worked miracles. Crazy people can get away with just about anything. You'd be amazed."

Charlene Walters was crazy, all right. Crazy like a fox. "The first time you called me," Barrie said, "you left the message 'He's done it before.' To whom were you referring?"

"Well, who do you think, dimwit? The President, of course. David Malcomb Merritt." She stabbed the tabletop with a broken, yellow fingernail. "He killed that baby boy, that little Robert Rushton, sure as I'm sitting here."

"What makes you think so?"

"Are you dense, or what? Don't you listen? Like I told you, he's done it before. He killed another baby. Years ago."

This was the information Barrie had come to Mississippi to hear. "I'm afraid you'll have to be more specific than that."

Charlene exhaled a plume of smoke. "David Merritt was working for Senator Armbruster. Good-looking hotshot, he was. Had women by the dozens. One of 'em got knocked up. Her name was Becky Sturgis. She had a baby boy while Merritt was off in Washington. When he come back, she sprung the kid on him. He didn't cotton to the idea of being a daddy and husband. But Becky, she'd made up her mind to marry him and kept pestering him about it.

"So one night, when her little baby was only a few weeks old, he went over to her trailer house to have it out with her. They got into one hell of a shouting match. The kid was squalling. He choked it to death.

"Maybe he didn't intend to kill the kid. Maybe he just wanted to hush his crying. But since he had killed him, I guess he figured he ought not to leave any witnesses. He beat Becky Sturgis to a fare-thee-well."

Snorting her sinuses clean, Charlene twirled the cigarette like a miniature baton. "There's no excuse for that sorta violence against women. None whatsoever. Even if I weren't a convicted felon, he wouldn't have got my vote, on account of it."

The tale was too much to absorb all at once, so Barrie cushioned her mind by thinking how interesting life was. The nation's history could very well be altered by this comically birdlike septuagenarian who was serving a life sentence for armed robbery and murder.

But who would ever believe it? Did *she* believe it? Charlene's credibility was as thin as rice paper. She could have invented this story to help fill her idle time. Robert Rushton Merritt's death had sparked her interest. Barrie's SIDS series had fanned the flames of her imagination. She'd found a sucker who would listen, who had come all the way to Mississippi to speak with her. Making up this story could be the best entertainment Charlene had enjoyed in years.

Or it could be true.

Either way, Barrie decided to proceed with caution. This could be the story of the century. If she blew it, not only her future but the nation's would be sacrificed to her ineptitude.

"It all sounds very . . ."

"Unbelievable," Charlene said when Barrie faltered. "You don't have to believe me. Ask ol' Cletus Armbruster."

"The senator?"

Charlene screwed up her wizened features in disgust. "He's the crookedest politician ever to walk the face of the earth, and that's saying something."

"He knows about Becky Sturgis?"

"Knows? Hell, girl, who do you think made the problem go away?" Charlene exclaimed. "Merritt went to him that very night. The senator took care of it."

"Senator Armbruster is a powerful man, but even he couldn't make two bodies disappear," Barrie argued. "Wasn't there a criminal investigation?"

"If you want to call it that," Charlene said with a contemptuous flick of her cigarette in the general direction of the ashtray. "Armbruster's pockets were crowded with city and state officials. He called in favors, is all. Becky and her little baby didn't mean shit to them good ol' boys down to the courthouse."

Barrie shook her head in disbelief. "Armbruster couldn't have been involved. He wouldn't have allowed Vanessa to marry David Merritt, knowing that he was capable of—"

"What planet you been living on? Course he would have allowed her to marry him. He fancied his daughter being First Lady." She hocked up a glob of phlegm and spat it on the floor. "Sons of bitches. All of 'em. They think they can do anything they want and get away with it. Folks like me and my old man, we had to pay for our crimes. But not people like Merritt and Armbruster."

"I'm afraid you're right," Barrie said. "If everything you've told me is true, it took place, what, twenty years ago? If Armbruster successfully covered a double murder, he would have covered his tracks equally as well. There's no way to prove it ever happened."

Charlene slapped the tabletop, startling Barrie and causing her to jump. "You're the stupidest gal the good Lord ever gave breath to. You think I'd spend my money calling you up there in Washington, D.C., and put my scrawny neck on the line if I didn't have no proof?"

Chapter
Forty-Five

"*It*'s better than you deserve." Bill Yancey leaned over the table, placing his hands flat on its smooth surface. "Provide us with evidence that the President smothered Vanessa's baby and was attempting to kill her, and you'll be granted immunity from prosecution."

Spencer Martin maintained his silence. Throughout the interrogation, he'd been admirably stoic, staring straight ahead, remote as a statue, as though detached from the circumstances in which he found himself.

The office was now cluttered with rubbish from several carryout meals and empty coffee cups. It was almost steamy with the tension generated during the long night and following day. Despite his protests, Daily had been taken to a hotel. Two FBI agents had accompanied him and were ordered to stay with him and see to his needs until further notice. William Yancey and Gray Bondurant had spent all day in that office, anxiously awaiting word from Barrie.

When she'd finally called from the Mississippi prison and recounted for them her conversation with Charlene Walters, Yancey had said, "We can't proceed without some inside help, and Spencer Martin is as inside as you can get." He'd ordered that Spence be brought in for questioning. Spence had come peaceably but had not yet cooperated.

Gray, who was against Spence's getting immunity, was being vindicated by Spence's stubborn silence. He had warned the attorney general that he'd have better luck getting statements from a turnip, and he'd been right.

"I told you this would be an exercise in futility," he said now. "That's why he declined your offer to call an attorney. He knew he wasn't going to say a goddamn word. You could torture him to death before he'd rat on David Merritt."

But Yancey wasn't yet ready to give up. "Mr. Martin, some of your former operatives are willing to testify against you to avoid prosecution themselves. You're implicated in several serious crimes, good for years in federal prison."

Nothing.

"Howard Fripp? That name strike a bell, Mr. Martin? It should. You're a suspect in his murder case."

Spencer didn't even flinch.

"He's not going to tell you a thing," Gray said. "He won't even tell you that I shot him and locked him in a root cellar. If he did, he would have to explain what he was doing out there. You're wasting your time."

Yancey ran a hand over his balding head. "Very well, Mr. Martin. This offer is good only for the next thirty seconds. If you reject it, you'll be subjected to a congressional investigation the likes of which will be unrivaled in American history."

Spencer Martin came to his feet. "If you had evidence of any wrongdoing on my part, I'd be under arrest. Don't try to strong-arm me again, Bill. It doesn't dignify either of us."

Yancey grumbled a curse.

Spence gave him a smirking smile, then headed for the door.

"Yancey, all right with you if I have a private word with him?"

It was clear that Yancey didn't like the idea, but he granted permission. Gray followed Spence out into the hallway.

As soon as the door closed behind them, Spence's nonchalance vanished. He grabbed Gray by the throat and slammed him against the wall. His face was ugly and flushed with fury. "I'd like to kill you for putting me in that fucking cellar."

Gray threw off Spence's hands and shoved him away. "But you won't. Because killing me would be stupid, and no one's ever accused you of being stupid, Spence. Not until now."

A flicker of interest appeared in his eyes. It was fleeting, soon replaced by his characteristic cynicism. "Who are you, the good cop?"

Gray shrugged. "Take this for what it's worth. You should have accepted Yancey's deal."

"Do you really think he, or anyone, could bring down David's administration?" Spence chuckled. "It'll never happen, Gray. You'll all be made to look like idiots for trying. You've aligned yourself with the wrong side, pal. We've been scrupulously careful. David's airtight. You know that."

"Whether or not his administration collapses is inconsequential to you, Spence. You'll never know one way or the other, because you'll be long dead." Spence's smirk lost some of its insolence. "Beginning to catch on now, Spence? You were in on David's plans for Vanessa, probably for the baby as well. So, as long as you're alive, he's not airtight. Once that occurs to him, you're history.

"David will find himself another Ray Garrett. Remember him? That nice young Marine assigned to assassinate me when I became an embarrassment to the Oval

Office? Too bad you're so goddamn self-assured you can't see the hazardous position you're in. Yancey's deal would have afforded you some protection."

"Go fuck yourself."

"Perfect, Spence. The defensive comeback of every dumb schmuck who has no other defense to offer." Gray opened the office door, saying over his shoulder, "Watch your back, *pal.*"

It was midafternoon of the next day when Barrie returned to Washington. A lot had happened in her absence. Dr. George Allan's attempted suicide had been reported on the front page of the Post. He was in a coma, his wife at his side.

"How'd they manage to keep it under wraps for two days?" Barrie asked.

"Out of deference to his family," Gray told her. "That was Neely's line anyway."

They were guests of the federal government in a comfortable hotel suite. U.S. marshals were posted outside the door. Bill Yancey was on the telephone in the adjoining room. Every once in a while, they caught snatches of his intense conversations.

"Poor Amanda. It must have been horrible for her to find him like that."

"The gunshot woke her up. She rushed into his office. If she hadn't, he would have died at his desk."

"I hope for her sake he makes it, and that if he makes it, he's not a vegetable."

"Either way, it's rough for her and the kids," Gray said. "What was the son of a bitch thinking?"

"I guess he was desperate and didn't know what else to do."

"There's always an alternative to that, for chrissake,"

he said angrily. "Yancey probably would have offered him a deal to turn state's witness."

"If he pulls through," she said, "I'm sure that's exactly what Bill will do."

She saw the consternation in Gray's face and remembered that he'd lost both parents when he wasn't much older than the Allans' sons. He also looked tired and haggard, unshaven and irritable. They were all frazzled. It had been an eventful forty-eight hours.

And there was no respite in sight.

At least Daily was out of harm's way and resting peacefully. He was in comparative luxury in another suite of the hotel. When she stopped in to see him, he'd grumbled about not being allowed to go home, but he was enjoying cable TV, room service, and the companionship of the two young FBI agents who'd been assigned to guard him. They were a captive audience for his tall tales about his years as a newsman.

Barrie glanced down at the copy of the *Post* on the coffee table and referenced another front-page story. "Would Spence be offended by the small write-up he received?"

"Flattered, more likely," Gray said. "He cultivated his mysterious persona. The less anyone knew about him, the better he liked it."

"I can't believe it." Barrie scanned the concise story again.

"I tried to warn him, but he wouldn't listen. It was only a matter of time before David took him out. The only thing that surprises me is how swiftly he struck."

"You really think Merritt arranged this mugging?"

"Mugging my ass." Gray shot her a retiring look. "Spence was dropped outside his apartment by two guys who all but had FEDS tattooed on their foreheads. What kind of muggers select a victim who's got that kind of heat around him? Spence was always armed. Besides his knife, he carried a pistol in an ankle holster. Whoever mugged him was aware of that. They knew exactly how to disarm him."

After what Barrie had learned in Mississippi, she didn't doubt Merritt's ruthlessness. Without a qualm, he could have his most loyal friend killed. Shivering with fear, she hugged her elbows. "We're on his hit list too, aren't we?"

"No doubt."

"Then what does he think of this?"

She indicated the third big news story on the front page, which involved her and Gray. Vanessa Merritt had gone on record saying that she had prevailed upon her friends, Barrie Travis and Gray Bondurant, to remove her from Tabor House. They'd been clandestine because of the hospital's strict policy against visitors. The confusion, resulting in Barrie and Gray being suspected of kidnapping, was absurd, she'd said from her hospital bed. Travis and Bondurant had delivered her directly to her father, who'd had a helicopter waiting. Did that sound like a kidnapping?

"I'm sure Clete scripted it and that David isn't happy about it," Gray said of Vanessa's statement. "It would have been convenient for him if we'd been shot as fugitives. But now he has no choice except to back his wife's account of the event. No one's going to disbelieve Vanessa and Clete."

"If I were John Q. Public, I wouldn't believe anything positive they said about us. Not after the incident in Shinlin."

He shrugged. "We've all kissed and made up."

So it seemed, particularly when the attorney general walked in and gave them the latest update. "Senator Armbruster wants to see you."

"Me?" Barrie exclaimed.

"What for?" Gray asked suspiciously.

"He wants to give her an exclusive. He says she's owed one."

"Exclusive about what?" Barrie asked. "What could it be?"

"Don't get excited," Gray said. "You're not going."

"The hell I'm not! I can't pass up an exclusive."

"You've already got one."

"Doesn't mean I can't have another."

Gray turned to Yancey. "Ever since Barrie got back, all you've done is talk on the telephone, while we've been sitting here with our thumbs up our asses. Why aren't we doing something? With what you have, you can end this thing now. March into the Oval Office, handcuff the bastard, read him his rights, and get it the hell over with."

"It's not that simple. We're talking about the President of the United States."

"I know who we're talking about," Gray shouted. "And he's a murderer."

"Calm down," Yancey shouted in turn. Then, in a more reasonable tone: "We all understand your desire to exact vengeance for Mrs. Merritt and her baby. If the President is guilty of the crimes attributed to him—and all evidence points in that direction," he added when he saw that Gray was about to interrupt, "then we must tread very carefully. We make one mistake, and he's scot-free. While we're waiting for lab reports, I see no harm in having Barrie talk to Armbruster."

"I'll tell you what the harm is," Gray said angrily. "He's as much a criminal as David. You heard what that Walters woman said. The list of charges against Clete is as long as my arm. Barrie could be walking into a trap that'll get her killed."

The attorney general shook his head. "Armbruster said that Mrs. Merritt is being released from the hospital this afternoon. She'll be there too, so he couldn't have violence in mind." Yancey turned to Barrie. "I gather you're game?"

"Absolutely."

"Where and when?" Gray snapped.

"The senator's house. Eight o'clock."

Chapter
Forty-Six

At precisely eight o'clock Barrie rang the doorbell. It was answered by a Secret Service agent who asked politely to see her satchel. He searched it, then handed it back to her and ran a portable metal detector over her.

Senator Armbruster came forward to greet her. He pressed her hand between both of his and said effusively, "I hope we can put all our misunderstandings behind us after tonight, Miss Travis. I've already spoken to your former employer at WVUE. As a personal favor to me, he's agreed to reinstate you. You can have your job back."

"Thank you, Senator, but I no longer wish to be employed at WVUE, especially as a charity case."

He smiled magnanimously. "Frankly I don't blame you. After tonight, you'll be able to sell your story to the highest bidder."

"I'm curious about the nature of this exclusive you've promised."

"Then I won't keep you in suspense any longer."

He led her into a lovely, tastefully furnished parlor. A cheery fire was burning in the marble fireplace. Vanessa, wearing a ruffled dressing gown and looking like the frail heroine of a Victorian novel, reclined on a divan. She was still attached to an IV.

Standing before the fire, one arm propped on the mantel, was the President of the United States.

No one had suggested that he would be here. There'd been no waiting motorcade or entourage outside the house. The only Secret Service agents in sight were the two who'd been in the entry when she came in, and she had supposed they were guarding Vanessa. She tried to mask her trepidation.

"Hello, Miss Travis."

She unglued her tongue from the roof of her mouth and said, "Good evening, Mr. President." She could barely hear her own words over the drumming of her heart.

"Hello, Barrie."

Barrie looked down at Vanessa. "Mrs. Merritt."

She smiled. "After all we've been through together, I think you should call me Vanessa."

"Thank you." Taking the chair the senator indicated, Barrie faced the three of them like a witness on the stand— or a condemned woman facing a firing squad.

"You appear to be feeling much better than you were the last time I saw you," she said to Vanessa.

"I am much better. How's Gray?"

Barrie shot a glance toward Merritt, but his expression didn't change. "He's shocked by what happened to Spencer Martin last night."

"As we all are," Armbruster said with insincere sorrow.

"Gray sends his regards," Barrie said to Vanessa.

"I can't thank the two of you enough for taking me out of Tabor House. Under George's care, I would have died there."

Barrie felt like thumping her temple with the heel of her hand. What was this, Wonderland? Was she Alice, who'd just tumbled through her mirror into an otherworldly tableau? Since stepping across Senator Armbruster's threshold, nothing had been as she'd expected it. For all the sense it made, their dialogue could have been gibberish. Surely Vanessa didn't believe that George Allan, acting singly, had devised to kill her.

Barrie saw no alternative but to go along with this bizarre script and see where it led. "Thank you for clearing up the matter of the kidnapping."

"It was a mix-up that needed straightening out."

As simply as that, Vanessa dismissed it. The senator interrupted an awkward silence by offering Barrie a drink. "What can I get you?"

"Nothing, thanks. What I'd really like is to get down to business. Why'd you invite me here?"

"We—the three of us—felt that we owed you this courtesy, Miss Travis." The senator was apparently the mouthpiece for the proceedings. Since greeting her, Merritt had said nothing, but she was constantly and uneasily aware of his baleful gaze.

"As I said earlier," Armbruster continued, "we want to clear up this unfortunate misunderstanding, lay it to rest. Because of all the ill-will felt by both sides, we're offering you an olive branch in the form of an exclusive story."

"What story?"

Armbruster looked at David, who glanced down at Vanessa, then at Barrie. "Vanessa and I are getting a divorce."

Barrie was too stunned to speak, but she didn't have to. He went on to explain. "Dalton Neely will make a statement to the media tomorrow at noon, although he doesn't know it yet. He'll read this letter from me to the American people. I'm giving you an advance copy." He removed an envelope from the breast pocket of his suit jacket and handed it to Barrie.

"May I read it now?"

He nodded. She opened the envelope and took out two sheets of stationery bearing the presidential seal. After a sugary salutation, she reached the body of the letter and began to read aloud.

" 'The death of our son took a terrible toll on Mrs. Merritt and myself. The demands of this office also have contributed largely to her unhappiness. Neither of us blames the other for the dissolution of the marriage. We accept our individual blame for its breakdown, although I must assume the larger share of responsibility. Countless times, being president superseded being an attentive husband.

" 'Vanessa is an incredibly unselfish woman. None other would have endured as much as she has for as long as she has. I have nothing but deep admiration and affection for Vanessa Armbruster Merritt.' "

Barrie stopped reading and raised her head. She might just as well have been looking at three formal portraits. Their features were frozen into perfect, perpetual pleasantness.

She returned to the letter. " 'Vanessa and I realize that you, the American people, will be as disillusioned and saddened as we by this turn of events, but no one is immune to this dilemma which is experienced by millions of families in our world community. We ask only that you make no harsh judgments and that you appreciate the honesty with which we're dealing with this unhappy situation.

" 'Following the example set by my father-in-law, Senator Armbruster, Vanessa and I have dedicated ourselves to public service. We plan to continue serving you in whatever capacity you'll allow us. Speaking for myself, more than at any other time as your president, I need your whole-hearted support. Thank you.' "

It was signed David Malcomb Merritt, President of the United States. Barrie folded the letter and replaced it in the official envelope. "Very eloquent, Mr. President," she said. After a beat, she added, "And very fraudulent."

"I beg your pardon?"

Barrie took a deep breath and mentally leaped off the high diving board. "You're not heartsick over this divorce, Mr. President. You're relieved. Because I'm certain it's part of a deal, right? A deal struck with Senator Armbruster and Vanessa."

"This is an outrage," Armbruster blustered. "You've surpassed even your audacity, young lady. We invited you here tonight—"

"Hoping that you could purchase my silence with an exclusive story about the divorce in the First Family. Sorry, Senator, no trade. No deal, Mr. President." She stood up and approached the divan on which Vanessa was reclined. "How could you settle for this," she said, smacking the envelope against her palm, "when he killed your baby?"

"I'm calling the Secret Service."

"No, Clete," David ordered, halting his father-in-law at the door of the parlor. "Let's have this out. Miss Travis has been slinging mud at me for weeks, influenced no doubt by Gray. It's time she heard my side of the story." Facing her, he said, "I did not kill Robert Rushton Merritt. I don't know how you reached that ridiculous and slanderous conclusion, but you're wrong."

"Vanessa intimated to me that you did. After the events of these last few days, I believe her."

"You mistakenly inferred that from something she said at a time when she was so depressed she couldn't think straight."

Barrie kneeled down so that she and Vanessa were on eye level. "When you contacted me that first time, were you clinically depressed? Or were you afraid? Did he smother the child while you were in the room, or did you find him standing over the body, pillow in his hand?"

"The baby died of SIDS."

Ignoring the President, Barrie grabbed Vanessa's hand. "Are you going to let him get away with murdering your baby and trying to murder you?"

"I'm warning you, Miss Travis, one more word and—"

"Your father talked you into this deal, didn't he? Wasn't it he who suggested that you maintain your silence in exchange for a peaceful divorce? Do you know why he urged you to accept that deal?"

"Because he knows I'm afraid," Vanessa said faintly. "I want out of my marriage to David."

"Be quiet, Vanessa," David shouted. "Don't tell her a goddamn thing."

Barrie appealed to her. "Why do you think the President agreed to a divorce when it could impede his chances for reelection? What reason would be compelling enough for him to grant you a divorce?"

Vanessa looked distraught, but her wide blue eyes were fixed on Barrie. "I . . . I don't know."

"Because your father threatened to expose a terrible secret if your husband said no."

"I'm warning you for the last time—"

"David, let me call in the Secret Service," Clete implored.

Barrie spoke above them. "Your father knows where the body is buried, Vanessa. In this instance, that isn't simply an expression. There really is a buried body. Of another baby. Born years ago to a woman named Becky Sturgis. That baby wasn't wanted either, so your husband killed it. And your father helped him cover it up."

Vanessa looked at her father. "Daddy? Is this true?"

"Of course not! The woman's a lunatic, Vanessa. Everybody knows it. You can't trust a word she says."

"You can't bluff your way out of this, gentlemen,"

Barrie said. "Shutting me up won't help. Too many people know. It's over."

"Like hell it is!"

Responding to the President's angry shout, the Secret Service agents opened the door. "Mr. President?"

Merritt impatiently motioned for them to leave. "Get out," he yelled. "This is private."

"Who's going to do your dirty work this time, Mr. President?" Barrie asked. "Dr. Allan tried to kill himself because of his contribution to your treachery."

"He tried to kill himself because of his own inadequacy. He's the Barrie Travis of medicine, a total screw-up. He couldn't even blow his own brains out successfully."

"What about Spencer Martin?" she said. "You had him killed last night because he knew too many secrets. Was he in the room when you smothered the baby?"

"You had Spence killed?" Vanessa cried.

David shot her a venomous look, then he said to Barrie, "I did not kill the baby. How many times do I have to say it? If Spence was here he'd tell you the same thing. I did not kill him. She did!" he exclaimed, jabbing his finger toward Vanessa.

Vanessa cried out in shock and outrage.

"Vanessa didn't kill her child," Barrie said. "No more than Becky Sturgis killed her baby son. You strangled him."

"Oh, my God. My *God*!" Vanessa wailed.

"That's right," Barrie told her. "Then he beat that young woman unmercifully. At least he learned one lesson from that experience. He learned to use more subtle tactics."

Vanessa rounded on her father again. "Is this true, Daddy? Did you know?"

Looking as flaccid as a deflated inner tube, the senator backed into a chair and plopped down on the seat. His posture was indicative of the guilt weighing down his shoulders, twenty years' worth of it.

Vanessa cried out as though in agony. "It *is* true. Oh, God! Why'd you let me marry him? Why'd you encourage me to have his baby?" She sobbed. "I wanted a baby so much." She looked at her husband as though looking into the embodiment of evil. "How could you kill him? He was so helpless, so sweet."

Merritt barked a harsh laugh. "You're such a sentimental fool, Vanessa. And so false. The baby was driving you to distraction. You couldn't stand his crying. You were inept at taking care of him, just as you are at everything. You didn't love that baby. The stuff that Gray squirted into you, and which you've so ridiculously romanticized now, was slime. It should have been flushed. That would have saved us both a lot of trouble."

Barrie was stunned by the ugliness of the President's words. Armbruster too was shocked into speechlessness.

But Vanessa was not. Eyes blazing, she came to her feet. She swayed weakly, but gripped the back of the divan for support. "You son of a bitch, it wasn't Gray. It was Spence."

"*Spence?*" Merritt exclaimed.

Spence? Barrie's mind reeled.

Seemingly unmindful of the IV tube in her arm, Vanessa moved toward her husband, dragging the wheeled rack behind her. "Yes, Spence. Spence!" She virtually spat the name in his face. "You thought Gray was my lover because you *wanted* to think it was him. A man of Gray Bondurant's inflexible sense of duty and right and wrong, sleeping with his best friend's wife!" She laughed tauntingly.

"Get real, David. Gray was only nice to me because he knew about your other women. It never occurred to you that it was Spence who was fucking your wife," she said in that same gloating voice, happy to destroy his illusions about the man in whom he'd placed so much trust.

"But he did fuck me. And I wanted him to. Only thing, the joke was on me. He wasn't any better at it than you are. He was a cold, heartless bastard just like you. He was actually glad that the baby died." Her voice cracked. "Spence wanted no part of him, and that broke my heart. But at least my son wasn't yours. At least I didn't have *your* baby."

Merritt slapped her.

That launched Armbruster from his chair. Roaring like an old lion, he charged his protégé. But with very little effort, Merritt shoved him aside. "You're a joke, Clete." David laughed. "You've got no power, figuratively or literally. You're a eunuch. You don't have the balls to bully me into making *any* decision."

Then, looking at his wife, he said, "I've changed my mind about the divorce, Vanessa. Not about granting it, but about the reason. I think it's time the world discovered what a cunt their sweetheart really is.

"As for you," he said to Barrie, "if you know what's good for you, you'll fuck off. And fuck Bondurant too, while you're at it. Although no doubt you already have."

He strode to the door and flung it open.

Gray Bondurant was standing on the other side of the door with Attorney General Yancey and a phalanx of federal agents.

"Mr. President, you have the right to remain silent—"

"What the hell are you doing here, Bill?"

Gray pushed past Yancey and Merritt and leaned down over the two women. "Are you all right?"

Holding the weeping Vanessa against her chest, Barrie nodded. "She's okay."

"What about you?"

"I'm fine. Shaken. He looked ready to kill me with his bare hands."

"I'd have killed him first," Gray said. His eyes held hers

for a five count, then he turned away and assisted in the business at hand, arresting the President and Senator Armbruster.

Merritt wasn't responding in a dignified, peaceable manner. In fact, he was raving like a maniac. He screamed invective at Yancey, but to Yancey's credit he maintained his cool while reading the President his rights.

Then Merritt began ranting that Vanessa, not he, had killed their son, and that anything he'd done since then had been to protect her. "She smothered him. It was her, not me. She's the crazy one."

"I caution you to say nothing more, Mr. President," Yancey said. "You're implicated in another crime in Mississippi."

"I don't know what you're talking about. Clete! Clete, tell them how sick Vanessa is."

Armbruster opened his mouth, but his lips were slack. His jowls jiggled when he tried but failed to form words.

"Senator Armbruster will have a chance to testify," Yancey told Merritt. "His testimony will be as valuable to us as that of the eyewitness."

"There was no one in the nursery except Spence, Vanessa, and me. Spence is dead, and she's lying."

"I'm not talking about the death of Robert Rushton Merritt," Yancey explained. "We have an eyewitness to the murder in Mississippi."

Finally, the attorney general's words seemed to penetrate the red curtain of David Merritt's rage. For the first time, he seemed to grasp the bleak reality of his situation. He glared long at Yancey, then turned to Clete.

Clete gazed back at the man he had made and had now destroyed, but at tremendous personal cost.

Merritt's eyes narrowed to malicious slits. "You sly son of a bitch," he hissed. "What did you do?"

The Exclusive

"Senator Armbruster was there when I regained consciousness."

Becky Sturgis's soft drawl filled the otherwise silent television studio. The floor crew had locked down the cameras. They were as immersed in her story as the millions of people watching it on TV around the world. She was staring down at her hands, which were clasped tightly in her lap.

"When I came to, I remember hoping that I was waking up from a terrible nightmare, but it was real. My baby was dead. His little body was still lying on the floor where David had dropped it. There was a lot of blood. I guess it was mine. David had hit me very hard."

"David Merritt, the President?"

"Yes, ma'am. Only he wasn't president then."

She wore a scarf to cover the permanent depression in her temple, where her scalp had been crudely sewn over her crushed skull. She was very self-conscious of the disfigurement. When Barrie met her, she'd been dressed in a prison jumpsuit. Tonight she was wearing a simple dress. Other than the scarf, she was unadorned.

"After he hit me that first time, I don't remember anything until I woke up and Senator Armbruster was kneeling beside me, feeling for a pulse in my neck. He was startled that I was still alive because David had told him I was dead."

"He'd also told Senator Armbruster that *you* killed the baby."

"I didn't," she said fiercely. "David did. And I told the senator the truth. He was very kind. He told me not to worry, that he would take care of it."

"What did he do?"

"He called a doctor, who came to the trailer and sewed up my scalp and gave me a shot for the pain."

"You weren't taken to a hospital?"

"No, ma'am."

"When were the police called?"

"Senator Armbruster called the sheriff's office. When the officers got there . . ." She began to cry. Barrie didn't probe. She gave her time to compose herself before starting again. "Senator Armbruster lied to them. He told them I'd killed my baby. He told them to arrest me. They took me downtown and started questioning me. They wanted me to sign a confession, saying I'd committed manslaughter. I refused. For a while."

"And then, you did."

"Yes, ma'am. Just so they'd leave me alone. My head was hurting so bad. I'd vomited a couple of times. I was bad off. So I signed a paper saying that I'd killed my baby. But I didn't. David Merritt killed him, and he left thinking he had killed me."

With Barrie offering very little guidance, Becky Sturgis told of the miscarriage of justice orchestrated by Senator Armbruster. He called in political favors. Within a matter of days, a judge sentenced her to life in prison. She was transferred from the county jail to the state prison, and there she had remained until two days ago, when Barrie learned of her existence from Charlene Walters. Attorney General Yancey had interceded with Mississippi authorities to have her brought to Washington.

Barrie asked, "Do you think Senator Armbruster believed David Merritt over you? In your opinion, did the senator honestly believe he was seeing justice served by putting you in prison?"

"I don't know," she replied honestly. "But I suspect he double-crossed me so David wouldn't get into trouble."

"You're aware that David Merritt has believed you dead all these years?"

"I didn't know that until yesterday. I guess the senator double-crossed him too."

To protect her objectivity, Barrie refrained from stating the obvious: Senator Armbruster had kept Becky Sturgis in abeyance should he ever need to use her as leverage against his son-in-law. Barrie had discovered her before Armbruster became desperate enough to need her.

"You've been in prison all this time, Miss Sturgis?"

"Yes, ma'am. My parole's been denied twice."

"Why? According to your records, you've been an exemplary prisoner."

"I don't know why, ma'am. The board just rejects me."

Barrie let the silence stretch out so that her audience could reach another obvious conclusion: Armbruster had seen to it that Becky Sturgis would never get paroled.

"A few years ago, you shared a cell with a woman named Charlene Walters. You told her your story."

Becky Sturgis nodded. "It was after David became president. At first Charlene didn't believe me, thought I was making it up. But when his baby died in the White House nursery, she began to think maybe I had told her the truth. Especially after she saw your series on SIDS. It got Charlene to thinking that maybe Robert Rushton Merritt was one of those babies who'd been murdered and it was made to look like SIDS."

"Miss Sturgis, this is the most difficult question I'll ask you tonight. I'm sure everyone wants to know why you didn't come forward. All these years you've been in prison, why didn't you bring it to someone's attention that you'd been framed and then coerced into signing a false confession?"

She shrugged, as though fully accepting the inconsequentiality of her life. "Nobody gave it a second thought when I disappeared. Nobody ever came looking for me. I hadn't lived in that town long. I guess folks figured I'd drifted out just like I'd drifted in. I don't have a family. Who was I going to tell?"

"Didn't you have a lawyer?"

"Yes, ma'am. They appointed me one that night in the sheriff's office, but he kept telling me that I'd be better off signing a confession. He said they might upgrade the charge to murder if I didn't confess to manslaughter. In a murder trial, he said, I might lose and get the death penalty.

"And besides, I was sick for a long time. I had headaches that would put me in the prison infirmary for days at a time. Sometimes I had blackouts and couldn't remember sections of time. It was a couple years before I felt like my head was on straight.

"That's when I started writing letters to the lawyer, but he only answered a few of them. Then he stopped writing back altogether. I tried reaching him by phone, but I was always told he wasn't there and he never returned my calls. One day this other lawyer—I've got his name written down somewhere—came to the prison to see me. He said my lawyer had died and that I wasn't to bug them no more. If I did, there'd be hell to pay from Armbruster, he said. By that time, David was a congressman. I didn't see the point in carrying on about it. Who would believe me over David Merritt and Clete Armbruster?"

"That's a good question, Miss Sturgis. Why should we believe you? What proof do you have that David Merritt killed your baby, beat you, and left you for dead?"

"None. But I can prove that he was my baby's daddy," she said proudly. "The day my baby was killed, I clipped a curl from his hair and trimmed his fingernails. I've kept them all these years in a little pâpier-maché box. Mr. Yancey has them now. He said they can run tests on them that'll prove whether or not David's the daddy. I didn't want to let 'em go, 'cause that's all I have of my baby. But Mr. Yancey promised to give them back soon as the lab is finished with them. People might think I'm lying, but my baby will tell them the truth."

Barrie couldn't think of a more fitting note on which to end the interview. "Thank you, Miss Sturgis."

She turned and faced the studio camera as it rolled in for a close-up. "According to Attorney General Yancey, preliminary DNA testing of the hair and fingernail parings has indicated that David Merritt fathered Becky Sturgis's son. This should go a long way toward getting her arrest and confession reviewed. Officials indicate that she'll be granted a long overdue trial. It's as yet undetermined whether David Merritt will be prosecuted for murder, although he's already been charged with obstruction of justice, along with Senator Armbruster.

"Senator Armbruster has been placed under house arrest. He officially resigned his Senate seat this afternoon. President Pietsch was sworn into office after Congress impeached David Merritt and demanded his resignation.

"The former president is also under arrest inside Blair House, where he will remain until Attorney General Yancey has had an opportunity to organize two full-scale investigations, one involving the crimes in Mississippi, the other the death of Robert Rushton Merritt.

"It's too early to speculate what the final outcome of this incredible story will be. Over the course of our nation's history, other presidents have weathered scandals, but there has been none to rival this.

"Whether or not his alleged crimes are proved, David Merritt fled the scene of a crime in Mississippi to escape the giving of testimony and possible prosecution. That in itself is a federal offense and was cause enough to bring his administration as President of the United States to an end.

"This is Barrie Travis. Good night."

"Hi. Come on in." Barrie stood aside and ushered Gray into the hotel suite where she'd taken up temporary residence.

"Thanks. I'm honored to be in the same room with you. You're a hot ticket."

"My celebrity hasn't impressed room service. It still takes them forever to deliver a club sandwich." She checked the clock. "Forty minutes and counting. Meanwhile, I'm starving."

"What's wrong with the lights?"

"Nothing. It seemed more restful this way." The suite was in darkness, save for one dim lamp near the window. The draperies were open, revealing the beauty of the capital at night.

Barrie was fresh out of a long, hot shower, wrapped from earlobes to ankles in a white terrycloth robe, compliments of the hotel. Her hair was still wet, hooked behind her ears.

"Saw your interview," he dropped casually.

She looked at him expectantly, holding her breath.

"It was good, Barrie."

While warming beneath his approving smile, she downplayed her success. "I didn't do anything. The story told itself."

"If not for you, there'd be no story."

"If not for Merritt and Armbruster there'd be no story. I didn't particularly enjoy what Becky Sturgis had to tell the world."

"Where is she now?"

"In a hotel. Bill has a couple of female marshals with her. She'll be returned to the prison tomorrow and will have to remain there until her case is reviewed by a judge in Mississippi."

"The interview was so touching, there'll be a public outcry for her release."

"At the very least, she'll be granted a jury trial. I'll be surprised if she's convicted. If she is, she'll probably be sentenced to time already served."

After a thoughtful moment, he asked, "What did CNN do to get you?"

"They topped everybody else's bid. What can I say?" she said, batting her eyelashes. "I can be bought."

"There's your sandwich," he said as he went to answer the door. He signed the bill and set the tray on the coffee table in front of the sofa.

"Amanda Allan called," she told him. "George is showing some signs that have encouraged the doctors. She's optimistic. She loves him very much and is willing to forgive him anything if he survives."

"I would expect that of her," he said. "How's Daily?"

"I'm covering his hotel tab now. I don't want him ever to go back to that dreary house. It's bad enough that he's dying. He shouldn't have to die there. Besides, I don't think any of us could go back without remembering those last terrifying days we spent there."

"Where will he live?"

She picked at the bread crust. "I'm thinking of buying a house. Something in the suburbs. With a mother-in-law room for Daily to live in. The insurance settlement on my town house was more than fair, and with the salary I'm negotiating, I'll be able to get almost anything I want. I could get a dog to keep him company when I'm not there. I think I'm ready to love another one, although I'll never replace Cronkite, of course."

"Have you bounced this idea off Daily?"

"He snarled something about his not being 'a fucking charity case,' but he'll come around," she said, smiling fondly. Having eaten a quarter of her sandwich, she pushed the plate away.

"I thought you were starving."

"Guess I wasn't."

"What's wrong, Barrie?"

"Nothing," she said impatiently. Then, reluctantly: "I don't know."

"You're right where you always wanted to be, on top of your profession with every network in the country clamoring to get you under contract. You can name your price. You had the interview of the century. I thought I'd find you guzzling champagne."

"That's what I thought I'd be doing too," she said ruefully. "But you'd be surprised what a downer it is to be the person responsible for toppling a president."

"You aren't the person responsible. David brought about his own downfall."

"You're right, of course. Up here," she said, tapping her head, "I know you're right. Maybe I'm ambivalent because of Howie. He was a casualty, and he shouldn't have been. I feel I'm indirectly to blame."

"Spence is to blame."

She gave a despairing sigh. "I guess it's sort of like

postpartum. After a hard labor, I've delivered the baby, but I'm not sure I love it yet." Averting her eyes, she said, "Pursuant to that, Vanessa called me this afternoon."

Gray looked at her inquisitively.

"She thanked me for handling the Becky Sturgis interview in such a low-key manner when I could have exploited the story, made it more tabloid." She paused and thought about that for a moment. "I suppose my restraint shows that I'm maturing. I've grown a lot, personally and professionally."

"Without a doubt."

"Anyway," she said, shaking off the introspective tone, "Vanessa's moving out of the White House tonight, but she's not sad to be leaving because it holds such terrible memories for her.

"Naturally she's shattered by Becky Sturgis's story. She kept repeating that she couldn't understand how her father could have had a hand in something so nefarious—my word, not Vanessa's. He not only covered up a violent crime, he allowed her to marry David. He *encouraged* it. She feels betrayed."

"Where has she left it with Clete?" Gray asked.

"She claims she'll never forgive him."

"Her rejection is no better than he deserves, but it'll kill him."

Barrie nodded. "She's promised Bill Yancey her full cooperation when he begins his investigation into Robert Rushton's death. Now that she doesn't have to fear for her life, she can tell the truth. David killed the baby, but it was Spence's idea to blame it on SIDS."

"Sounds like him. Keeping things simple was Spence's forte."

"Was Vanessa in love with him?"

"With Spence? No. She wanted from him what she wants from every man—attention and protection. Out of spite, she gave David a taste of his own medicine, with a man whose loyalty David thought was incorruptible. But when Spence turned his back on her, she took the rejection hard."

"And turned to you."

"For friendship."

Barrie rose and made a restless circle around the coffee table. "I'm not sure that's all she wanted."

"That's all she got."

"You could have told me."

"There was nothing to tell."

"That's what you could have told me."

"I didn't want Vanessa, and I never had her. There. Satisfied?"

"Yes. Was that so hard?"

He steepled his fingers and placed them across his lips, then studied her until she squirmed beneath his stare. "*What?*" she demanded.

"I think what's really got you down is that I haven't pledged my undying love."

She expelled an unladylike guffaw. "There you go, flattering yourself again. You have a bad habit of doing that, Bondurant."

"I'm here with you, Barrie," he said quietly. Then he reached out, grabbed hold of the belt of her robe, and slowly pulled her to him. "This house you intend to buy, how big is it going to be?"

"Why?"

"I've been offered a job in the Justice Department. Sort of a freelance job. Sounds interesting. I'll be spending a lot of time in Washington and will need a place to stay."

"I see." Her heart had picked up its pace. Her appetite had returned. In fact, she was ravenous. "What about Rocket, Tramp, and Doc?"

"I'll get somebody to watch them and the place while I'm away. There'll be plenty of downtime with this job. I'll get back to Wyoming frequently."

"You've got it all planned."

"Pretty much."

He tugged on the ends of the belt, opening her robe, then sliding his hands inside and resting them on her waist. His eyes held her transfixed. "You told me once not to look through you as though you don't matter. You matter, Barrie. Throw out all that emotional garbage your parents left you with. Your father cheated nobody except himself. You matter a hell of a lot."

Then he drew her down to straddle his lap, curved his hand around her neck, brought her close, and kissed her, sliding his tongue erotically into her mouth, sending her tummy plummeting and her spirit soaring.

His fingertips found her nipples tight and supersensitive. He pressed them, feathered them, molded her breasts while she wrangled with his clothing. His lips closed around one nipple as she took him inside her. She rode him with unabashed lust. Where had she learned to move like this? How had she come by this carnal skill to draw out his pleasure? From what pagan ancestor had she inherited this dark knowledge?

Nothing in her experience matched the way her body responded to his, or her need to pleasure him. Seconds away from her orgasm, he sensed it. "Are you going to start yelling like you did last time?"

"Unless you stop it."

"Not a chance in hell," he groaned. He gripped her hips and held them in place.

She gasped from the delicious pressure that created deep inside her. "I mean . . . unless you stop me . . . I might yell."

His mouth captured hers in another kiss, which disintegrated at the onset of their simultaneous orgasms. He buried his face in the cleft of her breasts. Her soft, staccato sighs made dash marks of erotic sound in the darkness.

Then she collapsed onto his chest, nuzzling his neck. He held her for a long time. When eventually he set her away from him, he brushed her wet hair from her face, traced her cheekbone with the tip of his index finger, stroked her damp lips with his thumb.

He'd never demonstrated so much tenderness, and tears came to her eyes. She whispered a single word. "Bondurant."

"You know," he said, "your voice alone makes me hard. It gets embarrassing."

Laughing softly, she leaned forward to take love bites out of his throat. "So it's accurate to say that you're definitely in lust with me?"

When he didn't respond, she pulled back to look into his face. He squinted, indicating she hadn't quite nailed it.

"Love?" she ventured weakly.

He merely looked at her, his eyes answering with their trademark blue intensity.

"Really?" she whispered.

"Don't get too excited. I'll never remember your birthday, or Valentine's Day, or anniversaries," he told her. "I'm not the hearts-and-flowers type."

She placed her hands on his cheeks. "Will you cheat?"

"No." His tone left no room for doubt. "Never."

"Then I don't need hearts and flowers."

"What about sex?"

"Sex I need."

Later, they lay together on their sides, spoon-fashion on the wide bed. The cool smooth skin of her bottom was nestled against the fuzzy warmth of his middle. His chin rested on the crown of her head. His arm was around her, his hand possessively covering her breast. Occasionally his thumb drifted across her nipple. Occasionally she raised his hand to her lips and kissed the spot that still bore faint teeth marks where she'd bitten him weeks ago.

She grew drowsy. Then just before falling asleep she spoke his name.

"Hmm?"

"You want to hear something ironic?" He didn't say anything, but she knew by his stillness that he was listening. "I loved my father. Desperately."

Softly, into her hair, he whispered, "I know."

Epilogue

The telephone on Barrie's desk rang. She glanced at the clock. Five minutes until she was due on the set. Time to take one quick call. It might be Gray. Frequently he called just before airtime to tell her to break a leg—preferably his, as soon as she got home.

Smiling at the possibility, she picked up the phone. "Barrie Travis."

"Saw you on TV yesterday. Did you color your hair?"

It was Charlene Walters. "I had it highlighted. Do you like it?"

"No. You ought to change it back the way it was."

Barrie smiled. Charlene was almost as famous as she. Her name had appeared in every story, broadcast or print, about the collapse of the Merritt administration. The prison inmate now considered herself Barrie's colleague.

"How are you, Charlene?"

"I've got gas. They fed us beans at lunch."

"I'm sorry to hear that. Listen, I'm due on the set in—"

"You must be walking on air, on account of what all you started."

Six months had passed since Becky Sturgis's resurrection. Trials were pending for Merritt and Armbruster.

Prosecutors were still organizing their cases. Defense attorneys were trying to scrape together a defense against overwhelming evidence and witnesses willing to give incriminating testimony in exchange for immunity or leniency.

"I don't take any pleasure in lives being destroyed," Barrie said. "Although I hope this will serve to prevent such unconscionable abuse of power in the future."

"I wouldn't count on it, people being what they are."

Barrie glanced at the clock. Three minutes. She placed the phone in the crook of her neck and took a mirror and powder puff from her desk drawer. There'd be no time for makeup. "It's been great talking to you, Charlene, but—"

"For myself, I wish they'd take the bastards out and hang 'em. After what they did to Becky, they shouldn't be allowed to go on breathing another day."

"If they're convicted, the justice system will punish them appropriately."

Charlene snorted her contempt of the system. "At least when I told you about Becky, you did something. It took you a while, but you finally got busy."

"Yes, well—"

"Not like her. She didn't do a damn thing."

"Well, she was in prison. As she said, there wasn't much—"

"Not Becky, nitwit. Mrs. Merritt."

Barrie set down her mirror and took the telephone receiver back into her hand. "*Mrs. Merritt?*"

"Ain't that what I said? Vanessa Armbruster Merritt."

Surely she'd missed something. With one eye on the clock, one on her mirror, and Charlene chattering in her ear, she'd missed a vital segue. "Are you saying you told Vanessa Merritt about Becky Sturgis?"

"*Duh!*"

"When, Charlene?"

"When what?"

"When did you speak with her—when did you tell her about Becky Sturgis and her baby?"

"Let's see now. It was after Becky told me, of course. Must have been shortly after Mrs. Merritt became First Lady."

"Charlene, if this is one of your tales—"

"You're my friend. I don't tell tales to my friends."

Barrie's mind was spinning. "Let me be sure I understand. You told Mrs. Merritt, the First Lady, about Becky Sturgis—about her involvement years ago with David Merritt?"

"All of it. Just like I told you. I told her that David Merritt had killed Becky's kid and that the senator had covered it up for him."

Barrie placed her elbow on her desk and rested her forehead in her palm to stop the room from whirling.

"I wrote her letter after letter," Charlene went on, "warning her that she was married to a killer, but she ignored me. At least I thought she did. Then one day, she calls me up here at the prison. Gave a false name, of course, but left a number where I should call her back collect. We talked for half an hour or more. Pissed off the ladies waiting in line to use the phone, but I told them to screw off."

The clock on Barrie's desk was ticking, but not as loudly as her heart. She swallowed a surge of nausea.

An assistant producer poked her head through the door of her office. "Barrie? Ninety seconds."

Barrie acknowledged the notice. "Charlene, didn't you tell anyone that the First Lady had called you?"

"Course I did!" she exclaimed. "But you think they believed me?"

The woman who'd been Robert Redford's college sweetheart and had borne Elvis's love child? Who would have believed her?

"So . . ." Barrie couldn't hold a thought. "So . . ."

"Barrie?" The assistant producer reappeared. "You okay? We're on in one minute."

"I'll be right there." Then she said to Charlene, "So after you told her the Becky Sturgis story, what did she say?"

"She said to keep it between us and stop writing her letters or she'd sic the FBI on me. I said she could come down here, meet Becky, and hear the story for herself, but she said no, she couldn't do that. She said it had happened a long time ago and that it probably wasn't true anyway. Made me mad as hell, me going to all that trouble to get in touch with her, and her not even heeding my warning. Less than two years later, she comes up pregnant. After what I told her, she still went and had a baby with that man. She must be crazy."

Vanessa Armbruster Merritt was anything but crazy.

Barrie, please help me. Don't you know what I'm trying to tell you?

What if her motive was plain ol', everyday spite?

I did not kill Robert Rushton. She did!

About that, David Merritt had been telling the truth.

She's the crazy one.

And in the words of Charlene Walters, jailhouse philosopher, *Crazy people can get away with just about anything. You'd be amazed.*

In a voice barely audible, Barrie asked, "Did you ever hear from Vanessa Merritt again, Charlene?"

"Only once. When she called and suggested that I call you."

SANDRA BROWN is the author of more than sixty books, of which over forty were *New York Times* bestsellers, including the #1 *New York Times* bestseller *The Alibi, Envy, The Switch, Standoff, Unspeakable, Fat Tuesday, Exclusive, The Witness, Charade, Where There's Smoke,* and *French Silk.* Her novels have been published in thirty languages. She and her husband divide their time between homes in Texas and South Carolina.